Skin

Flyover Fiction   Series editor: Ron Hansen

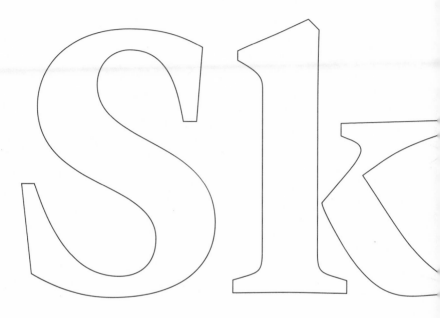

Kellie Wells

University
of
Nebraska
Press
Lincoln
and
London

© 2006 by the Board of Regents of the University
of Nebraska. All rights reserved. Manufactured in
the United States of America. Set in Carter & Cone
Galliard by Bob Reitz. Book designed by Richard
Eckersley. Printed by Thomson-Shore, Inc. ⊚

Library of Congress Cataloging-in-Publication Data
Wells, Kellie, 1962–
Skin / Kellie Wells.
p. cm. — (Flyover fiction)
ISBN-13: 978-0-8032-4824-3 (cloth: alkaline paper)
ISBN-10: 0-8032-4824-5 (cloth: alkaline paper)
1. Belief and doubt — Fiction. 2. Kansas — Fiction.
I. Title. II. Series.
PS3623.E47S57 2006   813'.6–dc22   2005019252

For Jaimy

CONTENTS

ACKNOWLEDGMENTS

Wholehearted thanks go to Jaimy Gordon, professional mensch, who once gave me a car, a plane ticket home, and who kept me moving forward with this book. I'd also like to thank Stu Dybek and Ellen Akins for their sage guidance, Shirley Clay Scott and Herb Scott just for being the good people they are, Peter Blickle and Katherine Joslin for their thoughtful readings, and a special thank you to Nancy Zafris, who recognized this novel in the short story it began as. Thanks are due Sarah Gordon, whose poem "Holding On" helped me launch a character into the ether, and the Kalamazoo Arts Council for funding a summer spent working on this book. Thanks especially to Ladette Randolph for believing in this book and Timothy Schaffert for his careful eye and enthusiasm. Lastly, I'm grateful to Joachim Siegmund, as well as the Free University of Berlin, for making me dream in another language during the writing of the novel and to my sister Jane for being my most ardent shill.

Prologue
Spiritus Monday

The air in What Cheer, Kansas, is gardenia scented year-round, even in the chill, white anonymity of winter, a perfume so heady and redolent it sets noses to twitching and muddles the thinking, throws the clock of expectations plum off its tock, prompts folks to marry in December, die in June, fills them to their gasping gills with a barren hunger no fecundity can ever answer. Just beyond the city limits, the nostrils broaden to the sulphurous reek of industry, the reassuring odor of people engaged in the production of objects, and tensed muscles relax beneath skin that recalls once again how to act, as bodies drive large, soft-seated cars toward reachable goals.

Rachel Loomis tries not to breathe. She stiffens her arms and wills herself to shrink, grow thin as paper. She imagines soon she'll be able to see her soul showing through, a faint glimmer near the jut of the hipbone, between her ribs; she'll wipe away the remaining tarnish of flesh and there she'll be all silvery with spirit, spit-polished and pure. She takes in only enough air to keep what's inside her afloat.

Ruby Tuesday watches her mother billow in the fragrant air, a handkerchief caught on a limb. When she grows up, she'll put her mother in her pocket. It will be warm and dark and tight in there and she thinks her mother will like the confinement. Until then she will sit in her front yard and listen to the rabbits singing. They loaf beneath the lilacs and juniper and hum when the wind blows. Ruby lies on her stomach and looks for a foot, a flash of fur. She knows they're in there, multiplying, multiplying! The singing grows louder every day.

Down the street, Zero Loomis lies in the field across from the house where he grew up, the grass sprouting around him. His mother sits on the porch and waits for his body to rise, waits for him to come back to her so she can feed him brisket, clean the grass stains from his trousers. He stares up at the sky, wavy with a smear of clouds and thatched with contrails. They are both suddenly reminded of the day he left the ground. He was flying a kite, a sturdy box kite he'd built himself, and it sailed so high it became a speck, a faint blemish against the watery blue, and he thought he might snare the moon if the wind held up until dark. His mother, Nedra, looked on and smiled, nodded when he looked at her, and in his mind she appeared in balloon-legged satin pants and curly-toed shoes, tassels and brocade, a veil that swelled when she exhaled like a magic carpet revving its engine, and he imagined she was a genie girl granting him a wish, ready to sate his longing to walk on the blue blue air. Then a puddle-jumper began to churn the air above them, and it loped along and descended to an altitude that caused Zero and his mother to look from sky to ground to sky to try to factor the difference. When the kite snagged itself on a wing and lifted Zero into the air, he faced his usual quandary from a new vantage point: he couldn't decide which was more threatening, earth or firmament. He thought perhaps he ought to let out his line as though he were just reeling in a giant trout, but he simply held tight and wafted across the plain. He watched the ground race beneath him then closed his eyes. Nedra looked on as her little boy was pulled up into the gauzy atmosphere, watched as his body became smaller, remote, eventually a matter of faith. When he touched down miles from where he'd been, he stood up on skinned legs throbbing with the onus of gravity and wondered when he'd ever rise again.

As Ansel Dorsett listens to his neighbor serenade the flowers in her garden, he has a vision: he looks up and sees the sky split, part its lips, a hidden mouth suddenly yawning, and out of the interrupted blue flaps a whiteness, a snapping sheet, the leaf of a blank book, a winged shape, a great bird, fierce dove, the Spirit descending upon him! It dips and drifts, does loop-de-loops, then dives full throttle and zooms toward Earth, aimed directly at him. He imagines the quadrants of his stunned face fixed by the crosshairs of a maniacal radar. Out of this breach in the sky comes a voice, soothing but stern, a voice toned to allay well-founded fears, and it says, *Please be seated as we begin our descent, and prepare to receive Me,* and then the engine chugs and buzzes, cuts out, and there is a rumbling explosion as the earth splits at the seams and rattles, the sound of metal tearing. Ansel crosses his arms in front of his face and is knocked to his knees, covered in a dusty radiance that eclipses all else in his sight. He gingerly offers his hands up to the light, reaching toward the sky that has only just been there and blue, loses his fingers in the burning white, but when he feels wings thrash his body, hears them beat the air, he draws his arms to his chest. He blinks slowly and surveys the wreckage around him: smoldering light piled everywhere, ragged light draping the limbs of trees, and he imagines a smoking black box, the indestructible Word, later stumbled upon by investigators, imagines them listening to exhortations from the cockpit, those last rasping words: *Behold, I come quickly*. Ansel falls to the ground, lies face down in the grass, and implores God not to devour the flesh from his limbs, sear him to spirit, leave him only with the afterthought of bones!

Ivy Engel watches her neighbor reach his hands into the air and then drop to the ground. She walks toward the gate and calls to Mr. Dorsett, asks him if he needs help, then remembers being scolded before for just such a charitable gesture. She steps behind the sycamore and hopes she isn't being a poltroon for letting a sleeping deacon lie with his face buried in his well-groomed fescue. Perhaps, she thinks, he's just quaking with Spirit. He is known to do that from time to time. Ivy stares at the petals of fungus growing from the bark of the tree. It looks to her like a mutant rose blooming from the sun-wizened cheek of an ancient elder. She thinks of the lightly fuzzed skin of her Grandmother Engel's face, the satisfying creases in the skin, well worn. Grandma Engel would say to Ivy, *Ich pflanze hier ein Küßchen*, and she'd lightly scratch the skin of Ivy's cheek, deep enough for the seed of her kiss to take root, give her a peck, and tamp down the skin's soil. *There, maybe it grows*. Ivy imagines the future of her face, sees it aging with time-lapse haste, folding and loosening, the faint scar on her cheek the only hint of a reckless youth. In this moment, Ivy feels as though she understands the outstretching of Mr. Dorsett's arms, like a plant yearning toward a meal of light, and she wishes she believed in or feared something enough to prompt her to do the same. She looks at Mr. Dorsett lying in the grass and thinks she sees tiny flowers pushing through the skin of his arms, blooming on the backs of his hands, in his hair, on his moving lips, blue and red and yellow petals covering him like a flowered suit of armor.

Mrs. McCorkle walks among her flowers, and she hums a song whose words evaporate in a mist as she tries to recall them. She hums all the more vigorously to compensate for the missing lyrics. In the yard next door, her neighbor stands still and stares pie-eyed into the sky, God's moony and smirking face dangling just beyond his grasp, she thinks, tormenting him. Mrs. McCorkle looks up at the sky and remarks that it is that curious shade of blue that threatens to gray at the slightest provocation. A little precipitation would not be unwelcome, would slake the thirst, she thinks as she regards the parched petals of her tulips, arid red and yellow tongues awaiting a whetting, the arousal that drink is. *Drink to me only hm-mm hm hm-mm.* When her neighbor falls to his knees, she looks again to the sky to discern what might have precipitated this penitent posture. The sky has in fact darkened, though it appears also eerily bright, like a harsh revelation, and the clouds seem to rush across the charred blue toward an invisible exit in the ether. When she looks again to her garden, Harlan stands before her, his big feet rendering violence to her sweet william, suddenly martyred beneath his heavy brogans. He motions her toward him, and as she takes a step, in his face flash the lives of other people, their histories and destinies churning kaleidoscopically, obscuring the comforting blue of her husband's eyes. Harlan's palsied hands reach toward her, and she singles out among the pictures twisting his face that of a flying boy, wispily gliding through the air like the seed of a milkweed. Then Harlan begins to dim and wither, a slight condensation warming the air and rising toward the brooding sky, and she misses him.

Elsewhere in What Cheer, silver disks spin in the air and glint in the occasional sunlight. Martin LaFavor wipes the drops of water from his glasses and watches his father disassemble the lawnmower. He wonders why his father has chosen to attend to Sunday's yard work today, why he's not out knocking on the doors of doctors and hospital administrators, pitching the wonders of pharmaceutical advancements. The lawnmower's guts are spread around him on the lawn, and Martin feels queasy when he gazes on the carnage. The lawnmower lies on its side like a tranquilized beast unaware that it will awake to its own messy dispersion, fragments unable to coalesce. Martin cannot help but be moved by the plight of the lawnmower. Periodically, Martin's father looks up and growls at the helplessness that his son's hands dangling at his sides confirm. Martin knows his father thinks he is a squandering of genes, genetic dross, Martin's very presence an excess, knows the story his father tells himself, that his own stout and indomitable sperm was seduced by the come-hither blandishments of a crafty egg concealing corruption within. Martin sees his mother standing at the window in his bedroom, looking vaguely aggrieved as her eyes follow a formation of geese pointing toward the other side of the sky.

Thin clouds prowl across the sky like cats stalking sparrows, and all the residents of What Cheer who stand in their greening yards, hands reaching out toward a trickle of sun, look above to see the sky eddy with the ylem of imminent consequences, kneel beneath the heft of sins they've yet to commit.

Chapter One. Ivy Engel
Compression Scars

Okay, so I live several blocks away from an electrical power plant, which is, I know, bad news. I saw that story on *60 Minutes*, or maybe it was *20/20* or *48 Hours* – one of those wake-up-and-sniff-the-scandal shows, hand-held camera wobbling on the shoulder of the crack cameraman in hotfooted pursuit of the story, shows that want to be the first to tell you the way you've been living your life all along is going to prove to be fatal – and now I'm checking my body every ten minutes for some sort of sign, early detection and all. I've moved my digital clock radio across the room, and I never stand next to the dishwasher when it's achurn. I'm playing hot potato with electromagnetic rays, dodging something I can't sense at all, and sometimes I have to pinch my arm and remind myself I'm on Planet Earth. I have this sneaking fear that somewhere out there in a remote pocket of the cosmos there is intelligent life, an easily amused race of beings sitting in a main street movie theater, watching me through 3-D glasses, laughing their scrawny, alien-green butts off. We all know that invisible peril burgeons around us, the weather itself a protean virus we'll eventually have to flee to Mars to antidote. Maybe it sounds cockeyed – of course it does – but I get the bona fide jeebies sometimes not knowing where to duck and what to cover. All these hidden assailants get to a girl. And now I'm wondering if the power plant might explain the week I've been having. Maybe a formerly loyal and punctual but now disgruntled employee at the plant vengefully pushed some big red button with the taunting warning: "Don't Push!" beneath it, and it unleashed stray volts that went wilding in my neighborhood.

Among other less worrisome events that have occurred in the past week: a colony of bats has settled in my backyard; my best friend, Duncan, has begun wearing only blue clothing; and my breasts have grown a whole cup size, as if I were just feeding them better. When I first noticed the bats, I had gone outside to watch the Roto Rooter men dig up the Dorsetts' backyard. Mr. Dorsett paced back and forth as the muddy men hoisted parts of the lame septic tank out of the hole. I admit I was sort of glad about it. I could tell Mr. Dorsett was embarrassed by the whole thing because he was stinking up the neighborhood. It was the middle of May and even though it wasn't sweltering yet, neighbors were shutting their doors and windows and turning on the AC.

Mr. Dorsett looked over at our yard periodically to see if my father had come out to watch the muddy gash that Mr. D.'s backyard was quickly becoming, and I'd wave and smile like we were old pals, old crew team cronies. Across Mr. Dorsett's yard I saw Mrs. McCorkle. She was kneeling in her garden, tugging at something. When she looked up, Mr. Dorsett waved at her nervously, and she smiled and yelled, "Hello, Ivy." I smiled back. I don't think Mr. Dorsett and Mrs. McCorkle were ever bosom chums, but for some reason Mrs. Mc-Corkle has found Mr. D. to be especially snubable lately, ever since Mr. McCorkle – who's a swell mensch, we all miss him – was put in the nursing home.

No love is lost between Mr. Dorsett and me either. When I was eight years old, he wouldn't allow his twelve-year-old daughter, Judy, to play with me anymore. He claimed he was afraid she would pick up infantile habits or her brain wouldn't be properly stimulated if she didn't constantly hang out with kids her own age (despite the slack-jawed, driftwood stare of the neighborhood cretins toward whom she naturally gravitated). Personally I think he didn't like me because of my unorthodox religious views. I think he was just steamed because I'd told Judy that when I prayed, I spoke to my stomach, because that's where I thought God was – on the inside somewhere, maybe perching on a branch of the bronchial tree or lying on the shores of the islets of Langerhans, overseeing the production of insulin.

Judy told me the next day she was poking herself in the navel, match-ing fingers to ribs, on the lookout for signs of a higher power hiding inside her, when her father walked in and asked her what in Henry's name she was doing. Judy, a hopelessly earnest and brick-headed lit-eralist, told Mr. Dorsett what I'd said and asked him if God in the pancreas wouldn't portend problems for the body later on (having just covered insulin and bile production in science class). She probably foresaw divine diabetes in my future and pictured my organs sagging from the weight of being occupied so intimately. I suspect she was hoping to locate the tumor of God inside her stomach so she could coax Him up into her arm or cheek or some other harmless spot where He'd be less likely to interfere with her bodily processes. Though she wouldn't have said so to her father, going to that church they went to, I think she was fretful about becoming God-clogged.

Mr. Dorsett was a deacon at a church where going to the movies, even a Saturday matinee of *Million Dollar Duck*, was a sin, although it was a-okay to watch television (all sources of venality apparently having been determined long before Philo Farnsworth began dissecting the images that would later litter TV screens, go figure). You weren't supposed to dance either. It was probably a punishable sin if you were even caught swaying a little, accidentally even (like when your mother is letting down the hem of a dress that was a bad idea when it was new, a dress you have no intention of wearing to some awards ceremony you have even less intention of attending, and your body, becoming fluent in movement, cannot be becalmed by lips pursed around straight pins entreating, *Hold still*). And music was definitely out unless the lyrics mentioned rising from the grave or the blood of the lamb or some such. I attended this church. Once. I sat between Judy and Mr. Dorsett. The minister didn't speak in a normal tone of voice; he bellowed, like he thought we all suffered from hearing loss (after several Sundays of that, I think we would have – probably an evangelical strategy for quick, resistance-free supplication: deaf lambs don't bleat back, a way to shut the mutton up). It seemed he kept looking directly at me, and I was sure the blank look he found on my face was spurring him on, his voice rising to an increasingly frothy pitch, the way people will gradually begin to yell when talking to recent refugees or immigrants from . . . Tunisia, or Finland, outer Mongolia, say, in the hope that if they bray the words, their listeners will somehow suddenly understand this language that's only recently been stuffed in their mouths and ears. I felt a little like a refugee myself, flung onto the shores of a land that was governed by laws more hostile, I was beginning to fear, than the one I'd fled. By the end, the preacher was leaning out over the pulpit and practically screaming the Word. His fists were often raised, like he was spoiling for a scrap, all too ready to go a few rounds with the lurking evil in the world, pretzel Satan into a half nelson, and it occurred to me that perhaps many a fundamentalist pulpiteer is really just a frustrated prize fighter. His face seemed to balloon as his sermon reached its shrill summit, and the thick folds of his cheeks flushed red. I don't think he was getting enough oxygen. He exhaled often enough, but I didn't hear him inhale much. He had gray, cowlicked hair that kept flying forward in an arc over his eyes as he shook and nodded his head. It's funny how some people think they have to look like they're having a stroke to convince you of the incontrovertible God's-honest truth of what they're saying. I remember shaking and kicking my feet during the sermon, and Mr. Dorsett slapped my knees.

So I was secretly pleased about this septic tank fiasco because I thought it definitely pointed to Mr. Dorsett's ailing karma. My friend Sai, who first gave me the skinny on karma, tells me it's not fair to be such a selective believer, and that's what I am I guess, fair-weather. I believe in it when I think people are getting what they deserve, which, let's face it, is pretty blue moon. But I have a hard time accepting the idea that famished babies with bubbled, empty stomachs are in that predicament because they were maybe contract killers or dirty despots or grubbers of ill-gotten gain in a previous life. She says this kind of thinking is wrongheaded, and that I'd probably feel differently if I'd spent any time around toiling hordes of starving people, your hungry huddled masses, if I were stripped of the privilege of three squares a day (I felt compelled here to point out that I'd recently begun to deny myself breakfast). She says I might look for different answers to questions that don't occur to a well-fed girl like me. Still, babies are blank, nearly smooth-brained, with a wrinkle for complacency, a wrinkle for fear, and a gaping ravine for hunger and thirst. So it's not like they'd learn a lesson or anything. I haven't mentioned this last part to Sai, because I'm afraid she'll lose patience and tell me I'm souring my own karmic destiny with such willful misunderstanding, which is what I always fear, a curdled fate.

Anyhow, as I watched Mr. Dorsett pop Tums like they were Sweet Tarts, I saw them, I saw the bats. I didn't know what they were at first. I was picking a scabby fungus off our sycamore tree, half-expecting it to bleed, and thinking it was odd the tree had some dead leaves. Then, a little higher up, I noticed these yellowish-brown bulbs dangling from the branches, and it appeared our sycamore tree had suddenly grown peaches, like it thought it might get more respect as a fruit-bearer.

I reached up to inspect one of these dead leaves, and as I touched it, an electric feeling zipped up my arm and across my cheek. This leaf was soft and angry, and it began to shake and screech. I instinctively fell to the ground, in case it got a notion to dive-bomb my head. It unfolded wings that were like little flannel rags, then this leaf and a few friends dropped from the tree and flapped away. As they screamed by, echolocating like crazy, I actually glimpsed their faces, these furry, crumpled, cartoon faces. They looked like one of those pictures you'd see in the backs of magazines or inside the covers of matchbooks, and if you drew it and sent it in, somebody, somewhere, for a small fee, would tell you whether or not you should go to art school.

I examined the tree more closely and counted fifteen masquerading bats total. Some hung freely on the branches, convincingly miming dead leaves, and others were curled up tight like tiny fists. They ranged in color from yellowish to orangish brown, but none were black like bats are supposed to be. After I fully realized what I was looking at, I got a little spooked, thinking maybe they'd gotten their coloring from blood feasts, like maybe steady plasma transfusions had begun to redden their skin and fur, the way if you ate ten pounds of carrots in an afternoon you might end up with skin tinted the color of cantaloupe. Then I noticed how beautiful the bats were. They looked like yellow flowers gone to seed. I reached up to touch one tucked beneath a leaf.

"You all right?"

My heart dropped into my Chuck Taylors. Mr. Dorsett. He's so stealthy – he scared the befreakinjesus out of me. You know how you're getting ready to touch something, maybe a smashed snake or an unidentifiable dark object lying in a corner, and some wiseacre emerges from the shadows and says something, or maybe your own stomach grumbles, and for half a second you think the mystery object spoke to you, you think, Jeezoman, I've just walked through the wall of another dimension? That's what I felt. Until I heard the gate close.

"Ivy?"

"Hi, Mr. Dorsett." I brushed myself off and bent forward so my hair fell over my doubly pierced ears, potential lecture fodder. "Too bad about your yard," I said. "Quite the terra carnage." I felt a thin smile spread across my face despite my best efforts to flat-line my lips.

"What were you doing?"

"I wasn't dancing." I thought of that old joke about fundamentalist Baptists, who won't have sex standing up for fear it will lead to dancing. Even though it had been eight years and Judy was now the sort of Young Republican Type A upwardly mobile urban professional overachiever I would never hang with anyway, I was still retroactively miffed at Mr. Dorsett. I didn't feel obliged to be overly civil.

"What were you looking at?" Mr. Dorsett moved in closer and looked up at the tree.

"I was just looking to, er . . . see if that new tree food was working."

"Tree food?" Mr. Dorsett stared intently at my face, as if he couldn't believe his eyes, as if my nose had just fallen off and a big tulip had bloomed in its place.

"A couple of months ago, we ordered this botanical grow food they were selling on TV. Comes with knives that can slice stone, or a Popeil Pocket Fisherman, I forget, if you order early. They say it's revolutionary. You sprinkle it around your tree and within a couple of months, you get fruit, apples or peaches . . . one tree in South Dakota even grew coconuts! Look." I pointed at the woolly orange balls dangling from a high branch. Mr. Dorsett shot me this dour no-nonsense look, like he'd had just about enough and if I didn't come clean soon, he was going to march me over to my parents and demand I be locked up in my room indefinitely or shipped off to a reformatory for inveterate smart alecks, in the interest of the community.

"Bats," I relented. The way he dropped his jaw and began to back up, you'd think I'd said jackals or two-headed goats. "Orange bats in What Cheer. Who'd a thunk it?" I shrugged.

Mr. Dorsett grabbed me by the shoulder and pulled me back from the tree. "Bats are dangerous," he said. "Disease-ridden."

"No, they're not," I sighed. I didn't like how Mr. Dorsett was all nosy and pushing me around in my own yard. "They're little, harmless bats. They get bad press, sure, but it's not like they're going to morph into Barnabas Collins or Bela Lugosi for Christ's sake." My heart raced as I uttered this last part – it came out of my mouth before I could put on the brakes – because I knew it was going to make the blood zoom in scandalized alarm to Mr. Dorsett's face.

"You listen here, missy – " Just then there was a minor explosion next door and black, foul-smelling glop started erupting from the hole in Mr. Dorsett's backyard.

"Looks like you got a gusher, Mr. Dorsett," I said, unable to pass up the opportunity to nettle him. "Maybe you've struck black gold. Texas tea," I called as Mr. Dorsett raced across the yard.

I decided to head over to Duncan's to tell him about the bats. I knew he'd think it was totally gravy that bats were roosting in our sycamore tree. Duncan is my closest friend. He moved to What Cheer from Medicine Lodge when we were both ten years old. The day after he moved in, he came over to my house carrying two box turtles he'd rescued from a busy street, and he let me paint a red "I" for Ivy on the back of one. We tried to race them, but they kept crawling in opposite directions. Duncan said that was their secret strategy, that they'd whispered to one another, "Odds are better if we split up." Duncan and I have been boon companions ever since. Now, nearly every day, Duncan's father will ask, "You two attached at the hip?" And Duncan's mother will wrinkle her nose and say, "No, dear. They're attached at the heart," and then she'll wink. Duncan dies a thousand deaths every time. His mom is super nice, but it's that brand of vigilant niceness that can grate on the nerves of adolescents and oldsters, people in age groups beyond easy sentiment. She's that type of concerned hostess that asks you every ten seconds if you're warm enough, cool enough, hungry, thirsty, etc., always on the lookout for ways to serve and placate. I think she took the gleefully self-denying good-girl lessons of *The Donna Reed Show* a little too much to heart when she was growing up. Once Duncan and I made signs that said IF THE TEMPERATURE IN THIS ROOM WERE MORE IDEAL, WE'D BE DEAD and WE'RE FULL AS TICKS AND COULDN'T POSSIBLY EAT ANOTHER MORSEL. We pasted them to popsicle sticks, and it wasn't long before we had occasion to wave them in response to the inevitable comfort quizzing. Mrs. Nicholson smiled and said, "Oh, you two," but she still asks.

Mr. Nicholson is a world-class cornball without equal. He's the kind of guy who steals little kids' noses and shows them, as evidence, his thumb held between fingers, tells them that eating beets will put hair on their chests, as if that were a perk, and assigns them ridiculous nicknames that make them feel as though they're wearing their underpants outside their trousers. Of course Ivy is an easy target; Poison is an obvious addition. "That girl's poison, Duncan," he'll say. "You better hope you never get the itch for her." Yuk, yuk. When I was younger, he used to call me "Intravenous De Milo," a pun he plagiarized from *Spinal Tap*, which he'd been forced to watch multiple times with Duncan, and he'd say, "I need a love transfusion, I.V." Then he'd make me kiss a vein. Once I said to him, "Boy, we'll never starve around here so long as you keep dishing that corn," and he quit razzing me, cold turkey, for days. I didn't say this with even an iota of malice, but I guess it took the fun out of it to have his behavior suddenly named like that, so now I just swallow it wholesale and roll my eyes like he likes. Mr. Nicholson calls their five-year-old neighbor, Jill Shipley, Henrietta, for no good reason except that it makes her stamp her feet in protest.

If the caption *What's Wrong With This Picture?* were beneath a Nicholson family photo, you'd pick Duncan out without a second glance. Duncan has nappy, brown hair that curls off the top of his head like it's trying to escape. It's buzzed short on the sides and if you look closely you can read the word "tattoo" etched in the skin over his ear. His favorite shirt is a Zippy the Pinhead T-shirt that says, *All Life's a Blur of Republicans and Meat.*

Some of the beef-necked deltoids at school pick on Duncan. When the principal's head is turned, they wear buttons that announce they belong to the *Fag-Buster Patrol*. The insignia on the buttons is a limp wrist jailed inside a circle and slash. They call Duncan fag-bait, make kissing noises at him, and say, "Bend over, Joy Boy, I'll drive." And I say, "You realize the implications here are much more damning for you." I whisper confidentially, "It's so obvious you're suffering from Small Penis Syndrome," socking it to them where they live. Then I put my finger on one of their clunky belt buckles (which invariably features the name of a truck or farm equipment manufacturer or the outline of a naked and buxom reclining woman), run it down the fly, and say, "You *really* ought to have that looked at." Of course they shoot back, agile and clever as the cottonwoods they resemble, with the snappy rejoinder, "Stupid lesbo" or "Shut up, cunt." These guys listen to Guns N' Roses instructionally and dream of the day they'll bury their girlfriends in the backyard. Real princes.

Then there's forward movement from mere simian to wunderkind and you get Duncan, who is boy poetry, utterly lyrical inside and out. His skin is white as Elmer's glue and if you look into his gray-green eyes too long, you'll slam your foot down because you'll feel like you're falling. It's like having a semi-lucid dream where you've just voluntarily stepped off a cliff, and one of the things you're thinking about on the way down is how they say you can have a heart attack if you let yourself splat because you're *so* into it. But me, I always bounce. I'm into it too, it's just that I believe in options. With Duncan, I know even death-defying feats are possible.

So about Duncan. After I watched Mr. Dorsett race around the heaving hellmouth in his backyard for a while, I went to see Duncan. Mrs. Nicholson answered the door, and she busted out crying when she saw me. "I'm sorry, Ivy," she said. "Come in." She hugged me hard and for a long time, like she'd just recovered me from a kidnapper, ten years and 40,000 milk cartons later. She pushed my hair behind my ears and cupped my face in her hands. "You kids are so young," she said, and I could tell her voice was only a few syllables away from giving out. "Duncan's in his room."

As I walked up the stairs, my mind raced, trying to compute the meaning of such a greeting. I became a little paranoid, my stock response to inexplicable distress in adults, followed closely by either blind self-blame or -defense, depending. I started thinking maybe Mr. Dorsett had gotten to them and told them he suspected I'd joined a strange new cult, a druidic splinter sect that worshiped at the altar of tree-roosting bats. Mr. Dorsett tended to see rank-smelling theological peril everywhere he stepped.

But as I entered Duncan's room, I instantly forgot what it was I'd just been sweating about, like some corrective, cosmic hand had reached into my head with a bottle of Wite-Out and painted over those brain cells. Duncan was lying on his bed reading *Death on the Installment Plan*, listening to Fad Gadget, a recent bargain bin coup, wagging his foot to the music. Somehow Duncan's skin seemed even paler, as if the glue had been watered down; his lips looked nearly blue against the incandescent white of his cheeks. "Hey, Dunc, what's up? Your mom's tripping."

Duncan stood up. "Look," he said and started unbuttoning his jeans.

"Is there some sort of planetary misalignment that's making people wig out or what?" I made a feeble attempt to avert my eyes. I'd actually always been a little curious about what kind of underwear Duncan wore – one of the few subjects we'd never braved. Striped boxers! He hiked his shorts up a little and pointed at his thigh, the scars from his moped accident. "You've shown me your scars before. They're cool. As you know, I don't have any good scars, except this fading one on my cheek. I can't compete." He turned around. The scars wound around his thigh and ran down his legs in widening, white lines past his knees. There were three lines that stopped at different places, as if they were racing. The lines were eerie, almost fluorescent against his milky legs. They looked like symbols or rebus, like they were trying to tell us something, like maybe they'd spell out a message when they reached the appropriate point, the meaning of life etched in inscrutable runes in his calf. Duncan put his jeans back on. "Jesus, Duncan. Your scars are growing, what gives?"

"So much for swimsuit season," he said. He tried to smile. I hugged him. I held him tight like Mrs. N. had hugged me. Even though Duncan had now put his jeans back on, I kept seeing those lines, as if a flashbulb had gone off and branded an afterimage on my retinas. I saw the lines lift off his legs and circle my head, curl in through one ear and out the other. I saw them slip under the surface of the skin on my face, tunneling a trail, making fleshy speed bumps across the pavement of my cheeks. I thought about the movie *Squirm* and the electrified worms that terrorized people, getting under their skin, literally. I wanted to make the droopy, gray crescents under Duncan's eyes disappear.

"Hey, Dunc, remember that scene in *Squirm* when that woman turned on the shower and the worms started oozing out the holes in the showerhead, and then she heard a noise or something and turned the faucets back off and the worms retreated?" I laughed.

"They think it's some bizarre thing called morphea, or scleroderma, they're not sure. They looked at pictures in these dusty books they hadn't cracked since medical school and scratched their chins. 'We're just general practitioners,' they told me. Not weird disease experts. But they think it's one of those one-in-a-million deals. Untreatable." Duncan pulled me toward him and kissed me. It was a kiss that was desperately thorough, as if he thought it might have some therapeutic or medicinal benefit. His tongue went everywhere, touched everything, took complete inventory. I believe if he'd had more tongue, he would have kept going straight on down to my esophagus, blazing a trail inside me.

I pushed him back. I wondered if this was one of his games. Sometimes Duncan is a magical thinker. He makes up these rituals and convinces himself that his wish will come true if he completes his task. Like if he can successfully throw and catch his boomerang twenty times in a row while juggling cantaloupes, it's a sign he'll get a full ride to Stanford, receive manna, there'll be peace in the Middle East, something like that. Spooky thing is is that it almost always works. I guess the psychologists would say it's just a self-fulfilling prophecy, but it's still kind of unsettling. I mean Duncan's no Nostradamus or Uri Geller or Tiresias or anything. His guidance counselor says he just has "an unusually strong sense of purpose," though when his counselor says this, he inclines his head forward and looks disapprovingly over his bifocals. They don't like you being too decisive too early, in case you really were meant to be a failure. They don't want to be accused of encouraging you to stretch yourself toward an impossible goal. Whatever happened to *To the stars through difficulties*? I asked my own naysaying counselor one day. I used to fall asleep chanting the state motto, *Ad astra per aspera*, so I'd be sure not to botch it on the compulsory Kansas history test we took every year at Oak Grove Elementary. If you ask me, they don't make Kansans like they used to.

"Morphea?" I said. "That sounds like science fiction. You're making this up?" I said hopefully. We sat down on his bed. I was beginning to get seriously creeped out.

"Nope."

"Is it some kind of sleeping sickness?"

"No. I don't think this was named for the god of dreams."

"Spill it, Dunc-man. You're making me nervous."

Duncan fingered his shorn scalp. "I don't know if you remember the finer points of my injury or not – who knew it was going to matter? – but these scars I got aren't from being cut open or anything like that, they're from the impact. You know, I got pressed up against the curb by the 'ped. The flesh beneath the skin was pinched and it sort of split or something. They're called compression scars." Duncan stopped and looked at me like what he had just said was dangerously illuminating, the key to sudden understanding, and he was waiting for me to utter a slow and knowing "Ohhh" and nod my head, paradise sacrificed.

"Yeah, keep going."

"I guess we should have held out for more insurance money. It turns out these compression scars can come back to haunt you, big time. They can lie dormant like some goddamned ghost wound hibernating in your leg. And you don't know, you think you're fine. You just think you got some awesome scars to show the grandkids later on when you tell them tales of your misspent youth. But then these scars, they like, come to life and spread across your whole body, and after they're done striping the outside, they can tear through your insides too and clip the edges off your vital organs like goddamned scissors. Fuck." Duncan bent over his wastepaper basket.

"Maybe you ought to go, Ive. I'm not feeling so hot. I don't have a stomach for tragedy," he said.

"Wait. I can't believe this," I said. "I've never heard anything like this before, and you know I've always got my ear to the ground for the weird and the one-of-a-kind. This sounds like some made-up disease from another planet, something you'd get inoculated for before traveling to, I don't know, Neptune or something. Surely there've been, like, scads of people who've had these compression scars, right? I mean how come I've never heard of this?"

"I don't know, Ive. Guess it's not topping the disease-of-the-week research priority list." Duncan clutched his arms. "They just don't know shit about it, fucking doctors. They're not even willing to commit themselves to this diagnosis. You could hear their malpractice-fearing knees knocking together every time they whispered the word 'morphea' to one another." Duncan began to rock slowly.

I twisted the spirals of hair that hung over his forehead. "Why didn't you tell me about this, about these scars?"

"Because. I didn't really know anything until today."

I felt my stomach start to knot in a way only a Boy Scout could appreciate, hundreds of tiny hands being wrung, pressing against the walls, twisting my insides into lariat loops and granny knots. "So is it for sure . . ."

"Time to feed the worms? Should I prepare for the big dirt nap?"

I nodded.

"They don't know. You could fill a thimble with what those bastards know about it. They said it might stop spreading and maybe it will never go inside. They said it could take a few months, a few years, few decades, maybe never happen, maybe happen tomorrow. Real conclusive stuff." Duncan looked straight into my eyes and softened his voice to a whisper. "I'm afraid to move," he said. "It's like I have this big rip in my pants or something, which should just be embarrassing, right? But if I move, I could die." He kept looking and looking at me, and I felt like he could see my thoughts, could see me thinking, *If you* die, Duncan Nicholson, I'll, I'll puncture an artery and sit in one place until I can come too. Those bottomless eyes. I steadied myself against the bed. I concentrated on the feel of chenille against my palm.

Duncan reached out and pressed his hand against my left breast, the larger one. "I don't want to die a virgin," he said.

I always thought this would be a meaningful moment, that I'd feel velvety needles prickle against my skin. But it wasn't like that at all. It wasn't like anything. I couldn't feel it. If I hadn't seen his hand on my breast, I would never have known it was there. My breast felt Nova-cained, heavy, but it definitely did not tingle, not a single goose bump, and I bump easy. I wanted to say, "Yes, Duncan. I love you, Duncan, er, take me," or whatever it is you say between panting breaths in moments such as these, moments that until this one I had only experienced vicariously through the lives of Chelsea Starling, long-suffering and secretly passionate nurse, and Vanessa Vandehorn, sexy rich girl bored with polo players and her MBA studies. But I couldn't. I couldn't even say something stupid like, "Could I please have a pretzel first?" if I'd wanted. My brain and mouth were momentarily disconnected. All I could do was stand up with my numb breast and paralyzed lips and walk out.

Things can get so strange so fast.

Chapter Two. Charlotte McCorkle
Ink Spots

The conventional view: old women, elderly *ladies* (broads) – land mines quaking quietly and out of sight, beyond utility in peacetime, waiting to be stepped on; shriveled figs wearing lavender, ever yearning for the past, as if it held some time-vanquished promise, waiting for death to creep in like bursitis. Lavender has never agreed with me, makes me look bilious. The instant I don a lavender blouse or scarf, people begin demanding I lie down and drink liquids.

Now that I've said this, your mind, wishing to fix me, gropes for a pole, pegs me for the spunky counterpoint, the fiery septuagenarian with gumption and verve, the other role available to an aging pigeon such as myself. I hope to exceed my age in meaning. I had fire when I was twelve, and thirty, before, between, and since. I am as worthy of good and bad press as any twenty-thirty-forty-something bungee-jumping chief executive sapsucker. I decline to be ground by your simplifying pestle into an easily digested set of sitcom characteristics you can swallow down without effort, relying on the peristalsis of those who've done the chewing for you, gullet-soothing gruel like the pabulum you've been led to believe I live on, toothless and soft-skulled. Fiddle.

I can see how these myths get spun. My dear friend Odella Norwood, pushing sixty for the last twenty years, no fresh tulip by most standards, claims to be just marking time until she can collect her Grand Reward. I have offered to help her expedite this process since I do not believe in hangers-on, but she insists it must occur naturally, otherwise she might be ineligible, disqualified, as though she were playing the Publisher's Clearing House Sweepstakes. What a swindle. She's molded herself to fit the propaganda, weak of spirit. I contend that despite the hype death is no more natural than NutraSweet or the breasts of starlets. There is nothing natural about incontinence and rigidity. I believe once folks begin thinking this way, they've clearly outlived their usefulness and need to be put to rest.

It is not so much a respite from the slow motion of swollen ankles or the ubiquitous odor of menthol that accounts for Odella's desire for death as her fun-in-the-never-ending-sun, resort notions of heaven. Her eschatological musings are corrupted by rewritten memories of a beautiful youth, her mind infested with gilt-framed pictures of heaven as scantily clad cabana boys whose fingers forever knead the lactic acid out of slack and weary muscles. As a concession to the more widespread myth, she is willing to imagine pearl-pocked gates, gold-paved paths, and sudden and complete understanding of All Things, but for Odella these lead to eternal vacation, Club Dead, where just thinking of oysters on the half shell finds them sliding down your throat.

I have my own ideas about the afterlife but am content for now to see how the beforelife plays out.

People's views of eternity do slay me. Ansel Dorsett and I have had many a heated confab over the hedges on this particular topic. Ansel is a devout member of the flock and full-time deacon at Shadyvale Baptist Church, and this affiliation naturally shapes what he is allowed to look forward to. Though he is not as long in the tooth as I am, somewhere in the twilight of his forties, his stodgy view of the world makes me feel girlish by comparison. I feel certain that Odella's hedonistic dreams of deliverance would cause Ansel an embolism (he's not terribly tolerant of divergent opinions, I have discovered, on issues concerning God or defense spending). I once told Ansel – and I did it, admittedly, just to see his eyes bug – that heaven for my recently departed Harlan meant singing Gershwin tunes and eating toasted cheese sandwiches, and for me it meant that these activities were not performed concurrently. The lines in Ansel's face let go, his grin sliding down his cheeks like rain on a window, and he said, "Sacrilegious levity, Charlotte, will earn you a ringside seat in Hell," then he whirled on his Florsheims and harumphed toward his house. I said, "You'll win no converts that way, you old sour-tongued devil." At this, Ansel bristled and turned around. "I bet Harlan's happy to be out of your sharp clutches," he said, then disappeared through the back door. I could tell by the arch of triumph in his back that he thought this would cut me to the proverbial quick. Ansel is one of the people trying to convince me Harlan is alive and well and slumming in some Godforsaken nursing home, foggy-eyed and supine from Thorazine and laxatives.

I know better. I killed him myself.

It was nothing personal. We each agreed long ago that if either of us became a heavy handful, the other had permission to do what needed to be done. Harlan's bones had begun to fossilize and his mind was gophered with holes, tiny gaps that made conversation a ponderous chore, especially if you had a fondness for clear, causal connections. Harlan suffered from Stiff-Man Syndrome, among other things. And I imagined I could see the waning muscles beneath the tissue-thin skin of his arms continually spasm and writhe like slow snakes, as if an electric current coursed right through him. Sometimes they'd twist with such vigor I was afraid they'd snap bone. Sirens at night make me remember his screams.

I wanted to drown him, let him be washed away in a summer deluge. That's how he would have wished to go, yielding to the pull of the water – as when the river emptied itself in 1951 – sinking through the cluttered floodwaters down to the buried streets, lilting beside light poles and water-logged cars. Logistically, however, this proved too challenging, so I fed him the Seconal, one after another, like bits of bread, Body of Christ, just as you might feed a sweet little bird, little twig-legged finch or warbler. And Harlan swallowed them happily, hungrily; he ate his death willingly and would have agreed, had he a mind to, that necessary actions were being taken. After a while, there hung in the air a smell like wet moss, the odor of an essence departing.

The day Harlan got work as a printer for Deluxe Checks, we went to the woods. We lay on the moist ground, on the lichen and club moss, green and vivid even in the shade, the lit-up color of tree frogs. The mulch of leaves and bark, the rhythm of our bodies, two airy halves of the same spore, adrift, pressed in efflorescence, in one long exhalation – it was the beginning and end bundled together. You could smell incipience and finality in the air. It floated in on the fecund breeze and clung to our skin. And Harlan said, "Charlotte, you are a happy fate, an open-eyed dream. You are my own heart," or some such sugar. Harlan knew how to sweet talk. He was grateful to have found a woman who could love a man with a glass eye, love him, in part, *for* his glass eye – the partial anopsia that assured she'd be only half seen by the body, half by something else – love that she could touch her finger to it and it would not water, would not move, always be cold and blue and stationary as sky. I could hold it in my palm, roll it in my hand, an overgrown marble. Sometimes I'd cup his eye in my hand and stare into it as if it were a fire or crystal ball, and sometimes I *could* see the future, see it foam up in the wear-brindled white.

Understand, I did not kill Harlan because he got ink on everything. He didn't mind that his clothes, his body, were indelibly stained, and neither did I. At times he'd come home looking like some sad old spotted animal, freckled with ink as he was, bruise-dark smudges hiding in such unlikely places as his nape or his ankles, under his eyes. Thankfully, he never saddled me with the onus of spot removal. I think he liked the stained figure he cut. He saw the purple-black blotches as visible testimony to hard work. Harlan was especially pleased by how ink under the fingernails made it look as if he'd been digging in the earth.

Harlan's sense of himself was forged by the barcarole of the printing press, the kachonka-thunk that daily filled his ears. Ink flowed in his veins, beneath his thoughts ran captions in backward type. Favorite music ensemble: the Ink Spots, "You Always Hurt the One You Love" and the "Cow Cow Boogie," melodies to make even a stiff old man tap his wingtips. In his sleep, instead of snoring, he would hum and click his tongue against his teeth, immersed in dreams of machinery. This simulated rhythm of printing, oceanic movement of the press – the solace of Harlan's melodic somnolence – it ordered my thoughts and rocked me to sleep.

Sometimes Harlan took me after hours to work, led me blindfolded to the old Linotype, guided my fingers to the metal letters, asked me what I felt. "Words mean twice as much backwards," he said. "There's more to understand." "Yadot," I said. "Tnedicca, erif, evol."

Here is something that may surprise you: the word cataract can mean both waterfall and occluded eye. When I was young, I lived within walking distance of a small cataract. I would bathe in it, hide behind the veil of water. The way the fall rushed across my body, I was momentum made flesh, skin and bones flowing, part of the original meaning of water, its etymology. I have not lived within walking distance of anything quite so lovely in many years, not that What Cheer doesn't have charms of its own to offer. Now a cataract is something that blurs my vision; now it is a milky curtain I try to see through. The world has gone dim. I don't mind the companionship of floaters. In the petri dish of my eye, trapped beneath the opacity, strands of life wriggle and list, paramecium. Maybe they're a sample, shards of what I will see when I die, fragments of God. Or maybe it's a tiny colony, microbial people struggling to hang on, aloft in someone's sight. Who's to say we are not floaters in God's eyes, making him a little less lonely behind his dimming vision?

Pah. Anyone who thinks I'm touched is welcome to look deep inside himself and see what he dredges up. Examination does not come cheap.

The doctors and pharmacists who keep me hitched to this iffy planet frowned wearily when I told them about the pictures of strangers' lives that cloud my eyes. So I don't tell anymore. I say only that the medicine is fine, yes, keeps my eyes clear enough, thank you. I see now sky and chair and dog and key, nothing more, and they smile with satisfaction at their curative powers, their sure-fire nostrums. But, to myself I say, it is an angel-fraught world we live in and you have only to look with discerning eyes to see this is so. Some are small, crafty, crouch in nooks. You must be careful where you step. They are not shy; they will nip at your heels or trip you. They'd just as soon see you fallen as upright. This is how they understand the world. Some are people-sized and walk among us. You've met them and thought there was something fishy about them. They make hoagies, they walk dogs. They live on warm grates or teach biology. They sweep up hair in salons and risk smiles as they pass you on the sidewalk. They are exotic dancers and people with allergies. There was one in my family.

I saw a billboard yesterday which announced, *She's coming, America. You can deny her no longer. Don't miss the message. Dial 1–800-Virgin-M*. A plaster-cast Mary stood there on the board with hands hidden inside the muffler of her flowing sleeves, head bowed, wimple rippling across her shoulders, gazing peacefully out at the turnpike, looking as tranquil as a billboard graphic can. I would hate it if the Blessed Virgin went to the trouble to appear and orate, prophesy, warn, whatever the tenor of this visit might be, and I were to miss it, so of course I called.

It was not Mary who answered, just a telephone emissary, a God-merchant hawking his wares. There are no direct lines to things divine. I have always suspected as much. The recorded voice said, "Hello, friend. Congratulations for taking that first step toward eternal salvation! These days salutary acts are not enough. These are tempestuous times we live in and they'll only get more so as we approach the millennium. The Virgin can help. Take her into your heart and grant her immunity from your skepticism. The Virgin Mary is scheduled to appear in Central Park" – scheduled to appear! Who is her booking agent? Central Park seems a questionable choice of venue for a well-known virgin – "on June 29th. Please leave your name and address to find out how you too can imbibe her heavenly wisdom. Rejoice! The time is nigh!" Honestly, it is not so much the actual message I distrusted as the delivery, the clipped consonants and too eagerly enunciated diphthongs, the rehearsed inflections. I did not want my suspicions, however, to deprive those more intimately connected to consecrated goings-on, so I left Ansel Dorsett's address. I know Baptists are, by their brimstone creed, not altogether fond of the sympathetic and placid Virgin Mary and tend to pass over stories of the annunciation and immaculate conception in favor of more hair-raising tales of tested faith and the hot posterity of the wicked, but I thought communicating with the Blessed Virgin firsthand might loosen his thinking, budge it a notch. I can see that behind Ansel's rigid veneer lies potential. I have glimpsed hidden spots in his mind, dark slicks of thought and memory that his surface thinking can't yet reach.

I see Ansel's septic tank has given up the ghost. A deep rectangle makes a gully of his yard, as though in preparation for a mass burial. When I go, I think I should like to be offered up to the wind and the birds rather than left to the designs of grubs and beetles; in Ivy's vernacular, I'd prefer a sky nap.

Through my kitchen window, I watch the white and yellow sky lose its shine. If my mind sticks by me till evening, I will see the early summer moon hanging low and pink and perfectly round like a dangling dollop of candy, glowing confection. It will hover over the skyline, dotting the well-lit **i** of the AT&T building, and make me feel nostalgic about menses. The loss of fertility is never easy. Fertility gives one's loins something to dream about, something to fear.

I spot Ivy sitting there on the picnic table. Ivy is my neighbor and a numinous spirit. She listens to people, too young to know better. She has recently taken to ogling trees. Wants to catch them budding perhaps. Ivy's beau, Duncan, is considered half-addled and bound for Bedlam by some, his ritualized compulsions and that bedspring hair of his, but I find him lovely in his own way, a kindred soul really. Ivy is delicate and gentle, could easily fit on the head of a pin. She is sheer and must be careful of strong winds. Duncan, despite his own airiness, helps her to remain anchored, I think, in the flesh of this moment. He is her ballast.

Ivy is talking with Mr. Congeniality (a.k.a. Ansel Dorsett). I can imagine their conversation. Ivy says something that causes Ansel's cheeks to redden and he scolds her and calls her "missy."

Ivy lowers her head so her hair will curtain ears so bangled with crosses and ankhs and silver studs the ears themselves look like accessories. She does not want to have to explain why she has decorated her temple in this way; Ansel will doubtless see it as defilement. If he only knew of the bright tattoo she will one day get, the word *God* emblazoned in a tiny script above her navel. The mere thought of this bodily graffiti and the lecture it would unleash could make Ansel fly in his dreams, fall hundreds of stories and bounce to the sky. Ansel lives for opportunities to wax sermonic, though his tongue often knots up on him in the heated zeal of the moment. Some day it'll limber up. Poor Dolores.

Ivy points at the tree she's been gazing at. Ansel looks up and then at Ivy, incredulity puckering his face. He is thinking, *The rod was spared too often with this one.* He is thinking, *Where are the parents?* and *Dissolution of the traditional family*, *Latchkey*, and *God save us.* And now he is wishing he could tell his own family of the strange dangers that percolate in his limbs. He is wishing he could tell his wife, but . . . he can't; his thoughts snag and slip behind gossamer walls. He is beginning to wonder if God's ways are mysterious for a reason or if the divine plan is really just chance, a spin of the wheel. These thoughts flow so swiftly through the fissures of his thinking, they are lost as quickly as they surface and sink back down to grope about in the gloom of the quiet geyser that is soon to blow.

Meanwhile Ivy dreams of mapping the moraines of a planet of her own making, dreams of activating the atmosphere by imprinting herself on its sandy surface, pressing her face to the landscape, encoding the mountains with her own countenance. Ivy glows, and she vibrates to the same harmonic as Harlan. Dreamboats both.

I dreamt of Harlan last night. He was partially covered in ink and looked cartoonish, like a shady comic book figure the artist had been filling in when the phone rang. Harlan was digging in the dirt with his ink-stained hands, looking for earthworms. I stood beside him, holding a lantern. He parted the dirt and dug and dug, and then he stopped. He had a look of determined perplexity on his face, as though he were fishing a diamond ring out of a drain. When he pulled his hands out, they were cut in many places, and blood ran from them thin as water. In the hole he'd dug were sharp triangles of glass, distinguishable bits of broken plates and figurines, jars and doorknobs. "Sand can only stay sand for so long," he said. He said, "Sometimes it's just easier to be transparent." I thought about this for quite a spell upon waking. I wondered if it were a message from beyond meant to ease my final passage or reveal the purpose of my remaining days. I cannot say for sure, but I think heaven is a place where blood means the same as milk or rain or wine, semantically democratic, and dreams are only a dialect of the language of wakefulness.

Harlan and I went to a photocopying convention some years ago when Xerox was in its adolescence. We were both quite taken with the immediacy and clarity of this mode of reproduction. It seemed like something from a future we'd never live to see, a future that included vacations on other planets and robots that whipped up perfect meringues, sweet and soft as clouds, while organizing your clothes by color, a future of distance and ease. While the other men danced with women who weren't their wives and the women drank drinks the color of their painted fingernails, Harlan and I snuck out to the showroom where the display models seemed arranged in a random fashion, at odd angles, like giant game pieces thrown on the board. We walked from one to the next, enlarging and shrinking, collating and double-siding, and the machines clanged and wheezed with this effort; the current technology was clearly doing all it could to keep up with the optimism and expectations of its developers, new model enthusiasm winning out over iron-out-the-kinks cautiousness. Still, we drifted through the room agog, wowed by the crude but workable genesis of advancements to come. We pushed button after button and swooned to the lights, to the symbols that meant *paper jam, add toner, check original*. Then it occurred to Harlan that he'd like to see how he would be rendered by one of these machines, which genes would dominate, which recede in this mechanical coupling. He lifted the lid to a deluxe model with all the options, pressed his hand to the glass, and lowered the lid, the machine ingesting Harlan to the elbow. He grinned and pressed the button. Light slipped out the crack and slid from side to side and Harlan said, "UFO." The copy of his hand was black, but you could see the lines and folds and scars. His hand appeared to be floating in water or air, fingers splayed, an amputated warning.

I put my hand against the windowpane. It feels to me as though it has some give. I think about sand and origins.

Chapter Three. Rachel Loomis
Rachel in the Mirror

The first thing on earth that could properly be termed 'alive' was a molecule with the unique property of reproducing itself. To do this it must have been able to break down complex molecules such as polysaccharides and use their constituent parts to build a mirror image of itself. – Dougal Dixon, *After Man: A Zoology of the Future*

Rachel Loomis holds particular beliefs:

Love. A rumor.

Money. A root. Whether of evil or good, you need a strong-snouted animal to find it.

Food. Held before the open mouth can lure tapeworms from intestines.

Birth. Not a miracle, not a pageant. Babies are smooth like seeds and sleep beneath the tongue of the mother until the sour taste tells her it is time to spit.

Breasts. Places bruises cannot be readily witnessed.

Blood. Has to be seen to be believed.

God. Invisible blood.

Sun. Velveeta.

Moon. A glow-in-the-dark flap (A) through a slotted black tarp (B) among pinpricks of stars. According to her father, an excuse for women to think they are the only ones who bleed. Avoid accidents and operations when it is full.

Skin. A tablet whose glyphs are read as clumsiness, an inner ear disturbance.

Heart. Something baboons and victims do not speak of at parties.

Angel. Band-Aid, sanctuary, pop star, mirror.

The angel was smart and beautiful. He had brown hair and hip-slung bell bottoms like David Cassidy, the dreamy TV boy on Friday nights, though he did not drive a psychedelic bus. He came in through the hole in the wall a poster covered. The poster showed a cat hanging from a tree limb by its paws, about to fall. The cat looked worried. The poster advised, *Hang In There, Baby!*

They played Triple Yahtzee. He did not let her win.

He asked her to marry him. She asked her eightball. *Signs Point to No*, it said. She said she was sorry. She said she had homework. She said, "Men change when they marry."

He was good to her. He gave her Charm Pops and chocolate coins and showed her how to play table football with a folded-up triangle of notebook paper. He didn't have to.

He told her what her body was capable of. He moved her hand across her skin, pressing it into her scapula and liver, the seedlings of her ovaries. He drew her a picture of her pancreas with flowers growing around the border. He told her to keep her heart a secret. "Shh," he said. He touched her finger to his lips.

He read her hand, veins and all. As he turned it over and fingered the telling bumps and ridges, she looked up into his eyes. They were dark gold with black darts like hers. It made her feel the way she felt when she looked in the mirror, hard, and saw herself seeing herself and said, "I am Rachel in the mirror," without really knowing what that meant, the edges of self growing all the more shadowy for being noticed, tunneling away from her. She felt as though she were deep inside herself, at the bottom of her feet, looking up, looking out.

"You will meet a handsome man and bear three children. They will yearn for the comfort of soft animals. They'll beg for hamsters and guinea pigs and parakeets and ferrets. You'll give in on the hamster. It could be worse. You will know people whose children beg for Gila monsters and piranhas and tarantulas. You'll be happy. You'll be very, very, very, very happy." This is what he told her, and she said: "I don't want to meet a man."

The angel put Razzle Dazzle Raspberry Lipfrost on his lips and kissed her on the cheek. She looked at the residue of the kiss in the mirror. It looked like pink wings. *Who is that kissed person?* she wondered.

He gave her baths and trimmed her toenails.

He was a perfectly agreeable angel in every way except that he could not play a musical instrument. At times Rachel had difficulty hiding the fact that this was a disappointment.

Once while he slept, she whispered into his ear, "I think I love you."

He opened his eyes and said, "I'll never be David Cassidy." "I know," she said, "but I can pretend." And she could.

And she can. Now when she hears cupboard doors slam, heavy books drop, feet stomp, shudders rattle, branches snap, glass break, the world settle and shift, she sees her angel again. He is older, more conservatively dressed, and seems sorry to have been such a poor fortuneteller.

Rachel sleeps in fits and starts, but when she wakes for good, her eyes are already open, and she finds herself looking at the very thing she looked at before her eyes closed, the window, her feet, the chair. If her eyes did close. She is never sure. Dry eyes are no indication.

She listens. She hears things that sound distant yet categorical. She imagines her ears are bionic, hearing things that are happening outside her room in other places, other zip codes and time zones, on the outside of her life entirely, maybe traveling light years to reach her ears, puncturing space and time; perhaps these sounds have been ricocheting through the universe since it first erupted into being. Or: she is hearing activity inside her own ears, inside her cochlea, her inner ear, stirrup and anvil, clicking with transmission, the internal communiqué. Perhaps there is a miniature world there, a tiny biosphere growing inside her, desperate for acknowledgment. She remembers well the lesson of *Horton Hears a Who*. Microscopic life in expendable places. We are Here, we are HERE, we are *here*! Boil that dust speck, boil that dust speck, boil that dust speck.

She hears things breaking. She hears things at the very instant of their becoming dispersing fragments of what they once were. She hears disunity, disintegration – dust-cloaked glass falling from sconces, knocked from end tables; world records faltering, cracking; mirrors splintering against walls, crockery against skulls, skulls responding in kind; the sound barrier pealing into stillness; vows and promises splitting up the middle; the brittle hips of old women crumbling. This unending clatter hovers above her and holds her awake at night, hostage of a clamor to which only she is attuned. She keeps her eyes open and seeing as long as she can, wide open, fearful the detritus of things that can't be mended will fall on her closed eyes, oscillating oblivious with dreams, and seal her, hermetic as quarantine, in sleep.

Though Rachel is still visited by her angel from time to time, she is no longer a child. She is an adult, a mother even, to a little girl of her own. Her child's name is Ruby Tuesday, and she is nine years old with hair dark and shiny as the wings of a grackle, a black rainbow in the sunlight. Ruby Tuesday sings herself to sleep. The sound is soft as fleece, and when Rachel lets herself listen, she slips into thinking it is a sound that starts with her, a sound that originates inside her own body – her pulse, her marrow churning. There are days when Ruby Tuesday will not sing or speak at all. She waits for the right opportunity. She is a patient child, a child who waits and watches and nods.

Rachel rubs people. She rubs their bodies, their skin and muscles, feet and faces. She kneads sickness and soreness right out of their limbs. Their pain leaves them and becomes part of their past, their history. It becomes stories they tell when conversations flag. She's not always successful, but people like Rachel because she is earnest in her work, and they feel a little better knowing a woman has tried to ease their suffering with her hands.

Rachel is not a trained therapist. She has taken no classes to learn to rub people the right way. She has no degree in the healing arts. She is not a faith healer. She does not demand that her clients display particular faith in anything, certainly not in her. She only asks that they conjure the departing pain in their mind's eye, see the disease or stiffness swirl through their bodies, dislodged, throbbing, brashly camellia-colored, see her fingers press those pockets of pain, crumble them like dried bread. They need only believe they are what they are – bodies, and feel what they feel – pain, rinse the mind of *tax attorney*, *brake shoes*, *oboe lessons*, *dry rot*, think *ow* and *elbow* and *mammal* and *ache*. Rachel follows her fingers, which know just where to press to make people wince and grin at once, does her work strictly by feel, subscribes to no orthodoxy save that which lies in her hands, sturdy hands that can point to and vanquish ache with the shaky certainty of a forked branch divining water in a desert. It's not the passing catechism of a faddish metaphysics, rather a brief subtraction of burden; a cleaving to the simple pith of being is what Rachel imagines she rubs her people toward.

Rachel is rubbing Liam Drabble. His blood pressure is high and his feet riddled with bone spurs. He does not like the medication he is on. He told Rachel it makes him feel slow and dull, as though he were wading through molasses. He does not believe Rachel can heal him, but he is smitten with the feel of her hands on his feet.

Liam lies on his stomach on the sofa, his feet curved over the padded arm. Rachel gently presses her thumbs into the arch of his left foot. She navigates carefully around corns and calluses. His feet are lumpy like bags of marbles. Rachel smells grass on Liam, freshly mown, and a hint of gasoline.

Ruby Tuesday sits in a kitchen chair she has dragged into the living room. The radio is on, an oldies station, golden hits of the sixties and seventies. A voice sings a frantic chorus, urging Joey to run, over and over again, to flee his girlfriend's violent father. Ruby hums and swings her feet. She will not sing a song unless she knows all the words to all the verses. She will not even part her lips. Rachel watches her as she presses her thumbs into Liam's toes. Ruby stares at her mother's hands and mimics their movement, smoothing and squeezing the air in front of her. She smiles eagerly, as though Rachel had just asked her if she wanted something, a chocolate kiss, a pony, some glow-in-the-dark fangs. Gifts are all the same to Ruby. She is more interested in the hand behind the offering.

Ruby Tuesday is different things to different people, puttying different chinks and cracks. She is Ruby to Rachel, Tuesday to her Uncle Zero. Her grandmother calls her Rachel. Her grandfather called her Pearl Friday or Daisy June or Peaches, and she could tell the nature of the gift he would give her by the name he called her: Peaches meant wax lips or circus peanuts; Pearl Friday meant a superball or folded-up rain bonnet; Daisy June meant tadpoles or ladybugs or water striders.

When the song is finished, Ruby walks over to Liam and kisses him on the ear.

Liam opens his eyes. "Thank you, sugar. I can feel these old frog flippers turning into the feet of a real prince now." Liam winks.

Ruby holds her hand out, as though for a tip. Liam pulls his hand out from under his cheek and slaps her five. She takes his hand and turns it over, traces the lines with her index finger. She squints her eyes. "You wanted to be . . . a dancer and raise rabbits for people to buy for their children on their birthdays and when they're sad. You like to play kickball and you like rhubarb pie but you sneeze a lot sometimes." Ruby nods. "Me too," she says. Liam starts to speak, and Ruby says, "Wait, I'm getting something." She folds his pinkie finger into his palm and touches the creases. "You will not marry a beautiful princess." Ruby frowns, cocks her head. "Sorry," she sighs.

Liam's smile fades as he says, "I was afraid of that."

Ruby says, "Can I come over and see inside your house?"

"Ruby."

Liam says, "Sure you can, honey. Ain't much to see, though."

"Can I see in your medicine cabinet?"

Liam looks back at Rachel and winks. "Sure you can."

"What kind of Band-Aids do you have? Do you have round ones? Round ones are best."

"I expect I got some round ones. I'll make sure I'm well stocked before you come over."

Ruby says, "Good," turns Liam's hand over and shakes it.

Rachel looks at Ruby but can't see her, can't make her out. She has tried. Her eyes send other signals to her brain. This space where a child is supposed to be – a little ghost, some spilled light, displaced air that moves through a room in the vague shape of a body. She is a dark moth, cellophane angel, darting bird too quick to see. She is all portentous sensation, tectonic shift beneath the feet, moist scent of ozone salting the air, tidal roar of water tugging the earth beneath it. A dusky animal at night, slung low to the ground, dark against darker, yellow eyes glowing. She is a gap, a roving lacuna Rachel is careful to step around, the carved opening in which a nine-year-old girl would perfectly fit, girl who sings between silences. Though Rachel clearly remembers Ruby's birth, the moment, the rending pain, the pudding of blood and membrane, she can't bring herself to believe in the resulting child. And Rachel won't touch what she does not believe, will not risk the fracture to prove Ruby is real and alive, prove she carries her mother's own unbreakable genes. Rachel reserves her touch, its dark heredity, for the resilient feet and hides of people like Liam.

After Liam has gone, Rachel stands in front of the picture window in her living room and stares out at her neighborhood. The houses are small boxes with tiny fenced-in box yards, one after another, as though the square were sacred. The yards are littered with things that no longer work or things that have been supplanted by shinier, new and improved versions, obsolete or past-their-prime objects that no longer have a place inside the box: dolls with hair that grows and shortens, air hockey tables, toilets, water heaters, perambulators, adding machines, typewriters, rocking chairs, vibrating beds, velvet paintings of clowns and wild horses, lamps that once rained oil. These artifacts, low-rent suburban vegetation, lie in permanent limbo because their owners waffle, cannot commit themselves to either owning or disowning them. Rachel looks at the debris and feels a vague desire to pull the stopper on this residential bog of dissatisfied, careless consumption, watch it eddy round the drain and be sucked away to the hidden reservoir of ugly living, irreparable actions, the rising swamp of disposability. But people cannot abandon their half-attachments to broken objects, she knows, any easier than they can set hapless lives, graying with disappointment, by the side of the curb.

Ruby sits in the yard with an oversized, Day-Glo orange comb, a prize Zero won for her at a carnival. She runs the comb through the grass, as though she were sitting on a giant green-haired head.

Rachel walks to the phone and dials her mother.

"Hello?"

"Mama."

"Rachel? Why don't you and Rachel come over?" Rachel knows her mother thinks of Ruby as her second chance, the child who will redeem her, redeem them all. Nedra cannot bring herself to use the name that would rupture the illusion. "All this food's going to go begging. It needs to be eaten. I wish people'd quit bringing it over. Every day something – a rump roast, Rice Krispie squares, fresh asparagus. *Had some extra. Thought you might like it, Nedra.* Still trying to feed me. Honestly. Course you can't say anything."

"Ruby's playing outside." Rachel cradles the phone between her shoulder and ear, cracks her knuckles. "How are you feeling? Are you sleeping at night?"

"I get enough sleep to get me through the day. I read where adequate sleep is believed to be one of the best ways to insure longevity. The doctor in this article even said he recommended sleeping ten hours a day! He said that would add several years to your life if you did that. But the way I figure it, you'd end up sleeping through those extra years anyway, so what's the point?"

"Are you still having headaches?"

"Dr. Ingram says it's natural. He said they're a symptom of grief and they'll stop in time. I read about a man today who had a hole in his head that closed up when he bathed in those waters in France. Will you go with me to take flowers to your father?"

Rachel lets the word symptom sit in her ear. She says, "Why don't you ask Zero?"

Silence, then, "Your father, he . . . loved you, Rachel. Didn't always show it proper, but . . ." Her voice quavers, as though it were holding something heavy, something it couldn't quite carry. "He suffered . . . hard knocks and . . . worked for years, those . . . long hours . . . jobs that broke him . . . so we'd never want . . . a man needs . . . good provider . . ." Her voice trails to silence.

"He showed it," Rachel says. She sees her father's large, hard hand crusted with callus, a hand big enough to palm her head like a basketball, this hand a symptom of his love.

Chapter Four. Ivy Engel
Baternoster

The sun was going down and the cicadas were throbbing. I wondered if the sound bothered the bats, if it disturbed their sleep. Maybe it got in the way of their navigational vibrations, sent them diving in the wrong direction. I sat very still on the picnic table. I decided to keep an eye on these fraudulent leaves. My brain was still buzzing from the strange bomb Duncan had dropped. Morphea. It sounded like the name of a host of late-night horror flicks – Morphea Bloodletter or something. I know I should have stayed with Duncan and tried to comfort him somehow, but I had to bolt. An anaesthetized girl can do more harm than good.

The bats were still dozing. Mr. Dorsett still had a septic gorge in his backyard. I considered mentioning something about sky-tram rides across the malodorous chasm next time I saw him but decided against it. I guess I felt even Mr. Dorsett deserved a break. He was probably at church praying his head off, begging God to have mercy on his crummy plumbing.

I watched for signs of life from the wrinkled, brown leaves. You couldn't even see them breathe. I thought about their metabolism, how it must slow during sleep so they can preserve energy for flying and foraging. I imagined their lungs as delicate bubbles, filling only once or twice a minute, their button-sized hearts beating slow and steady as a bathroom sink drip.

I thought about Duncan, about Duncan before all this. I thought about the night we rode our bikes toward a storm. The lightning in the distance was constant and bright. We counted the seconds between lightning and thunder and stopped riding when the flash and bang were almost on top of each other. We parked our bikes and walked along a dirt road that sliced a field of corn in two. The air smelled hot, burnt, and my mouth tasted like metal. We stared silently at the lightning, appreciatively, like we were at a laser show. You didn't have to be looking in the right place to catch the silver zags either, because they were everywhere. And then I noticed the fireflies that hovered over the field, a blanket of yellow blinking above the corn in an uneven rhythm, a floating net of intermittent light, bright and fleeting stains against the black sky. I don't know how long I'd been holding my breath, but all of a sudden I started gasping. Duncan pulled me toward him. He widened my mouth with his hands, turned his head, and matched his mouth to mine. I was surprised at how well we fit together, no overlap, better than clasped hands. Then he breathed. He just breathed. I took his breath in my lungs and held it there. I wondered where his tongue was and what it was doing, but it was only air that passed between us.

My stomach burbled with the memory, and a strange feeling like lit fuses sparked and trailed from my nipples down to my thighs. I wished Duncan were here touching me. I was sure I would feel it.

The dead leaves began wagging. The bats were dropping off one by one and flying in an erratic, noisy mass above the tree. The sycamore suddenly appeared a lot healthier. Up in the air like that, the bats looked like jittery little birds. The streetlights snapped on. The bats flew over and circled the lights, swooping into the buzzing glow periodically, feeding on mesmerized moths and June bugs, those nighttime pilgrims that foolishly worship at an altar of fatal light.

Then I heard screaming, and my first thought was, Oh no, they've gone and attached themselves to someone's carotid artery. This was clearly the residue of Mr. Dorsett's repulsion. And then I could hear it was Mrs. McCorkle's voice. "What?" she yelled as she moved slowly across her backyard toward the pit of tamed sewage in Mr. Dorsett's yard. She kneeled at the edge and looked in. "Harlan? You in there?" She wrestled a spidery root out of the mud wall. "We'll have to clean this mess up. Mercy. Come on now," she said. She walked back to her house and disappeared through the back door.

Then I heard screaming again and things shattering. I walked around front and across Mr. Dorsett's meticulously groomed lawn toward Mrs. McCorkle's. She was yelling at some invisible person, something about bluebells and pork roast, and smashing glass on her driveway. She lobbed an armful of plates and cups and jars onto the concrete and shook her fists in the air. She ran into her house and pulled her gauzy curtains off the rods. She ran back outside and started ripping them into thin strips, like a maniacal maker of kite tails. She spotted me at the end of her driveway and looked at me with narrowed eyes and tense lips, like she wanted to club me. My heart was pounding hard inside my chest, as though it wanted to get out before it was too late. I felt my vision clouding. I was totally clueless as to a reasonable plan of action. I knew Mrs. McCorkle had these spells if she forgot to take some kind of medicine. I think she intentionally neglected to take it sometimes just because she was bored or lonely and needed her other self for company. Once last summer Mr. Dorsett was about to get into his car to leave for work when she ran into his driveway and started clobbering him over the head with a newspaper. She'd thought he was trying to steal her gladiolas. I admit I thought it was sort of amusing at the time, but now it felt like the whole world had completely kooked out, schizoid squared, like the planet had wobbled clean off its axis, and it was beginning to spook me but good. I wondered if some unstable isotope had been released into the atmosphere of What Cheer, or some volatile chemical that could take a once uneventful Midwestern existence and turn it into something Lon Chaney would surely star in if he were alive (something Morphea Bloodletter would introduce on the late-night Creature Feature). Or maybe the magnetic field reversal was finally here. Life, as I had known it, was seriously out of whack.

"You," Mrs. McCorkle said, still sneering at me. "You. Where's Harlan? What have you done with him?"

"He's at Medicalodge South, Mrs. McCorkle, the nursing home? Remember? He's been there for a couple of months." I stretched my arm out toward her for reasons I can't begin to understand. I think the only reason she would have taken it would be to rip it out of its socket and beat me over the head with it. Mrs. McCorkle snorted at me and ran inside. When she came back out, she held a large ceramic vase and a wall mirror. I backed up into the street. Mrs. McCorkle threw the vase and mirror into the pile of shards. The crash was loud and sounded final; glinting splinters of mirror shot across the pavement like sharp bullets of light. She smiled and kicked off her shoes. She raised her dress above her knees, and I could feel my panicked stomach trying to push free of my doomed body. "Don't!"

She hopped onto the sharp rubble and pranced around like she was stomping grapes, smiling and stomping, dress in hand, as though she were just entertaining tourists with a quaint, old-world custom. Then she went down on her hands and knees.

I think I may have screamed, but I couldn't hear it over the thunder of muddled thinking. I walked unsteadily toward Mrs. McCorkle, my legs springy like pogo sticks. I made myself think, willed thoughts outside this scene to come into my head. I thought of the bats, wondered if they were watching and if they were glad to be bats with their breezy lives, hanging in trees, eating easy meals, ignorant of the unseen perils of power plants, compressed skin, and old age. I would have traded places with them at that moment. I wanted to rise, lift up and out of this life, and would have given it all up – Duncan; my bootleg albums, Soft Boys, Captain Beefheart, the good old noisy, collectible stuff strategically swapped for at used records stores; the archive of articles on UFO sightings and the Viking Voyager expedition I'd been compiling since I was a kid; my memories of Grandpa Engel, his teeth;

my face; my breasts – the whole caboodle. Would have given it up in the beat of a tiny wing.

Steady, I told myself. I made my way slowly to Mrs. McCorkle. I saw my chance and grabbed her off the razory debris, wrestled her to the ground, which was no easy feat. Criminy, those age-withered arms and legs held surprising strength. At first I was afraid if I handled her too rough, I might crack her bones, and then I was afraid she might crack mine.

I finally wore her down and began picking the spurs of glass from her hands and feet. She held her hands up and smiled like a child who has made a mess of herself with spaghetti sauce or ice cream. She looked pleased that we were both now covered in blood. Mr. Myers, next door on the other side, finally came out to investigate the commotion, and when he saw the blood and shattered glass, he started running around the yard, shrieking, "Oh my god! Oh god! Oh my god Effie!" He picked Mrs. McCorkle up. She was playing itsy-bitsy spider on her shredded fingers. I could tell she was ticked when he made her lose her place. He carried her inside his house. My stomach finally made its way up into my throat, and I spit bile into the bloody grass.

I wished the bats would swoop down and pick me up by the collar and carry me off to some cold, quiet cave and feed me flies.

Duncan came over the next night and apologized like mad for being so pushy and forward and unromantic and all. He said the uncertainty of his body's future gave all things nascent and physical a kind of guerrilla urgency. It made me feel crummy because I thought I should be the sorry one. I mean, I was the one who had abandoned him in his moment of need. It wasn't like my sense of propriety had been wounded or anything. I think I just went concrete at that moment; maybe I was scared his skin might start falling off if we did it, like that grisly film of the aftermath in Hiroshima they made us watch in sixth grade. The captured shadows branded onto walls, the charred bodies, and all those people in the hospitals. And they just filmed it like it didn't even matter that the people whose bombed bodies they were documenting were completely raw, almost jellied; they let the cameras roll. I always wondered what those cameramen had eaten that day, pears or sweet rolls, rice cakes, carrots, whatever, and if they had been able to keep it down. What did they do when they were finished shooting that evening? Did they take a bath? Did they touch themselves? Did they stare at their skin in the mirror, waiting for it to move? Needless to say, this is not an association you want to make just before your premier sexual experience.

"I think you're going to live through this, Duncan," I told him. "I'm sure of it."

"Yeah, what makes you so sure?"

"Well, last night I had this dream that we were old, ninety-five if we were a day, and we were sitting on a porch swing attached to this gnarled tree that I'm sure didn't have nearly as many rings as we had wrinkles, and 'Take the Skinheads Bowling' was playing in the background. We were talking about the concert we went to last week like it was the good old days. And then we started comparing scars. We both had scars all over our pruney bodies. I had a cool fish-shaped mark across my stomach. You were impressed."

Duncan smiled. "At night I look at my legs and watch my scars. I see them disappear, like someone pulled up the plastic sheet on a Magic Slate. Voilà, new skin."

I noticed that Duncan was clad head-to-toe in blue. Usually he wore four or five bright and competing colors, and you could only look at him for so long before things started vibrating, visually speaking. But today he had on a navy blue bowling shirt that said "Earl" on the pocket, blue jeans, blue Converse high tops, and a blue bandana around his ankle; a small, blue marble dangled from his ear. "Say, what's up with this color-me-blue look?" I asked.

"It's chromatherapy," he said. "I saw it on Oprah or Sally Jessy, somewhere. Different colors have certain effects on you emotionally and physically. Red is a stimulant. If you surrounded yourself with red, you'd constantly be doing chin-ups or something. Blue is supposed to be healing." He shrugged his shoulders.

That's one of my favorite-favorite things about Duncan, how he gives anything or anyone a chance, withholds judgment until he's seen for himself. He accepts without complaint the absurdity that's as prevalent as ether and knows anything is possible, even good weird things.

I told him about the bats and about Mrs. McCorkle. Duncan loved Mrs. McCorkle because she always said outrageous things even when she *remembered* to take her medication. Once she told us if she were president, she'd impose capital punishment only for excessive chatter in movie theaters and dawdling in line at the supermarket. "That would rid society of an insidious element," she said, "*and* help defray the population explosion." I think she meant it too. Duncan wanted to send her blueberries and winding vines of morning glories.

I showed Duncan the bats. They were resting again, their withered foliage shtick.

"Are you sure they're bats?" Duncan asked. I pointed to the peaches near the top and showed him the ones clenched tight under leaves. "Wow," he said. "They're awesome. They look sacred, ancient. Like something from a cave painting." Duncan's voice began to crack. He gently placed both his hands on my breasts. "Do something for me," he whispered.

My breasts were tingling, hot-wired, bubbling with current. "All right," I said. I closed my eyes.

"What do these bats eat?"

I opened them again. "Insects mostly."

"What time do they start feeding?"

"I don't know. Around sundown." I began to wonder what it was I was going to end up agreeing to do. I had a feeling it wasn't what I'd originally imagined consenting to.

"Green and yellow are good colors too," he said. "Restorative. I'll be back," he said, walking away. He turned around. "Tomorrow night."

When Duncan showed up, he was wearing only a busy madras pair of Bermuda shorts – no shirt, no shoes, nothing else. I hoped his scars wouldn't glow in the dark. He was carrying a blinking jar full of fireflies and a coffee can full of dead bugs. "Will you humor me, Ive?" he asked.

"This isn't going to involve, like, chicken blood, is it?"

Duncan smiled and shook his head. "What are your 'rents doing?" He had this very serious look on his face; he looked sort of like Spencer Tracy in *Guess Who's Coming to Dinner*, like he was getting ready to make an eloquent speech on a touchy subject.

"I don't know. Watching a miniseries or something."

"Will they come outside for any reason?" Duncan grabbed my arm like he wanted me to think before I answered.

"Not likely. Unless the couch catches fire."

"Good. What about the Dorsetts?" He nodded his head toward their house.

"I haven't seen them. I think maybe they left town."

"Cool," he said. "Where are the bats?"

I pointed to the streetlight; a dark halo circled it. "A couple stick around the tree and dive at the porch light occasionally."

Duncan took hold of my shoulders and led me under the canopy of the sycamore. He raised my arms and pulled my T-shirt over my head.

"Couldn't we at least use a tent or something?" I asked. For most things you can count me in; my name and the word "trooper" come up a lot in the same sentence, but an exhibitionist I'm not. I don't even like to undress in front of a mirror.

Duncan spread my shirt on the grass, pushed me down to my knees, then lowered me gently to the ground with my head in his hand, as if he were baptizing me. Out of the corner of my eye, I saw a bat dive into the light. Duncan took the dead insects out of the coffee can and arranged them on my stomach: a June bug, a cricket, some flies and moths.

"Duncan, you know, this is weird."

"I know," he said.

"I refuse to eat them, if that's what you had in mind." My stomach itched, but I was afraid to scratch, like any movement might activate the insects and make them bore into my navel or something, as if Duncan had preprogrammed them. Stepford bugs.

"You don't have to eat them," he said.

I was relieved. Around Duncan I do things that under any other circumstances would lead me to believe I'm certifiably off my noodle.

Duncan sat down next to me. He took some fireflies out of the jar, held them between his fingers, waited for the blink, and crossed himself, smearing the phosphorescent abdomens onto his chest. He lay back. I felt a little bad for the sacrificial fireflies. Duncan scissored his arms and legs like he was making snow angels, only I guess they were actually earth angels, invisible. "Close your eyes," he said, "and do like I'm doing." I flapped and kicked, and it felt sort of nice, like I was a low-flying, upside-down bird.

I felt something brush against my stomach. My skin was sparking, crackling with heat. I felt my stomach and my heart lift out of my body, finally striking out on their own. My legs shook. I let myself feel it.

Chapter Five. Charlotte McCorkle
Mrs. McCorkle's Ascent

Somewhere in time a child is wishing she were asleep, hidden from the calamity she associates with opening her eyes. I can see this child clearly. Her face is scarcely bigger than my hand. She sits in a field with a man, watching cars clank down the rutted dirt road.

The man bites into the little girl's forearm and says, "Rachel, you flinched." He says, "Daddy loves you."

The little girl looks at the teeth marks on her arm. *It looks like empty parenthesis*, she thinks. *Didn't hurt, didn't hurt.*

The man leans back on his elbows. He pulls up handfuls of grass. "This is your beautiful hair," he says. He lets it fall through his fingers. He laughs. "See, the earth's scalp is smarting, but it doesn't make a sound. Listen."

I don't know this man, this child. I don't know this place.

The little girl looks at a meadowlark sitting on a fencepost a few feet from her. She remembers reading about the state bird in a book about Kansas. The meadowlark sat on a fencepost just like this one, next to a picture of the state flag with its rippling motto: *Ad Astra Per Aspera*, to the stars through difficulties. Thereafter they were linked in her mind, the bird and the flag, and she decided that the path of migration of meadowlarks bent magically toward the moon, an arduous trek. She says, "I can read the minds of birds." She stares into the meadowlark's black eyes. "He's thinking, I wish my children would bring me presents. He's thinking, The breeze from the big cars is nice."

The man pinches the child's leg and smiles at her silence.

Of course being a sporadic seer can stoop the spirit at times.

For this they give me drugs, tranquilizers and anti-psychotics, anodynes for second sight, so at night all I can see when I fall asleep are the brightly colored liquids of apothecary decanters. There is madness in this world, I don't deny it, barking, moaning, self-mutilating madness. But in a world where perfume is sprayed into the pink and pinned-open eyes of rabbits to test for resulting irritation and blindness, where illiterate men, men who promise to remain so, are sought to do janitorial work, to clean up after nuclear physicists who may have absentmindedly tossed out top secrets with the evening trash, it's a fine line, a pot and kettle skirmish.

For my mother there were different labels. At first it was the vapors, later hysteria, the megrims, female trouble, dementia, doldrums, melancholia, floccillation, brain fever, she was moonstruck, bedeviled, shatterpated, splenetic, corybantic, chapfallen, had bees in her bonnet, rats in the attic, all diagnoses pronounced in hushed tones. I wanted to understand how other people saw her. I could see that her unhappiness was an embarrassment to them, an unforgivable breach of uxorial protocol, bad manners plain and simple. *Hystera*: Greek for uterus. Ancient Egyptians believed hysteria was the result of a malcontent uterus with a bad case of wanderlust. They thought the uterus unhitched itself and floated and drifted like the seeds of a milkweed, roaming, searching for who-knows-what, something to fertilize. It sometimes comforts me to imagine that a part of my mother escaped for a time. The symptoms of hysteria varied depending on where the organ landed. I believe my mother's uterus eventually touched down in water, mistaking it for limitless sky, and found that it could not swim. I believe it was a welcome relief, this watery exit.

Harlan went out peacefully, a babe in a cradle, easy as crib death. He slept his way into the next world, not noting how the outline of his life was shifting, jerking occasionally as though he were only sleeping through a thunderstorm. I watched his bony chest rise and fall, barely displacing the air around him. His mouth was agape, rounded as if in surprise, and I could see the thin thread of air that moved through him. As his chest stilled, mine heaved, breathing for both of us now. There were no final words or sounds, no rattle or sputter, no fluids attesting to the ebbing of life. Just muffled quiet, the silence of being under water. I twinned the O of his lips with my own and waited. Two men came and took him from me.

Ansel's pit appears to have sprung a leak. A thick, black fountain of bilge gushes in the air as though from a special breed of subterranean whale. Ansel is running back and forth in front of the hole. He is thinking, *How can I subdue this foul geyser?* and *Raw sewage, Cleanliness, Godliness, How have I come to be here?* and *God save us.* He is realizing he's up to his wobbling knees in the muck of the mundane and that there is no one who can save him.

Time for me to close the windows.

This house is beginning to feel small, the air is close. I feel hemmed in, compressed. The furniture appears agitated and out of breath. The cushions on the couch pulse anxiously. They long to be sat upon by Harlan. I haven't the heart to break the news to them. Harlan's La-Z-Boy rocker/recliner, normally recalcitrant and squeaky, sits silent. It knows something is amiss for it has not been properly rocked for months now, and it knows the bones that occasionally stick in its open maw do not belong to its beloved. Recliners are not easily duped. The possibility of mutiny looms large and palpable in this living room.

I rest my eyes, and behind the wrinkled paper of the lids I see figures lying in the grass. I cannot see their faces, but their bodies are young and fluorescent. Small, black birds fly and dart and circle dim lights. The figures move their arms and legs like water striders. Blink.

On the television, there is a talk show. The guest is the talk show host herself, an echo that grates. This woman, the guest, the host, blond, white teeth, taut calves, linen suit, is here as a cautionary tale. She speaks of the perils of breast implants. They can shift and travel and pad your shoulders or they might leak or burst, emptying out the contents never intended to course and bubble through the human corpus. To counter, there is a smattering of success stories in the audience. Women whose pert breasts bear a resemblance to any variety of fruits (wax?), a gamut of shapes and sizes and buoyancies spoken for, all the latest mammary models. They sing the virtues of being allowed to shimmy closer to someone's idea of beauty. (*Big Breasts, Big Business: The Blossoming Industry of Breast Implants – The Bosom Boom! Next on . . .*) The discussion now rotisseries around whose idea this is. Attempting to raze the walls of long clung-to notions, stone by stone, is labor too strenuous for these old, opaque eyes to watch. The beauty of aging: the pressure to be cast from a certain narrow mold of comeliness fades and frees you up to think bigger thoughts.

Into my eyes drifts Zero, the wash and rinse boy at the beauty parlor. I see him afloat in the air, hovering above a flat mattress, rising slowly closer to the ceiling, where a movie poster conceals cracked plaster. Bells ring and he drops, sinks back into the anvil of flesh.

It is time for my constitutional around the yard. I must chat with my flowers lest they leave me for a kindlier caretaker. I weeded today, a necessary trauma my lovelies must endure, painful maintenance, the horticultural equivalent perhaps of having your gums scaled, and I have only my less-than-dulcet voice to offer as anesthesia. "Drink to Me Only with Thine Eyes" seems to have a nice narcotic effect. Dear glads, I do miss you, too early yet, will see to you later, sure to be enchanting as always, your ascending shots of blossoms, a Roman candle frozen as it flares. The neighbors covet you. I see it in the wily whites of their eyes. Not to worry; I have one peeper peeled at all times. You'll be no one's nosegay while I'm still upright. Hello, sweet william. Chin up. You're in the pink. No more frost to fear. (I find a bit of jocularity feeds a flower good as fertilizer.) And my nasturtiums, my little firebrands. From the Latin for nose torture. So called because when ingested you produce a burning sensation in the proboscis. Of course, it is rather an afterthought of a defense. The flummoxing beauty of my candy stripe phlox. Good work, troops. Salutations, my petulant tulips, who bloom impetuously at any hint of warmth. I long to stroke your thin, green throats. The Audrey Hepburn of garden flora!

Ivy has finally left her post, most likely to visit her dear Duncan. The plumbers appear to have subdued the fountain of muck in Ansel's yard. After all the money Ansel will have poured into calming this angry spewage – he will choose a spare-no-expense, top-of-the-line tank – his temper will be newly inflamed when he discovers the city plans to dig for sewers soon. Of course Ansel puts no stock in my prescience, so it wouldn't do a lick of good to apprise him of this.

I do miss Harlan's hedge of vegetables. Harlan had an especial affection for his modest corn crop. He would reverently lay the ears, his adoring offspring, in a wheelbarrow and swaddle them in a blanket. He would bring me out to look at them, though it was understood I was not to touch. Only he was permitted to fondle their feathery silks at first. Harlan would kneel, close his eyes, and run his hands across the soil, as if he were a blind person learning the language of a new face. His tender cultivation paid off. Word got out about the heaven hidden inside those husks, and folks traveled a far stretch to sample the sweet white flesh of Harlan's legendary love children, his green growing kin.

Touch is an underrated sense. We are tyrannized by the visual, and nearly as often led around by the ears, but what if we lost tactility, what lesser creeping creatures would we be could we not feel? The texture of soil is one I too quite favor. It ranks high, among scars, scabs, and bark. When I was a child in Montana, I had a friend, Luella Sanford, whose right arm had been badly burned in a grease fire. The landscape of scarred skin on her forearm seemed to me so beautiful as to be ornamental. I loved to run my hand over the drawn and puckered terrain of that skin. The cooling lava of bunched flesh was patterned and perfect, mathematical, mesmerizing as a spinning pinwheel. One night I stayed with the Sanfords and slept with Luella in her bed. I was so excited to be that close to her that my own skin flushed red and began to itch. I felt the stiff ticking of the mattress pressing into my legs. When I thought Luella was asleep, I pushed the quilt back and gently laid my head on her arm. I rubbed my cheek against the blossoms of scar, the thick petals of skin. Luella awoke and began to cry. Deformity's just another shape, I wanted to tell her.

I smell a pan heating on the stove. Hello? Wonder if someone's been in here heating milk in my absence? Gaslight. Hello. A skin has begun to form across the surface. It puckers at my touch, like the tight cheeks of a new facelift, makes me think of Margaret Huggins' mug that looked permanently windblown and startled after the surgery. I think it is now wholly unsuitable for consumption. I do enjoy the rockabye sedative effects of a glass of warm milk.

Kansas is not dairy country, though we claim our share of cows, our share of the cow pie, Harlan would quip. This neighborhood was cattle-covered once, some time ago. When was that? The world all spinning simultaneity. Time seems to me now little more than God's way of preventing everything from occurring at once, an imposition I balk at. I believe I read something to this effect on the chest of a young man. The sagacity of T-shirt aphorists is sometimes surprising. So I haven't much of a mind for dates, but the heyday of the cow in Wyandotte County was sometime prior to the Nixon administration but long after the once-upon-a-time of mythical beginnings. I can recall when the landscape was once so thoroughly measled with the creatures, dotted with their slow, brown bodies, they seemed to be part and parcel of a lumpy topography when viewed from above. Urbanization has since herded them toward greener pastures on the perimeter of town, which, I suspect, is perfectly agreeable to the cows. However, due to some sort of legislative chicanery, a grandfather clause, a few blocks from here one lone, hill-of-beans cattle ranch remains, though the lowing grows fainter by the year.

Rural and urban ways have been known to collide here, such as the time the marathon runners' course intersected with that of a group of wayward bovines moseying toward the besaged field across the way. The angry knot of runners jogged in place and jeered the animals, ignorant of the rules of right-of-way, and you could see in the stretched lines of the joggers' bobbing and furrowed foreheads, lines of frustration no amount of endorphin would erode, vows of revenge to the tune of secret and endless nights of cowtipping and the reintroduction of red meat into their diets.

I too feel it is time to emigrate, feel as if I'm on the brink of some movement, the precipice of a long drop. The blue and silver brocade of the sky (it is a Vincent Van Gogh sky, swirling thick and wet, as though you could reach up and touch it and it would stick to your hand) swoops around me as if resentfully aware of its role as background, and I see myself as a photograph waiting to be taken – the present turned into the past the instant it is trapped on film, frozen stark staring into the headlights of time, pesky time, chopped into representative mile-marking bites and history a repeated dream, a song I can't shake, a story I carry with me as I look for the perfect vellum and quill with which to transcribe it. Tsk.

The wind swells and seems strange today even for Kansas wind, which is wind mostly unchecked and untamed by the bunched-up carpet of hills. It has a tint to it, as though viewed through yellow spectacles. A jaundiced breeze. It smells of lilacs and brisket. Cicadas churn and hum and slip out of themselves. I have a fondness for finger-ing the fatigue-green mottled armor of the cicada's carapace, though it will not tolerate this for long without the restraint of pinched wings.

Word of caution: *never* carry a rabbit by its ears. The day rough-handled hares turn deaf and cease their silent singing is a day we'll all learn to rue.

Corn. Ears of corn. Harlan confided to me that "corn is to vegetables as spiders are to insects as whales are to fish," logic which left me just this side of bewildered. Ears of corn, a figure of speech I tell Harlan. Needn't fear the auditory powers of vegetables. Deaf and silent as sleeping things.

Harlan aims the TV remote at me and presses the mute button, mistaking me for the Motorola. I'm the real thing, I say. See me.

Mercy me, words and pictures and smells! Salad days of my think-ing. Cognitive stew.

Popko, Stewart, whom I loved as none before him at the age of ten because he seemed to glow, ambling about in his own personal globe of light, and because he could converse with owls by rolling his tongue into a hollow log and blowing. Hoo-hooo. They had wonderful nighttime colloquies, the treetop cantabile of hoot owls a melody he could translate and sing himself. He would share with me the stories these wide-eyed birds told him, primal secrets dipping far beneath the surface of empirical knowledge, secrets about the species-propagating responsibility of sensing the distant movement of mice in the dark, the burden of forward sight, and the tingle of instinct in talons.

It was fear that accompanied bathing in that long ago claw-footed tub. Wary was I, as a child, it would wake up, flex its creaky feet, and carry me off into the middle of town, displaying for all to see the mouth-shaped birthmark on my chest, an indelible kiss. Harlan loved this part of me and it was for him alone to love, even then.

It is dusk and time for Harlan's return. He's been coming home later and later since his boss, Mr. Notley, passed on. Harlan works himself into the ground, until his edges are visibly frayed, but never a word of complaint. He is a fine man. Perhaps he has stopped out back to jaw with the corn and the crows.

The sun is sliding loose and oblong down the sky like an egg thrown at a wall, trying to ooze away unnoticed. I know how it feels. A pyramid of mud sits next to an empty square in my neighbor's yard. Bomb shelter? The days of duck-and-cover with us again. It all comes back around. I do hope Harlan's not been digging again. Sometimes he buries small secrets in backyards, but this appears to be a doozy and will surely cause the neighbors to pitch a fit. Harlan? Better check this dug-deep cranny in the earth. There's that lovely child sitting on the picnic table. Her name, her name . . . floating around somewhere, darting behind the clouds in my head. Best not wave till it settles on my tongue so I can speak it. *Mersey shoats and dozing goats and idle rams eat . . .* Harlan? Goodness, who *is* that making such a fuss? Are you all right? Where have you disappeared to? Heaven's sake, it's hardly dignified for me to be snooping about my neighbor's backyard in search of a grown man.

Good gravy Marie, this is indeed a sizable concavity! If I kneel on this grassy pallet, who knows when I'll be properly upright again. Leaning is my limit. My, it is deep and smells of putrefaction. Harlan?

Are you in there? Roots poking through the sides to see what gives. We'll have to clean this up. Merciful heavens. Come on now.

A woman, old woman cloaked in a dimming nimbus of light, sitting in the grass. Her legs outstretched, the soles of her feet bleed and glint in the failing light. Her fingers twist around one another and climb the sky. This woman looks worn. Her face, I wish to feel her face.

Beneath the thin fabric of her flowered shift, the skin on her back bubbles and splits near the curves of shoulder blades and wet, brown feathers emerge, crumpled and slick and slow as birth.

Her eyes, white as a near-blind dog's, but she sees things all the same. I've witnessed these eyes before, looked through them. Her sight gropes forward, lists, returns. Those boiled-egg eyes look through the past to see what comes next, look behind to see what's ahead, the loop of being, look and look at the air. They see an old woman with outstretched legs, seeing.

Things! Roiling and cracking beneath my feet. The earth itself. My life has been what it has been. Nothing more. You divide who you are by who you have been and accept the quotient. If not, you're left wishing you had time to do more than wish and you become the empty space between living and then what.

So I will clear this life of its hard evidence, the everyday indictments that give it heft, must clean house, perform an ablution on the outward edifice, this exoskeleton that has held most of my days in its dark jaws, will flush out the accumulation of the mundane, the day-after-day objects that bear testimony to gravity, the breakable matter of living, will empty this life for where I am headed there will be no appetite to feed or thirst to slake, no reflection to see, no call for the dinner service, the looking glass. The things this house has seen. Make my life light and earn the air so to find my love Harlan dispersed in atmospheric thinness, cells gathering and grouping long enough for me to fix him in my flickering eyes, and we'll erupt and fill the air with the mist of who we are next.

I collect the bones of this house, break them, crush, scatter them across the earth, pry loose the cloying ligaments until this skin of living, this temporary shelter, slumps in on itself! Then I'll float up and wheedle the currents, breathing easier in the new altitude.

I fancy the screech and crackle and splat of things breaking back to their discrete parts, their origins, the world cracking open into the egg of its start. Oh!

Voices coalescing. Parts of myself saying their piece, parting words, and I see an angel in my driveway, wearing sneakers, shadowed and sleek. Maybe she is Harlan's familiar. Maybe his captor, a precocious, bored seraph already disenchanted with the new whoosh of wings, the wonder of flight. She glows, lit from inside, so bright, she burns my eyes. Cannot look directly at her. Bits of God drift and swim through her system like the squirmy-celled organisms in lake water. She knows something. She's done something with Harlan. Where is Harlan?

Her mouth opens, lips shift and look familiar, but I don't speak angel, cannot decipher the sounds that escape. This one, she reaches for me (I long to be felt but am afraid). What if she is not what her outstretched arms suggest? Mustn't let her sniff my fear, mustn't waver.

Shattered remains wink in the evening pink light, diamonds in water, refracted again and again.

And there is this, all that is left, this desire of the flesh to know that it persists: I want to feel the ruins of this ordinary life press hard into my feet and my hands, want to feel my skin give, feel my body slip and lodge between the angles of light.

The diamonds are rapiers, hot, the comfort of nerve endings, reassurance of pain.

I am as a child amidst her first textures, the feel of her own fingers. Feel the skin on my back begin to pucker and part, bones shift and slide and rise through me.

Red spreads around me bright and everywhere: the red of spilt sun, the red of indelible ink. It is wet and sticky, lovely.

Life clings to me –

Harlan, my sweet easy Harlan, I miss your inky fingernails, your purpled hands. I love your feet and your lips and your white, white belly. Harlan, my soiled Harlan: a dream I have when I'm awake.

Chapter Six. Rachel Loomis
Ullalulla

Rachel lies in bed listening. She can hear Ruby in the next room singing herself to sleep. Ruby has taught herself another song from old Christmas records. *It came upo-on the midnight clear, that glorious so-ong of old, from angels be-ending near the earth to touch their ha-arps of gold.* Rachel stares at the woven ring that dangles beneath the window shade. It is set against the black sky outside her window, a cored moon guiding the waxing and waning of her thoughts. The night air is swollen with the whirring of cicadas. The sound is loud, and she feels it on her skin; it crawls with prickly legs along her arms and into her ears. Rachel feels her father, feels him hanging in the dark air of the room. She craves his noise. His hands.

Her angel comes, crosses her gaze, sits on her bed. He has aged since she last saw him. New lines crease his cheeks and the skin of his arms looks wind-beaten, as though it had been exposed to extremes of weather. The angel smiles. He picks up the glass of water from the nightstand and throws it, dutifully. Water and glass burst against the wall and shard the air. Rachel watches it explode and catch the light like a magic, fast-blooming flower, transparent orchid noisily racing through its life cycle, lovely. The angel peels back her sheet and lifts her leg to his mouth. He bites her calf, and she exhales soundlessly. He claps his hands against her face and shakes her head. Sound roars and rushes and loops through her ears like a carnival ride and blows a small hole through her forehead, a hole she can feel with her finger. "I love you," she says, "I think," reaching out for his lips. Things slow and grow quiet. Her angel's face is ashen, the color of old meat, and his lips move, but she cannot hear what they say. He releases her face and holds her hands.

See these hands? Her father. He sits beside her bed on a chair he is too big for. *These hands love you,* he sings the words. She sees him, so close, sees him rubbing his hands together. For warmth? Cleanliness?

His eyes gape, but he doesn't look at her, reminds her of a fly. *They want to make sure you take in all the feeling you can. Pleasure's stored in these beat-up palms and fingers.* Holding them up, arrested. *Pleasure for the pair of us. Symbiosis* – he accents the second syllable with a long I and Rachel thinks *kumbaya*. He lays his hands on his own cheeks and rubs gently in circles, as though he were putting on rouge. *These hands are the real thing, angel, and you'll know when they've touched you, when they've pinched your skin and slapped you, you'll know you're alive. They brought you here, to this world, this home. This little bed. They caressed and squeezed and pulled you into creation. The sounds they make against your skin, it's music, child. It's what living sounds like. These hands are crazy for you, crazy-crazy for you, darlin'.* He moves his hands down his throat, across his undershirted chest. *Hands, they want to marry you, angel face. Most people aren't even alive, stiffs, don't live wakeful, numb and hard, they feel with their small brains and not with the very sap of themselves, and then they deafen themselves to their own irrelevance. But you, pumpkin, I'm giving you the gift of feeling life the way it was meant to be felt, all dizzy and physical, filled with blood and sensation. Because that, child, is what we have on the dead.* His hands move down to rub his thighs. *'Good' is a word you have to arrive at a meaning for on your own, and the feeling that heats up these fingers when they gather your skin,* he rocks and closes his eyes, *they grow so strong with the sweet feel of drawing that life-granting substance to the surface, the lovely contrast of the colors after that show you felt something, skin all bubbled up like hot tar pavement in summer – that feeling is powerful good!* This last word comes shivering out of his mouth, and he holds her hands between his, rubs them together, meets her eyes. *Can you understand?* His voice gets quiet and trembles when he says, *So much love! So much love for you, my baby doll, my little sparrow, my sugar cake,* thinning to an inaudible whisper.

The first blow is the only one Rachel ever feels or hears. The rest is a silent movie she experiences secondhand, in memory, seen from below, crouched beneath the looming action, an insect, pebble, particle of dust. Tonight it is an openhanded slap against her bare thigh. The large, red handprint makes her think of cartoons, of Bugs Bunny's outline left behind as he runs through the wall, a desperate exit, the shape of his fear, the gap between calm and chaos, a hole the blue sky shows through like an insult. She hears the first moan. After that, the soundtrack of her father's love plays for his ears alone. When his hands have had their fill, giving and receiving all the love they can bear, her father cries out, and the music on the radio downstairs rises in volume. *I love you I love you I love you so much chicken love you so so much listen to how much listen.* He takes the objects from the tray he has brought with him, collected for this purpose, sacrament of love, and throws them: a mixing bowl, a mirror, a paper weight, a travel clock. Rachel knows there are crashes and frightened cries, but she hears sounds like bells or birdsong or horns or laughter, and when the tray is empty, she reaches tentatively for her father's arm, strokes it as though it were a napping cat, until his love-cramped hands only jerk and clap and shake themselves to sleep in his lap.

Land's sakes! You are certainly prone to uncleanliness, child. The weary voice of her mother. She is bathing Rachel, scrubbing her feet. *You're not my kin. You're from the Black Feet tribe.* She moves the washcloth up her legs and settles on a bruise. *Where does all this dirt come from?* The rubbing is hard and hurts Rachel. She pushes her mother's hand away. Her mother finds another bruise and scrubs it harder. Rachel pushes her hand. Her mother finds a scab and says, *Your skin is like tree bark in the summertime.*

Rachel grabs her mother's wrist, pushes her hand, covers sore spots. *Please, Mama.*

Stop it, Rachel! We have to make you clean. Her mother folds her soapy arms on the bathtub, hangs her head. *If you were just a piece of soiled carpet, I'd know how to clean you. A little soda, good as new.*

Rachel says, *Please.*

It is later that night and Rachel sits on the floor, gently rubbing her arms and legs, feathering her fingers against the skin until bumps rise, as her mother reads to her and Zero from a magazine. Rachel's mother cleans office suites. In her buildings, there are doctors and dentists and architects, insurance and farm service and travel agencies. And they all have rooms where clients or patients or policy holders wait. To forestall their boredom and impatience, these rooms are stocked with assorted magazines: *Parents, Highlights, Field & Stream, The New England Journal of Medicine, Ladies' Home Journal, National Geographic, Glamour, Popular Science.* Rachel's mother brings old issues home, where she reads article after article, collecting facts and tips like trading stamps, as though she might one day be able to swap them for one big insight – information about trolling for walleyes and the pathogenesis of non-insulin-dependent diabetes mellitus and inventive ways to prepare okra.

Rachel and her mother play Waiting Room. Her mother reads to her and helps her fill in puzzles and answer surveys. They fill out subscription cards under made-up names and addresses. *Smithsonian* goes to Juniper Hopewell of 777 Redondo Drive and *Newsweek* to Billy Bob Thundershoes of 1313 Mockingbird Lane. Rachel thinks about waiting. She wonders what it is her mother waits for, wonders if she reads to keep from thinking about it, to keep from seeing the expectant wariness that ages her face.

Rachel stands on the couch and looks at herself in the big square mirror that hangs on the wall, reflecting the other side of the room. The mirror makes the room a visual echo of itself and sometimes tricks Rachel, making her think she is on the other side.

Sugar, Sugar – The Archies. Rachel speaks to herself. She makes lists, lists of possessions and dreams and names and food, favorites and wants and fears. She catalogues her life, the world. She is indexing her forty-fives, announcing the names to herself as she writes:

Gypsies, Tramps and Thieves – Cher
Heartbeat, It's a Lovebeat – The DeFranco Family
Beach Baby – The First Class
Seasons in the Sun – Terry Jacks
Brand New Key – Melanie
One Bad Apple – The Osmonds
I Think I Love You – The Partridge Family
Life Is a Rock – Reunion
Little Willy – The Sweet

She has a round, pink plastic record case with Disc-Go! in relief on the top. The base is black plastic with a spindle that spools the records in a stack. Rachel imagines it is a thin arm accessorized with flat, black, space-age bracelets. This is Rachel's favorite pink possession. She prints the names of her records neatly on notebook paper and tapes the list to the handle. She hides the case deep in her closet.

Another list – Favorite Names, Boys: *Ambrose, Chevy, Derek, Elmo, Louie, Moses, Pierre, Poodebaugh, Winslow.*

Girls: *Brandy, Crystal, Druscilla, Gladys, Hyacinth, Libby, Marvina, Ruby, Torey, Tuesday, Willette.*

She even has a list of her lists, an index of her order. At night, she lulls herself to sleep by naming and alphabetizing and categorizing, cross-referencing her thoughts. She sees each idea, each person or picture that comes to her mind, as a recipe card that goes in front of or behind the last.

Rachel continues to wander, weaving about in her past, and she stumbles forward into recent events, hears her mother's voice say, *Come now. It's your father.*

When she arrives at the house, he is lying on the bed with his hands folded across the pale mound of his belly. *He wouldn't let us call an ambulance,* her mother says. She has been crying. She clutches her elbows.

Pillowcases cover the dresser mirror. The bedroom window is open. The closet door is open. All the drawers of the dresser stick out and appear demanding, as if waiting to be fed.

Her father's eyes are closed. There is odor, a loamy stench. Her father is naked. Her mother has begun to wash and groom him. She has combed his hair; it is so neat and thick, it looks like a hat, a soft helmet surrounding his sallow face.

Her father is dead, a massive coronary.

Rachel begins rubbing her father's feet. They feel cool and hard, ceramic feet.

Her mother grabs her arm. *Don't! You can't raise him!*

Rachel pushes her mother back. *Go,* she says. She looks into her mother's eyes. They seem strained, as though they'd been forced to look too closely at something. They look pushed in and empty, small, blue basins. Rachel grips her mother by the shoulders and walks her out of the room. *Go downstairs,* she says.

Rachel returns to her father's room, closes the door behind her. She begins to rub her father's legs. She rubs and presses, the knees, the shins, the thighs. She shakes the sickness off her hands and moves to his arms, first the right, then left. Then his stomach, his chest, his shoulders and groin and face. The skin feels cool and moist beneath her fingers, like clay. She pushes against the putty of her father and looks to see if it will hold a new shape.

Then his hands. Her rubbing hastens. The skin remains blanched and cool. She pulls hard on the fingers. Nothing. She claps each hand between hers. They fall to the sides. She bites down on the heel of one hand. *Come back.* She begins to pound on his chest. *God.* She punches him in the groin and stomach and slaps her hand on his thigh. A sound comes out of her, a gravelly keening. She picks up the lamp from the night table and lobs it against the closet door. The crash is loud, and a riot of white powder drifts through the afternoon light that slants across his feet. The effect is stunning. She is somewhere else, another country, another planet. Mercury or Venus, close to the sun. She's floating through the air, through a miracle. The atmosphere is immolation and avalanche all at once.

Still, it's not enough.

Rachel hears the television go on downstairs. She feels a remote satisfaction in this, in making this happen. She opens her mouth, leans over her father's face, cries out, a creaky plaint, an unoiled hinge. Her chest aches, and it feels as though there are multitudes inside her, angry people marching out of her lungs and larynx, falling from her mouth. *Can you understand?* Rachel moves to her mother's dresser and pushes bottles of perfume and fingernail polish and hand lotion and cuticle remover from the round, gilt-edged mirror they sit on. She marvels at the fact that the mirror, which has sat on her mother's dresser for as long as she can remember, has survived until now. She looks at the walls of the room. White walls, no scars, blank white walls. She carries the mirror with her and crawls on top of her father's body. She drapes herself over him, matching him part for part, over his distended belly, the final sheet. She lays her face sideways against his and holds the mirror beside them. She sees his ear and his hair; her eyes, her nose, squeezed lips; her neck, his shoulder. Rachel sees herself in the mirror, her image fusing with her father's, skins mixing. It is difficult to distinguish the dead parts from the living ones. Her cheeks are not kissed or bruised but pallid, lifeless as his. Rachel drops the mirror. She picks up her father's hand and covers her face. She stares through his fingers at the wall, closes her eyes.

And this is how nights pass, Rachel sunk deep in the quicksand of history. Though she snags herself on chain links of time, she can't imagine what happens next. A future curls in front of her, sticking impudently out like a darting tongue, daring her, mocking her. She can't see it, but she knows it's there.

She knows but doesn't believe. Knowing is no trick, no boon, no balm. She knows her father loved her.

What Rachel also knows is that people believe strange things about death, things accepted without being taught or preached, things that get passed on through dreams or genes or food.

To rid her grandfather's corpse of the cancer that had crept through his living tissue, Rachel's grandmother put a pound of butter on a plate, their wedding china, and placed it atop the coffin overnight to soak up disease and leave the body renewed and ready to rise when the time came. Then she pitched the poisoned butter, plate and all, in the mortuary dumpster.

Rachel's mother once read to her from one of her magazines a story about a community of people who believed Death held a roster of the names of the living, which he used to guide him in his work. When someone died, all the members of this community would change their names to befuddle Death and hamper his progress in reaping until he could revise his list. For extra insurance some changed their names monthly or weekly. Others tried to steer fate by living without names entirely, erasing themselves, answering to nothing.

Rachel's mother believes the soul flies out of the flesh fast like a scarf caught on a stiff wind and that all measures should be taken so that it doesn't tumble back into the body. Windows and doors are kept gaping, knots and ties and braids and tangles are loosened, undone back into a career of straight and flat. And mirrors are covered so that the spirit doesn't falter amidst a double take of its own departure.

Tonight when Rachel finally sleeps, she will sleep deep and dead for a time, and then her mind and nervous system will click on like backup generators, and she will dream. One of her dreams will buzz loudly in her head, make her spring to like a Murphy bed, act as her alarm clock. The dreams Rachel can't bring herself to sleep through, the ones she cannot allow to twist to conclusion, are the ones she has just before she needs to wake. She is afraid these dreams will tell her that the life she thinks she has already led is the life yet to be lived.

Rachel will dream of her father. She will see him laid out in the polished mahogany casket she and her mother chose for him. She will look at his body, the deceit of his hands clasped calmly, surrounded by creamy upholstery, and she will wonder what color the thread is that forces intimacy between her father's lips and gums. She will wonder what has been done with the blood that was drained from his body, the organs he no longer neglects. She will wonder if the fluid that now flows through him, inflating his skin, keeping his skeleton afloat inside him, will eventually drain and soil this satin fabric that frames mourners' final memories of him. She will think of the plight of the coffin, the lambent grain of its wood soon to be kept secret beneath the earth. And she will wonder what will happen when the tiny organisms that expedite decay drink of her father. She'll see them in her dream mind turning on one another, covering and silencing one another like hands over mouths, swallowing one another whole until there is one mass, one creature that feeds on itself.

She will focus on her father's strange pink complexion, the powdery pancake foundation, and the thought of draining blood will thrust the notion of vampires into her thinking, compelling her to reach into her purse and pull out a compact. She'll snap it open and hold it over her father's face. She will see her father's face appear in the mirror just before it disappears behind the humidity of his breath.

When Rachel's eyes realize they are open, they will look through the circle of the window shade's pull, and she will see the eye of her angel blinking, wet and penitent.

Rachel doesn't know what she believes, but she knows her father would never allow other people's desperate theories about death or soul or sin or butter to prevent him from gorging himself on this life, and she knows too that fear of the pain of purging in the next did not seize him until he began, belatedly, to finally question what followed living and breathing and feeling on earth.

The world in so-olemn stillness lay to hear the a-angels sing. Ruby's voice.

CALLING ALL ANGELS

Go into this child's room. See that she is bleeding. Gently kiss the blood from her lips. Fold your wings around her.

Sit beside her in front of the television and watch cartoons and game shows. Unwrap candy coins and slip them into her mouth. Rub her feet. They are small and smooth as polished stones. Let her chew on your feathers if she begins to grit her teeth.

At times you will lose patience. You will wamble and flap at your own limitations, and molting feathers will twist to the floor. She will gather them and make a picture to comfort you. She will trace her hand on construction paper, a sweet hand small enough to fit comfortably inside your mouth, and she will glue your fallen feathers to the outlined fingers. She will fashion the body and head and wattle of a turkey out of brightly colored kernels of Jolly Time popcorn. She will affix toothpicks for legs and feet. This will make you wish you could inhale her, breathe her all the way in, hide her in a window-clear satchel of lung until it is safe to exhale, marsupial breath.

You will want to be all things to her, lick her clean as new, but you are only witness. You can but dance her in circles and braid her hair and let her watch you sleep.

She believes that behind every gesture lurks its opposite, its dark twin: hidden inside every caress is the violence that gives it purpose; inside every blow is its attendant caress.

As she gets older, your role will change, grow more difficult. She will want you to absorb absences, straddle gaps. But you are without mass, the absence of absence, food that will never fill the stomach, and a covey of you could not plaster the lack.

Do what she requires, even if it hurts.

Dream, dream of her flying beside you. See her smile at her sudden skill as she navigates the air. Teach her to dodge turbulent currents, rub rain from dark clouds.

Lip-sync a love song for her when you wake.

Chapter Seven. Zero Loomis
Zero Overhead

It may well have been because three people that evening spat the word "fuck" at him during abridged conversations that Zero knew he must float.

1. "We're a not-for-profit organization and any contribution you make would be tax-deductible."

"Yeah, deduct this, you sorry fuck, and get a real fucking job!"

2. "Hello, may I speak with Mr. Everett LaMountain, please?"

"Fuck off, you bastard! I told you Mr. LaMountain died six months ago. You can't get blood from a dead horse!"

The last call was an experiment, and Zero disguised his voice. He called a friend who didn't know he was now telemarketing:

3. "I'm sure you've heard about the tuna industry and how they'd decimated the dolphin population. Public pressure has finally brought about federal regulations forcing them to revise their policies and practices, and we have a – "

"Oh, like they won't find a way around *that*. Like they won't just fish in unregulated waters and employ migrant fishermen they'll pay in fish heads or rancid chum or a delectable assortment of marine life conveniently euthanized by the latest tanker spill or biohazardous dumping. Anyway, I'm afraid you've mistaken me for someone who gives a rat's raggedy ass. I say nuke the goddamned dolphins and those bleeding-heart whales and spotted owls too but leave *me* the fuck alone, pal!"

His friend's hostility didn't surprise Zero particularly. He'd heard him hector phone solicitors before. Once he overheard him describing to a representative of AT&T the grisly end she would meet if he were ever again the someone she tried to *reach out and touch*. Zero couldn't help but notice the delight his friend took in this rebuke, and he had the feeling his friend had been spending long days beside the phone just waiting to slug the sloganeer with her own sentiment. Zero's friend is a performance artist who sometimes slaps himself in the face with raw flank steaks on stage. It's a persona. Still, their conversation depressed him a little. However predictable the abuse, and despite countless opportunities to adapt, Zero had never warmed to being the object of scorn.

There's something about people ruing the day they met you that makes the body want to be weightless, Zero thought, walk on the moon.

And he felt discouraged too that he had not yet found an honest and forthright way to persuade people to donate their money, sad that his earnest soft-sell was an approach openly scoffed at by his high-strung coworkers, who successfully solicited money for a gamut of gimmicky products and fly-by-night organizations from even the most hardened resistors of phone swindle. They called him "Chinchilla" and said, "You know what happens to chinchillas, don't you? There's no future in being soft!" The time-share condo operators were the most velvety-voiced and slick. The woman in the cubicle next to his told him about a telemarketing seminar she'd gone to in Tulsa in which she learned useful and easy-to-implement techniques to increase her sales. One veteran salesman, she said, told how he'd boosted his sales of hearing aids by looking in the phonebook for people with antiquated names like Eustace or Emmaline, Ulysses, Obadiah, then speaking very softly into the phone when they answered, whispering his pitch so that the customers would say, "What?" or "Pardon?" to every word he uttered, thereby demonstrating their need for his product.

That night, Zero turned the light off in his bedroom and undressed.

He louvered his blinds so the moonlight angled through the slats like a stationary searchlight trained on him. He lay down on his bed striped with light. He raised his head to look at his body, the striations of darkness and illumination, and thought he could feel the moon's heat; he imagined broad, hot fingers splayed across his body. He looked at the alternately dim and glowing skin on his thighs. His legs were thin, dark with hair, and long. He wondered if anyone would ever wish to touch his abdomen, kiss his knees. He thought this would feel pleasant, give his stomach a sense of purpose it now lacked. He imagined himself the night's prisoner, outfitted in the striped duds of a jailbird. He felt quietly reckless.

When Zero was sixteen, the woman who administered the eye test at the DMV asked him to meet her after work, "*If* you pass the driving test," she said with the stern and provisional tone of one who prefers paperwork to customer service. Her upper lip was bristled with tiny dark hairs; she had lead-colored eyes streaked with yellow and a knob of graying black hair at the back of her head. Zero imagined turning it, gaining entry. He thought there was something primitive and inaugural about her; something of the origins of existence skulked in her smile, a big bang of crooked, stained, ivory teeth. He longed to know more.

Zero aced the test. She took him to her house. The sex they had felt hereditary to Zero, determined. It felt like they were two parts of a larger mechanism coming together, clicking in place, facilitating something outside themselves; Zero believed he was, diminutively, in service of the churning of the universe. She would not kiss him. She stroked him and pulled him inside her, then later placed her hands on his pointed hipbones and pushed him out, removed him, as though he were a spent part, an emptied cartridge. This made Zero feel sentimental. He looked at her lips. She sighed and said, "I see you need succor," and pressed his cheek to her chest. The heat and moisture of skin flushed from vigor warmed his face.

Zero had often thought he might like to be in such intimate proximity to another body again. But, as a rule, he kept at least an arm's length between him and the next carcass, never tailgating: bodies scared him a little. All those different zones and sensitive moraines, it was confusing.

He lay back and closed his eyes, felt his body sink into his comforter. He rolled his eyes back as far as he comfortably could. His eyelids began to twitch, and he adjusted the angle of his blackened stare. He breathed deeply and thought about clouds, pictured the suggestive and raveling gauze of them. The word "cumulus" flapped through his mind, V'd like a seagull. "I am weightless," he told himself. "I am zero mass. Nothing. Nothing can hold me down."

He felt himself move, felt his feet tremble first, his calves, felt his body making decisions it had not been faced with before. The air quivered around him, and then he felt himself break loose like a balloon dislodging itself from the limbs of a tree. His hair fell away from his ears, and he squeezed his eyes tight and exhaled. The hair on his arms sparked with tiny volts, stood straight, magnetized toward the ceiling. He felt a slip of air glide between his backside and the comforter, and he hung there, tottering in the air, imagining himself a puck imperceptibly aloft on the steady pin streams of an air hockey table. As he tightened his buttocks, he visualized himself being pulled upward by an unseeable force, dangled by an airy thread emanating from the curious spinneret of his own navel. His arms and legs felt like vapor, more breath than flesh. And then Zero felt distinctly the ponderous anchor of living begin to lighten and lift, felt the dubious, stitched-together confetti of matter disperse, felt the flinders of being fling themselves wide. The tiny buried center within every molecular speck of himself rattled with his notice. He felt his DNA untwist, unfurl, and fade, and he thought, My body is air soluble, gravity no match. They will have to scrape me off the sky. Zero's body throbbed, mortised to the superlunary, empyreal purlieu of being.

The phone rang and Zero felt his body drop into his bed, a stone, a baseball, a shoe, imaginable matter. He'd forgotten to unplug the phone. Shit. He'd never shed the flesh if he couldn't anticipate how the spirit could be startled back into its skin. Willed dissolution of matter was a delicate business requiring absolute silence. He knew this.

Zero let the answering machine do its job. He sometimes thought he sensed a bitterness in the red glare of the display that invariably announced, "o Messages." It was his mother. She wished he would come over and eat some food. There is too much. It will spoil. Zero stared at the ceiling, at the *Wings of Desire* movie poster tacked there. Without his glasses, it was only a floating, dark square. He felt pleasantly abstract.

Zero preferred his day to his night job. During the day, he was one of the shampooers at 2001: A Hair Odyssey. Zero loved having his hands in water and hair. He loved scrubbing scalps, running soapy fingers through wet hair. He imagined they were the rain-soaked pelts of sleek and sleeping animals, ocelots or cheetahs, minks.

He found most things about the salon soothing: the pouting lips of the black porcelain sinks; the carousels of rattail combs; the constant and variegated dusting of hair on the floor; the sound of chairs being pumped, hoisting heads closer to scissor-ready hands; the exotic fragrances of jasmine and jojoba. He even took strange pleasure in the sting of perm solution in the air.

Zero fed his fingers, like sticks to a fire, into the springy silver hair of Mrs. McCorkle. He loved the sterling coils of her mop, flattened at the back from sleep. He also loved the hair of the women who came in the Care-A-Van on Saturdays, residents from the retirement highrise. There were several women with hair bright and unnaturally blue, some almost turquoise (the experiment of a rogue stylist banking on the failing vision of milky eyes), like the water of the log ride at the amusement park. Those women, with their cosmic, welkin curls, were often lured into a brief nap by the sleep-inducing pulse of his fingers. But Mrs. McCorkle stayed wide awake and told him stories.

On this day, Mrs. McCorkle wore bandages on her hands and oversized, Velcro-strapped shoes to accommodate the dressing that wound around her feet and ankles. Though she usually entered the salon mobilized by her own will and legs, today she had been wheeled in by a nurse. The nurse and Zero had lifted Mrs. McCorkle into the chair in front of his sink. Zero could feel his face twist as he looked at Mrs. McCorkle's mummied hands, and the nurse whispered, "She had a little accident." She smiled at him. "I'm going to duck into the dime store," she said. "Back in a bit." Zero was worried about what lay beneath these bandages, worried about the meaning of Mrs. McCorkle's escort, but he didn't want to pry. And the salon prized efficient detachment in its prep people. He reclined the chair and eased Mrs. McCorkle's head into the sink as gently as if he were placing a newborn infant into the arms of its mother.

"My nephew Gabriel was thin like you and had very nice hands and feet. A fetching fellow. Did I ever tell you he was an angel?" She lifted her head slightly, looked at Zero, then relaxed back into the sink, closed her eyes. "I know what you're thinking – Gabriel, angel, an old dame's delusion. They've already tried to incarcerate me for such thinking." She held out her gauze-padded palms to him, as though for an inspection of cleanliness. Again she raised her head from the sink and looked into Zero's eyes. "I see you, kid," she said and smiled. Zero gently persuaded her head back into the sink.

"He was . . . born an angel, your nephew?" Zero asked, non-committally.

"Yes, but it wasn't apparent until puberty."

Zero pumped piña colada-scented shampoo onto his palms and massaged it into Mrs. McCorkle's scalp. He could feel life and resilience in her hair, not the usual damage, the brittleness bred by blue rinse and dandruff shampoo. Mrs. McCorkle had a little dandruff too, but did not attempt to exterminate it with harsh chemicals. Zero imagined tiny, grayish flakes falling on Mrs. McCorkle's shoulders like bits of drifting ash, salting her neck and back, flakes that would prevent most people from wearing dark colors.

Mrs. McCorkle's stomach began to grumble. "That's the sound of a poisoned clairvoyance," she said. "Such as it was. This medicine disagrees with me. Your fingers are soothing to this aging scalp. Sometimes I think my thoughts will fly right out of my head, maybe put someone's eye out."

"How did you know?" Zero asked.

"About Gabriel? We always knew there was something unusual about him. It was obvious even to strangers he was special, but we didn't understand how special until his wings began to show. When we are in the midst of a celestial burgeoning that walks among us, we tend to look the other way, hope we'll be spared. He was a strange child. Eyes big and blank as peeled onions but gray like thunderheads. He was always doing things that made him sad, rebelling against what he sensed he would one day have to accept. He would kick a cat clean across the street then bust out crying and repent by fattening that confused and wary feline on cream, stroking and scratching it until it purred the purr of a forgiving bliss. His parents would discover money missing from purses or dresser tops one week, and the next it would be returned with interest accrued. He'd scream at his sister, then he'd scream back at himself on her behalf. There was talk of multiple personality sickness, though in those days we just spoke of it as a many-faced form of madness. Lunacy, as you probably know, has always been much more commonly identified with women, so we all resisted thinking this way. I suppose being labeled demented is the predictable cross one has to bear when he is both human and something else. There are, of course, imposters.

"Gabriel was always trying to push a part of himself away, keep himself at arm's length, but this part always came snapping back at him like a plucked rubber band."

Zero thought of his father, of all the times as a child he'd been pried from his father's leg and pushed away as though he were a leech, a barnacle, hampering his father's ability to swim. He thought of the time when he was six years old and dared to venture into his father's room. It was during one of those afternoons in which the noises upstairs battled with the cranked volume of the television. First Zero went outside and pretended to send bottle rockets blasting out of the clear, green glass of an old 7-Up bottle as he waited for the house to still. There was a thick sadness inside him, a weight in his stomach, holding him down, stunting his growth, keeping him short and invisible, he was sure. He didn't know why he felt so heavy and small, but he knew the noise inside his house came from something both terrifying and magical, like Willy Wonka's glass elevator crashing through the roof of his chocolate factory and tearing across the sky, and Zero was certain it was something his father might reveal to him if he could prove to his father he were worthy.

When the house finally grew silent, Zero wrapped his too-big gun belt around his waist, buckled it, and walked with the spread-legged gait of a TV cowboy to keep it from falling and binding his legs. He secured his cap gun barrel-down in the holster and walked into the house, up to his father's room. His father lay on the bed in his white, ribbed tank shirt and boxer shorts. Zero stared at his father's body, the rising and falling hill of his stomach. He felt an urge to climb on the bed and bounce on his father's belly, to crack him open like a geode.

Pop! Zero shot the cap gun in the air; a thin snake of smoke coiled out the barrel. His father's body jerked and he opened his eyes. Zero grinned and shot again and again. Then he held the gun to his own head. He'd seen this in movies, a game of bravery. He pulled the trigger. The gun snapped, felt hot against his temple. Zero's hearing tuned slowly out, turning into a hiss of static. He dropped his gun and cupped his ear. It was ringing now, a manic switchboard of muffled sound. A fire blazed inside his ear, and his head felt wobbly and loose, leaky, like a cracked egg.

Zero walked to his father and laid his head on his stomach, the place where shirt and shorts parted and hair sprouted on the bowed belly. His father rested his hand on his head then pushed him off. "You are a ruined boy," he growled. "Nothing, a void. Out."

Zero walked out of the bedroom holding his ear, afraid the shrill whistle was now trapped inside him.

Zero squeezed the water out of Mrs. McCorkle's hair. His ears ached with memory. He stared at the lines in her slackened cheeks, neatly parallel as if marking off geologic ages. He wondered if there really were a race of sorrowful angels, mongrels, part human, wandering loose in the world, and he forced his father's face, impassive as glass, from his thoughts.

"Of course when the wings began to sprout, Gabriel's calling was hard to deny. It started at his hips, two sharp, bony structures that pressed their way through his skin and bled like anything. Gabriel was up in arms about this angelically renovated physiognomy and had these little inklings of wings surgically removed. Wasn't easy finding a sawbones for that job, I can tell you. But." Mrs. McCorkle sat up. Water ran down her face and slid into the channels of flesh ringing her throat. "They grew back."

Zero toweled Mrs. McCorkle's head and neck. He looked at her bandaged arms. She seemed to him to be descended from a large, flightless bird. Poor wounded emu. He sensed an electrical stinging in his hips, but this was not entirely unpleasant. He felt for the protrusions of bone. He usually deafened himself to stories of pain or injury because he had difficulty controlling his empathic responses, which had doubled him up and blurred his vision on occasion. Once when he was seven, a neighbor boy who'd somehow gotten wind of his vulnerability tied him to a chair and made him listen to the story of the crucifixion. *They spiked nails through his wrists and ankles, Zero, drove them clean through bone, through veins and tendons and everything. They flogged him with a knotted whip until it split his flesh. Creatures came down from the hills at night and lapped up the blood. We have to make sure it wasn't in vain*, the boy said, smiling. *We must make sure our sins are worth it*. The boy stopped when Zero's hands and feet splotched red and his eyes rolled to white. Zero's arms and legs and chest and forehead throbbed for weeks after. If only someone had finished the story, he later thought, had told him about the resurrection, the body stitching itself back together for another round. There's nothing so reassuring as a theatrical flouting of common sense.

Zero loved movies, old ones, safe movies with safe stars like Dorothy McGuire or Merle Oberon, no slasher films, gory horror films dripping in ichor, no films with hospital scenes or anything more than tears of romantic emotion jerked from the viewer. Zero also liked foreign films. He liked how the act of reading subtitles made him feel distant, secure, wrapped in the dark custody of the movie theater. It gave his brain another distraction; immersion in words made him feel less at the mercy of the visual image.

Zero wondered what an angel's body would feel like to human hands. He couldn't help himself, he imagined the narrow hips of this boy, Gabriel, the extra appendages poking through like fingers testing the air outside, blooming with feathers. The hips seemed to Zero like the wrong locus for such anatomical pomp. "Shouldn't the wings be in the back?"

Mrs. McCorkle dabbed at the moisture around her eyes with her gauze-bundled hands and said, "Well, that was the rub. He was deformed, you see. Maybe it was from those years of resistance, who knows. The wings came in all cockeyed and sickly, curling out to the sides like corkscrews with shriveled, musty feathers, and each time they grew back they came in more gnarled and in less and less likely places. His body grew knotted with scars, a map of failed aerodynamism and rejected godliness."

Mrs. McCorkle looked dead into Zero's eyes. "No," she pronounced. "He wasn't a mere freak of nature, a collision course of genes. People instinctively gravitated toward Gabriel. He was magnetic. If we took him to a department store or an amusement park, in a matter of minutes we'd be surrounded by people who were embarrassed and confused by their overwhelming desire to touch him, be witnessed by him. Once his parents took him to Worlds of Fun, just after the grand opening, and Gabriel was desperate to ride the Finnish Fling, that round barrel that whirls as the floor falls out. He was crazy for that lovely inertia. But they had to halt the ride midway through because the barrel began to wobble. Somehow the people had stacked and rolled themselves on top of one another like wooden matches. Either side of Gabriel was caked with bodies. They dropped at his feet as the spinning slowed."

Zero felt apprehensive about knowing anything more about this boy, this, this hybrid creature, felt it was dangerous, but his curiosity voiced itself before he could check it. "What happened to him?"

Mrs. McCorkle stared down at her bandaged hands, wet coils of hair dangling near her creased eyes. "He killed himself. A terrible end. He was tired of his family, all of us, pushing him to pursue this avocation for which he'd been chosen. He lay down behind the back tires of his father's truck, waited for him to back out of the driveway on his way to work. His note said, 'I'm only human. See?'"

Zero felt a tumescent pressure in his head as he thought about a truck moving over the modest hillock of a mixed-breed boy.

Mrs. McCorkle said, "You float, don't you, Zero?"

Zero looked into her eyes, reflective panes of green glass. He thought if he stared long enough her eyes might crack and shatter, and he could reach his fingers inside and pull her out, her bones and organs knotted together and endless like a magician's rope of multi-colored scarves, mere illusion, like God, willed belief – the heart, the pelvis, the lungs, the femurs, the liver, the kidneys, adrenals: invisible parts taken on faith until they falter; then the outside is cut open, the certainty cracked, the secret blue of air-stunned blood turning red, faith obsolete. Zero thought of Schrödinger's cat. He imagined opening a box and finding a stout, caramel-colored cat coiled and stiff, front paws raised in reaching. Or maybe it would be empty, like the magician's box, contents waved away with a wand, absence the measure of success. Or perhaps there would appear an enchanted eightball, like the one his sister, Rachel, had as a child, displaying the floating message: ANSWER HAZY. TRY AGAIN. Everything a puzzle, nothing an answer.

"Sometimes," Zero said. He saw himself in Mrs. McCorkle's eyes. He saw his cheeks and nose broadened by convexity, black glasses, his eyes floating in hers, layers of vision, seeing and seeing and seen.

Chapter Eight. Ruby Tuesday Loomis
Denomination: To Be Ruesday, Epizootic

OF RACHEL, GRANDDAUGHTER OF NEDRA

Ruby Tuesday gazed at the constellation of freckles on her arms as she sat on her grandmother's lap. Her grandmother, Nedra, patted the sides of her legs and said, "You're Grandma's little chicken, aren't you, Rachel darlin'?"

Ruby thought about her grandmother's neighbor, Mr. Markovich, whose chickens flew up into his trees at night and roosted on branches. They sat still and clucked softly and some curled their heads behind into the pillows of themselves, and Ruby thought they looked like big, exotic flowers blooming brown and red and white and yellow, camouflaged flowers pretending to be chickens for protection against greedy beetles and grasshoppers. Ruby traced the thick blue veins that branched out from beneath the flowered shorts along the moon-white thighs and knees rocking her up and down. The veins blazed trails down her grandmother's legs like little rivers and creeks, tributaries in search of headwaters.

"Shall I read you a story, chicken? I read an article about newborn stars. It's all about these subatomic particles and optical images they have now of, um, let's see, what was it again?" Nedra rooted among the magazines on the table next to her then flipped through *Scientific American* with one hand. "Images of a radio-emitting galaxy from ten billion years ago. By the time the pictures reach the lookers' eyes, they're already that old. It takes them that long to travel to us. Slow as cold Karo syrup."

"Maybe those pictures don't count anymore. Maybe they changed things up there and we don't know it yet. There could be space babies who turn into purple plants. Or giant rats. Or maybe they're just like Earth people but they drink out of flowers and have tails and sing instead of talk. Or maybe they only allow talking on holidays or at bake sales." Ruby hummed and jiggled her throat with her finger, a manual vibrato. In a bobbing monotone she said, "Do you have any stories about gorillas? If you couldn't see me, you'd think I was talking into a fan. It's cutting up my voice like the blades. Ahhahhahhahh. I like it when the fans are turned on. It sounds like the cookie factory we went to on our field trip." Ruby took her finger away from her throat and pressed white spots into her grandmother's legs. She watched the pale circles shrink and disappear, fill with color again. They reminded her of the television. She loved to turn it on and off, on and off, then stare at the screen until the last pinpoint of light burned itself out. "Or a story about serial killers? I know a boy at school who has these collector cards, with cartoons of killers on the front and words about their crimes and lives on the back. There's this one killer and he only killed nurses, and this other one used zodiac signs to know who to kill next. I'm Gemini, it's twins. He would have killed me fifth, I counted. Maybe he killed two Geminis just to be safe. Joshua said his dad said the killers are unbalanced. He said the front part of their brains is smaller than the front of nice guys' brains."

"Good gravy Marie!" Nedra said. She gathered Ruby's hair into her hands and combed it with her fingers. "You oughtn't to have your head filled with such upsetting information! You only have so much room in your noggin" – she gently thumped the top of Ruby's head – "for a limited number of thoughts and you don't want to waste them on serial killers for Pete's sake. You don't want nice thoughts elbowed out by ugly ones, do you?

"I could read you a story about cowbirds? Would you like that? You're fond of little birdy-birds." Ruby nodded. Nedra pulled *National Geographic* out from under *Family Circle* and rested the magazine on Ruby's legs. She thumbed through the pages and found the article. She held the magazine to the side and read: "'Blinded by instinct, a mother blue-winged warbler feeds a brown-headed cowbird chick that has hijacked the nest. Brazen imposters, cowbirds foist their fast-hatching eggs on the unattended nests of other species, duping countless songbirds whose own young then suffer from neglect and starvation. Surveys show cowbirds are on the rise in some Illinois forests, virtually every wood thrush nest has been saddled with their telltale speckled eggs.'"

Ruby said, "Oh," covered her mouth, and chewed on the heel of her hand.

"'At Fort Hood, Texas, biologists have killed thousands of captured cowbirds with auto fumes in a bid to save the heavily paratized,' no, 'parasitized black-capped vireo from extinction.' Gracious."

Ruby looked at the picture at the bottom of the page of asphyxiated birds lined up in neat rows like a package of Fig Newtons. She stared at the black slits of their closed eyes, their stiff legs and curling feet. She imagined the birds being fed to the exhaust pipes of old cars. Her tears fell on her grandmother's legs.

"I'm sorry, sweetie. I had no idea this was going to be such a sad story. We'll just turn the page and find something more cheerful."

Ruby stirred the tears in circles on her grandmother's floury white thighs, wishing they would turn to paste so she could glue the pages of the magazine together. "It's not fair," she said. "Why don't they find them new homes? They don't kill people that leave babies on doorsteps or give them to be adopted. They could double-dog fool those cowbirds right back. They could put pretend birds in nests. Why don't they just take the eggs out before they hatch and grow up confused?"

"Well, sometimes, muggins, they have to take drastic measures in order to keep things under control."

"Why?"

"You wouldn't want us to run out of those precious little songbirds, would you? I understand you're a songbird yourself. I hear you've recently developed quite an impressive repertoire of Christmas tunes." Nedra squeezed Ruby's shoulders. Ruby stared at the dark space where her grandmother's legs met.

"Just because the cowbirds don't sing doesn't mean they aren't nice birds." Ruby karate-chopped her hand against her grandmother's knee, watching for reflex. "Maybe they don't sing because their real mamas weren't there to teach them how. They grow up alone and they're quiet. They can't figure out why they don't look like their parents. They feel bad all the time because they're off-key, like Mrs. Landers says to Clarence Routh, so he plays the recorder. But what if cowbirds can do other good stuff we don't know about? Maybe they can see things singing birds can't see. It probably makes those other birds mad and everything because the cowbirds are always looking into their lives. I bet they can hear better than other birds. I bet they're good listeners. What good's a singing bird if there aren't any listening birds around? They can even hear things growing and crawling, like lilacs maybe. Or slugs. They have supersonic ears – they can hear . . . what's the smallest alive thing in the world? Or maybe they're just better dancers than singers."

Nedra said, "Well, that's quite a fanciful little story, Rachel honey, and it's good to use your imagination sometimes, but in the real world, things just don't work that way. Sometimes, even though it might not seem fair, you've got to sacrifice the individual for the greater good. Don't they teach you that at school? Maybe it's too early." Nedra kissed her granddaughter's cheek.

Ruby whispered, "*Ruby* honey."

OF PEARL FRIDAY, PEACHES, DAISY JUNE,
GRANDDAUGHTER OF H. JACKSON

When Ruby was four years old, her Grandpa Loomis gave her an Etch-A-Sketch. It wasn't her birthday or Christmas and they weren't on sale. On it he had drawn a heartbeat with the neatly creeping peaks and plummets of a healthy rhythm. That same year, he gave her a Rubik's Cube key chain. Neither of them could solve the puzzle, could get the colors to line up and change from patchwork to planes, but they would take turns twisting the cube, pretending they knew a secret combination. Their secret, they both agreed, was that they preferred those tiny squares of color mixed and random.

When Ruby was five, Grandpa Loomis made her a miniature dollhouse out of balsa wood. It was a toy for her Barbie doll. Before he glued it together, he drew tiny pictures on the walls and floors, pictures of windows and sinks and chairs and paintings and dogs and rugs and lamps, pictures the size of thumbtacks. Ruby set the house on her dresser, and she placed P.J., the doll with the smooth rubber skin and bendable limbs, beside the dollhouse, on her stomach, her pert and smiling, blond-pigtailed head resting on swiveling hands, forever gazing into her own personal miniature dream home. Ruby imagined Barbie doll dreams. She pretended that as P.J. lay admiring her dollhouse, she dreamed of the day she would have a couch of her own to sit on, a dog of her own to pet and feed, a window to open and close. At the moment, P.J. had none of these things, though she did have an orange and pink beach van with folding chairs and inflatable water raft. Ruby inherited all of her Barbies and accessories from Rachel. Some had still been wrapped in cellophane when Ruby got them, and the prices on the yellowing tags seemed so low Ruby wondered at first if there was only fancy candy inside.

When Ruby was six, her grandpa gave her a pet turtle the size of a silver dollar. The turtle's house was round and made of transparent plastic, and a moat of water circled an island in the middle. There was a brown and green plastic palm tree and a gray, plastic rock. Ruby saw the turtle's dream. The turtle dreamed of privacy, so he could step out of his shell now and then and scratch the rubbery hide of his back against sticks and rocks and welcome the sun onto his wrinkled stomach.

When Ruby was seven, her grandpa gave her the following: a gumball machine; trimmings he'd saved from a haircut; a box of cinnamon Tic Tacs; walkie-talkies; Bugs Bunny Band-Aids; a plastic half-sphere filled with water, glitter, and a winter village; a box of colored toothpicks; ear muffs; sea monkeys; partially popped bubble wrap.

When Ruby turned eight years old, her grandpa gave her an illustrated book about animals of the future, *After Man*. She wondered what comes after man in the alphabet of existence. After man, woman, she thought. After woman, girl, gorilla, eggplant. And before? *We stand here before God . . .*

Rachel watched and trailed behind Pearl Friday, Daisy June, Precious Peaches.

Ruby loved her Grandpa Loomis. She loved the gifts he gave her, but more than that she loved the chafe of his big hands as he placed the gifts in her open palms. She felt the rough, callused skin brush her hands, and her fingers would tingle and fizz, as though her circulation had stopped, the blood slowing to a ticklish crawl.

When Ruby was newly nine years old, she carried a tray of food to her grandpa, who told her he was resting his quarrelsome joints. There was a dinner plate filled with thick slices of ham, scalloped potatoes, and snap beans. Also on the tray were a purple thistle in a thin vase, a jelly jar full of ice water, a biscuit and butter, some Apple Brown Betty, and a wint-o-green Lifesaver, whose magic spark-in-the-dark powers – visible when quickly bitten – Ruby could not wait to show her grandfather. Ruby had insisted she ready the tray and carry it to her grandpa by herself. She walked carefully up the stairs, testing each step tentatively before committing to movement, and made it all the way to her grandpa's door before a small bunch in the rug caught her foot and pitched her forward. Ruby held tight to the tray, but the plates of food flew and clattered sharply, sounding like a toy machine gun as they fell to the floor and cracked against each other. Ruby stood up and covered her mouth with both hands. Grandpa Loomis widened his eyes and mouth, but the sound stayed inside, and he clutched at his chest as if stanching a wound. Ruby walked to the side of the bed and touched her grandpa's arm. His breathing slowed, and he looked past Ruby to the doorway and said, "Sorry, child. I'm sorry." Ruby laid her hand on top of her grandfather's and spread her fingers.

"Starfish," she said.

OF TUESDAY, NIECE OF ZERO

Ruby Tuesday felt the tree-torn sunlight roll down her cheeks like drops of warm water as the zoo train rounded the monkey house.

When Zero had asked Tuesday if she would go with him to the zoo, he told her it was important to him; he said there were monkeys he had to see and square things with. He had to make peace with the primates, he told her.

Zero pointed to the building and said, "Bet we'll see a few of your relatives in there, hey Tues?" He bared his clenched teeth as if showing a dentist his overbite and shook a limp hand in the air. Before he could emit monkey sounds, Tuesday said, "We'll see everyone's relatives in there."

Zero dropped his hand and relaxed his lips to a grin. "Better not let Reverend Falwell hear you say that, missy, or we'll end up with prayer in the zoos." Zero laughed and Tuesday smiled. Zero was often cracking himself up, and Tuesday was happy to be there when he did.

The train stopped near the reptile house, and Zero and Tuesday got off. In front of the house was a fenced-in area where small children rode on the backs of sea turtles, gouging the shells with their invisible spurs. Most of the children giggled and kicked, but one child screamed so loudly her turtle disappeared inside itself. The child grew silent, laid her head against her grooved saddle, and knock-knocked. The

other turtles lurched and staggered randomly and reminded Tuesday
of polite, slow-moving bumper cars.

"How about a turtle ride, Tues?"

Tuesday shook her head.

"You're right. Where to?"

Tuesday walked and Zero followed her. "Can't we work up to this?"
Zero asked. Tuesday shook her head.

Inside the monkey house, Tuesday walked slowly by the chimpan-
zees and mandrills, the spider monkeys, gibbons, and orangutans. She
stopped in front of the gorilla cage. The gorilla paced back and forth
on his tough knuckles, his eyes following Tuesday as he cantered. The
weathered black skin of his chest and face looked like dusty leather and
Tuesday wanted to touch it. She moved close to the glass, and Zero
touched her shoulder. He bent over and said into her ear, "I think the
King of the Jungle has eyes for the Terrible Tues."

"He's not happy," she said. "He's flabby and tired, like Grandpa
when he got sick. His joints ache, and he misses things. He misses
the way his heart used to beat in the jungle. And he's . . . I think he's
daydreaming. He's thinking of new and improved gorillas, gorillas
that fly, on this side of the glass." Tuesday looked up into Zero's eyes.
"He's wishing for wings." Tuesday saw this in her head, saw the gorilla
flying around, wheeling through the enclosed air, grazing his slick belly
against rocks, knocking into the ceiling, the stony walls, and finally
thudding against the clean glass, a mean trick, a solid pretending to be
sky. "Let's be quiet," she said. Zero kissed Tuesday's ear and they walked
on, Zero toward another exhibit. Tuesday stopped and watched him.
He walked toward a noisy group of brown monkeys, who leapt and
swung with the fervor of windup toys. She watched Zero fold his
hands together and incline his head slightly forward. He held a finger
up and touched the glass.

Tuesday thought about the gorilla again, and then she thought
about flowers. She remembered something her third-grade teacher,
Mrs. Romanchuk, had told her class. She told them a story about
flowers and light. Mrs. Romanchuk lived in a nearby town smaller than
What Cheer, a place where there were dirt roads and duck crossings

and slow-moving vehicles and big fields of floppy-necked flowers, and one of these fields surrounded the drive that led to her house. Hundreds of blue and purple and yellow flowers sprang up on either side of the drive, and Tuesday pictured the flowers pressing against the gravel path, the row of flowers that edged each side stretching toward the other, yearning across the flowerless expanse.

Mrs. Romanchuk said that several weeks after her husband had started working the evening shift, she noticed that some of the flowers refused to bloom, and strangely their timidity was not random but patterned. The closed-up flowers, tight as pursed lips, arced in neat rows, cutting a wide swath to the right of the driveway. And these flowers never opened, never risked the vulnerability of blooming. So Mrs. Romanchuk went to the library, looked these flowers up in a book, and discovered that they were special flowers requiring uninterrupted nightfall, the privacy of darkness in which to unfold. When her husband turned into the driveway at night, the headlights of his car arced across the flowers like a sickle, dooming them with illumination.

Ruby Tuesday knew this was a story meant to illustrate the wonderful things people could discover in libraries, but she wanted to know more about the flowers, about what had happened to them after the story ended. She wanted to know what Mrs. Romanchuk had done with this library-book knowledge. "Did you cover the flowers? Did you make your husband take the bus?" she asked. Darren Crenshaw suggested she take a flashlight out at night and draw pictures and words in the field. Mrs. Romanchuk laughed. The children laughed. "Does he turn his lights off now before he gets to the flowers?" Mrs. Romanchuk smiled and smoothed her skirt.

Tuesday watched Zero and waited for him to start walking. She caught up to him and said, "Okay?" He nodded. Before they got to the exit, they stopped to see the lemurs. Zero read the placard of information beside the window and said, "From Madagascar." As if in wistful response, the lemurs cried, and Tuesday felt the skin on her arms prickle with bumps. Zero's body jerked. The chirruping cries were shrill and hollow, like bursts of air allowed a slow escape through the tautly stretched throat of a balloon. They sounded like loud, mournful babies, but not from this world, not human – space babies, spirit babies, extraterrestrial ghosts, doubly spectral. Tuesday pressed her hands against the glass.

"Yipes," Zero said. "What the hell kind of sound is that?"

Some lemurs were black and agile with a white burst of fur circling their faces; others were reddish or gray with ringed tails, draped over limbs. They leapt from bough to bough and swung into position with peculiar grace. They moved with careless ease, oozed along limbs, like a thick liquid spreading, spilled syrup. Tuesday thought she saw pools of faint light following them. They seemed to her indestructible, immortal, and that, she thought, must be why their cries sound so sorrowful. Their eyes were glass balls, wide, open, watching.

"Well, I'm thoroughly depressed now," Zero said. "I hate displays with moving parts. Unless it's a telethon, numbers flipping by at high speed can only be bad news." Tuesday looked over at Zero. He was standing by the exit, watching numbers click and click as they tallied the number of acres of tropical rainforest being destroyed every minute. Tuesday walked over and stood beside him. He said, "I'm sorry to break it to you, Tues, but the world is *fucked up.*"

"I know."

"I think you have a right to know. But don't tell anyone I told you."

"I won't."

Zero shook his head and whispered, "Christ on a crutch," as he hugged Tuesday to his side.

Tuesday had heard Zero say this before and had been meaning to ask him. "Did Jesus break his leg?"

"I don't know, Tues. Maybe. It's just an expression, when you're disgusted and don't know what else to say. It's probably not something you should repeat."

"Before or after he rose again?" Tuesday liked the idea, not that Jesus had been in pain, but that it was possible for him to feel it, the everyday scrapes, possible for his bones to break. So he'd have to be careful, like the rest of us. She had wondered about Jesus's body before. She'd always imagined his skeleton made of indestructible rubber, unbreakable and with maximum bounce like a superball.

"Let's blow this clambake, Tues, what do you say?"

Tuesday looked back at the lemurs. Their long, plush tails curled in the air above them as they floated along the branches.

OF RUBY, DAUGHTER OF RACHEL

Ruby is:

the backward love in evolution
Band-Aids and breath mints and tiny seeds
beautiful tumor
the breath of animals on cold glass
day after tomorrow
dulcet death-bed aplomb
God and begonias
a maple filled with singing chickens
a pitch only gorillas can hear
precious stone
quadruped in private
quicksilver shadow that can't be touched
silent nights
singing nights
what lemurs dream
a word in your sleep

Sometimes late at night Ruby wakes and can't soothe herself back to sleep with a drink or a song. She goes into Rachel's bedroom and watches her. She puts her face close to the sheet that covers her mother's body and follows the slow billow of breathing. She touches Rachel's hair and pretends her mother is a magic horse whose dreams cure sick people. At the end of the bed, she gently uncovers her feet and stares at her mother through the space between them. She squints until the tiny bit of illumination that drifts in from the bathroom night-light is enough. She tries to imagine what her mother would see if she were to awake. A tiny winged face, her own naked feet poised for flight. Then Ruby walks to the side of the bed and leans close to Rachel's face. She puts her lips as near to her mother's ear as she can without touching it and whispers, "Ruby, Ruby, Ruby, Ruby . . ."

OF RUBY TUESDAY, NEIGHBOR OF MR. ABATISTA

Ruby Tuesday's neighbor Mr. Abatista is dying and she is sad. Mr. Abatista's backyard is a garden filled with vegetables and flowers and herbs. Whenever he saw Ruby T. passing by, he would harvest something to give her, sunflower, rutabaga, watercress, thyme. Sometimes he would rub mint or marjoram onto her wrists, and she would smell fresh and edible, like something that deserved to be eaten or slowly sipped. Once he gave Ruby Tuesday a zucchini he said he'd grown especially for her. It was as long as his black Lab, Lorenzo, and as big around as her waist. Mrs. Abatista gave her things to eat: eggplant with spicy tomato sauce, skinny spaghetti with mushrooms and pungent cheese, blood oranges, tuna fish and Twinkies. Ruby T. was in love with eggplants and Bermuda onions. She wanted to marry them. She thought their brash purple skins, defying rough grocery store sackers to try and bruise them, marked these vegetables as something a person should pray to, ask for guidance. It was clear to her they knew something other vegetables did not.

Ruby Tuesday plucks some dandelions, white clover, chickweed, sorrel, the closest things to flowers or fancy foliage her own yard offers, and goes to see Mr. Abatista. When Mrs. Abatista opens the front door, she looks smaller than usual and the skin on her face hangs loosely, as though she were shrinking or preparing to shed. She pats Ruby's hand and leads her to Mr. Abatista's room. He lies in a large bed whose headboard is painted and seems to tell a story about mountains and horses, people dancing, and grapes. There are machines around the bed that drip and tick, clear tubes that disappear beneath the sheets. Mrs. Abatista leaves the room and Ruby Tuesday walks to the side of the bed. She holds the bouquet out, and Mr. Abatista takes it with a slow hand, lays it on his chest. He smiles and rests his hand on Ruby's shoulder. Ruby lays her head on his chest, next to the flowers, and he smoothes her hair and pats her back. "*Bella bambina.*" The sound of his heart thumps in her ear. It sounds insistent, not like something that will soon stop. She is glad she got to hear it.

Ruby knows Mr. Abatista is going to die soon, but she does not know what she must do. At Vacation Bible School, they taught her about death, about how the body gives up the soul, which pries itself free of the flesh and floats toward the bright light of Jesus. She imagines Mr. Abatista's spirit, weightless and silken like the seeds of a milkweed, exiting his garden in a chariot of eggplant led by a team of lemurs. She nods and begins to sing, her voice sharp and clear as a piccolo, but quiet; she is careful to hit each note gently, as though her voice were a hand tentatively touching a slumbering body. *Sleep in heavenly pe-eace, sle-eep in heavenly peace.*

When she stops singing, she notices Mr. Abatista's lips have trembled open and then she sees that Rachel is standing at the end of his bed with her hands held still on the tops of his feet. Mr. Abatista begins to cough, a hoarse, wet cough too big for his body. Ruby thinks it is his spirit trying to skin itself, trying to split open the husk of flesh and fly free. Rachel touches Ruby's shoulder and leads her out. As they pass Mrs. Abatista, Ruby drops a watermelon seed into the pocket of her apron. Mrs. Abatista stands watching her husband's body spasm. She grips her elbows and closes her eyes.

Ruby plays with safety pins and Band-Aids and Tic Tacs, mints shaped like tiny eggs as though laid by a miniature chicken or reptile, and she tells herself knock-knock jokes. Sometimes she anticipates her own knock and says, "Who's there?"

"How did you know?"

"I heard the steps creaking," she says.

"Oh."

"So, who's there?"

"Dwayne," says Ruby.

"Dwayne who?"

"Dwayne the bathtub, I'm dwowning."

Ruby sighs. "That's an old one," she says. "I heard it last year."

"Yeah."

Or:

"Knock-knock."

"Go away," she says.

"No."

"I know who you are."

"Knock-knock," Ruby says.

"Okay, who's there?"

"Apple."

Ruby yawns and says, "Apple who?"

"Knock-knock."

"Apple. I mean, who's there?"

"Apple."

"Apple who?"

"Knock-knock."

"Orange you ever going to leave, Apple?"

"You ruined it," she says.

"I know."

As Ruby Tuesday tells herself jokes, she arranges the Band-Aids and orange, white, and red Tic Tacs in symmetrically circular patterns on the floor. She hooks the safety pins together in a chain and weaves them through the circles, the lobes of infinity, a pictograph only she can read. Then she hops around the design on one leg, picking up mints and popping them into her mouth. If Ruby Tuesday's grandmother is present, she will say, "Rachel, be careful, honey. You're going to choke. Why don't you play with your Kiddles?" If Zero is near, he will point to a part of the circle and ask, "What's that?" Once Ruby T. answered, "Dead dogs." Zero said, "What?" Tuesday said, "Digging for heaven. And their mama." Zero said, "That's deep, Tues." She said, "When animals die, they look for God in the ground. Dogs eat grass 'cause God soothes a sour stomach." If Rachel is present, she sits and watches Ruby, rubs her own aching hands.

Chapter Nine. Zero Loomis
Desire's Zoo

When Zero was ten years old, he went to the Swope Park Zoo on a field trip with his fifth-grade class. It was spitting rain outside when they arrived, so the children had to eat their lunches on the bus. Zero was excited. He couldn't eat. He sat staring out the window at the wrought-iron gates to the park. The bus was filled with the rustle of paper sacks and the smell of cheese puffs and peanut butter, cream filling and pimiento loaf. Zero clutched his lunch in his hands and kept his eyes on the grassy entrance, looking for wildlife, escapees.

The teacher, Mrs. Albertson, who was plump as a partridge, always wore tropically flowered print dresses, and kept an embroidered handkerchief tucked beneath her wristwatch, moved thickly down the aisle between the green vinyl seats, policing cleanliness, on the lookout for crumb-dotted mouths and plastic baggies carelessly dropped to the floor. The extent to which neatness counted with Mrs. Albertson was legendary, and only the most congenitally slapdash and slovenly hobbledehoys dared to pollute in her presence. Zero knew Mrs. Albertson was somewhat partial to him as he had entered the fifth grade with an already well-developed sense of tidiness, the contents stored in his pelican-pouched desk at school organized by shape and color. Zero watched the bus driver fidget beneath a yellow sign that read, NO EATING OR DRINKING ALLOWED. He wanted to bolster the bus driver's spirits by showing him his unopened sack. He could see him visibly wincing at being saddled with a busload of scofflaws. This sign was flanked by another that pictured a young girl and boy with index fingers held before pursed lips. The caption read, QUIET! PLEASE. Until recently, Zero had thought these signs were somehow related, that they were always meant to be read together, and this idea had created confusion for him as to the true meaning of "allowed." When Mrs. Albertson reached Zero's seat, she said, "Lost your appetite, Mr. Loomis?"

"I'm not very hungry," Zero said.

"Are we feeling unwell?" she asked and put a hand to his forehead.

"No, ma'am. I was just thinking about the monkeys." He looked up at her expressionless face then ventured, "I've always wanted to meet a real live monkey." He looked again at her puss of granite. "Ever since I found out I used to be one, I mean humans. Ever since I found out humans used to be . . ."

Mrs. Albertson frowned and held her hands in front of her. "We don't meet monkeys, Mr. Loomis, we observe them."

"Yes, ma'am." Zero reached into his lunch bag and pulled out a corn chip. He held it up for his teacher to see and put it in his mouth. He chewed quietly. Mrs. Albertson moved to the next seat. Zero knew that when on the hot seat with Mrs. Albertson, the best course of action was always to reassure her with routine and servility.

As they entered the primate and reptile dome, the zoo guide, whose nametag bore a yellow smiley face and the name "Todd," explained the habitat was a new and healthier design and had only been open a few months. Zero wondered if the well-being of the animals had really improved in that short time. There was an expansive airiness to the habitats, as though to allow for the flight of a large and gangly bird. Hanging doors in the back walls permitted the animals to escape to enclosed, peopleless areas outside. Sunlight streamed through the glass cupola above and made the shiny green leaves of the plants and trees, around which the walkways curved, seem wet and slick, waxen. Zero touched the feathery leaves of an acacia tree blooming with white puffs. Todd explained that this tree was not indigenous to Kansas. Beyond Todd the zoo guide, who was backing his way through the tour and pointing to things with wide, exaggerated gestures, was the first monkey stop: macaques.

Zero, at the rear of the group, looked over the wall into the crocodile pond. The crocodiles cruised steadily beneath the surface of the water, eyes like tentative periscopes rising through the calm wake carved by other snouts and toothy maws. "See level," Zero said aloud and chuckled. The girl in front of him turned around and said, "Shut up."

Zero had not listened attentively to Todd's speech about these animals, which he now referred to as "crocs." At the end of his speech, he had said, "After while, crocodile," and the children laughed and groaned. Zero had listened instead to the screech and chatter of the monkeys as they flung themselves from branches and leapt onto rocks.

Here he was, finally at the edge of the monkey exhibit, within spitting distance of his origins. There were no bars or glass separating the watchers from the watched, just a short stone wall that rose to Zero's shoulders. Intersecting with this was another wall and a long drop that separated the monkeys from the crocs. Zero could hardly believe he was breathing the same air as honest-to-goodness monkeys, chattering macaques. Zero's mother had often read to him about these creatures from the now dog-eared pages of old *National Geographic*s but had as yet never made good on her promise to one day take Zero to meet (he was sure she had used this word) them in person, mammal to mammal, monkey to boy.

" . . . any of several short-tailed monkeys of the genus macaca." The children laughed. Todd smirked, clearly still young enough to be amused by the word for shit in another language but old enough to know his pay could be docked for encouraging misconduct in children. *Monkeyshines*, thought Zero, a word his mother used only when his father wasn't within earshot. "They hail from southeast Asia, Japan, Gibraltar, and northern Africa. Rhesus monkeys are macaques. Does anyone know what they're famous for?" Todd asked. Some kid said, "Peanut butter cups?" and the children howled into their hands. Mrs. Albertson twisted her handkerchief and glared at one boy as harshly as if he were covered in vegetable peelings and candy wrappers. The monkeys' screeching rose in pitch. Zero raised his hand. Todd said, "They were used in experiments that led to the development of a vaccine for polio." "I knew that," Zero said. The girl in front of Zero turned around and said, "Shut *up*."

"You might have seen one of these fellows earning his keep with an organ grinder. Sporting a little red hat and tin cup?" Zero pictured a small macaque, the fur under his chin worn away by the strap of his hat. He saw him bouncing and capering at the end of a rope, shaking a cup at the feet that rushed by. Zero felt vaguely outraged, almost as though he could break rules, possibly two at a time. "We'll pause here for a moment so you can observe the macaques in their perfectly replicated habitat, and no feeding, okay?"

Zero looked at Mrs. Albertson. She was wandering away from the exhibit with her hands clasped behind her back. Zero huddled as closely as he could to the space at the wall nearest a tree. Its branches sagged and waved with the weight of the perched monkeys, who were scouting one another's heads for edible nits. He surveyed the tree and saw he was being studied by a young monkey, who began to mirror his movements. Zero scratched his head and the monkey scratched its own. Zero covered his mouth and the monkey did the same. Zero clapped and the monkey clapped and screeched. The monkey slowly crept along the branch, and as it moved farther out, the limb bent closer and closer to the wall. It felt to Zero as though his heart were swelling as it knocked against his chest. He kept his eyes on the monkey's eyes, shiny little eightballs that could see the future. The monkey's lips spread, and Zero could see its corn-colored teeth. Methodically the monkey put one hand, one foot, in front of the other, curled its tail around the limb. The monkey was near the end of the branch, close enough for Zero to touch if he stretched, and Zero's knees began to ache. The monkey picked up its small, black hand and reached it out, held it out toward Zero. Zero raised his own hand and leaned across the wall, trembling with the strain. He heard someone say, "Don't!" as he stretched toward the macaque. Zero could already feel the rough skin igniting the fuses of his own fingers as they touched, could feel his hand ticking, about to explode; he could feel the coarse fur brush against his palm. A pleasant sensation burned in his stomach, and below his belt. This monkey was so beautiful! Plush and lovely, someone he might choose as a mate in a different kind of world. Monkey hand and human hand yearning across time and space, the rope of evolution taut and observable – Zero saw this all in the meeting of their digits, and his head swam with the immensity of it – then the monkey grabbed Zero's finger, pulled it to its mouth, and bit.

The sting that zagged through Zero's finger caused his hand to yank and snap back reflexively, clipping the monkey across the jaw, and the little, brown macaque, whose ancestors had been hunted and caged and forced to beg at the ends of leashes, who'd given their lives in medical experiments, whose bodies had curled in knots for the sake of vaccines, this monkey fell backwards, off the branch, out of the tree, bouncing feet over head off the stone wall separating one habitat from another, one diet from another, and fell into the pond with the crocs.

There was an abbreviated squeal and a splash followed by the churning of water as the crocodiles raced toward the afternoon kibble this tiny monkey would quickly become. Zero stared into the water that boiled and reddened, crocodile jaws snapping, legs rowing, bodies twisting toward their small share. The girl standing next to Zero shrieked, the chatter of the monkeys became a fevered clanging, a thousand spoons against metal pots, and Zero shouted, "Shut up!" his knees giving beneath him.

Zero shed gravity like a heavy coat and floated with a feather lilt toward the ceiling. Bent bolts of spackled cracks came into focus. He was buoyed up and hung in the air just below the movie poster, his chest rising and falling beneath **Wings of Desire**. He could see it all clearly, even the small print: "**A CO-PRODUCTION ARGOS FILMS, PARIS •** Road Movies, Berlin Together With **WESTDEUTSCHER RUNDFUNK, KÖLN . . . .**" He hovered face-to-face with the golden and towering, winged statue, whose head was crowned by an eagle, its spread wings an echo of ascendance. On the shoulder of the statue sat Bruno Ganz, "Damiel," who gazed down through the atmospheric mist at the trapeze artist for whom he would fall, straight to earth, for whom he would shuck the worn wings of his near-divinity. Zero saw it all so clearly just before he passed through the tarnished silver clouds.

What appeared to Zero first as he rose through the thin, foamy air was the face of his father, yellowed and shiny like a votive replica, a wax mask. His father smiled weakly and a handful of gray heart, knotted and gnarled as a fist, appeared beside him. Zero reached out to touch the heart and it sizzled into nothing, cotton candy on a tongue. But he felt something clutch his reaching hand, and in the blank space where his father's head had floated appeared a little, mangled monkey. The monkey's patchwork fur was tufted or missing, shredded in spots, matted with blood. An eyeball was absent, he had a ravaged mouth, no feet, a Manx tail, but the leathery hand that clung to Zero's seemed whole and unscathed. Zero's stomach slipped, his mind pitched and heaved slightly like a toy boat caught in a bathtub squall, as he began to imagine his body beset by a maelstrom of teeth poised to cleave and consume. Just as Zero reeled with the first scalpel-hot prickle, the monkey's body knit its own regeneration, skin and fur rewoven and sleek, blood tucked back into veins, blue with rejuvenation, eyeballs popped into sockets, feet shot from ankles, the curling party-favor tail grown to size, ready again to coil around limbs – a time-lapse wonder! The repaired monkey pulled the finger into his mouth and Zero flinched, but the monkey's mouth was soft as water and warm. Zero's body responded with a monkey-do shiver of moist heat. They locked eyes briefly then, and the monkey faded like a developing photograph exposed prematurely to light.

When Zero finally saw the angel, he realized he had been staring at his feathered chest for some time without recognizing it as a body, thinking it only a shape spun from clouds. The angel's eyes were large dark openings in his face. The bright enamel glint of his cheeks reminded Zero of that dangerous second following a solar eclipse, and it made him blink, fear blindness. The angel's face bore an expression of studied concentration, as though he were finally remembering, after years of practiced disregard, a seminal event. But these observations were diversions, thoughts that gave Zero's mind time to calmly sail before attempting the boggling navigation of: the wings.

Everywhere. Countless pairs. All sizes and mutations. Tattered. Monstrous. Unspeakably beautiful. Tiny white wings wagging at the tips of the angel's ears, eternal butterflies; two sparsely feathered spires lancing his neck, the victim of a mad if venerable picador; perfectly shaped pairs in miniature crowding his chest with feathery white hearts and fig-leafing his genitals; out of his back, two burdensome structures wandering in sharp angles, without logic, this way and that, flagged at the ends with two large drooping feathers, as if to warn tailgating angels to back off. And more, every pore and orifice below the chin appended for crazy flight.

Zero said, "Gabriel." He wanted to feel those feathers. He wanted to feel them brush his knees and open the closed places in his body, pass through him, tearing like hot nails, feel them die violently, all blood and sun, then feel them light as nucleolus rise up inside him like resurrection, scattering on the wind, the pollination of a restive demi-divinity.

"You are zero mass," said Gabriel, grinning. Zero reached out to touch his cheek, and Gabriel held up his hand, small and clean and free of feathers. *Nothing up the sleeve*, this gesture seemed to say. Gabriel lowered his arm across his midriff, his fingers disappearing in a white ruffled hyperbole of wings. He pried loose the front of himself as though he were opening a refrigerator door. Behind the feathered breastplate lived damaged skin slick with black oil and blood. Zero held a hand to his chest and felt a sudden pressure wrench the breath from his lungs. With the other hand, Gabriel again swung himself open, peeled back the damage, revealing the clouded sky behind him. The hole in Gabriel's body gaped at Zero and released the pressure in his chest. Gabriel rotated around, his arms holding open the doors of himself, the final wings, inverted, ready to lift him. Zero felt dizzy and his nose tickled and burned, as though he were breathing carbonated air. This puzzling triptych of feathers, blood, and sky made Zero think of his father. He heard noises, things shattering in the distance, tiny bones and hearts, and he looked through Gabriel into the seductive emptiness on the other side and felt suddenly, startlingly sad, and thankful that his father had not loved him, so sorry his father had loved his sister too much.

Zero let go and floated through the gates of Gabriel. He turned and hung in front of him and felt Gabriel's breath on his own lips. Closing himself around Zero, embosoming him in the portal of himself, Gabriel kissed him. Zero accepted his lips and his sweet angel tongue, pressed himself into the musty feathers, and as a bell rang below him, he did not fall but flew further up, up and up into his own hot body.

Chapter Ten. Ruby Tuesday Loomis
Evolution

Tonight Ruby is visited, as she often is, by the future animals from the book her grandpa gave her, animals who will live fifty million years after all the humans and their parking lots and salad spinners and cellular phones and encyclopedias and ballpoint pens and espresso machines and oil refineries and ankle weights and collapsible cups and hibachi grills and garbage barges have stopped ticking and sunk into the earth, fallen to the floor of the ocean. They come to her and crowd round her bed, and even though they are animals out of a book, out of a man's head, she recognizes them, knows their origins.

They come to her, leave the safety of the great coal forests, and swarm her room, fill it with symphonic growls and clucks. The animals fly or slink or amble in then puff and preen and rest on their adaptations.

The desert leaper, a big-eared, pink-skinned hopper whose taut hide sags after the stored food of her own body runs low – it is Mrs. Abatista and she hops, her body weak and shrunken, into Ruby's room, dependent on her front feet to drag her forward. The flower-faced potoo, whose open beak and pointed tongue mimic the red petals and pollen-ready stamen of a flower, luring the easy nourishment of insects: Mr. Abatista glides in, perching on the withered back of the depleted leaper.

The tick bird is clever, lays its eggs in the insulated spinal nest of the cleft-back antelope. It rides the beast's bony ridge, waiting for chicks to hatch, leaving the work of warmth and protection to the makeshift nest's stiff hairs: Grandma Loomis walks in on her fragile, see-through legs and roosts on the end of Ruby's bed. The vortex, a large and thundering sea creature, uses its mighty beak to strain meals of plankton from the water it rules: Grandpa Loomis glides through the doorway and fills the room, rests on the cool wooden floor beside her bed.

A juvenile parashrew's tail is umbrellaed with woven hair, which he opens for a single flight when he reaches sexual maturity: Zero drifts through the air, the thatched hairs of his tail ballooned in flight, and drops onto the comforter.

The wingless skern uses its webbed feet and slender legs to paddle itself along on the boat of its belly. When the skern hears volcanic rumblings, she knows it is time to bury and abandon her eggs in the heated sands, offspring she will know only through the pictures she carries in her faraway head. Baby skerns believe sand to be mother and live with the hope that one day the sun's incubation will turn them to glass and they will shatter back into small grains when the time comes. Rachel rows into the room and propels herself up the side of the vortex, careful to avoid his massive beak.

And there are other animals, animals whose complicated human pasts Ruby can only guess at, who come flooding into her room with their bony plates and their whiskered bills and their leaf-shaped backs, swimming and flying and burrowing their way into her night. They all gather and agree not to eat one another long enough to warble and coo a song, a quiet melody Ruby's ears will remember when she is sleeping in warm sand.

And now Ruby Tuesday is praying to eggplants and onions, saying thank you oh eggplant for all the gifts I've received, thank you thank you oh onion for being so purple and good, and she is singing, a song from the radio, about the inedible fruit of a beautiful tree, and she is thinking, thinking she is a lemon, something with lovely, bright skin on the outside and a scent that makes one search for iced cookies or cream pie or a cold drink, but an inside that can't be sampled, can't be swallowed with open eyes. Not yet. When the tongue's buds blossom with possibility, with what comes next, when they are ready to taste the future, to stare into God's hot mouth, the mouth of a little girl rounded in song, then Ruby Tuesday will fill the parched maws around her with her flavor, and her mama will say, *Ruby, my Ruby Tuesday, my little lemon drop, come let me eat you, let me lick your sweet bones*.

After listening, rapt with curiosity, to the church's teachings, Ruby has decided that mamas must learn from Jesus, must eat their baby girls like vanilla wafers, so they can all be born again and again and again. Ruby hopes next time she will have a cat and her mama will brush her hair and her grandpa's heart will keep beating and her mama will touch her, knead her like bread dough, and Mr. Abatista will grow giant eggplants that keep him from coughing and she will marry an eggplant and her grandma will forget how to read and will bake bread from her floury thighs and Zero will live and work in the forests so people can breathe and gorillas can swim, swim to the moon, and Ruby Tuesday will be a watermelon, sweet on the inside and filled with speckled seeds.

Ruby takes the offerings from the cup beside her bed: an orange seed; some bird seed she took from a feeder; the gooey pink seeds of a pomegranate; a sunflower, pumpkin, and apple seed; grass seeds; lemon, nasturtium, and watermelon seeds. She puts each one on her tongue and swallows it whole, dosing herself with potential growth. When she is finished, she drinks water and rubs her stomach and tries to imagine the wild crop that will grow there, winding vines and fruit and birds and flowers will grow, all crazy commingling colors growing in the garden inside her.

Chapter Eleven. Rachel Loomis
Jesus's Skin

Such a woman is the infected carrier of the past—before her the structure of our head and jaws ache—we feel that we could eat her, she who is eaten death returning, for only then do we put our face close to the blood on the lips of our forefathers. – Djuna Barnes, *Nightwood*

When I was a little girl, my mama drilled me with her own personal catechism for survival. She said, "These are some things you will learn. Love," she said, "it's a balled-up fist you hit yourself with, but you like it that way 'cause the beauty of contusions is that they disappear." She said, "Money, the need of it, the want of its breathe-easiness, can kill a man sure as a loaded gun held to the head. And God? God's a shrimp of a word with a big meaning, an equation bigger than our brains can cipher. He keeps to himself. It ain't his place to say. Some days he looks like your daddy. Some days he looks like dirt. No one can look him straight in the face without burning his eyes out his head. He's got to let you bleed – he don't like it, but he's got to – lest you not learn how lovely it is having blood to let." She said, "The sun'll set you on fire any chance it gets. The moon grows full like a woman, but don't be deceived. It won't help you empty yourself."

The moon was swollen the night my mama had me. She stared out the car window at it as my father drove her to Bethany Hospital. She said it was too full, looked like it needed to be lanced, drained of light.

When the nurse offered me to her, she wouldn't hold me. She turned away from my seceded body still glassy and slick with blood. She said she saw sorrow, clear as illuminated thread, woven into the tight shawl of skin that wrapped me, Wednesday's woeful child.

That night she hemorrhaged hard, blood rampaging out of her, fleeing the body it had buoyed. Mama told me one doctor said had she lost even another teaspoonful she'd have been "strumming a harp and waving to us from the beyond." He said that. A doctor. A man who rubs elbows with death every day, sees it – in some form, if only lurking, a precipitous gas – more often than he sees his daughter, his son, misses recitals and spelling bees in order to forestall it, keep it from eddying around the ankles of the infirm. I imagine him, this doctor, rattled in the operating room, hissing, "Quiet! What *is* that racket, that pling, pling? Oh, Mr. Pendleton, liver didn't take, a pity," waving his starched white surgery cap at the ceiling like a bon voyage handkerchief.

Comfort should hurt, not numb you with foolish myths. Mama once read me a story about a woman who had no pain receptors. She could feel no pain. Pleasure or bare sensation fizzed on her skin but never the hot welling that rides a sore spot. She never knew when she'd bitten her lip too hard or stubbed her toe to breaking unless someone else was witness to the raised or gaping signs of injury. Her body hoodwinked her, shielded her from feeling the chafe of rough life. She died, this woman. We all do, of course, that's not the point, but most of us go out in violence, don't we, even if it's quiet, a private racking between our shedding skins and our selves? She didn't even know she'd been stabbed in her sleep, by an angry lover who knew her body's secret. She'd been dreaming, I bet, a dizzy reel throwing the same pictures over and over onto the screen of her mind: stars, burning and scalpel sharp, dropped from the sky and fell into her mouth, their glinting needle points lodging in her teeth and gums, hot stars falling and filling her up, entire constellations, choking her. Spitting stars onto her pillow, she woke up, turned on her lamp, and there it was, bright and everywhere, startling, trying to sneak away, free of the veins and flesh that had channeled and dammed its wandering. What good is blood to someone who cannot feel its escape? It was bound to betray her in the end, demand a reckoning. All her blood outside her, spreading out, as though it had gone for a walk and lost its trail, couldn't find its way back inside, her very own blood soaking the sheets. Too late. She felt no pain. How disappointing! Dying was so like living, a pedestrian chore, but messier, sticky, something someone else would have to clean up in the morning. This woman, staring at the blood puddled on her bed, her heart slowing, draining of beats, she probably thought about the recent white sale she'd neglected to bargain hunt at, the costly linens she'd have to replace. It's not such an extraordinary story.

It's not that I don't believe in things, God, harps. It's just that genuine succor's not cheap. You have to steel yourself for it. That's the benefit. One hand cuts and the other daubs iodine. They both hurt.

I was nine years old when I left my home and walked without knowing where I was going. I walked and walked, out of my neighborhood, out of What Cheer, Catalpa County, into the next. It was storming in the distance, one world over, breaking open the dark-clouded sky next-door to the dry, bright blue that hung over me. I walked toward the lightning, toward the zagging silver that split the sky at the seams, those hidden stitches revealed only in the unraveling. I thought there would be something for me there, a small rip in the earth's topcoat through which I might slip away and vanish. That's what I wished for that night, to be hidden, unseeable, like the Invisible Man, detectable only when wearing clothes, his face all air beneath his bowler.

I walked, and people honked as they drove by; some slowed and asked me questions. A girl out walking alone, with a determined gait, on a stormy night – it makes people nervous. I cut across a field, a wide square that stretched beyond the reach of my eyes. It was yellowed and brittle like some forgotten keepsake and burnt to exhaustion; the empty stalks sagged in the hot air. The too-late crows hopped along the stumpy rows, running with wings spread when I came clicking by. My ears closed themselves to their fractious blatter. Quick and shifting, fireflies blinked their fleeting beacons in the dusk light, like eyes of hidden creatures opening up in a cartoon night. At the end of the field, there were trees, tall oaks pinched together. I threaded my way through the thick trunks and kept looking up as I walked, watching for the crackling glow.

I saw shapes in the distance, moving beneath a light, dark forms pulsing. As I neared them, the shapes came clear. I saw the angels feeding, saw the light, heard it buzzing above them. They knelt beside an animal, something dead, a deer. I walked closer. Their mouths were ringed in red; there was blood in their hair, on their chests. Their bodies, children's bodies, were crusted and muddy beneath the blood, in camouflage colors, browns and greens. The grass and leaves and bark of their bodies were betrayed by the tattered saucer of light that floated above them, showing them to be muscled and torsoed, mammal. They dipped their mouths and ate from the animal's belly as though it were a split melon. They saw me and raised their hot white eyes, kept feeding. One angel sat back from the rest, pitching sticks, pulling weeds. When he saw me, he tossed a twig at me. He stood up, stared, started to walk toward me. I fell to my knees and curled into myself, turtled in my arms and legs, as I had read you were supposed to do upon startling a wild animal. He tapped me on the shoulder with a stick and sat beside me, and after a moment, I sat up. His eyes were like small flashlights, discs blown out with light from the inside. He shined them on my bruised legs, and I pushed at the luminous circles. He looked away, punching holes in the darkness beginning to droop through the trees. I pointed at the other angels. He said, "I'm not hungry." He said, "Take me with you."

When I got home, I could see through the windows there were policemen in the kitchen, drinking coffee, taking notes. As soon as the screen door snapped behind me, my father ran to the living room and grabbed my hands. His face slowly ballooned and turned red. He squeezed my hands hard, and I felt my fingers crumbling, felt the bones flattening. I imagined myself becoming a paper girl, thin with sharp edges, able to float to the floor and slide beneath doors, able to hold the secret, scribbled thoughts of others on my body. One of the officers stepped behind me and pulled my body into his legs. "Take it easy," he said. "She's all right." The other officer pried the tight gloves of my father's grip from my small hands. My father's face deflated a little then opened up like an unfurling fist, and he laughed. The blood swelling his cheeks thinned. Sweat ran down his neck. The angel stayed outside, looking in. The light of his eyes pooled faintly at my feet.

My mama said, "Gentle men will never leave you, but violent men will love you more."

1967. My father said something like this: "You have to watch, Rachel, this is history we're witnessing, it's playing out right before our eyes, thousands of miles away, right on television, goddamned television! You need to see what life looks like outside the narrow city limits of What Cheer. In places like Vietnam, the stakes are huge, boundaries, tyranny, deep historical wounds. Gorgeous. Watch." Then my mother said something like this: "Jackson, are you sure we should let her watch this? She's awful young to be thinking about war." My father stared hard into my mother's face. He kept his eyes locked on my mother's, and then suddenly his arm came flying toward me, loose, as though he were trying to throw away his hand, a live grenade. His fingers exploded against my mouth. Mama stayed quiet and tried not to look stricken. She picked up a magazine. I sat perfectly still, sucking my lip. My father looked at me and rubbed the dribbled blood from my chin with his big thumbs, smiling warmly.

My father had tried to enlist. He hungered after the dutiful anger,

the gunfire, legal and imperative, the injury, the possibility of not sur-
viving. He failed his physical – heart arrhythmia, chemical-weakened
lungs that rasped with each breath, impacted sinuses, various other
bodily shortcomings. My father fled his home when he was thirteen
years old and wandered around the country performing any unskilled
task that would keep him afloat another day. These jobs often involved
prolonged exposure to pesticides or high concentrations of chloroflu-
orocarbons, or the simple poison of men on the make taking advantage
of his youth and desperation. I imagine him performing these jobs defiantly, daring dangerous molecules to trespass his flesh, inviting them
to step outside and trade blows. His health was in chronic decline.

Every night we watched the news on television. Sometimes we ate
Swanson TV dinners on TV trays in the living room. We chewed and
swallowed quietly as we watched and listened to the war coverage.
Newsmen walking alongside soldiers dressed like the jungle, thatched
huts blazing, people running and screaming, soldiers ushering crowds
into green thickets, young men smiling and blowing kisses to people
at home, stretchers sagging beneath bodies, helicopters slicing the air,
everyone mad at Charlie. Sometimes my father would turn the sound
down and just watch the pictures. The men on the screen were so small,
flat and untouchable, their guns G.I. Joe-sized. I didn't understand
what those tiny men and their tiny actions meant to my large father, his
enormous hands and thick arms. But I loved Walter Cronkite's head
as it filled the screen and wagged its moustache. Even when he too
shrank, standing next to a map, I was comforted by his deep and even
voice, his steady pointer.

At the TG&Y store, I spotted a pyramid of silver bracelets on a table.
Etched in the metal were the names of men officially listed as Missing
in Action or Prisoners of War. Mama bought me a bracelet and an
authentic Mexican jumping bean, which came in its own red plastic
box with a clear lid that clasped shut. The jumping bean snapped and
plinked against the plastic. The name of my soldier was: *Lt. Col. James
Patrick Halloran, Missing in Action 04–26-66*. Each night at the end
of the news, a series of names would appear, identifying soldiers as
released or confirmed dead. Each night I sat with the jumping bean I

named Patrick, clutching the bracelet in my hand, waiting for my own tiny soldier's name to appear so I could break the stainless steel bracelet and free his soul from the war. After the first week, Patrick's popping had started to slow and eventually ceased altogether. And I had to hide my bracelet as the sight of it angered my father. I knew he too longed to be missing, bravely absent.

Sometimes my father held me on his lap and clamped his hands on my arms, shaking my body and emitting staccato machine gun noises, aiming me at the end table, the television, the front door, my pregnant mother.

One night the television showed a small dark man in a plaid shirt standing still, stony. His hands disappeared behind his back. Another man with his back to the camera held his arm out, pointing a gun at the little man's head. And then the man's head burst open and blood flew. He crumpled to the ground. It happened silently, the volume down. My mother screamed and grabbed me off the floor, squeezed me to her chest. My father rubbed his hand across his mouth. He looked up at my mother, eyes wide and slow moving, clear. My mother shook her head and said, "Leave her be, Jackson, please. It ain't right. She's just a baby." My father stood and held out his arms. My mother shook her head and pressed my cheek harder against the small bulge in her stomach, as though she were trying to squeeze me through a tight opening, reverse my life. My father took me from her, pulled me out of her arms, and held me in his lap. He kissed my cheeks and ears and rocked me back and forth. He wrapped his body around me, as though he were shielding me from cold weather. He whispered, "Life is war, a constant skirmish. And you're a foot soldier, a grunt, born to sacrifice if you're not careful. You have to steel yourself against it. The world's radioactive, child, a bomb that would like nothing better than to scatter your cells. But inside you, in here," he thumped my chest, "inside the veins and tissues that shield you, it's Eden!" He kissed me again and again.

That night he came to my room after I'd gone to bed. He stood in the doorway and said, "My father landed at Normandy." He walked to my bed, squeezed my blanketed feet, said, "Brought me back souvenirs, couple of thumbs, bayonets." He held out to me a small gold gift box. I lifted the lid. Inside there was a brownish finger surrounded by bloody cotton. I backed up, pressing into my pillows. The finger wiggled and my father laughed. He turned the box over, revealing the hole in the bottom, the rest of the finger attached to his hand. He pulled his finger out of the box and licked it clean. He said, "Whatever doesn't kill you . . . ." He threw my lamp against the wall.

One night on television, a reporter asked a young man, "What do you like best about piloting the Cobra?" and the pilot replied, "It's kind of like a hard woman: it's something you can't like very well, but you can love it."

My mama said, "God made women weak so men would have something to spend their surplus strength on. We often ignite the battles men love to wage. But don't worry, Jesus loves you just the same. He turns a blind eye to anatomy, he won't hold your deficiencies against you. Anyway, looks to me like Jesus, what with his delicate hands and feet and building and carrying his own cross and all, is just this side of being a girl himself."

Because of the angel, I could see my father's dreams. He was a lens that magnified the urgent stories lurking in my father's head, in his heart. I walked into my parents' bedroom. My father lay on his back, snoring quietly. My mother was turned toward the wall; moonlight spilled across her lavender snood, her gently heaving shoulders. The angel stretched across my father's body, stomach to stomach, chin to chin, sucking in his exhalations. I saw my father's dream as though it were a film. It spooled through the angel and came shining out his eyes, projected against the headboard. My father walked through a hot and swampy tangle of foliage, cutting green stalks with a wide blade. His face and arms were black and oily. He heard a noise he didn't make, branches shivering a few feet away. He stopped. His eyes shone dimly, small gaps in the black air. Quietly, he reached for his gun. He emptied his rounds into the blank night in front of him. Something dropped into the water. He waded across. When he got to the body, the face came clear in the shallow murk, the features slowly filling themselves in, as though he were watching a photograph develop, the black and oily skin, the cleft in the chin, dark hair floating around his head like flames. It was his own face, his own body. He felt for the wounds in his chest and abdomen, tasted the blood on his fingers. He picked the soldier up out of the water. As he drew the body closer to him, he saw that the man was naked and so fair, almost see-through, fragile as glass. The man's hair seemed to weave itself around his head in a barbed wreath. He was frail, this man, like a woman, thin and hungry-looking. There were holes in his wrists. My father cradled him, pricking his forehead on the thorns. A shot rang behind him and something hot bored into his back. He slumped into the beautiful, dead man.

I went back to bed and took the soldier bracelet out from under my pillow. I ran my fingers across the words, the numbers. I wanted to store the information in my fingertips, a tactile memory safe from my thoughts. I imagined myself taken prisoner by short, flat men with small eyes and guns draped across their backs. They'd torture me, demanding the name of my soldier. They'd drip water on my head, slide bamboo beneath my nails, spin the barrel of a partially loaded gun in front of my eyes, hold it cocked against my head, just as my father had described, but the secret was hidden, inscribed in the tips of my fingers, readable only in their prints, where the enemy would never think to look. I broke the bracelet in half, wishing, pretending I could free sad men from capture and fear, free them from blind nights of walking through perilous swamps.

My mother sent me to church so I'd be assured of one gentle day a week, but she did not know about the stories we heard in Sunday school, stories of a furious, flood-heaving God, and an evil giant, conniving, hair-cutting women, and sacrifices, plagues, bad luck, and sore skin, testing the love, fidelity, patience, and faith of scared people. It all seemed so hazardous, so tricky. How could you ever be sure you were doing the good thing? And how much was enough, when would it be clear that you meant well? It was in Sunday school that I decided the safest way to live in the face of daily hazard was to remain silent, inoffensive, and to go limp at the first sign of assault, offering the body up to the caprice of the creator, the attacker.

In my own dreams, I saw Jesus, his brightly lit head filling the television screen, smiling. He stood up and pulled from the ceiling a map of the world, then he floated unsteadily above it, as though he were being dangled by a thread, and pointed down at the map, saying, "Cease fire. The offensive is finally over." And then he began to bleed, his eyes and his nose, his hands. He said, "It doesn't hurt, doesn't hurt." He chewed on his long, soft hair and held up two fingers. "Peace be with you," he said, his face suddenly dark and sad, menacing in its disappointment.

I asked my mama about the communion we took twice a year at our church. She said, "Yep, the body of Christ is there for the eating. It cleans out your invisible insides, like a soul colonic. He takes all your sins upon his own shoulders. That's the kind of stand-up fellow he was."

"What are my sins?" I asked.

She said, "Well, your tally as yet don't amount to much, but just being born, being human, makes you fallen, because of what some other folks did before you came. You know about how Eve sullied the garden for everyone else. That's why women have to bleed, why we have to die. That there's the wellspring of suffering. It's a fall into skin, into the flesh."

I said, "Jesus had skin." I wasn't actually sure if this was true, but, as I couldn't see how it could be otherwise, I risked it. Mama sighed at this observation so I added, "Did he fall into it? Who died for his sins? Whose body did he eat? What about all those people between Miss Eve and Jesus?"

She said, "Well, Jesus, he had the big sponsors, God, the Holy Ghost, and so on. Seems the crucifixion, you know, evened up the score for him. Must've covered all those other folks in the balance too, retroactively. It gets fairly complicated. Best not to worry yourself with the logic of it."

"But if no sparrow falls from the limb of a tree unless it's God's plan . . . that's what they told us."

"That'll get you nowhere quick, girlie-girl. Nothing but a tail-chase." Then she dipped a napkin in water and rubbed from my cheeks dirt only she could see.

I longed to tell my Sunday school teacher, Miss Aurora, that I knew where God lived and what he ate and that if you were quiet and thought about something else, the sting of his blows quickly passed. God the Father lived at 4820 Key Lane, I didn't tell her, used Tres Flores hair oil to slick back his downy, dark hair, and carried a picture in his wallet of himself as a boy standing next to a wire-haired dog balanced on two feet. He ate fried mush for breakfast and had a tattoo on his right arm of a shapely woman in a grass skirt who hulaed stiffly when he flexed his biceps. H. Jackson Loomis is my father's name, H equals Howard. Our Father who art in heaven, we prayed, Howard be thy name. The only other Howard I knew was a boy in my class, Howard Gaither, who was much too small and quiet and nearsighted to be a compelling God. Clearly, it was my father we prayed to. I'd met more than once with the wrath of God and survived. This is what I believed.

Chapter Twelve. Martin LeFavor
Graft

I am not a simpleton despite my father's contention to the contrary. This was my father's explanation for my indifference toward the vocation of pharmaceutical and general medical accoutrement sales, the pursuit of which would mean following in my father's footsteps, filling my father's orthopedic shoes, I've often quipped to myself. Many times my father has said to my mother, "Martin is a mental gimp, a lame-o, a retard. There's none of that psycho stuff on my side, Helen," at which point he has arched his eyebrows and peered over the top of his glasses in a sort of facial indictment. The reason for my father's charge was my refusal (as he saw it; I would say inability) to converse with him on any topic. I was stymied by his presence. He had an enormous personality, my father did, a bully of an aura. I was eclipsed by him from any proximity and rather than balk at this dwarfing shade, I welcomed it.

There were, of course, sides of me my father never saw. For example, after a certain age, having passed out of a chubby infancy into a lithe adolescence, I was never seen naked by my father. If I even removed my shirt, he turned his head in disgust. He could not stomach seeing my inner architecture press against the smooth tarpaulin of my olive skin. I was and am undeniably bony, though I think it was the purity of my skin that repelled my father. I am unblemished, nary a wen, pock, or scar anywhere.

My friend Duncan told me my family was dysfunctional and said that if I weren't careful, I would one day end up parading pain on daytime talk shows in front of yearning housewives and jobless sad sacks.

My father's name was Art, which, if you'd known him, you would surely have agreed is ironic. Art did not imitate life – he throttled it before it had a chance to throttle him.

Art and I had our hearing checked at the shopping mall each year during the health fair. At the speech and hearing booth, as I sat beside the oversized model of a human ear complete with detachable auditory canal and demonstrative hammer (malleus), anvil (incus), and tympanic membrane, I would hold up a finger to indicate in which ear the tone had been sounded. Sometimes the nurse tried to trick me by sounding five tones of varying frequencies in a row in the same ear. I always scored perfectly. The fact that I did not miss even one infuriated Art. Art had long been convinced that my reserve stemmed from an impudent hearing loss. This year he missed three, and the nurse informed him this was normal for a man his age. Art hated it when someone told him he was normal for a man his age. The nurse also told him that it is the higher frequencies that go first, making it difficult for the elderly to converse with women and children. The nurse smiled the smug and sunny smile of a handsomely pensioned public servant; Art scowled. Clearly, he did not appreciate this bit of health trivia.

At the health fair, there were tables on which shiny, square placards were displayed. On these placards were questions about the body, questions about melanin and pheromones. You flipped the cards over for the correct answers. Art always missed the one about skin being an organ. This year he asked for confirmation that there was not in fact a misprint. "You can't have a skin transplant, can you? You can't be a skin *donor*. How can it be an organ?" he argued. "Actually," began the nurse. Art's radioactive glare made the words shrivel in her throat.

Art's health IQ was generally in the subnormal range despite the fact that the questions changed only slightly from year to year. Mine was always in the expert range. I say this with little pride as it was only ever a source of aggravation for Art, another aspect of my character that chafed, the hair shirt of his son's maddening expertise. Art insisted this was just my idiot-savant specialty. He said there were a handful of morons, and he claimed to use this word, this time, in a purely medical sense, who had been compensated by God with one amazing gift, like being able to play the piano by ear, read bus schedules at a glance, instantaneously compute the day of the week of any historical figure's birthday, et cetera. My gift, he said, was an intuitive, unearned understanding of anatomy.

Of course, deep down, Art realized I was neither mentally nor auditorily deficient, as my teachers had all assured him over the years that I was bright and well behaved, the civilized life of any classroom, the polished apple of any teacher's eye. But he reconciled himself to our near monastic silences and my lack of ambition in the hawking of blood thinners, bronchodilators, and the like by thinking of me as his mentally incapacitated son, brimming with genes from my mother's side.

This year Art and I encountered an unidentified flying object on our way home from the mall. We saw a pervasive, yellow glow blinking through a copse of cottonwoods, as though a million synchronized fireflies hovered in the branches. Art pulled over to the side of the road but glared at me incredulously, as though this were just another elaborate health fair ruse, another test to flunk.

As we walked toward the jaundiced light, Art startled me: he began to sing. He sang "Bringing in the Sheaves," and it occurred to me that I had never heard him sing before. He had a lovely tenor voice, whose lilting vibrato verged on tenderness. At that moment, I felt almost remorseful, albeit prematurely, for I suspected this trek toward the glow could come to little good. Any unexpected collision of elements that makes brutish men sing is to be feared, in my book.

We finally came upon the curious, well-lit object, big as a building and rectangular as a shoebox. It was unidentifiable, certainly, not saucer-like in the least, but grounded in a clearing. The yellow light was bright and left me seeing black, spinning circles in the intermittent darkness.

Art and I walked slowly closer to this woodland anomaly until finally we passed through the side of it, calmly, evenly, atom by atom, as though we did this sort of thing routinely.

Stepping through what had appeared an impenetrably solid surface gave me gooseflesh and left me with the unsettling feeling that the very matter of me was recombining, cells ashift beneath my skin. Once fully inside, we were encircled by a group of people, aliens I suppose, looking, however, remarkably human, childlike. They all grinned congenially and had enormous, black, welcoming eyes, big as salad bowls and perfectly round. They looked like those paintings of big-eyed, elongate children one used to see in the pediatric wards of hospitals. They were strangely beautiful and naked. The parts of them I saw were all familiar to me. They had hair and genitals and navels and toenails and knees. Their skin was skin but seemed too loosely wrapped, making it appear as though they might shed at any moment.

Art was particularly silent and without expression, one might even say catatonic.

A small, red-haired girl walked up to me and laid her hand on my groin. I did not resist this gesture. Odd greeting, I thought, but, well, all right, when in Rome . . . . She pressed and her hand disappeared inside me. I felt a tingling in my bowels. The girl smiled. She asked, "What is your name?"

"Martin," I replied. "And yours?"

"Nancy."

"Pleased to make your acquaintance," I said. I wondered if she were familiar with this punctilio. I wondered what sorts of compulsory pleasantries were bandied about where she came from. Useful information for the polite traveler. I felt a fluttery pressure near my kidneys.

"Likewise," she said. "Your internal organs are in top form, Martin."

"Thank you very much," I said, thinking this encounter was far more instructive than the health fair.

She removed her hand and began pinching my forearm. Her hand remained clearly visible outside my arm, which was a relief. "Any prostheses?"

"Not to my knowledge," I said. We smiled.

She turned to Art, who began singing again. She turned back toward me and said, "He has a lovely voice."

I nodded. She asked me his name. "Art," I said. "Diminutive of Arthur."

"Art?" she called. Art gave no response.

"He's a bit hard of hearing," I told her.

"Art?"

Art stopped singing and faced Nancy.

"Art, I'd like to ask you a few questions." He nodded. "Are you on any medication?" He shook his head. "Art, I'm going to listen to your heart now. Don't be alarmed." Nancy laid her head against Art's chest. Her dark eyes became pink-rimmed, a signal of some sort, an ocular barometric diagnosis. "Did you have rheumatic fever as a child, Art?" Art nodded. "Your heart murmurs," Nancy said. "Do you know where your heart is, Art?" He placed his right hand over his left breast, a patriotic understanding of anatomy. "That is incorrect, Art." Nancy moved his hand to the center of his chest.

While this examination took place, the gape-eyed group of small and well-behaved aliens looked on and appeared to scribble observations now and then on clipboards. I thought I saw a brunet wink at me and was slightly taken aback until it occurred to me that, in all likelihood, this half-blink did not mean the same to him as it did to me. I could well imagine those large eyes might be in frequent need of lubrication, but perhaps alien eyes only dry out one at a time. Clearly, great mysteries coursed beneath the extraterrestrial skin, drooping from their bones like melting wax.

He did continue to stare admiringly, however, or so it seemed, at my hands.

Nancy returned to me and asked me to remove my T-shirt, which I did.

She clenched and stretched her fingers as if preparing for a piano recital then smoothed her hands along my arms and my chest. Her hands were cool and damp and soft as washcloths.

At this moment, Art, my father, began reciting the Preamble to the Constitution. I can explain neither this nor the singing nor, for that matter, his altered disposition.

"We the people of the United States of America, in order to form a more perfect union, establish justice, insure domestic tranquility . . ."

I looked into Nancy's eyes; my convex reflection pooled in the centers of those wide spheres, dark as wet asphalt. She shrugged.

"It's all right," she said. "It happens." Then she turned her head and continued moving her hands along my chest, as if to memorize the terrain of my body, its smooth surface, its peaks and vents.

"Provide for the common defense, promote the general welfare and . . ."

She said, "You are lean and slight. You do not lift weights or engage in manual labor. You are not at all thick with muscles." And then she did something that, even despite the unpredictable circumstances, surprised me very much. She placed my hands on her naked breasts. I admit that prior to this moment I hadn't much taken note of them, what with the disorienting peculiarity of having stumbled upon a UFO and all. I mean, that is to say, it's not that I don't like breasts.

"What do you feel?" she asked.

Quite honestly I felt weak in the elbows, though I thought this an inappropriate response as I was sure she meant "feel" in the tactile sense of the word. "Heat," I said. "You are generating a lot of heat." Almost as if she'd been sunburned, though she was quite without color.

"Skin – it is our warmest organ."

"Our largest," I said, and I reminded myself of a parent bragging about the rudimentary accomplishments of his firstborn offspring.

" . . . do ordain and establish this Constitution for the United States of America."

"We need your father's skin," Nancy said.

"I doubt he can get along without it," I said, not a bit facetiously.

"No," she said. "That heart of his is going to be giving him a great deal of trouble soon."

"We have ways of treating these things. Medical technology. Pharmaceuticals. In fact, he probably peddles the very drugs he'll be prescribed."

Nancy shook her head, and I noticed that her saucer-eyed followers now echoed her movements. "It's better this way." She took my hand. "Your mother will actually be happier, eventually. She'll appear aggrieved at first, maudlin, but after a time, she'll join clubs and buy a dog. She'll recarpet the living room and wear loud prints if she likes. You'll become friends and talk openly to one another. You'll tell her of your first sexual encounter and she'll share her genealogical discoveries with you. She'll reveal to you that there have been, in fact, two well-documented cases of stubborn dementia on your father's side of the family."

This prophecy produced in me something akin to vertigo and by the time I came out of my spin, I found myself outside the glowing box, alone. I knocked on the wall. My hand made barely a sound against the hot, silvery, unassailable surface.

And then something was kindled inside me. Suddenly I could feel each of the parts of my body discretely. I could feel my pancreas and my toenails, my spleen and adrenal glands. I could feel my brain creasing inside my skull with this intimate knowledge. My brain felt distinct, fully formed, steaming with self-awareness. I could feel my heart fueling the pith of me, valves fluttering open, ventricles sleek with blood. And I could feel my skin, each pore and follicle, and was strangely reassured by the sudden understanding that this spare wrapping of organ is quick healing and tough.

It struck me as curious that acute awareness of my inner anatomy had been catalyzed by this otherworldly encounter, by a world light years beyond my grasp.

I have not told my mother what happened. I do not believe it is a story that would comfort her. Of course she fills in the blanks for herself; she cannot help but wonder if oats are somewhere being sown, if a midlife love interest, or the hope thereof, has wooed Art away. I offer her the alternative point of view that perhaps a search for a son more to his liking accounts for his disappearance.

The only people to whom I've confided this story are my friends Duncan and Ivy. Ivy has a particular interest in UFOS, and I knew she would be an open and attentive listener. The expressions that crimped their faces as I spoke told me that though they found it difficult to completely and unquestioningly accept the truth of my story, they believed that I believe it, and I suppose that is all anyone can ask of another.

Pictures of my father have begun to appear on the backs of advertisements that come in the mail. This is a service usually reserved for missing children, but my mother convinced the advocacy group to make an exception. Words crown my father's head, asking HAVE YOU SEEN ME? Beneath the bluish picture are the pertinent statistics: name, dates of birth and disappearance, height, eyes, hair, weight, sex, and a toll-free number. On the front of the card is an advertisement for the original first five episodes of *The Andy Griffith Show*, now on videocassette. The titles of the shows are "The New Housekeeper," "The Manhunt," "Guitar Player," "Ellie Comes to Town," and "Irresistible Andy," and the caption beneath the photograph of the small town sheriff and his deputy reads *Pull up a chair and get a bottle of pop . . . It's time for Andy!* It is unclear whether these were once lost episodes, episodes taped then stored unwatched in some secret, moldering vault where controversy and dark implications are hidden, but every time I look at this card, I half-expect the caption to read, HAVE YOU SEEN US?

We are all lost to someone.

My father's absence is just that. Where once there was a person, now there is air.

Chapter Thirteen. Rachel Loomis
Digesting the Father

1976. My mother took Zero and me to see the Bicentennial Freedom Train. Zero was excited. He'd say, "Betsy Ross was thrown out of the Quakers after marrying an Episcopal upholsterer." He'd say, "Robert Peary left a trail of torn-up flag after reaching the North Pole." "Mrs. Mellunbruch made me the class vex . . . vexil . . ." he'd look at his hand, "vexillologist," he'd say. He'd been marching around the house, whistling "The Star-Spangled Banner" for weeks. To Zero, the Bicentennial meant extra field trips, commemorative quarters, and strange celebratory pastimes. His class at school had volunteered to be part of the Catalpa County Bicentennial Beautification Project. They traveled around the community painting fire hydrants, turning them into important men of history and melting pot representatives: Patrick Henry, a black dentist, a white lumberjack, Sitting Bull. In honor of his visit to the Freedom Train, Zero rubbed a temporary tattoo on his cheek that said *Spirit of '76.*

When we got to the train, we had to wait in a long line to board it. It seemed like the whole world was awash in red, white, and blue. People wore flag-mimicking hats and shirts and pants and shoes; they painted red and white stripes on exposed body parts. One woman had stuck a dozen miniature flags in her tall, ratted, blue-black hair, as though she were staking a claim to herself for her country, christening the colony of her head. On display in the field beyond the train, an old, red fire engine framed against the blue and white sky made this patriotic fervor seem like a conspiracy of cosmic proportions, bigger than now, bigger than Kansas, the sky itself colluding. Men dressed up as Revolutionary War soldiers were swathed in blood-soaked bandages and slings, and limped as they smiled and shook the hands of the waiting people. They stopped in front of Zero, who smiled up at them, happy to see historical figures passing out souvenirs. "Here you go, little nipper," one of the soldiers said, handing Zero a balloon. My mother smiled to see her child chosen, and Zero pointed to the man's arm swaddled in gauze and said, "Does it hurt?"

"War maims and kills," the soldier said, drawing out his words thoughtfully, "but tyranny's wound runs deeper than the musket's." Zero applauded and offered the man one of his treasured Bicentennial quarters. The flustered soldier limped on.

The drill team of a local high school danced alongside the crowd and began performing, as a marching band played a medley of songs. I recognized "Saturday Night," "The Hustle," "Jive Talkin,'" "Fame," "Louie, Louie," and "Philadelphia Freedom." For their finale, they played "Yankee Doodle Dandy." The girls seemed to me so strange-looking with their constant smiles and thick makeup. All their eyelids were bright blue, their cheeks the color of ham. They wore glossy hose beneath their short, jauntily pleated skirts, and bobby socks, and they shook their pom-poms with such natural frenzy these bursts of shredded plastic seemed an extension of the girls' arms, as though their very hands had exploded and frayed, become decorative, an appendage naturally selected for girls suited to drill teams. Their cheerful, synchronized movements scared me a little, and I looked away.

We slowly moved along the Preamble Express to the back of the train, where a splintered sign read *Enter Here for Freedom*. Just as we were about to step onto the ramp leading into the train, an elderly man in a dusty, black suit with a worn top hat and bow tie walked up to me and took my hand, and I wondered which consequential American man of history he was meant to be. His face was pinched and wizened and he wore delicate, gold, wire-rimmed spectacles. He said, "Have you found Jesus, little sister?"

A man behind us said, "Why, pal, 'd'you lose him?" People in line snickered.

The old man ignored this and stared at me. He said, "Have you given yourself to God?"

My mother pulled my hand away from the man and held me by the shoulders. "Excuse us," she said, pushing me and pulling Zero onto the ramp.

"Listen, my children, and you shall hear of the midnight ride of Paul Revere," Zero incanted, hopping from foot to foot.

I turned around and looked at the man's small eyes. "God?" I said. I wanted to hit his clean-shaven face, make the glasses fly from his nose. "God's insatiable," I said. The man stepped back and narrowed his stare.

Once on the train, the man behind us leaned forward and said, "Events like this bring 'em out of the woodwork, hunh?" He rolled his eyes. My mother smiled at him and pushed us onto the moving walkway. My mother understood men who had missions born of difficult histories.

Slowly, we were carried past the exhibits in each of the cars, the floor inside moving while the train itself remained stationary. There was too much to see and hear, memorabilia in glass cases, animated displays, Americana stacked and ordered, voices and music, two hundred years of history crammed into twenty-three minutes and ten train cars, dizzying. George Washington's personal copy of the Constitution with his own notes in the margins; Amelia Earhart's scarf and goggles; talking mannequins representing far-flung immigrants; an old dental drill; trophies and medals; Dorothy's dress from *The Wizard of Oz*; paintings and sculptures, machines; Abraham Lincoln's rocking chair sitting in a theater box, ominous and empty behind the velvet rope; a chunk of moon; everything, the world, nothing, just things, artifacts, time collapsed, debris, achievement's flotsam, the collectible jetsam of progress. I had never liked museums much, the way objects are displayed in cold suspension, unable to reach you, torn from time and place and purpose, sitting there smug and dusty and inviolable from another world, expecting you to understand. I felt the same traveling through this crammed and jumbled history of my country. "Happy birthday, America!" people shouted randomly. Who am I, I wondered, that I come from this? How have Marilyn Monroe's cement footprints shaped me, carved me into an American girl?

Zero was spellbound, taking it all in, swallowing the chaos, hungrily, silently, moving his eyes over every inch of display, a sensual lingering, as though his eyes communicated more than simply visual details, as though they did the work of roaming fingers as well. He held my hand and squeezed it as we rolled into each new car. My mother crossed her arms and clicked her tongue and said things like, "Well, will you look at that! An Arapaho headdress, who knew, lovely, my word," and "Fred Astaire's *actual* hat and cane, seeing it in the flesh, never thought it could happen, I'll be."

The one item that gave both Zero and me a start was an enormous sneaker, size twenty, Converse high-top, former shoe of a basketball player, B. Lanier. That is a shoe I want to be descended from, we both thought. With feet that large, mythically big, you'd be guaranteed a spot in history, and you'd certainly be always safe, never fall, anchored by Paul Bunyan-sized feet, you'd be worthy of God's love, no question. With feet like that, the jeopardy that surrounds us would surely drop away, like shed skin, a phase overcome, broken through and stepped out of. Zero lined his foot up next to mine. "You're winning," he said.

I left the Bicentennial Freedom Train feeling less certain of who I'd been than when I entered it, but I knew now what to pray for: huge, historical feet.

A foghorn sounded as we left the grounds, and people in line instinctively cheered. "Marian Nettleton, you're the four-millionth visitor to the Bicentennial Freedom Train!" roared a voice over loudspeakers. People whooped, the high-pitched chainsaw buzz of noisemakers filled the air, and I heard a child scream, "She's the Queen of Freedom!"

When we got home, my father was sitting at the kitchen table, crying. "Jackson," my mother said, "what happened, what on earth's wrong?" Panic shrilled her voice. My father grabbed me by the waist and buried his wet face in my stomach. "I need to talk to Rachel," he said.

"Why, Jackson? What's the matter? What has she done?"

"I'll talk to you, Dad," Zero said. "Look, Dad. I pulled out one of my baby teeth. It wasn't ready to come, but I made it. It kept bleeding for a long time, but I didn't care. Look at the hole, Dad. I didn't even put it under my pillow or anything. I just did it for the hole." Zero opened his mouth and bent down next to my father's face. "Look."

My father pushed Zero into the wall and raised his head. "Leave us," he said.

My mother took Zero's face in her hands and pulled him out of the kitchen as though she were leading a pony. I looked at Zero's eyes and saw that they crawled across my father's face and arms and hands as they had across the exhibits of the Freedom Train, starvingly, wide.

My father sat me down in the kitchen chair across from him. He asked, "What'd you learn?"

I said, "I don't know. There was a lot of different stuff. Things from movies, sports." I shrugged. "Stuff from war."

He seemed to brighten. "Tell me one thing you learned."

I hesitated. I didn't know what my father wanted, didn't know what response would prove I was loyal and loved only him, had given myself wholly to God. I imagined myself looking at two wires, trying to decide which would disengage the ticking box, the blue one, the red, then clipping the red and seeing everything fly apart, slow and dreamy so I could see the patterns of dissolution, atoms dispersing like blown bubbles, the blast blooming through the kitchen ceiling. I said, "Tyranny's wound runs deep."

There was silence, then the weather around my father seemed to change; a kind of darkness passed across his face and his cheeks went slack. He said quietly, "I love you. Rachel." When he said my name it was a sentence in itself, a full-stop statement. I felt cowed by the heavy syllables that were me. "Has any father ever loved a daughter more? Has any father . . . Sometimes . . . I want to make you strong, is all. So they can't . . . can't get at you. So . . ."

"I know."

He looked at his lap, slapped his hands against his thighs, rocked forward. "Did they teach you that this country . . ." he paused, looked up, smiled, "this free and equal opportunity republic of ours," smile flattening, eyes lowered, "feeds off men like me?" He spoke dispassionately, as though he were discussing an approaching cold front, his voice soft and polite. He stared at the stretch of linoleum between his shoes. "Did they include that part of the story? What special mementos did they use to document that?" He looked up, just to the side of me, at my exposed ghost trying to skulk away. I could feel his eyes outlining an electric fence around me so that nothing, not even my thoughts or breath, could escape. "Tell me."

Suddenly a picture slipped into my mind, an image of God, my father, as a tapeworm, coiled endlessly inside my body that wasn't mine to claim at all but just a host for Him, sustenance to keep Him from becoming small and extinct, this body a never-ending meal. I saw the worm unwinding inside me, sending strands of himself into every bend and crevice, the pink putty of his ravenous body coursing through every limb, stretching inside my throat and legs, filling my abdomen, my pubis, my limited, tottering feet. There was nothing left, no claim unstaked, no cell or organ in which I could closet the last kernel of self. I had become so strong I was beyond body, elbowed out into the thin ether, where I was finally, beautifully, invisible, a slip of atmosphere, untouchable, beyond knowledge, beyond falling.

Over the years, Mama had been worn slick. She grew weary of my survival. When her own wisdom finally gave out, she relied on that of women's magazines and pithy plaques displayed in kitchens. She said, "Once across the lips, forever on the hips." She said, "Why should a man marry the cow when she gives out her milk for free?" She said, "Men seldom make passes at girls who, girls . . . I forget." "Oh Rachel honey," she said, "wait till you have a strong man and a sweet little baby doll of your own. Then it'll all come clear. Life *is* war. Make hay between air raids. That's the best I can tell you."

My angel has dimmed his eyes and shifted shape and before me lies my father, Jesus, soldier, my God, all for one, the final shored-up fragments. His body is lifeless and stiff. He does not look like he will rise again. Gray and slightly shriveled, rotting fruit. He does not look like someone who can hurt me. I can feel now that I have been hungry. I will feed myself with his sins, with his transforming flesh and blood, his transubstantial body. I will take his iniquities inside me and swallow up his voracious appetite with my own, wrap my mouth around it quick before it gnaws at my lips and takes hold, swallows what's left of my dimming face.

Digesting the Father

And the body speaks. It says: *Take, eat: this is my body, which is broken for you: this do in remembrance of me.*

So I pluck off his ears and his hands. They resist at first then give, like the leaves of an artichoke. I press them into my mouth and chew. They taste like nothing and lodge in my gullet; the things they have heard and held, the surfaces they have struck, stick like small bones in my throat. I swallow and swallow until the last of the recalcitrant flesh passes down. I tap his forehead and out pop his eyes. I roll them in my cheeks like jawbreakers. Their fishy slickness helps them to slip down my throat. My mouth fills with a bitter brine, the unseen washing to the surface, sights the eyes have blinkered themselves to. My mouth floods and I spit pictures onto the floor.

We all make an appearance in the hidden diorama of the eyes: my mother, Zero and me, and a blurry scene, a large, limping man in overalls, my grandfather? Me at seven in my lavender Easter dress with white crocheted gloves and black patent leather shoes, hiding my left eye beneath my lacy, white hand, smiling so pleadingly my mouth looks like a foreign object floating beneath my cheeks, incongruous, as though it had been donated to my face, a secondhand mouth worn only for special occasions; Zero, a thin boy, with cowboy hat and chaps, wielding a cap gun, a look of befuddlement buckling his brow; my mother, pregnant with me, her hands clasped in prayer atop the wobbly altar of her stomach; the big man shooting a BB gun at a small dog again and again, laughing, the dog twisting and bouncing; my mother and me beneath the pin oak, matching dresses, matching faces, arms outstretched, empty and stiff.

I look at the yellowing soles of my father's feet, shiny and smooth like tallow. The toenails are thick and slightly vaulted, the toes tumored with corns. The skin on the top of the feet is soft and pale, virginal, the thick blue streams of veins ornamental. His feet are not large, not the kind of feet that would never let the body fall. And then I see these feet shrink, hinged to the ankles of a boy. The boy wears special boxy, brown shoes with braces lining the legs. He sits next to a man in uniform. The man takes a drink from a bottle then kisses the boy on the lips, filling his mouth with stinging liquid. The boy sputters

121

and coughs, the man laughs, slaps the boy's knee. The man holds a bayonet, begins clicking it against a metal brace. The boy's lips move, but his mouth is soundless.

And then these feet enlarge, outgrow the shoes, the guiding stays. They're attached to adult legs that walk back and forth in front of a crib. An infant sleeps on its stomach. The man stops and touches the baby, pokes at its plump arms and legs. He runs his finger across the soles of baby's feet, no bigger than quails' eggs. He looks outside at the blurry world, through the rain beaded on the window. Rain has been falling steadily for days. The river is rising, flood conditions. He remembers the last one, years ago, remembers debris floating down the streets, people sitting on roofs. He didn't own anything then. There are large blocks of wood stacked in the corner should the crib need to be raised. This man won't be bullied out of his home by a little water.

The man rubs his face, can't decide where in the house he should be, wonders if his presence might be more keenly felt if he were gone, piling sandbags on the banks of the river, protecting, slowing the water's advance. The man stands with his hands in his pockets, stares at the silent baby. He looks at the baby's legs, imagines them kicking, churning the water. He will teach this baby to swim. The younger it learns to navigate the fickle tides, the better off it will be. Or perhaps it could teach him to breathe underwater. Surely it hasn't forgotten this stunt yet. He would like to learn how not to drown, how to inhale and stay alive, longs to learn the secret of the baby's primitive instincts, its leathery, resilient fragility. He lays his hand gently on the baby's head. His hand all but covers it, the tender grapefruit. It would be so easy to pluck it from the soft stem of its neck, save it the trouble. The man stands still, blinks and breathes. His pupils slowly dilate in the weakening light.

I snap off my father's arms and his legs, push them into my mouth whole, like a sword swallower. They thrash as they go down, beating against the inside of my chest. The internal organs I fill myself with one by one, pancreas, kidneys, spleen and intestines. I choke on the liver. It takes small belts of blood from the cup of blessing to ease it down.

The worm inside me stirs.

The heart is tough, doesn't care to be swallowed. The arteries, hardened and full, stick in my teeth, tire my jaws. I chew and chew on this gummy organ, chew it to paste, chew its troubled history of beats.

The dismantled body begins to tick inside me.

The brain I tear into pieces, small bites, shredding the rubbery diary of his experience of the world into single moments. I pop them in my mouth, tablets of bygone life. I chew on his sexual experiences, his violence, his sickness, his boredom. I grind up his beliefs, belated fears, disappointments, his famished love.

I am thick with my father, my own cells displaced, floating to the side.

I pull the scarf from my dresser mirror, offer it my body bloated with sin and origin. It accepts and I see thin, hot skin blistered with the green pocks of a fretting leprosy, the scall of a swallowed father. This offering of marked skin burns with the afterthought of my father's hands, feels the murmur of air as the hands whisk quickly through it, always in motion, imperiled fish fleeing, feels the warm sting of them against small parts. I watch my father's face stretch the skin of my stomach, lips and nose, closed eyes, pressing. I pass my hand across the bloat of my belly, feel his lips parting beneath my skin. I open my mouth to the mirror, offer the food of me to the coiled fluke inside me, entice and dupe it with the nourishment of its own shell.

I take a deep breath, inhale my scattered self, and the godworm inside me slips out of my mouth. It spirals out and out like an unraveling sweater, pale ribbon, loop after loop, twisting and slopping onto the floor. I see the wet, pink flesh in the mirror, watch it spill endlessly from my mouth. The end of it snaps my face as it scurries from my body. I feel dizzy and sick, strong.

I press my sore lips together. The mirror shows a woman, shrinking to form, intact, pale skin, thin. I miss my father. My soldier never came home. God doesn't scare me. I'm tired.

Chapter Fourteen. Ansel Dorsett
Grasping the Constellation

A historian who takes this as his point of departure stops telling the sequence of events like the beads of a rosary. Instead, he grasps the constellation which his own era has formed with a definite earlier one. Thus he establishes a conception of the present as the "time of the now" which is shot through with chips of Messianic time. – Walter Benjamin

As I sat before the kitchen window watching men shovel dirt into the breach that had once been my backyard, I felt a twinge of sadness, the kind that accompanies the passing of a casual acquaintance. Strange it was, I knew, but there had been camaraderie in that emptiness, that growling belly in the earth, now filled and sated with a new tank. My wife, Dolores, would, I suspect, have been displeased had she heard these thoughts, heard me thinking in what she would no doubt have deemed a fool manner. Dolores watched me closely and waited, with the forever-clasped hands of a stoic, for a change. She is a patient woman, Dolores, patient as those secretive desert flowers whose petals God peels back when least you expect it, after years of deprivation. So patient her limbs, when at rest, fold in neatly like a napkin and the constant and close company her lips keep often sets my eyelids to twitching. They say a watched nut won't crack.

There was sod to be laid and grass to be mown, but the blades of my Snapper had grown blunt. I should have attended to this while my lawn was torn asunder, but my mind had wandered to places more distant and shaggy than my own backyard.

They had taken my neighbor away. Dolores and I were on retreat when Charlotte, through the neglect of medication, created such a stir as to have landed herself in Bethany Hospital. Mr. Myers left word for me to see to her plants and garden during her absence. Charlotte and I were rarely of the same mind but found we could come together over living things, our common ground. I missed Charlotte, thorny as our exchanges often were. Something inside me was ignited in the presence of Charlotte McCorkle, a sensation I now longed for. The cloud-shaped stains on her driveway crowded my dreams at night.

Dolores stood beside the refrigerator looking at my back. I could feel the press of her stare as distinctly as if it were tiny hands inching up my spine.

The retreat had been a successful spiritual cleansing, an ablution of the soul, a purification that made prayers feel more honest on my lips, but it seemed somehow to have acted as a wedge between Dolores and me, an excuse to forgo speech. It was as if an intermission from the time spent talking the talk that saying nothing was, a break in the continuity of our polite dissimulations, took it to a new level, took it to silence. Clearly, this could not persist indefinitely, though I'd once read of a pioneer couple who cohabited without speaking for thirty years. Toil and routine can render a body laconic.

Perhaps as a sort of peace offering, a tithe to outward appearances, and in the misguided hope that my brooding could be wooed away so easily, fearful my midlife eyes were wandering, Dolores had taken to perming her hair and rouging her cheeks, hair and cheeks I could no longer bear to look at.

"BLTs tonight?" she asked. "I got some fresh corn and tomatoes from Hart's Farm this morning. They had burpless cucumbers and near-seedless watermelons. How do you figure they take the burp out of a cucumber?"

I turned around and stared at the veiny, white tops of her moccasined feet. I imagined the thick, yellowed nails of the toes that twitched beneath the beaded leather, toes I sometimes longed to take in my mouth. "Dolores, I have come to a decision," I said. She unlocked her fingers and cupped her elbows. "I think I shall take a respite from eating the flesh of pigs and cows." Dolores's eyes flashed a look at me I could not quite read. She held her eyes tight on me and looked afraid to blink. "Health reasons," I said. "You ought to consider doing the same." Hurt appeared in those anchored eyes. The sense of betrayal that results from dietary decisions made alone blazed in her muddy brown irises. "A sight healthier for the animals in question too," I said, levity that fizzled and fell to the floor between us, brown tiles we stared at as though debating whether or not to swab them clean. "Blink," I said. She did. Sometimes she forgot and her eyes burned of a night.

"You'll be eating only fish and chicken then, like Maralee Withers?"

"And legumes and grains and vegetables and fruit. Everything else will be the same, Dolores, just no beef or pork."

"Legumes? L*egumes*, Ansel? What *have* you been reading? And what about salmonella? You increase your chicken intake, you up your risk of becoming deadly sick with salmonella and mistaking it for a strain of flu."

Dolores was ever fearful of that hoodwinking species of fatal illness that masquerades as something less serious, something to which you are likely to pay no mind until it is too late. "I'll take my chances." This seemed to me a most peculiar line of discussion, though I could figure no way to reroute it. Dolores advanced toward me slowly, clutching and releasing her hands. She placed her hands on my shoulders and said, "What is it, Ansel?"

The faint ammonia smell of her hair and the feel of her breath on my throat very nearly made me pitch backward. I gripped her arms and moved her back the distance of my reach. I said, "I simply do not want to burden my arteries any more than they already are, Dolores. I feel a heaviness in my chest." The need to leave the house and get out from under those bewildered eyes pressed against me palpably.

It seemed of late the instinct to flee had been kicking in all too routinely, though what it was I hoped to escape eluded me as surely as the answers to all the questions by which I'd been recently plagued. I recollected my one crack at preaching, my short-lived charade as a spiritual authority, Reverend Rawley down sick with bronchitis, a rasping call from him asking if I might fill in. My heart fluttered as I whistled for my godthoughts, corralled them like scattered sheep, tried to gather the various notions about the Almighty and Man, heaven and hell, good and evil, I'd thoughtfully tended for so many years. And the day of delivery, that day all the oxygen seemed to rush out the tilted windows of the church as I began to speak, floundering in the sizzling, airless atmosphere that caused me to gulp breaths between words. I started with talk of the quick and the dead, not what I'd planned, but what fell from my lips as they parted. I was thinking of the men in my family, myself. The dead need our comfort, I said, need consolation and advice as to how best to spend this trying interim as they wait to rise, wait for the auditing of the lives behind them. It's not easy, this sinless slumber. Dying alleviates some burdens, I said, the burden of insolent, unpredictable flesh for example, but hovering in between begs the new question of what to do with a spirit grown restless without its body to occupy it, corrupt it, hold it in place, how to keep the soul from splitting in the absence of an organizing corpus, this a new headache. *But the end of all things is at hand: be ye therefore sober, and watch unto prayer.* And what of the living? I asked. Those left behind swarming the surface of the earth, whose collective weight keep it from flinging itself back into God's face. What hope is there for the rank-and-file likes of us whose actions are so pettily fallible? *And above all things have fervent charity among yourselves: for charity shall cover the multitude of sins.* We with our white-collar pilfering of photocopies and paper clips, our overindulgence at all-you-can-eat food bars, garden variety sins we succumb to daily. Charity? What have we to give? What does it mean to live even remotely godly in the face of such mediocre temptations? Is it worth it to try? Is it? And with this, the last wisp of air in my lungs left me as the congregation began to shift in the pews and murmur to one another beneath cupped hands. Brother Beaufort took me by the arm and ushered me from the pulpit, cuing the organist to cut in with a brisk rendition of "Up From the Grave He Arose," and I slipped out the back before the service had finished.

This memory did little to diminish the desire to abscond, so I dropped my arms and walked. I walked out of the kitchen, through the living room, out of the house. I knew this would alarm Dolores, but I could not keep my feet from moving forward, carrying me with them. I didn't know what came next, where it was I was to go after this curious exchange with Dolores, this strange leaving, but for a second, a mere snap of the fingers, this aimless exit made me feel oddly dashing and cinematic, a silver-screened dandy, faithless rake; I knew, however, I could not wrest myself free of my life so easily. To try to escape my own flesh would only anchor me more thickly in it. And anyway, though Dolores's concern and self-improvement were a reflection of my own growing discomfiture, the origin of my unsettling hardly lay with her. I needed to stop and sit and let my mind go, let my thoughts run to where they'd run if unfettered, destinations distinct from sewage and salvation.

As I descended the concrete steps to the driveway, I breathed the world in and it smelled unfamiliar. It smelled warm and soft and sweet, the scent of something newly extinct. It made my head feel light and empty, woozily drifting, like those rainbow soap bubbles children blow through round wands. I did not care to feel so insubstantial; I could not think of where to go. I thought I might head toward church. I have always felt at peace among the hymnals and hardwood pews and the colored motes of dust that tread the evening slant of glass-stained light. I rescued the keys in my pocket out from under some saltines that had come with the soup I'd let grow cold at lunch. But as I got into the car, started it up, put it in gear, it became clear to me my feet would have none of this. They were headed toward parts more foreign and wild and strong-smelling, a place with pluck and thunder. They were leading me by the leash of my body. "Verily I say unto thee," my feet whispered, "walk where we walk and we'll take you where you're going." So I went.

Chapter Fifteen. Zero and Mrs. McCorkle
Random Acts

Zero wheeled Mrs. McCorkle down the ramp and toward the van lent to him by the Catalpa Heights Retirement Highrise. As accommodating as this was, he didn't care for these dreary digs and hoped they were only temporary lodging for Mrs. McCorkle.

When Zero had arrived, he waited in the antechamber to be buzzed in, and a small bald man with brown spots measling his face and crossed arms – spots so orderly they seemed appliquéd – wearing puckered pants barely held in place by a cinched and lolling belt Zero couldn't imagine ever having fit him, this man stood stone-stern and scowled, shook his head, clearly revved by the false authority the locked door gave him. Zero wondered if he'd been a night watchman or perhaps the super of a large building. He appeared to Zero the type to delight in petty importance, the officiousness of handling keys.

When the door buzzed open, the man quickly snapped it shut, his hand a rickety spider leaping. Open, shut, open, shut. It took Zero three tries before, pretending to turn to leave, he whirled back and wedged himself through the brief opening. The man pushed against the door and growled, excited by the new challenge. Zero was afraid to resist too forcefully, afraid he might send this rabid featherweight rolling through the lobby. Finally, another resident came to Zero's aid and pried the old man from the door. "Sorry," the man said. "We've had some trouble recently. Erdman's always on the prowl for intruders."

Then on the elevator, Zero noticed the stain and smelled the lingering after-odor of the shit Mrs. McCorkle told him someone had deposited in the corner one day last week. "This return to infancy in some of the inmates is irksome," she had said. "Not something you herald with a celebratory shower." And the depressing furniture in the lobby of Mrs. McC's floor, garage sale castoffs of mismatched, worn-wool plaids, ripped leatherette, in colors so uncomplementary they made Zero's stomach ache. He looked at the bulletin board hung on the wall between the elevators. There was a sign-up sheet for birthday-cake-baking volunteers: *January Marguerite*, *February Elsa*, *March Ruthann*, and so on. The months of May and October were left unclaimed. There was also a "For Sale" notice for crocheted antimacassars and Kleenex cozies. And yellowing obituaries with phrases underlined in pencil: *a member in good standing of Oddfellows Lodge #272*; *she was the eldest of ten sisters*; *had been active in both local and city politics*; *became a member of the Ziegfeld Follies at the age of fifteen*; *rebuilt his business after the flood of '51*; *known to his friends as Laredo Bob*; EDITOR SUCCUMBS TO HEART ATTACK; etc. Zero felt a stabbing loneliness deep in his abdomen.

As Zero secured Mrs. McCorkle into the back of the van, it occurred to him that inviting her to see his friend Id perform might have been ill-advised. He'd just wanted to get her out of this dismal bivouac. And he wanted to talk to her about Gabriel, her nephew, the angel. The hall would be dim and smoky, the people affected. In the volatile atmosphere Id fostered, the audience might feel free to lob insults at an old woman, hold her responsible for their joblessness, obstinate hair, broken homes, their crooked teeth, their lack of rhythm. Id liked to foment mob anger and wasn't choosy about where it landed. His own anger was unfocused, seemingly random, a roulette spin of chance umbrage. He couldn't make out who the enemy was for sure, but he knew there was one afoot, and in an effort to turn the tables on the evil du jour, and to seem an anticipator of trends rather than a Johnny-come-lately, he was willing to strap a different villain to the tracks from week to week according to the whims of the crowd. When Zero was in attendance, Id would sometimes tilt the show in the direction of Zero's concerns, a gentler attack. Zero had known Id Weird né Edward Moody since third grade and he was the only male friend of Zero's who would hug him or slap him on the back when he saw him, thunk him in the chest and call him "Bro."

Zero said, "You know, I was thinking maybe you'd rather do something else on your night out. My friend can be a little loud and, mmm, well . . . evangelical? In his own way, but . . . and the place he's appearing at is kind of, uh . . ."

"Squalid?"

"Yeah, squalid. Definitely. Id gives me free passes all the time, so it's no big deal if I miss the show tonight. I know his shtick."

"Well, if it's not an embarrassment to you, I'd like to go. I'd like to see you in your element. I'm not afraid of a little anti-establishment squalor."

"You're sure?"

Mrs. McCorkle nodded and pointed a bandaged hand forward.

Zero rolled Mrs. McCorkle into the VFW hall and quickly snagged one of only four small tables on the floor – Id's strategy. He thought people were easier to incite if they were on their feet, ready to slam and pogo up into the dark heaven of their angst, and a standing crowd allowed him the illusion of being more rock star than stand-up comedian. The table was up front and to the side of the stage, a proximity Zero was only willing to risk because Id had promised him he'd tired of spraying chicken blood and Readi-Whip and Silly String on the audience.

The last time Zero had been to the VFW hall, he'd come to see Jazz Butcher play, and a drunken young woman had followed him around all night, lifting a T-shirt that said something about *Random Acts of Kindness* and exposing tiny breasts with pierced nipples. This did not arouse Zero; the looped nodes of flesh made him think of door knockers for little dolls. Toward the end of the night, he noticed a guy staring at him from across the floor. He had tousled black hair matted in places from calculated neglect, a goateed chin, and ashen half-moons under his eyes. He wore clothes that appeared as though they'd lain wadded in a bag for some time, and he gestured with vulnerable-looking hands, agile mitts somehow bright in the dimly lit hall, phosphorescent with grace, so lovely Zero imagined they could effortlessly play an instrument fashioned from the bones of small birds. Zero smiled at him just as the woman slid into view and flashed him again. "Please stop," he said. Another woman appeared finally and forced her friend's shirt down. She laughed and said, "Sorry! She took her econ final today, and it kicked her ass in, you know, like, a totally comprehensive way? She's sort of decompressing, nothing personal." As she ushered her friend away, Zero saw that the disheveled, goateed fellow now had his arm around someone, a child-sized person of indeterminate sex.

The first band Zero had seen here years ago, one of the first all-ages shows, was the Cramps, and when the singer palmed his crotch and went down on the microphone, holding the entire silver-mesh bulb of it in his mouth, Zero involuntarily fell to his knees; his hands flew to his chest. People moshed in front of him like raging animals trapped in the tornado of their own vigor. Then the power was cut and the lights came up and an elderly man walked to the stage, his hands held out, poised to thwart assault. Someone had filched a WWII German coal scuttle helmet from the display case downstairs, where the aging vets hid and drank, bemoaning, Zero figured, the financial necessity to lease their hall to the loud and thrashing antics of teenagers clearly in need of war. "We don't want your fucking Nazi memorabilia, man!" someone yelled from the crowd. "Your, like, souvenirs of conquest." The snarling guitarist said, "Shut the fuck up and show some respect, asswipe. You raised in a goddamn barn, Kansas-boy?" She twirled her hair and narrowed her darkly outlined eyes at the crowd. She reminded Zero of female characters he'd seen in comic books, women who frightened him: teeth bared and seething above crossed arms with sculpted biceps and spiked bracelets, but also sporting cheerily buoyant breasts and angular art deco eyeliner, a rushing river of limned curls.

Zero hoped no such excitement hung in the air tonight. He felt strangely close to Mrs. McCorkle, and he knew it was more than the intimacy of his hands in her hair, the tactile knowledge of the topography of her scalp. He didn't want her to think he was just some misguided, self-absorbed kid, someone who knew nothing of the world outside his own body, his own thoughts and urges. He wanted to tell her that he sometimes felt a threatening energy detonating behind him, floating so close it stepped on the heels of his shoes. He felt Mrs. McCorkle could see him, know him, like no one else, as though she had X-ray eyes that burned through the layers of false flesh and bone to the real him, the absolute Zero, illuminating his wispy essence. "Can I get you a drink?" Zero asked. "Some pop?"

Mrs. McCorkle shook her head and scanned the hall. The space was beginning to swell and stir with people.

When Id finally walked on stage, he did so without introduction, and it startled Zero. Id wrote his own intros, which were generally comprised of apocryphal stories that painted a cartoon portrait of his hardened singularity, his rebel moxie – stories of, say, a childhood growing up – forever at a stoic angle to the terrain and interminably chilled – on the arduous slopes of the Himalayas, unclanned, outcast, a target of Sherpa ire; or: raised by warrior rats in the sewers of New York City, navigating waste and hostile, pistol-packing sewer workers. But tonight Id sidled out without flourish and sat on his wooden stool. He was naked but for a pair of glittery cardboard wings spray-painted silver, and a cigarette. When the audience fully took notice, they hooped and whistled and circled their fists in the air. Zero felt heat crawling up the back of his neck, rising along the thermometer of his throat like quicksilver, a febrile blush that neared his cheeks. A young man wearing a T-shirt that announced in broad black letters THAT'S MR. FAGGOT TO YOU stood on one of the tables and yelled garbled words about clothes as oppressor, a tool of The Man, and someone else rallied the cause, saying, "Before that shit came down with the snake and the apple, man, Adam was a dude, the body, you know, like, beautiful. Naked rules!" Zero feared there might soon be an outbreak of sympathetic nudity, but the audience laughed and snickered and hissed at the speaker of this sentiment, pushed him to the back of the crowd. Zero looked at Mrs. McCorkle, who sat silently with her mummied hands crossed in her lap. Her wounds were apparently healing, the layers of gauze thinning steadily. Her hands made Zero think of slumbering rabbits, worn out after a day of dodging coyotes or the cameras of tenacious naturalists.

The crowd grew silent, and Id took a long drag on his cigarette. He bowed his chest out, exposing the tattooed defibrilation paddles caged by a circle and slash. Though it wasn't visible tonight, Zero had seen Id's other tattoo, an anarchy symbol that had been etched into the back of his scalp with a sewing needle and India ink and which only emerged when he shaved his head. Id crossed his legs and rested his elbows on his knee. After exhaling, shooting a gale of smoke toward the ceiling like a triumphant fire-eater, he said, "Time to take the bullshit by the horns, I say to you my fellow travelers. What's up with this *angel* shit, anyway?"

"It's a delicacy in equatorial Africa!" a voice yelled. The audience laughed halfheartedly, noise that sounded to Zero like thin glass breaking.

"I don't think you're taking me seriously here, punkboy," Id said, "mosh rat with your fashionably ripped jeans," launching his cigarette in the direction of the voice. "I mean what *is* the goddamn fin-de-millennia fear that lurks behind these innocuous little wings? What are we afraid of? What won't we let ourselves see?" Id pulled a small string at his shoulder and the pieces of cardboard flapped, snowing glitter. The crowd applauded, Mrs. McCorkle nodded her head, Zero felt an erection rising.

"I mean you *have* noticed this seraphim epidemic, have you not, this plague of cherubs? Worse than freakin' locusts. Jesus, those annoying pocket edition books boasting true angel stories?" Id's voice grew artfully fey. "Did you hear the one about the people whose car breaks down in bumfuck Sahara nowhere, sun roasting their hapless asses, no water, no signs of life, but they're suddenly saved by a mysterious elderly farm couple, Ma and Pa Beneficent, dressed and austere à la 'American Gothic,' sans pitchfork naturally, and whose sepia-fading images the angel-grace recipients later spot on the wall of the greasy eatery miles down the road only to discover the couple has been dead for forty years, gasp! Henry, what can it mean? These Dell Classics at every checkout stand in the nation amidst the last-minute final offer necessities, flashlight key chains and miniature sewing kits, the divine barcode just waiting to do its part to drive the sanctified GNP up into the heavens, fucking glory to God in the highest.

"And the TV shows and movies and that insufferable fair-weather monk babble, Gregorian goddamned chants that drone pretentiously on in the background of PBS-subscriber-bag-toting bug-up-their-pre-Raphaelite-classical-ass bookstores." Id stood up and started to pace, breaking his rapid-fire Roman candle delivery. Applause, applause. "Record club sale price CDs shipped by the thousands with friars float-ing penitently among the clouds. What is this shit? Fucking Michael Landon, man, lost without his Half-pint, Pa Ingalls speeds along that Highway to Heaven, selectively resurrecting a few of life's many road-kills. TV kills, man." Id raised his arms in a pleading X across his chest. "Can you feel my pain?" The crowd howled and applauded athletically.

Zero felt hot and small, targeted, sighted in the cosmic crosshairs of this attack, culpable. He hadn't mentioned anything to Id about float-ing, about Gabriel. Still, he felt now he had somehow disappointed Id; even though Zero was only vaguely familiar with the bits of popular culture Id was lampooning, he felt he had not measured up, had too

readily floated into the feather-safe warmth of his battered Gabriel. He
began to grind his knuckles into his legs, chewed on his lips. Id barked
into the microphone, but Zero's mind scrambled the words, wouldn't
allow them to sensibly group, collect meaning.

After a while, Id's gestures became grander, broad brushstrokes of
dismissive arm-waving, conscious bravado, and Zero could tell his rant
was reaching its crescendo. Mrs. McCorkle put her wrapped hand on
Zero's, still a fevered pestle pounding itself into the mortar of his thigh.
He stopped mashing his fist and listened. Id paced wildly across the
stage, his body all vibration. He began to tear at his wings. " . . . I
mean, where are the dark angels, the fallen angels, the Halloween yang
to all this Easter-sweet yin? Pretending that our demons are dead,
that we can hear the whir of wings behind the close call that every
day of sheer survival is, gives us only the illusion of sanctuary. No
more dirty reds under the bed, hallelujah brother! Christ. Don't let
yourself be bamboozled by the mellifluous tinkling of Gabriel's horn,
Jack, those boo-boogity threats are out there, they're just reds of a
different color. I say to you now, heads up, the evil's a comin', and
I demand equal time, tales of tiptoeing, pointy-eared imps that slap
bacteria onto meat with arbitrary cosmic precocity. Dark, hooded figures that tamper with road signs, sending Rand McNally-failed motorists into the quicksand-urban-nightmare-snuff-film of their choos-
ing, where the violence and poverty burn so bright the tinted windows
of your Beemer can't hide you, don't even cut the glare. It's only just,
we need a remedy for this fair-feathered panacea, little snake oil, the
time is nigh for millennial mutiny!" And with this, he turned his now
wing-free backside to the audience, spread the cheeks of his buttocks
and out shot a springy, red tail, sproing! like the gag-gift snakes that
leap, upon opening, from deceptively decorated cans. "Wake up and
realize!" Id wailed. "And remember, kids, don't dream and drive!"
Over the speakers, the Chamber Brothers' "Time Has Come Today"
began to rise in volume as Id flung the sparkling remains of his wings
into the audience like a magician who has turned a dove to confetti,
scattering the evidence of his alchemy, the loaves, the fishes, among his
hungry acolytes. And then he made his exit, tail tossing behind him.

Zero sank into his chair as the crowd broke open, a too-full balloon that snaps at the lips as it pops. They stamped and rumbled their feet and fists to the jungle-bird shrillness of their voices. Zero imagined the vets downstairs sucking on beers, gazing at the ceiling, shaking their heads. He looked at Mrs. McCorkle. Her eyes were unreadable, locked and distant. They reminded him of the early morning test patterns signaling the dawn of another day of television, another Farm Report.

The howling applause finally ebbed and people began to dance. Zero scooted his chair closer to Mrs. McCorkle's. He said, "I'm sorry about this, this . . . kind of an insane idea on my part. I don't know what I was thinking. I . . ." Mrs. McCorkle shook her head. She raised her hand and maintained her stare. Zero couldn't imagine what those eyes were seeing, what her brain was thinking. Zero felt fallen, implicated by Id's monologue, a contributor to the world's ills. And he was a joke as a chaperone for this old, wounded woman. He craved redemption. He was now thoroughly bewildered and lost, wandering the endless desert of his own dark soul. He would always be a disappointment to people, would always feel all the wrong things. He said, "I saw your nephew, Gabriel." Zero looked at his lap, ashamed, excited, dizzy. He gouged his palm. "His feathers. I touched them." Mrs. McCorkle took Zero's hand and nodded, though she continued to gaze at the stage.

She opened her mouth, exhaled slowly. She said, "There's a woman and a man. The woman has lived with this man for most of her adult life. They live alone, never had children, and they cling to one another, but the clinging is a kind of organic attachment – not desperate – like creeping vines twining. They gild one another, shingle the soft surface of the other, blend and grow. But the man falls ill and starts to live in such a way that he's all exterior, his vulnerability mushrooming beyond her capacity to conceal and protect, haywire blood and muscle and brain wave. He is all body, lost inside, malfunctioning. He shits and he bleeds and cries, and she washes him, rocks him to sleep, where he twitches with dreams so incipient, she knows he sees only dark shapes darting." Mrs. McCorkle does not move except to tighten her grip on Zero's hand and breathe. "And the woman, she looks for the man inside his body, looks for the pocket of failing flesh he's hiding in, but she cannot find him. All flickers of this man she knew have disappeared. And she feels weary and disheartened, all alone with his empty body, feeding it and cleaning up its mess, this helpless, ailing house pet." Mrs. McCorkle looks at Zero. "So she kills it. She has to, you understand. If she lets it keep going on like that, it will make her forget the beautiful man who once lived inside. It will make her forget. And if they both die forgetting, it will be as though, it . . . the body will have won, will have swallowed the spirit whole. They won't remember to look for one another when it's over. Ever after they'll see only what's in front of them. They won't know to grope, won't remember what it is to be reached for. They have known each other, *actually*, this man and this woman. They have peeled the perfunctory skins away, the falsifying rinds, and seen themselves, the gorgeous absence. This is a story of the necessary measures and unpleasant acts of true love.

"She needs now to raise this man."

Mrs. McCorkle's body folded in a bit, as though this held-in speech had been inflating her. Zero didn't know what to make of Mrs. McCorkle's words, but he raised her still healing hand next to his face. He felt a sour sickness turning inside him. He shifted in his seat. His body felt gnarled and seared. And doomed, so small, the body of a mangled monkey, evolution interrupted. I will never have skin thick enough to weather this world, he thought. Discrete wants began to pulse inside him. He wanted to unzip his stomach and tuck Mrs. McCorkle behind his ribs. He wanted to loosen his genitals and free them, send them scuttling into the world to find their own way without him. He wanted to kill his father, his recently dead father. He wanted to flay him and glove his own body in his father's durable hide. Gabriel throbbed in his ears, on his skin. He felt Gabriel's slick lips on his throat. He shuddered. He wanted dead angels with sad, sad stories to leave him the hell alone.

Chapter Sixteen. Ivy Engel
Ivy in Kansas

Depending on what it is you're looking for in a homeland, Kansas can be a tough state to grow up in. Smack dab in the middle of the country, it hasn't any hope of ever being on the cutting edge, unless that mysterious fault line in Missouri splits the country up the middle like those Richter-heads keep promising it will. For some reason (and with the notable exception of Duncan), anything with even a smattering of outlaw charm, the cachet of the recklessly new and untested, originates on the coasts. Such is the remedial fate of the hemmed-in. By the time the wave hits the Conestoga trail inland, it's been bastardized to within an inch of its former full-blooded verve. And it has taken so long in arriving that back at the daring outskirts it's already part of a retro revival that resurrects and romanticizes trends seemingly as immune to a second life as puka shell necklaces and Plexiglas shoes with water and live, punch-drunk goldfish in the platform heels. There must be something about breathing sea-salted air that breeds hipster genes and forms antibodies against the stalwart conformity that holds people in place. Not that I don't think there aren't jerkwads and mediocrity aplenty outside this cinched Bible Belt. Much as I dream of escaping this artery-hardened heart of the Midwest, I don't know that being a barnacle, a coastal dweller, would necessarily solve any of my problems. And anyway, my sights are set on more distant geographies, places not accessible by minivan.

Once I was watching the weather on local news when their technoid weather graphics were on the fritz. They had to revert back to the prehistoric era of meteorology, the days before Doppler Radar and Accuweather, and use plain old maps and pointers. The weather guy was working with one big map of the United States, probably on loan from the nearest grammar school, and it was apparently a big puzzle because when he pointed to Kansas, he tapped it a little too hard and it fell out of the center of the map, right onto his shoe, leaving a gaping whiteness in the middle of the country. For some reason, I found this comforting, the idea of the whole landlocked state just tearing itself free, a kind of cosmic secession. I'm ready for the earth to shatter.

I admit that ever since I first heard of the Viking Voyager, I've had a thing for Mars. Ivy Engel, space sleuth, hit the library and devoured all the articles she could get her Martian-hungry hands on. Most of the writers turned up their noses, stuffed with empirical data, at the notion that those photographs showing what look like pyramids and a wall and a human face are evidence of intelligent life on Mars. A trick of light or tectonics, they said. The whim of sandstorms. As if Planet Earth were the only place where advanced brains could possibly grow. Break me. Fortunately I'm no scientist; in fact, people expect very little from a fifteen-year-old girl in the way of so-called reason and rational thinking, and I use this to my advantage. It frees me up to believe things that would otherwise distinguish me as hopelessly non compos mentis, two enchiladas shy of a combination plate as Duncan likes to say. I can risk extravagant thoughts. The world would be a different place if everyone could be a fifteen-year-old girl for a day.

I think about this when I'm sitting in Mrs. DeFries's home-ec class, which my guidance counselor, Mr. Stratton, assured me would come in handy *even if one day, Ms. Engel, you end up* CEO *of a large corporate enterprise*. I wanted to wipe that shit-eating grin off his sweating, bread-doughy face and smear it all over his white shirt. I smiled back, trying to exude time-delayed irony that would only hit him later as he shoved chipped beef and creamed corn into his gap-toothed gob. It's pointless to discuss your future with a man whose desk displays a rocking, rectangular box filled with chemicals and colored liquid meant to simulate a small cross-section of ocean and a WORLD'S GREATEST UNCLE statuette. And anyway, I was pretty sure Mr. Stratton was getting some kind of payola from the local ju-co because community college was as far as his vision of a student's future reached, that was the broken-record extent of his counsel on higher education. *Go to ju-co, go to ju-co. A four-year college could be tough for a kid like you*. He even said this to Duncan, who everyone knows is an Einstein-in-the-making – I'm sure one day Duncan's brain will be packed so tight with smarts he'll forget the simple mechanics of using a fork, like Albert E. himself.

But as for home-ec: since the alternative, making footstools and spice racks in shop class (populated largely by the seriously y-chromosomed), didn't appeal to me either, I was stuck in June Cleaverville. I have nothing against housewives, mind you; I mean, I believe they should be salaried. It's just that that weird assumption behind the need for marriageable young ladies to know how to make the perfect blintz gets under my skin. Sometimes school genuinely sucks, period, and it has nothing to do with hormones or peer pressure.

It is in home-ec that I dreamt my first dream about Mars. While staring at a botched bodice only Thumbelina could wear, I wondered what the rubber soles of my sneakers would sound like tromping across that red and angry landscape. "Going on a diet?" Mrs. DeFries asked. She liked me because I was constantly providing an outlet for her sarcasm. She picked up my overworked seam-ripper and smiled. I imagined her using it to pry open my skull and gasping upon discovering the shriveled part of my brain where sewing skills are supposed to reside.

So instead of matching naps or being wary of selvage, I dreamt of a pilgrimage to that cold and hostile planet, where my tiny, space-helmeted face would gaze at the mysterious monument of a past civilization, a giant humanoid mug whose sandy lips would move slowly, stiff from millennia of disuse, and say, "Step into my mouth, Ivy. This is where you belong." And I would be overwhelmed by the carved-in-clay resemblance: the same crooked nose, same silly eyes big as soupspoons, same freckles, moony cheeks, thick lips prone to stumbling. Eureka! The progenitor puzzle solved, I would think. Like most children with the healthy tendency to balk at their parents' pat answers to questions regarding the meaning and origins of life, specifically their own, I have always suspected my leaf on the family tree to have been secured via adoption or alien insemination.

When I was five years old, a spring sprang on my hobbyhorse and it bucked me, flinging me forward into the corner of the coffee table. I slammed into the sharp wood and opened a gash in my cheek that made all my relatives cry. Until that moment, I was said to have a perfect face, the first in my family. Most of my blood relations claimed to be victims of a family disfigurement curse; however, except for my grandfather's furry cauliflower ears, these claims of deformity were invisible to me – scars drawn with disappearing ink and invented as explanation for mean little lives, empty of fireflies and true love. But mine was real, a serious scar by all accounts. When the wound healed, a horizontal line cut across my right cheek and stopped short of my mouth. Like me, it was a blank waiting to be filled in: The capital of South Dakota is _____. π^2 = _____. Religious Affiliation (optional): _____. Over the years I have grown into it; it's more of a hyphen now, a dash bridging my dimple and mouth.

At the time of the accident, Grandmother Engel wept. She said, "Oh, *mein Gott!* How you will now suffer! The hands of men what paw you and always the smell of sour soup!" She thought my potential for a life of luxury and adoration had been kiboshed by my newly flawed beauty, and she tried to cover it up with greasy, pink makeup, a poor color match, making me look like I carried around an extra smile, an understudy, in case the one with teeth wore out.

My grandmother was what she, herself, would call a corker. Me she called beautiful treasure and little mouse and living doll, names she exchanged for weeping at the sight of my ruined face. I also began to cry whenever I glimpsed myself in a mirror, or in her eyes, until my Grandpa Engel said, "You are lovely, my little rabbit. Men will look at you and know you have strength. Come, watch Handsome Harley Race. He's fierce like nails." Then we watched the local version of All-Star Wrestling and cheered when the masked wrestler who had sailed in on a chorus of boos seemed a mere headlock away from a three-count that would win him a huge, gold belly plate of a championship belt. And we cheered for the good guys too, Danny Little Bear and Rufus R. Jones. We just liked to cheer, the victory in our voices as jubilant as a storm of ticker tape and confetti. And Handsome Harley Race *was* handsome with his vanilla-ice-cream-colored hair and mouth full of sunny teeth.

I realized that faces are important.

My Grandma Engel had a face like an old apricot, lightly fuzzed and round, ravined from fear and age and worry, but cheeks a rosy orange color you couldn't help but want to taste. I secretly wished for a face like that, so I could touch the chamois-soft cheeks whenever I wanted. If I tried to touch Grandma Engel's chin, she would slap my hand and call me a little goat. "Ch, ch, ch! You want you should have age on your hands?" she'd say. "It does not come off."

At night, my grandpa's face folded in like a collapsible chair, and I would sneak into the bathroom and stare at his teeth clenched and floating in the glass of fizzing water. I was fascinated and soothed by them, the way some people find mesmerizing comfort in swimming fish or fire. I looked for other removable parts stored in bottles or boxes but found only false eyelashes, locks of baby hair, hardly in the same league as simulated teeth wedged in rubbery pink gums afloat in a watery chamber.

I did not yet understand my grandfather's dentures to be a sign of age, decay, the body giving out, had little knowledge of death or serious injury, physical debilitation. Even when I was a little older and Grandpa Engel died, the idea of slipping out of this world permanently still didn't register amidst the murk of persistent innocence. It was my first death, and I thought all that funereal hoopla was just ceremony, that he'd eventually wake up. I'd seen so many cartoons and movies in which people were magically resuscitated. They'd pull the escaped Self back inside slumped bodies, push themselves back from the craggy edge of death and rise up, back into Being. Like those vegetable tufts of a Chia Pet – even though you know it's seeds you're spreading on the bald back of that clay sheep, they spring up so quick and lush they seem to come from nowhere, life out of nothing, the green surprise that life is to a kid. And then there was Jesus – I knew how successful he'd been; I'd heard by then of his grandstanding comeback. I'd also read about water-breathing aliens who crashed near a lake in Wisconsin and who looked lifeless at first inside their celery-green skins but woke up when splashed with water. So when I stepped up on the stool next to the casket to say good-bye to Grandpa Engel, I poured a Styrofoam cup full of cool water onto his salmon-pink face. I stared at his sealed eyes and mouth and waited for them to blink and sputter back to life. But when I pushed at his lips to see if he'd taken his teeth with him, Mr. Simmons, the funeral director and mortician, saw me meddling with his handiwork and he shrieked. My father grabbed me off the stool and pulled me away from the casket with such brusque haste you'd have thought I was a baby reaching out for a swig of Clorox.

This is a story my parents love to pull from the bulging archives of family foibles. It's the first story out of the vault when, at Rotarian mixers, parents begin swapping tales of the misguided precocity of their offspring, and it is a story that is likely to outlive me. At my own funeral, my children and grandchildren will stop grieving long enough to look at my dry old dead face and laugh as they remember the Legend of Rehydration. I know all about Life and Death now, and a few of the alternatives – Rapture, reincarnation, cryogenics – but I'm holding out, as long as I can, for something better.

I miss my grandpa's face. I dream about his teeth.

My parents, well, they're just parents. They're pretty much by-the-book guardians, forever doing what's expected. They monitor my progress in school, smile or frown accordingly, and tally my growth on the doorjamb, try to make me wear a skanky hat and scarf in the winter, tell me not to take drugs or have premarital sex, force-feed me liver and squash. They don't beat me in the name of Jehovah or rent me out on weekends to heavy-breathing, out-of-town businessmen with a taste for veal, or tabloid junk like that. Unlike my friend Martin, who believes his father disappeared in a spaceship, we'll probably never have an occasion to meet a dysfunction-hungry talk show host. They're a little older, my parents, came together after failed first marriages. I think fear of failing a second time is the epoxy that keeps them together. As far as I can tell, my relationship with them is evolving according to schedule. I mean, they do things I can't even understand or condone: they willingly choose to belong to groups with names like Optimists and OptiMrs, drink mixed drinks with men's names to relax – Harvey Wallbanger, Tom Collins – before breaking out the Thighmaster, and they recently became members of a moronic country club so exclusive

I think they had to take a polygraph to join, probably had to trace their dopey lineage clear back to the prelapsarian salad days. Another measure of what I consider to be their burgeoning midlife madness is our yard, which is under the strict herbicidal supervision of Chem Lawn. I can't even lie down in the grass anymore and stare up at the summer stars without risking a serious rash and probably disfigured offspring down the road; you can almost feel your genes recombining inside you when you whiff that noxious spray. Life in What Cheer's pseudo-'burbs grows increasingly surreal with each fiscal year, especially when you've got wandering cows and chickens just two streets over causing lost or out-of-town motorists to swerve and curse. But the 'rents like to pretend they're living at their summer villa in the Poconos or the Berkshires or some other place rich TV characters tend to vacation, wearing conspicuously colored clothing on the links, foxtrotting spontaneously across the parquet floor. On their way out of the fifties, I think old Tom and Pauline got trapped in the turnstile. Actually they haven't been the same since the waning of the Cold War. I've heard them talking wistfully about ducking and covering and Cuban missiles. Their fear once had a bull's-eye. They could point to it on a map.

And me, I wear clothes, listen to music, and read books that cause them to fear for the future, both mine and the country's – I'm flattered – and offer sweeping disparagements about the "youth of today." Currently, we're at a stalemate that's probably headed toward peace talks, but if they pull another fast one like joining that country club all the hair on the left hemisphere of my head is history, and there'll be a permanent embargo on civil relations.

Predictably, we shoot off in different directions and disown each other in public, though we smile, sometimes euphemistically, for all family photo ops.

So, okay, all in all they're good eggs, "huevos buenos" Duncan (a.k.a. Diego in fifth period Spanish) calls them, if a little too smitten, in my opinion, with the two-car garage dream de los Estados Unidos.

Chapter Seventeen. Ansel Dorsett
Sermon on the Prairie

My feet carried me, via the worn accelerator of my Valiant, to a place I'd never been, not even in dreams. When the car came to a halt, my hand lingered on the shift then threw it in park, and my feet carried me out into the remaining scraps of sunlight. My feet walked me over to a deserted expanse of land strangely cratered with sloping holes like miniature volcanoes. It made me think of pictures I'd seen of the surface of the moon, and as I stepped onto the dirt of this land, as I felt my foot sink into a new geography, a queer reverence rattled through me, clip-breathed and shaky. The sparse and occasional vegetation that poked through the otherwise bald ground looked like two days of beard growth sprouting on a lumpy, featureless face. "Why hast thou brought me here, Feet?" I found myself asking.

My toes flexed in rejoinder: *Relax, Old Salt. The earth is yours for the inheriting if you'll let go your ghosts.*

My mind raced and teetered, and I felt as if I were standing on the hem of the next part of my life. And then I began to see things and hear things that made my eyes water and blink, made me open my mouth wide, as if I'd risen too quickly to a new altitude. It was the clickety barking that reached me first, the growls and chirps and points in between. Finally the source of the chatter, the sources, began to poke their small brown heads from the holes, and then the holes fairly erupted with the jittery wag of their bodies as they leapt to the surface and stood stiff and still with the physique and posture of bowling pins, paws drooping, gently sniffing the air before darting back into their own little pockets of earth. The longer I stood and stayed silent, the louder their dialogue grew, an escalating ululation that shook the air. I was standing on the noisy edge of this world of prairie dogs, who sniffed and twitched and filled the air with the specialized clatter and clang of voices that ricocheted through the innermost channels of my ears, whizzing bullets of sound, and I could see in the swivel of their heads and the tautness of their tails that there was serious communication traversing this plain. I could hear it clearly: love poems and grocery lists, aspersions and curses, commandments and limericks and warnings and lies all flew off the ends of those furious lips.

These dogs barked and growled and chattered their teeth like something wound too tight. The mantra of their alarm made me woozy and hot, and my feet began to ache as if I'd walked for miles in someone else's shoes, someone's size nine Florsheims on my size ten feet. I felt my knees begin to give and was compelled to exhort, "Friend! I am friend to the prairie dog!" As I said this, I wobbled out among them, weaving about their holes, arms outstretched, seeking I can't say what exactly – forgiveness, acceptance, succor, to have my arms' aching emptiness confirmed. Who knows what small, stumbling gestures mean to a man grown suddenly dependent upon glorified ground squirrels for guidance? I yelled again and laid my hands on my chest as if to suggest, *Oh, brethren, fur-bearing friends of the flatlands, we are all the same on the inside, just a heart beating, a soul writhing.* Counter to church teachings, I was inclined to believe there'd be rodents and reptiles and birds and all order of creatures (save maybe snakes and jackals and bats, those sinister miscreants of the animal kingdom) in the heaven in which I planned to end up, all perished four-legged, winged, scaly-skinned critters awakened and rising with the rest of us at the time of Judgment. I bellowed with vigor as if the amplified timbre of a befuddled faith could communicate my benevolent intent. "Friends," I cried, "I'll not fill your holes with dynamite or flood them with water or place poisoned dates at the mouth of your dwellings" – I was well-acquainted with their plight. But they scrambled like spilt marbles, their fevered screeching pitched glass-breaking high. I watched forlornly as they scattered to safety.

I suddenly felt abandoned and false, a confidence man so transparent even downtrodden hounds of the prairie could sniff his boondoggle, and was bereft of theories on what to do next.

I looked down at my feet, which seemed to be shrinking and swelling, then shrinking and shrinking, leaving me, my anchors, my emissaries, growing too small to hold up a man of my size, smaller and smaller, not even fit for a toddler, disappearing beneath my ankles, and I screamed as I tottered, "Feet, don't forsake me!" and fell hard to the ground.

For a length of time I have no way of measuring, the world went black as pitch, and I felt pulled into the deepest cavern of being inside myself, the very nucleus of Self, as though I were staring at the backs of my own pupils. My mind revved itself inside my skull, and I could feel it as well as I could feel my hands or lips, feel it stretching against the choke chain of cortex, attempting escape. And then I saw my brain clearly, cask of my mind, saw the furrowed bulb spin and saw my father's face rise up and shape itself from the spongy clay.

I was ten years old when my father retired to his bedroom one evening and stayed there. Stayed. The remainder of his days. He said he was weary and his legs hurt and standing was simply no longer on his agenda. He felt he'd done enough standing and walking and moving about and figured he'd take the rest of his life off, give his feet the vacation they deserved. People talked, of course, there's no shortage of hushed opinions when a person veers suddenly off course, but it made some kind of sense to me, to my ten-year-old thinking, and secretly I looked forward to the moment when I could follow in my father's inactive footsteps. Life gets tiresome and feels ruefully pointless at times and a body does just hanker to sleep through it until it's time to rattle on to the next stage. That is what I thought then, and I can't say as I've been much dissuaded from this view since.

But then my father's eyes lit up a cloudy yellow like a tornado sky, and I knew some change was brewing. Late one night, I heard a scream and a sound, the dead weight thud of a fallen body. My mother was known to sleep through hailstorms and flapping shutters, and my sister, Genevieve, lived with her husband and baby girl in a house down the road, so it was up to me to investigate. I ran into Papa's bedroom and found him sitting upright on the floor next to his bed with his legs slung out in front of him. His arms were folded across his chest, and he was scowling and muttering sounds my ears could not cobble together into words. I knelt beside him, and he looked at me suspiciously, as though an old debt or feud stood between us. I touched his elbow and said, "Papa?" and then I pointed to him and said, "Papa," a shibboleth to let him know I had no part in whatever it was had provoked him.

At this he let loose his face and the lines of his cheeks sank southward. He put his hand on my shoulder and said, "Don't know who's responsible, Ansel, but it weren't a bit amusing. A mean-spirited prank is all." He patted my cheek and said, "I trust you were in no way involved in this, Ansel. I know you love your papa and would never conspire to harrow him who helped bring you into this world."

"No, sir," I said, still puzzled as to what it was I had not been a part of, and began to feel a bit nervous, the way I felt when, out of the blue, I was asked by a teacher to remain after class, triggering my mind to click through the memories of all my recent actions as I tried to determine if anything I'd done was worthy of private reproach.

"We'll get to the bottom of this, you and I," Papa said as he nodded and tapped me on the forehead.

"Yes, sir," I said. "And what is it we'll be getting to the bottom of, sir?" I dared.

"Why, this," he said, and he held out shaking hands, as if dispensing alms to lepers, above his right leg. "Someone has practiced cruel chicanery, macabre monkeyshines, hiding this hideous leg in my bed, this dead and hairy lump of flesh, this amputated club. To whom does it belong? This is a question what begs a prompt answer. Call the newspaper, check the morgue! Who covets my immobility so he has seen fit to divorce himself of this lifeless appendage and slip it under my covers as I slumbered? Whose cockeyed thinking has led to this demented gambol, Ansel, whose?"

"Sir?" I looked from his legs to his bed to his legs again, and then at my own legs folded beneath me, in search of the physical evidence that would help these queries make sense. I felt dizzy and hot, my feet ached, and it seemed to me that being ten years old was not nearly as easy or enjoyable as I had imagined it would be when I was nine.

"What's most bedeviling is that when I heaved this fleshy log from my bed, I fell out with it." And then my father's look changed again, the lines in his face drooping further, as if his cheeks might drip right off the bones and into his lap. His brows tightened around his eyes, and he looked as if he were on the brink of laying bare the mystery of something as big and curious as the meaning of life, the meaning of death, the exact weight of the moon, or duckbill platypuses.

The next morning, Mama sat me down in front of her, bony knees to bony knees, held my hands in hers, and said, "Time I told you of your paternal heritage." And so she did. She told me of the legacy that afflicted the men on my father's side of the family upon entry into their sixth decade. At fifty-two, my father's older brother's arms began inexplicably to sprout mushrooms. Out of nowhere, the dirt-brown fungi rose up on Uncle Dudley's wrists and biceps, and a fairy ring circled his left elbow. News of it hit the local papers and made him more than a little self-conscious, and with that came the scientific inquiry, but no earthly reason could explain why the flesh of Dudley's arms saw fit to conduct and nurture the spores of toadstools. This eventually sent him into a full-tilt funk, and he took to thinking he was meant to be in the ground, immersed in soil, so he lately spent his time burying himself up to the neck in yards and parks and gardens, trying to spruce up the local flora with his own troubled corpus. We hadn't visited Uncle Dudley for several years, and all I could remember of him was the dirt that lined his neck and darkened his fingernails, and that, at the time, I had hoped might set a new precedent with regard to cleanliness, relax the rules, point up the excess of the weekly scrubbings I dreaded.

My Great-uncle Emmett, at fifty-three, my mother continued, began swallowing pebbles. He claimed his gizzard was on the blink and his digestion troublesome and believed they would help to churn his food into passable particles. Over time the pebbles he ingested increased in size, and the autopsy showed his beleaguered stomach to be weighted with a millstone big as a man's fist.

Grandpa Jacob, fifty, amputated his left arm up to the elbow when the *Ojo de Dios*, glaring Eye of God, his wife had made him from crossed sticks and colored yarn blinked and told him The Great Redeemer frowned most punitively upon the defiled temples that housed tattoos of naked women, as Grandpa Jacob's left forearm had.

Mama stopped there, but I could see in the angle of her gaze and the set of her jaw that there was much more, that this behavior was old as an heirloom, that it stretched back and back to a time when my ancestors were scratching pictures of bison and bears and big, round moons on the walls of their dwellings.

"The men in our family," Mama said, "do not go gentle into middle age. I give you this history, Ansel, as a preventative measure, in the hope that this knowledge might help inoculate you against the mayhem that lurks in your body, a midlife virus waiting to ambush you." Mama had been a polio survivor and such analogies came readily to her.

Back at the here and now, my head thumped with these thoughts, and I imagined I could feel the blood vessels in my head constricting as if trying to squeeze my memories back, rope them off, corral them into that hibernating part of my brain for which spring never comes.

I sat up, and my field of vision quickly filled with black spots. I closed my eyes, hoping the darkness might harvest the spots from my sight. When I peeled my eyes again, I saw the scarred plain and its five o'clock shadow of sage and bluegrass, but it was quiet, tranquil, no audible trace of the earlier ruckus, so incredibly quiet, as if this land had been born that way, bred for silence, sound and noise naturally selected out generations ago.

And even though I saw the grass gently bending, the wind made not a whisper in my ear, and I began to wonder if there were such things as prairie dogs and ancestry, oracle feet and God Almighty and genetic predispositions. The click of my joints as I came back to my body and the gurgling in my stomach made me feel like a terrible trespasser on this solitude. I felt thick with human frailty and like Jesus in the verse known to many simply by virtue of its brevity, I wept.

I don't know how long I sat with my head hung low and shoulders hunched, but when I looked up, the sun had begun to bleed and oozed across the horizon with such flourish, such shameless bravado and easy beauty that it seemed to me the sun was clearly grandstanding, that the day had only existed, the sun had only bothered to come up, to provoke this pink and dramatic demise. It made me wonder. Then I noticed noses poking out of holes and paws groping tentatively as if looking for light switches. My feet reared on their heels, and it was then that I was assailed by a vision, a memory as clear as if I had stepped forward right into the dank vault of my past.

I lost a good forty years in that lift of my head. I was ten years old again, and she sat before me as she had done that day wrapped in a thick and soiled, zucchini-green wool coat, an army-issue blanket with buttons, in the middle of May. She sat beneath the cottonwood with a face and neck creased with dirt, but her hands were white and ninety-nine and forty-four one-hundredth's percent pure as Ivory soap and were held out to the sides, palms up, as if waiting for some bounty to fall, bits of sky to grace her. Her hands were at stark odds with the rest of her. They bobbed and hovered, seemed almost to float, and I wondered if she actually had arms; maybe they were rubber hands, the kind found in magic shops, maneuvered with sturdy wires, I speculated. The hands were not so much white as scrubbed colorless, like a skinned rutabaga. At the ends of her outstretched legs, her red-galoshes-covered feet wagged back and forth like competing metronomes. I thought of my father's legs, the lifeless one lying still and eternal, a corpse awaiting burial, the other inching away as if from contagion, and I could tell right then and there this woman knew something I needed to know. There was something about her, the sheer carelessness with which she sat under that tree rocking her feet, that set her apart from other vagrants and workaday citizens like myself groping feebly for some understanding.

I remember the very instant the clouds of my thinking began to part and I saw her for what I imagined her to be: as my eyes focused on her long, wavy hair, silver as new cutlery, and moved to those diaphanous hands poised to stoke smoldering spirits, I saw clearly she was canted ninety degrees in the direction of the divine and that it must be a genuine, card-carrying angel I was gawking at, a guardian messenger come to save me from my life, and I believed that if I approached her with the instinctual devotion and reverence and conviction of a lemming nearing a cliff, I might leap into the lap of wisdom. I saw heaven in her ruddy, smudged cheeks as distinctly as if she were a red pushpin on a map of the firmament. Cherub or seraph, it didn't matter; whatever the taxonomy, she was most certainly set apart and I felt sure she could help me find answers. And then another smack of understanding smote my face, and I thought I had it, thought I finally understood it all, the whole kit and caboodle of unresolved conundrums. I got the meaning of the squirrels that lately littered our town; the picture of Christ on the cross that hung in the Emerald Avenue Church of God, the thorny brow that had begun to bleed real blood and attract the chronically infirm; I understood my mama's recent interest in the bumps on my scalp and the shape of my head, her inherited belief they foretold the path I should follow and weaknesses of character I should work to eliminate; began to make sense of the plum strangeness of being ten years old; and I even began to fathom my father's recumbent resolve and the lead weight masquerading as his leg. And maybe, just maybe, sort of retroactively, flipping back through time as only the foreknowledgeable can, with this careworn angel also lay the answer to my whole tilted lineage.

It seemed as though the murk was beginning to clear, as if recent days were just a dream from which I could now open my eyes and awake. Maybe it was even that this Angel Lady was causing these mad shenanigans. Not intentionally, of course, just that her nearly divine presence here in our town, a basically God-fearing town, had kindled things, made them spin and sent them sailing out of their normal orbits, made them point in confusing directions the way a compass will do when within kissing distance of a magnet. Or the way downed power lines can cause a cow to make a lyrical sound like singing, and even though others hear it, they fear its eerie sweetness and won't let mention of it creep into conversation. Once even, after a spring squall, Mr. Pacheco's favorite milk cow led him, his hand in her frothy jaw, to the ravine where the near life-drained body of a missing child lay. The child recovered, but Moon Baby's tail snapped and snapped, swatting at invisible flies, the lowing so melancholy and soft like water slipping across smooth stones, and then she fell to her knees and on her side and sank into the next life. Mr. Pacheco sobbed and rocked in reverence when news of the storm-severed power lines and the strange antics of cows in the next county hit the paper here.

Yes, I thought, this is just like that, the visit from this Angel Lady, but on a slightly grander, more spiritually charged scale. Surely we would all soon be carrying the onus of precognition and heroism in our imaginary udders and swooning into the destiny of a chosen people. Perhaps my father was a stationary apostle leading the mission on which our town was unwittingly embarking.

As I walked toward the Angel Lady, I could see her seeing me. I imagined myself growing less blurry in her eyes as I approached, gaining definition with each step. She began to smile as I neared her feet, and though it appeared that angels do not brush regularly, if at all, I felt comforted and privileged to be looking at her teeth. It was reassuring to know an angel could leave a dental impression if called upon to do so. I could hardly believe my good fortune at having stumbled upon the very origin of chaos and knew shortly, if I listened closely, I would be so much savvier, otherworldly wise, better equipped to get at least base hits from life's endless curve balls. She didn't look a jot like those benign paintings or statues; she was not chubby, childlike, winged, or naked; she was not backlit and I heard no harps, but I knew deep inside me she had seen things, things that had scorched her vision. I felt charged to the marrow and it was the same feeling I was pricked by when I knew, before the doctor or midwife, my sister's baby would be breech and blind and a girl, the same feeling I got when I exhaled a thin swell of labored breath at the same moment Grandpa Jacob suddenly, without warning, and with the complacent rattle of natural causes, breathed his last. These things I knew I kept to myself as our family was already plagued with distinction. So I began cautiously, not letting on to this Angel Lady that I knew the nature of her elevated rank. "You know things," I said simply. "You can help me, help us."

She nodded and patted the earth beside her. I sat down. Her silvery hair waved slightly in the breeze and reminded me of a school of slow and graceful fish. She took my hand, spread it open, and smoothed her fingers across the palm. My hand was not as clean as hers, and

I felt heat bump along my arms. She said, "Pardon me," spat in my palm, and stirred the saliva in circles. "The dead develop a powerful thirst," she said. "It's hard to imagine how it will be slaked when the time comes." She looked at me without grinning or frowning, and I remained quiet. "They make a terrible noise when it rains," she said. She looked straight into my eyes, a look so potent I felt it bore through the back of my head. I wondered if she were seeing the forsythia behind me. I sat still, wanting to get this moment right. I sensed there was a fine line between grace and desolation.

I stared back and thought I saw tiny outstretched hands in the centers of those eyes, tugging me into her gaze, and I had the feeling I needed to steady myself lest I swerve from my purpose, so I said, "My papa doesn't recognize his own leg?" though it sounded less like saying than asking.

She continued to rub and study the spit. After some minutes, swirling the saliva this way and that, she said, "For pulmonary complaints, sleep in a room over a cowhouse. Consumption makes us forget the flesh, induces amnesia of the body, and this is a danger. We are consumed with forgetting, with stepping out of the casing we think holds us back. But we *are* material creatures. The ripe smell of cowlife can rouse you to this truth."

Unsure what to make of this prescription, I added, "He thinks it's someone else's leg."

She closed and opened my fingers, examining the knuckles. "Your hand looks at you and wonders who you are, wonders why the wrist from which it swivels seems so unfamiliar. It forgets it slipped food between your lips, scratched your knees, held your chin, wiped your bottom. The memory of this intimacy floats just beyond its grasp."

The little hands I saw in her eyes seemed to push themselves through the black of her pupils and she said, "Cattle are important to this community, and they're happy to help. Cows know more than they let on. Years of sacrifice have lent them a clarity of vision.

"Slaughter a cow, slit the belly, and while the steam still rises from the carcass, thrust your head inside and draw the folds of flesh around you. Inhale. This will lift disease from the body and allow it to recall its substantiality. As it stutters back to life, be prepared to indulge its sodden whims."

I felt dizzy and my stomach complained. I was swimming in the brackish waters of a mission that had grown no less murky for being divulged. Perhaps this angel had been sent for another; perhaps I had stumbled upon someone else's salvation. Hardship was in no short supply in this world and certainly not in this county, to which the hobbled throngs at the Emerald Avenue Church of God attested.

"There now," she whispered, rubbing my belly. She smiled. "You're quite a fetching youngster," she said, "and clean." She pulled a plum out of her pocket, breathed on it, wiped away the breath with her thumbs, and held it out to me. I took it and looked at its new-bruise-colored skin. It looked suddenly foreign and inedible in its smug purpleness, something you might paint a picture of or arrange in a bowl and display on a coffee table, but not something you'd put in your mouth. It would be too sweet, too much to bear. "Go on," she said, and she pushed my hand.

"Here's something, lambchop, you may one day need to know." As she said this, she tapped my knee with her index finger. I bit into the plum, which turned out to be tart, and I felt I'd been duped by its beauty. "When I was a little girl, I fell down an empty well." A jumble of odors slipped into my nose as she leaned toward my ear. I smelled grass and urine and smoke and cat and smells I could only identify by category: sweet, musty, rancid, pungent. "Here's the lesson," she whispered. "From the pit of a well, through your conical view, you can see stars in the sky in the daytime, see them sparkling and snapping against the blue like sunlit ripples in water." She sat back and smiled. "Empirical data," she said. "Most folks don't have an opportunity to find this out, and those what do often perish before they can spread the word." She said, "It's important not to let what you think you know eclipse what you see. Otherwise the messages might start coming in garbled and mixed." She ran her clean hand down my leg. "You might hold your own body at arm's length."

These words registered somewhere inside me and though I saw my father in her warning, it all seemed far too complicated for a ten-year-old brain to decipher. I tried to imagine what it was my father hadn't let himself see, what daytime stars he'd blinded himself to, what neglected sight now rendered his body a stranger. I realized I simply didn't know my father well enough, didn't know what his days had been made of, to answer these questions.

I noticed the squirrels weaving and limping in front of us. The squirrel population had recently burgeoned to such proportions that people began finding squirrels or evidence of squirrels in unlikely places. They turned up so often in peculiar hideaways that one could now distinguish the startled cry that meant *surprise encounter with squirrel* from all other kinds of yelps and yowls. Undernourished juvenile squirrels would lie in wait in Folger's cans full of nails, poking a head out as a hand went rummaging through; they'd scrounge in canisters of flour, looking like emaciated ghosts as they padded slowly across countertops; they'd root through the springs and fiber filling of car seats and chatter weakly when sat upon; they'd perch on the sleeping chests of children and tug at their lips until a shriek sent them scrambling out the open window. Many a town meeting had revolved around methods of extermination, but there was enough dissent and general disagreement that steps were never taken. So people sealed themselves in their houses at night and tested the waters of every aspect of their lives with a timid and tentative toe, fearful of the ubiquitous rodent underfoot.

As the squirrels inched closer, I could see their sides heaving, revealing tiny ribs between breaths. Their eyes seemed to say – seemed to speak to me personally – *Eat or be eaten*. And I was suddenly struck with strong feelings for these squirrels, love call it, true and absolute, for these skinny, indigent creatures, and I found I did wish to eat them, swallow each and every furry body whole to keep them from succumbing to their own gnawing, insatiable hunger.

Angel Lady smiled and laughed by way of a snort. Who is she? I thought. Who is she really, this smudged and rumpled woman whose words so confound me, this sanctified blatherskite? Do angels know too much to make sense to a ten-year-old boy? It was in the midst of this quandary that a cascade of her specialized wisdom fell from her lips. As she spoke, she moved her hands back and forth in front of her, fluid as sea grass, motioning the squirrels hither.

"When a calf comes into this world, you feed it a magnet, and as it grazes, the magnet will pull metallic debris to that stomach. Nails and staples and tacks, filings and bits of barbed wire will collect heavily in one spot, and in this way will the cow's strange taste for metal and iron, known to farmers as 'hardware disease,' be controlled. Apprise the butcher of this so that when the animal goes to slaughter, this magnetized heap can be removed and sold for scrap, a supplementary income." She stopped and slapped her knees and turned her head toward me. The squirrels continued to weave and watch.

"Listen up. Sheep are no proponents of modern conveniences and will not drink from running water, which is why the Lord only leadeth his flock beside still waters." She hiccoughed. "Beware of the blood rains. There are parts of the world where they've already begun. People halt in their tracks and let the red water roll down their cheeks and stripe their vestments as they wait to hear the thunderous clomp of the hooves of the Four Horsemen, which is as good a promise to wait for as any." She paused. "But you're maybe looking for more practical advice." She stared back at the squirrels and went, "Pssst." The squirrels held their distance. "When you're old enough to fancy the girls, snail divination can augur her whom you're meant for. Loose the snail among the whitening embers of the hearth, and in the morning, follow the sticky turning of the trail in the ash, and it will reveal the name of her to whom you will become betrothed. Or so they say. I can't say as I've had much success with this myself.

"If your father cannot reacquaint himself with his flesh and passes on, you mustn't forget to include all in your mourning. Tie pieces of black crepe to the stems of plants, cages of birds, boxes of bees, ears of dogs, cats, and rabbits lest you lose them too. They are sensitive and vulnerable to the exodus of spirits. And cover all mirrors! But now I'm telling you things you already know." She stood up and fished through the pockets of her coat and came up with handful after handful of acorns and berries, which she flung toward the fatigued flotilla of squirrels. The ravenous rodents erupted into sound and motion and reminded me of that terrible folktale of a tiger who chases a boy around a tree in circles so fast he turns to butter. These squirrels scattered and darted and leapt with such fury, I knew they could not remain solid for long. "There can be comfort in chaos," she said. "Don't let it scare you." But it did.

Angel Lady pressed her hands to her cheeks and then held them in front of her face, staring at the dark streaks that now trespassed across her white palms. Finally she coughed a terrible racking cough and said quietly, "You have the power to save small lives and in this will you find relief and deliverance from him whom you wish not to be." She placed her hand on my face, and I felt the streaks of dirt branding themselves onto my cheek.

My knees trembled as if I'd climbed to heaven and back on my own spindly legs; I was not confident in their ability now to carry me away. I pitched the plum into the confusion of squirrels and felt my knees unhinge and lever my legs into action.

I ran and ran, into this very moment, into the body of the man who now lay thickly ensconced in his own uncertain skin, trying to remain rooted, maintain a sense of gravity on this lunar landscape, during these fateful remaining days preceding his fiftieth birthday. I sat up and felt the throb in my head keeping time with my heart. Slowly I arose, and in the dim light of dusk I began. "Pssst," I said. "Pssst, pssst. Hello, hello, hello. Pssst, phtt, parumpitypumpum," I whispered, cajoling sounds I hoped were laced with the magic of my mission.

Then slowly the craters bubbled with brown heads atwitch with curiosity. I held my arms out before me and spoke:

"Blessed be you hungry dogs, for you shall be filled with sage and thistles.

"Blessed are you creatures when ranchers shall hate you, and when they shall separate you from the company of sheep and cattle, and shall reproach you and cast out the name prairie dog as evil.

"But woe unto you who quibble over your own boundaries and the paths of tunnels for you shall be subject to the appetites of badgers.

"But I say unto you which hear, Love your enemies, do good to them which hate you. Love those coyotes and kestrel hawks, and honor the waning numbers of the black-footed ferret.

"Bless them that curse you and pray for them which despitefully use you. Bless those humans who drown and poison and blast you from this earth and do so because they hold no sway over the real threats.

"And unto him that smiteth thee on the befurred cheek, offer also the other.

"And as you peaceable dogs would that humans should do to you, do you also to them likewise.

"Give, and it shall be given unto you; good measure, pressed down and shaken together, and running over, shall humans give into your flea-bitten bosom. For with the same measure that you rodents mete withal it shall be measured to you again."

I paused to notice my congregation was no longer subterranean. They stood before me, stretched tall and rapt, paws hung in front in a somnambulistic gesture of devotion, and I felt warm, my feet tingled. As I parceled out a final pearl, I was consumed with that same soul-seizing love I'd felt for those scrawny squirrels as a boy.

"The guidance of the blind will find you in ravines and alleys and all range of places not commonly trod by your kind. Never fall in line behind the unsighted step of a mole, no matter how attractive the galaxy of his exploded nose might be."

With this my flock thumped their tails against the ground and pointed their noses to the sky. I pulled from my pockets the cellophane-wrapped crackers from a meal not eaten, bread not broken, unwrapped them, crumbled them with a grind of my fist, and scattered the particles among my flock, saying, "Forsake your sage for the body of Christ. Nibble of his toes and his beard, liver and lips," the word made flesh made sustenance. "Ingest the holy protein of his Being, and as you consume the body and commune with the spirit, in this way will you be sanctified." The magic hummed and snapped around me, the air charged and thick with the current of grace.

The prairie dogs wiggled and wagged in preparation for the prairie dog days of the rest of their lives! Then slow as backward molasses, they rose from the ground, one by one, noses pointed, paws slack, whirling slowly, drilling the air, cloud-bound and gentle bullets, heaven-seeking missiles of holy rodent, and I sank into the soft earth, lower and lower, watching the sky bloom and darken with the little, brown bodies of my flock as they floated up, caught on the wind, drifting through the evening air, obscuring the disappearing horizon. As they floated farther away, the constellation of them winked in the dusk-dull light.

I blinked and blinked and into my vision came the neatly combed hair and fretful face of my Dolores, and she said, "Please, Ansel, come home. Please. We'll have a nice white fish and steamed carrots or baked chicken and parsnips. No brisket or tenderloin if you'd rather not. Come home with me now. A quiet dinner. Salmon patties and three bean salad, please come . . ."

Chapter Eighteen. Zero and Mrs. McCorkle
The Singing of Crocodiles

Zero drove Mrs. McCorkle to Medicalodge South, periodically lifting his eyes from the road to gaze at the bulging moon. It looked to Zero like the glaring end of a film projector, shining the world through its lens, projecting Earth onto the screen of the cosmos, projecting him, a hazy holographic image. Mrs. McCorkle was silent most of the way, staring out the van's window, her head slightly tilted, perhaps studying the moon as well. Finally, she spoke. "In 1951, when the flood came pouring into the streets of Silver City, Harlan wouldn't believe what his eyes told him. Even though the water edged up his ankles, and strange objects—baby doll, canteen, tackle box, cowboy boot—came floating into his shop, he sloshed about nonchalantly and sat at his Linotype, wouldn't concede this watery interruption. The water nearly reached his waist before he paid it any mind at all, and then he gasped, as if suddenly startled, and scrambled atop his press, the loyal captain. People floated down the streets of Strong Avenue in makeshift boats alongside the flotsam of their daily lives, random objects adrift and bobbing as if waiting to be plucked from the barrel by a giant mouth. We were all unanchored, afloat in this strange soup of who we had been. People were crying and moaning, shivering inside their soaked clothing, but it felt comfortable to me, like we were setting sail for uncharted parts. I was happy to be cleansed of accumulation. I'm drifting yet." As Zero listened to Mrs. McCorkle's voice, he kept checking to see if the moon was watching, and he thought he saw the sky blink.

When Zero and Mrs. McCorkle got to the nursing home, a tall, thin, silver-haired man in a bathrobe and slippers stood staring out the front window into the dark parking lot. He opened the door for them, and Zero wheeled Mrs. McCorkle in. The man smiled and tipped his head then returned to his vigil.

It was after visiting hours, and Zero had to talk the night nurse into letting them into Harlan's room. It was quickly clear to Zero that this nurse was not the sort to forsake rules lightly, but Zero suspected from the way she nodded and rubbed her collar as he spoke that growing dissatisfaction with her job had caused her to look for just such an opportunity to toss caution aside, so he leaned farther over the counter, saying, "It's their fifty-second wedding anniversary. We drove all the way from New Mexico." He grinned but saw skepticism flicker in her eyes, then added, "They have children there." Zero chose the state carefully, a place distant and exotic, a double-word state; a redeemed place, once old, now improved; a place the Kansas mind would likely swirl around with topography envy. He hoped she was a native.

She said, "New Mexico! Mercy! You must be thirsty!" She pulled at her hair. "I just love those mesas out there all painted up and jagged. We took a trip to California when I was a little girl. My daddy didn't care a whit for the natural world, so I didn't get to linger long on the visual splendor. Daddy said it was just God playing with dirt, no call to get so excited.

"And you all live there all the time! You get to gander at that handsome landscape every day, those buttes and bluffs and canyons and such? Does it get old, all that beauty?"

Zero shook his head. "Scorpions," he said. He was now nervous and looked to Mrs. McCorkle for reinforcement. She was holding her hands out to the sides, testing the imaginary water rising around her wheels. Zero had never actually been to New Mexico and was afraid he would clutch, say "humid" when he meant "arid," confuse Taos with Tahoe, if he had to sustain this ruse for very long. When he'd leapt headlong into this lie, it hadn't occurred to him he might have to verify it with convincing details. He was sure he would betray himself, sure the words NEVER BEEN ANYWHERE would be written in the furrows in his face. He wished his friend Id were with him. Id could make a person believe he'd been to Mars. He'd pull out persuasive souvenirs, adapting whatever he had in his pockets. He'd talk knowledgeably about the unusual flora, making up, on the spot, his own taxonomic distinctions. Weeks of phone soliciting had still not turned Zero into the ace dissembler Id was naturally.

Fortunately the nurse did not press him further on the wonders of New Mexico, and when she said, "Okey doke," he felt himself slump with relief. She buried her face in a magazine, rather theatrically Zero thought, signaling she was blinding herself to their after-hours caper.

Zero wheeled Mrs. McCorkle into her husband's dark room. He flipped on the light, and Harlan sat up in his bed, pulling against the restraints. He blinked his foggy eyes. His white hair fuzzed out around his head in a staticky aureole. He licked his lips and lay back against his pillow. Mrs. McCorkle gently wheeled herself to the side of his bed and pulled back his covers. She put her hands on his strapped leg. He stretched his hand down and tugged at her bandage. She patted his ankle. She took the pitcher from the night table next to his bed and dribbled water across his waxen feet, his hand. Harlan smiled. Mrs. McCorkle sandwiched his hand in hers. She said, "You sleep now. I'll row."

Zero slipped out and went to the recreation room across the hall. It was lit by the glow of the television set and a small, orange lamp. Spread out on card tables were sewing cards and yarn, puzzles and magazines. Zero sat in a stuffed swivel chair close to the TV. A woman he hadn't noticed stood up, clutched a hand to her abdomen. She announced, "It's late!" and scurried out. Zero stood and peered down the hall, but she was gone. He turned up the volume and sat down.

On the television, a group of women sat at sewing machines in the parlor of an old house. As they ran their machines, a muffled bellowing sounded. The women looked at one another in alarm. Some bent over and eyed the pedals of their machines suspiciously. This was a reenactment scene. The actresses feigned surprise, dismay, holding their hands to their cheeks. The narrator explained that Singer sewing machines hum at B flat, a pitch that makes crocodiles keen.

Zero watched and pieced together from the rest of the story, a true story, that a wealthy man had secretly kept crocodiles in his basement, illicit pets, he loved them. When he and his wife decided to move from Michigan to the more agreeable climate of Florida, the natural habitat of his beloved hobby, the man had to find homes for his reptilian children, and so this man's story got out. News of his eccentric pastime, and the symphonic lowing his wife's sewing machine induced, made its way to scientific research communities and inspired curious zoologists to try to catalyze the mournful bleating of crocodiles using a well-tuned tuba.

The first attempt failed, the crocodiles unimpressed, logy as usual. But after certain variables of the experiment were modified, a more reverberant venue chosen, the tuba player tried again, and now the jaws of all the crocodiles began to creak slowly open, silently, as if it were only an epidemic of yawning, then the oddly melodic rumble churned the water, the air, the low ripples of sound so melancholy Zero thought the bellowing must surely be interpreted as animal despair and regret. He knew he was projecting, anthropomorphizing, transplanting his own fractured heart into their armored chests, but he couldn't help imagining they bemoaned the weighty burden of having such sharp teeth, huge maws, amphitheatres of carnal savaging, appetites so ravenous, inclusive, even monkeys – innocent, intelligent, sacrificial, ancestral – had to walk softly around them. But the crocodiles' lyrical bellowing seemed thoughtful to Zero, cautionary, the call of conscientious sirens warning the auditor to turn back lest he wreck his vessel on the craggy rocks of their unending hunger. Zero knew what it was to be hungry. Large appetites, he thought, are certainly to be feared.

❖

Zero sat on Rachel's couch as she rubbed his shoulders. He thought about Id's naked body, the anal punch line of his tail, about Mrs. McCorkle, the things she saw and her tender love for a lost husband, about the singing of the crocodiles, and the phantom wings that had haunted his back since his encounter with Gabriel. He could feel them waving in the air behind him as he walked, spreading decoratively as he sat. He felt them now, parting and lifting, moving out of the path of his sister's hands as she pressed her fingers into the knots of pain stitched loosely along his spine.

"What have you been doing, Zero? Feels like you're storing stones under your skin."

Zero shrugged his shoulders and felt something moth-soft brush his ear. It made his hearing whine to silence, then a deafening buzz filled his ears. His eyes watered. He turned over, sat up, and took Rachel's hand, held it to his ear like a medicinal cloth. Then he cradled it in his lap and stared at her pale arm. His ears roared with noise now, big noise, loud and stampeding, his head splitting with sound, thick with pressure, as though the atmosphere in his head were bearing down in the expectoration of a new planet. Distinct blares and crackles filed into his ears: the hubbub of midtown traffic, jackhammers exploding through concrete, lawn mowers razoring across suburban yards; stereophonic, sensurround screams all swelled in his ears, sounds he had conjured as a child to drown out his father's silence or the upstairs clamor he was supposed to pretend not to hear. Zero felt a long-welling infection breaking loose inside him, sorrow and longing colliding like demolition in his chest.

He saw Rachel's lips moving, her hand on his cheek. He touched her wrist and her elbow, pressed her thigh. He said, "He touched you here. With those callused fingers. He always pulled you toward him. I didn't look, but I knew. He hit you. His hands' shadows, still there." Zero traced his finger around phantom bruises, shattered capillaries. Rachel jerked away. "Maybe if he'd spread it between us . . ." Zero's voice, a sound he could only guess from Rachel's reaction was making its way out of his mouth, finally dulled the pealing tintinnabular chaos in his head to a hum.

Zero looked at his own arms. "It's like he *signed* you. He wrote himself onto your body. He wanted to see himself there, in your skin, didn't he? See himself continued. You were his slate." Zero pressed bloodless circles into his skin. "Am I blank? I don't know what to touch. I wanted to be worth his violence."

Zero looked up at Rachel. "Rache?" Her eyes appeared dark in the diminishing light of the room, as though they were all pupil, sinking into her head, eyes dropped down dark wells, out of reach.

Chapter Nineteen. Ivy Engel
Ivy on Mars

Kansas was once under water, the whole state submerged, gasping for air, dreaming of the day its soil would sponge up the blood of abolitionists and border ruffians, waiting to feel the record-breaking weight of the Largest Ball of Twine, floating in the amniotic fluids of prehistory, suspended in brine like my grandpa's teeth. Sometimes Duncan and I go down by the river and look for fossils, make up stories about swimming across the prairie, backstroking our way through slender, bending stalks of sunflowers, our phototropic mouths surfacing to drink in light. I get caught up in these visions of Cambrian Kansas, and then Duncan says I need to learn to be where I am when I am there or risk becoming nebular fizz; I am always dreaming I'm somewhere else. At this very moment, in fact, I picture myself as a trilobite, the inaugural trilobite, primordial arthropodan Eve, who looked at the sea through the first eyes to peel themselves to the world, and I wish my fossilized face would protrude in relief from an outcropping of Kansas limestone and be discovered by a future girl, a commuter to Mars.

Get *over* yourself, I think, but my face is thick with fate, plain as age or mood or beauty.

A more recent feature of my facial imperfection is a mercurial condition known as geographic tongue. It is an icky affliction but mercifully covert. It seems mine is an extreme case. Even the dentist lost her bedside cool and said, "Yawps!" when she saw my tongue. Some of the papillae on the tongue swell up and redden, form strange shapes, and you do look like you've got a map in your mouth. It's a fitting name, not like morphea. It's a little painful, but it goes away, and they have no idea what causes it, estrogen maybe or cayenne pepper, but it's not fatal. For me and Duncan, easily entertained by all things bodily, it has been an endless source of fascination. We are oral cartographers, anthropologists of the mouth. We give the countries names and chart climatic conditions and indigenous wildlife and wait for the continental drift that will erode them from my tongue. It's like time-lapse geologic history, oral history, nations mapped in silence, disappearing in utterance.

Under my bed, I keep a shoebox full of clippings about Mars and UFOs. I began this collection when the Ghost Lights started appearing at the quarry a couple miles from my house. A double helix of light was spotted twisting in the air before separating and zooming right over the heads of the watchers. More than a few people claimed to have witnessed this on several occasions, and suddenly UFO enthusiasts from all over started traveling to What Cheer in hopes of glimpsing these spectral lights. This created a hubbub for a while. There was even a guy who set up a sno-cone stand at the quarry, and he sold these plastic luminescent necklaces filled with an oozy pink and green substance that held its nuclear shimmer for weeks if you kept these circus souvenirs in the freezer.

So then there was an article in the paper about this woman who lived next door to the quarry and claimed she'd been visited by the Ghost Lights' pilots. She said they "walked in through the back door pretty as you please" and sat down at her kitchen table. She sat with them. And then she said she felt the strangest sensation, like a warm hand cradling her heart, and she had a peculiar and overwhelming impulse, one she'd clearly never had before. She reached back in her head with her fingers and pulled her eyes out of their sockets, plucked them straight out, and laid them on the kitchen table, next to the salt and pepper shakers and napkin holder. It didn't hurt and she didn't bleed. Her eyes rolled around on the table and aimed their line of sight like little searchlights at the beings seated in front of her. She could see them so clearly now. She could see they looked exactly like her.

The person who wrote the article made much of the fact that this woman had been a single mother whose only child had died the year before from a head injury sustained by a blow from a baseball and made little of the fact that her body was altered after this visitation: the sudden and inexplicable blindness (though her eyes had been safely returned to their sockets), the eerie graying of her skin, and the equally doctor-befuddling disappearance of the large, premature liver spots that had covered her hands and arms, appearing shortly after the death of her son.

So I had this dream the other night that I kept my eyes in my pockets and when I took them out to look, they were covered with lint and I had to lick my thumbs and clean them off. When I put them back in my head, I found myself holding a fish bowl filled with water and colored rocks. Then I saw a pair of miniature dentures floating near a plastic treasure chest, whose lid kept a bubbling rhythm like breathing as it opened and closed. I sprinkled in food flakes and the teeth zipped to the water's surface. The bowl turned into a big silver cup and I saw my stretched and dangling face mirrored in its shiny curve. And then somehow I realized that the face in the cup was the real one and I was the reflection, and the mirrored Ivy said, "Face it, girl. Destiny is as destiny does. It's time to trim the fat from fate." My clean eyes began to spin in their sockets.

I awoke short of breath and couldn't slow the frantic chainsaw buzz of my mind. I was thinking about the girls in my high school, all sentenced to the aegis of Mr. Stratton, the ones who would get pregnant and drop out, thinking they'd get their GED after the baby, and who would marry a boy, the one they'd been dating since ninth grade, a boy who would go to Taps every night of the pregnancy and come home to their basement bedroom in his parents' house smelling of beer, cigarettes, spearmint; girls who would have the baby and then three more while their husbands, on line at Proctor and Gamble, inhaled fumes that made them cross and near tubercular, these girls who would eventually divorce and join NutriSystem to try to lose the weight they'd gained during the marriage so that they might attract one of their ex-husband's friends, women who would live in clapboard houses that smelled always a little of mildew and baby mess and who would eventually get jobs at Walgreen's that allowed them to buy discounted Maybelline cosmetics, which they would use to cover up the blueprint of mundane despair their faces were, the place where the unhoped-for shape of their lives was etched in sharp lines, brightly colored faces that would stare out front room windows at their children playing and wait for the day they could show calmness and strength when their pregnant daughters quit school, when their teenaged sons moved brides into basements.

When you live on the unending flatness of the plains, terrain so level balls refuse to roll even when pushed, you make your own hills.

Before Grandma Engel died, she told me about a woman named Etoile who could tell me things about my life if I touched her face. She told me I should go to her when I felt like my skin didn't fit anymore, or when I couldn't remember where I came from. Once, just before she died, Grandma Engel took me to Etoile's house in Rosedale. I didn't go in, though. I sat outside on the sagging stoop poking holes in the dirt with a stick. The neighborhood scared me a little; except for the occasional chicken scratching in the crabgrass, it was so different from mine. There were rusted carcasses of cars and trucks in almost every yard, and the sky looked more yellow in this part of town, like it had a liver condition or was stained from years of neglect. Etoile's house was on a dead-end street that swooped down into vine-covered trees and never came out.

Years later I would ride my bike through Rosedale looking at the boarded-up bell tower of an old house where a rich baron-type was said to have slit the throat of his young wife, who was so good and beautiful he could not bear to let her live in an undeserving world. I would ride right up to the wrought-iron fence and spook myself senseless. I also looked for the animal genetics laboratory. It was rumored to use the unlikely locality of Rosedale as camouflage for dodging animal rights activists, who were always monkeying up the works, foiling their experiments. I had heard tales of two-headed cows too mammoth to stand on their spindly legs and giant chickens big as make-believe, chickens previously thought to live only in the ink of cartoonists or the wandering minds of out-of-work surrealists. Fortunately I never found the laboratory.

I had also heard stories about Rosedale being home to a community of Satan worshipers. Dogs and cats from surrounding neighborhoods last seen ambling toward the bottoms were never heard from again, so the stories went, clear evidence of either sacrificial misdeeds or leash law fanaticism. If you ask me, people are scared to death of the plain old poverty there that stares them dead in their upwardly mobile faces. Being dirt poor sounds too much like a road they themselves have come close to taking, whereas worshiping the Devil creates a rickety bridge they know they'll never cross, shoves those ragtag cretins right out of the realm of reasonable pathos because, after all, Devil-loving folks deserve all the blows they receive, deserve inadequate shoes and poor nutrition, deserve never to know the satellite joys of eighty-two channels. I don't know, I don't mean to be high-horsing it or anything and maybe there really are people in Rosedale begging Satan to let them Win, Place, or Show, reap a dark harvest just once, guzzling blood and signing over the deed to their threadbare souls for some measly break in this life, but me, I can tell you, I want out from under it all—I just want to meet a nice Martian who'll feed me home planet gumbo and tell me mythic stories about creatures whose hair lights up and sparkles like stars when they want to be kissed.

Etoile's short hair coiled on her head in pin-curled circles so flat and thin they appeared to be drawn on by a child, scribbles of bark-brown hair. Her eyes were cloudy and big behind her thick glasses. She was thin but had tight muscles in her arms, and seemed so young, maybe twenty, which meant she had been a child when my Grandma Engel first went to see her. Her cheeks were startling, quilted with shiny welts, as though she'd been stung by hornets. I imagined her face a foreign surface I could travel across, my bare feet sinking into her skin as I scaled the soft dunes of her cheeks.

She took my hand and led me into her tiny kitchen. I smelled Pine-Sol and fried onions. We sat at her table. I thought about the woman who took her eyes out for the aliens—momentous things happen in kitchens. Etoile sat in a chair covered in sunlight; her face was so slick with illumination it looked like glass. She tapped the tabletop and I laid my hands on the swirly, red Formica surface. She held my hands and said, "Did your grandmother tell you about my gift?"

"She just said you could tell me things, help me see stuff," I said.

She nodded. "I have to tell you the story," she said. "When I was a child, I got the fever that no amount of begging or bloodroot would curtail. On the third day, my face began to pucker and lump with sores the size and shape of thumbs. They spread and took root in the deep layers of my cheeks until the sixth day when the fever finally broke open. The heat fled, but the blains welled up and bloomed like little flowers. The petals of skin opened out. Mama pressed wet, rough leaves to my face and tarred them with a thick, malodorous gum. Papa made her stop. He said, 'This child's sight has been sleeping beneath the topsoil.' His own face and back were knotted with scars, though what he saw was in the past, terrible things buried deep, beneath memory, things people didn't want to dig up."

I got goose bumps all up my arms, and I was thinking how this was making Duncan's rituals and the bats and even Martin's story about his father seem sort of ordinary by comparison. I still wasn't sure what Etoile's prophetic specialty was so I guessed garden-variety spirit rapping and asked, "Could you tell Grandma and Grandpa Engel I miss them?"

Etoile smiled and said, "Your grandparents are dead, Ivy. I don't jaw with the dead."

"Sorry," I said. I wondered if I had just insulted her, if she felt misunderstood, like a serious ceramicist being mistaken for someone who makes ashtrays fashioned like hollow swans or pickle-shaped relish dishes. Mr. Egbert, the art teacher at school, was just such an artist, and he often wore an expression of disgusted forbearance when called upon by the PTA to sculpt fundraising gewgaws.

Etoile picked up my hands and put them on her face. She pressed my fingers into her bumpy cheeks, and I felt like I was about to do something illicit, something I wasn't old enough to do, something maybe no one was old or experienced enough to do. "Close your eyes," she said, "and look." Right away my eyes filled with flashing color; my mind quaked with pictures erupting too quickly for me to discern anything but bleary shapes. For a second, the faintest paranoia twitched in my temples, but, like my grandma had, I suddenly trusted Etoile completely and wanted to go where her face would take me. Etoile continued to push my fingers, one by one, into the scars on her cheeks, and it felt like pressing keys on an instrument, like the making of soundless music: I was playing her face.

This symphony of pictures became less frenetic and the shapes gained distinct edges, dimension. It was like a big roulette wheel slowing to the point where you could see the number you'd bet on flashing by. And then there it was, right there infecting my closed eyes: I saw the face on Mars, the infamous visage, and me, face-to-face, big to small, flesh to clay, I stood at its chin. And I saw the scar on its cheek! It was my face, there it was, plain as day, it was *my* face on Mars.

I knew I was meant to go there, meant to make peace with that hostile atmosphere, meant to end up in a place where I could carve out my own wobbly trek through the world and there wouldn't be anyone there to grin at me knowingly as though he could read defeat in the scar on my cheek. Maybe I'd take Etoile with me and together we'd say, Beauty is a stretch of skin whose perfection can be witnessed in the sickness it survived.

Just as I began envisioning Etoile and me loping along in our hovercraft sneakers, the picture changed. The face started roiling and shifting, as though there were fists beneath it punching a new shape. The face was aging, drooping with time, like those artist renderings updating the faces of disappeared children so you can see the direction their brows and noses and hairlines and chins are likely to go in, if they're going at all, which is only a dream really, a guess at the future, speculation filled with the hope of growth.

The face was wrinkled, the scar was gone, and I noticed people, everywhere, the planet suddenly crawling with them. They stared at each other as if they all knew a secret, casting furtive glances and talking over their shoulders. Mars was fraught with humans, cripes! I'd carried them with me, like a virus.

There was no escape.

Then the Ivy who is the Me I'm seeing through Etoile's face crawled up on the crumbling chin, scaled the eroding nose, and leapt into space, flying off the planet into the thick cosmos, and I flap-flapped toward the tiny sphere below, the place that I came from.

I will tell this to Duncan, and he will say, "It's clear, Ivy. You don't have to be Houdini to see that the trick of escape is being where you are at the very moment you're there," and I will be so much there at that moment that I'll be pulling the words from his mouth with my embattled tongue.

Etoile took my hands from her face, and I opened my eyes. She smiled. The sun had moved and now it angled across her head and lit up her hair like the spiraling filaments inside light bulbs; her hair fizzed with bright and hovering circles, nesting stars. Her mouth looked like a moth poised for flight. I blinked my eyes and touched my scar. I kissed her on the lips.

Chapter Twenty. Ruby and Martin
A Girl and a Boy, Some Trees

It is Saturday morning, and Ruby Tuesday pokes at the milk-bloated hearts and stars and clovers and moons bobbing in her cereal bowl. She transplants them onto a paper towel and leaves them to dry so she can swallow them whole later, plant them with the rest deep in her empty stomach. She puts on her sneakers and stuffs Band-Aids, magic markers, and a small bottle of Elmer's glue into her knapsack. She grabs a banana, some peanuts. She's going into the woods.

Outside, she walks down the dead-end hill toward the place where the street stops and the trees grow thick. She pretends she's a gorilla who has lost her memory, a gorilla afraid to lift off, confused and grounded, unable to bloom. She spots a hedge apple and a piece of green glass lying in a ditch. She picks them up. "Are you my mother?" she asks the hedge apple. "No," she says. She squints at the sky through the bit of broken bottle. "I'm a gorilla and I am lost." She holds the glass in her palm. She says, "Can you tell me my name?" "Tomorrow," she replies. "But I want to know now," she says. "No, that's your name, lost gorilla. Your name is Tomorrow." Ruby nods. "Oh," she says. "Oh, oh."

She reaches the edge of the woods and finds the rough trail of trampled grass and moss flattened, she guesses, by the feet of truant children escaping to makeshift forts and cigarettes and imaginary histories. Ruby picks up a branch ruffled with fungus and holds it in front of her like a flashlight. "Hello, hello, hello," she calls. "Hello, hello, hello," she quietly echoes.

The trail turns to dirt and knotted roots, and Ruby walks carefully, sidestepping the beginnings of trees and plants bending toward the trickle of sun that slips between branches. Every now and then, she reaches into her knapsack and tosses a peanut behind her. She knows in the wilderness it is important to leave signs of yourself behind, to mark your trek. And she hopes she might draw out wild animals, summon them to her with the scent of salted nut. Mr. Abatista, who lives close to the woods, has a salt lick in his backyard, and she has seen deer leap out from the tree line as if they were touching down from another world and edge their way slowly closer until the smaller parts of them were discernible, their noses and white throats, their quick tongues flickering, stealing a taste of salt.

As Ruby continues along the trail, birds swoop and chatter, chirps and clicks of alarm telegraph across treetops, an occasional squirrel spirals up a trunk. Ruby stops to inspect an insect resting on the weedy growth that arcs over the path. It has a fizzy green body bright and volatile-seeming as the commingling of two chemicals meant never to be mixed. It makes Ruby think of Mr. Science and the once-a-month lyceums at Oak Grove Elementary where he performs his "Wondrous World" magic with aluminum foil and string, soda cans and coat hangers. "Common household items are full of undreamed-of secrets," says Mr. Science. Ruby prefers the lectures of Officer Friendly, who teaches children how to crouch and roll in the event of a fire and shows them slides of bicycling boys and girls whose use of helmets and hand signals earn them "Certificates of Merit" from the City of What Cheer Police Department. She knows Officer Friendly is not as flashy or popular as Mr. Science, but she loves the bright shine of his shoes, patent leather oxfords that reflect the auditorium lights, making it appear as though he has slow comets at the ends of his legs. And she especially appreciates his big-bodied willingness to roll on the ground.

Ruby fixes her eyes on the cellophane wings of the insect, opening and closing, steady and even, a heartbeat, a breathing thing. Ruby opens and closes her mouth in unison with the rhythm of the wings. The wings are see-through and brittle; on the outer curve of one a tiny wedge is missing, as though an even tinier bug had taken a bite from it. "Are you on your way to a dance recital?" Ruby asks. "Are you on your way to heaven? You look unhappy," she says. "Are you waiting to be extinct? We all are. You're a nice bug. I'm a gorilla and I have lost my way."

"My father called them moon bugs because they look rather as though they've swallowed a sample of moon," a voice says. "Which, it occurs to me now, was uncharacteristically fanciful of him."

Ruby turns and sees a man lying on the mossy ground on the other side of the trail. She walks over and looks down at him. He wears jeans but no shirt. His sneakers are muddy. He's very thin.

"How do you do?" he asks.

Ruby blinks, stays quiet. She drops her knapsack and plants herself beside him, cross-legged.

"My name is Martin. I hope my partial nudity does not offend. I seem to be having some difficulty keeping my upper body clad these days. I don a shirt and then thoughtlessly remove it. It's not that the fabric scratches, mind you, or is in any obvious way inimical to my skin. Rather it's as though I believe my chest and abdomen might yield

174

some secret if I were to keep watch. I know this must sound strange."

"Common household items are full of undreamed-of secrets," Ruby says.

"That certainly has the ring of truth to it, doesn't it? And one is less likely to catch cold searching for answers in, say, Saran Wrap." Martin grins weakly. Ruby nods. "One noteworthy discovery, however: insects seem altogether uninterested in my flesh. No bites, no stings. I am told that mosquitoes are particularly attracted to the fluctuating sweetness of diabetics. Fortunately my blood sugar maintains itself within the normal range."

Ruby takes a banana out of her knapsack and dangles it over Martin's face.

"Too much potassium makes me maudlin," he says. "But thanks."

She peels and begins to eat it. She says, "Mama has scars and crooked bones. She rubs people good as new. She's in the phonebook."

"I'm quite fortunate," says Martin. "I haven't any noticeable physical imperfections whatsoever. My body's smooth as satin."

Ruby asks, "What about on the inside parts where it's hard to see?"

Martin says, "Pardon me?"

Ruby says, "My grandma has scars on her vocal cords. We can hear them but only the doctor can see them, and they're tough and thick like toes. They keep her from singing." Ruby says, "Sometimes people think I'm a girl, but I'm not. I'm a gorilla."

Martin nods and says, "Hence the banana."

Ruby smiles and drapes the emptied peel on a sturdy weed tree. "Daffodil," she says.

Martin turns his head toward Ruby and looks at her. He says, "I dreamed about my father last night." Ruby nods and finishes off the naked fruit. "I'd like to tell you about it, though perhaps you're not old enough. You're not very big. You must be quite impressionable. I certainly wouldn't want to be responsible for a loss of innocence or a scarring incident you might one day recount to a therapist."

"I'm old," Ruby says.

"How old?"

"I'm Tomorrow. Old as next week."

"All right then."

Ruby fishes her bottle of Elmer's glue out of her bag and unwinds the orange lid. She looks at the grinning bull on the bottle then takes Martin's hand. He turns his head back to stare up. Ruby squeezes the glue onto his palm and spreads it around with her finger. She blows on his hand as he starts his story.

"I dreamed I dissected my father. He was spread out on a slab of black wax, straight pins driven through his hands and his legs, holding his body taut." Martin stops and turns his eyes on Ruby. "Let me just say that after much consideration I've concluded that Christ does not linger behind this dream image. The pins were utility, necessary to the task, like the skewering of a grasshopper's thorax, the pithing of a lab frog's spine. One never sees comparisons to crucifixion drawn there." Martin casts his gaze to the treetops again. Ruby looks up at the slivers of sky, the bright blue and white thatched with branches.

"And with an exacto-sharp finger, I sliced him down the middle, carved an indelible axis. Then I pried him open like an old carpetbag and looked inside. My steely fingers flashed in the glaring lights above me and then glinted against something white in the otherwise dark cavity of my father. I looked closer and discovered a repast of cheese and crusty bread, slices of pear and squares of chocolate tastefully arranged on what appeared to be a lovely piece of bone china. *Contents of stomach*, I recorded on the clipboard in my head. Of course I realized this did not jibe with my father's customary Friday night meal of polska kielbasa and sauerkraut, spreading wetly across a floral-patterned plastic plate. Someone had been here before me, stolen his last meal, I thought. With the skill of an ice fisherman, I quickly cut an opening in my father's head and out spilled dozens of photographs of my father at varying ages: a smirking child, a flexing man, a tuxedoed dancer in full grin dipping my mother. It was too much. I didn't know this person whose body gave up its secrets so easily, revealing a blithe and tender history I could never have inferred from the present. I snapped my father's body closed and began carving my initials on his chest, as though he were an aged oak. I carved *Martin loves Arthur, Marty + Arty, M and A Forever*. I kissed the bloodless cuts."

Ruby gently peels the stretchy glue from Martin's hand. When the map of his palm is free of the skin, she turns it over in her own hand and studies it. "Hmmm," she says, "Uh-hunh." She touches the network of lines in the ribbed mold. She says, "You will make coats for cold people." She says, "Your father will touch you. He'll touch your stomach and your lips and other sore spots. He'll roll you up in his hands and pat you down like a snowball. One day," she says, "one day you will die." She shrugs her shoulders. "Me too." Martin closes his eyes.

Ruby takes the magic markers and Band-Aids out of her knapsack. She selects yellow and blue and draws small x's on Martin's bare chest and arms. Then she covers them with Bugs Bunny Band-Aids. She crosses his arms on his chest and sings: *And ye beneath life's crushing load whose forms are bending low, who toil along the climbing way with painful steps and slow, look now for glad and golden hours come swiftly on the wing: oh rest beside the weary road, and hear the angels sing.*

Martin looks at Ruby and says, "I didn't realize gorilla girls had such melodious voices." He puts his hand to her cheek. "Care to marry me?"

Ruby lays her head on Martin's stomach. She stares at his bony sternum, touches his hairless chin. "I better not," she says. "I just remembered something."

"What did you remember?"

"Ask me who my daddy is."

"Who's your daddy?"

Ruby sits up, looks around, says, "You. Daddy with the sad dreams." She presses her finger against his forehead.

"Me?"

Ruby nods.

"How do you know?"

Ruby points to the glue-print and says, "It says so right here." She rummages in her knapsack and pulls out a peanut. "Take this. It'll help."

Martin takes the peanut. "And the mother?" he asks.

Ruby looks behind her. The lichen and saplings stay green and silent; the full-grown trees gently stir, as though a waking giant exhaled calmly above them. "The bug, there, on that weed." She points. "Moon bug. You met in the doctor's office. You were getting a flu shot and she was having her tonsils looked at. You fell in love with her wings. You thought she was beautiful and you thought she could teach you to fly. She took you to church, and the light that fell through the colored glass made your cheeks warm. They felt like pancakes. The man in the purple robe told you stories, about how God makes you bleed and itch so you'll think about your skin and the skeleton bones inside making it shaped like you, and you'll think about who gave them to you, about who lets the blood come out when you get cut. Then you sang songs, and you were so loud the other people in church covered their ears. I came when no one was looking. Everyone put their faces in their laps. They chewed on their knees. My mama coughed and there I was, a little gorilla. I was stuck in her throat the whole time." Ruby holds the palm print over one eye and closes the other. "That was when the world was small." Ruby pats her hands on Martin's cartoon wounds, making singsong sounds as she taps his abdomen, a fleshy xylophone.

Martin sits up. "I have something to tell *you*," he says.

"Shhh." Ruby pushes him back to the ground, puts her hands over his eyes. "You're dead," she says. "But I can help. I can make you well, and then you'll be little, but I'll be your mama. I'll wash your hair and feed you with raisins." Ruby peels the Band-Aids from Martin's body and sticks them to her knapsack. Then she licks her thumbs and rubs the blue and yellow x's, wipes them dry with the sleeve of her jacket. When she is finished, Ruby surveys her canvas. Martin's flesh has a peculiar tint to it. It reminds Ruby of the seasick color the sky turns during late summer storms, the sky she has stared at from the safety of basement windows. "You're cured," she says. "Your sores are all gone. Rise up, rise up!"

Martin opens his eyes and sits up. He takes Ruby's hands. "Listen. We're aboriginal, you and me, incipient, inaugural. Thoroughly inchoate. We're incunabular, you understand, protasis, the genesis of genesis." Martin kisses Ruby's hands. "And: we are conclusion. We're fait accompli, apodosis, the end of the circle."

"Okay," says Ruby.

Martin says, "There are aboriginal peoples who have a lateral sense of kinship. Familial relationships stretch outward like roots, benevolent tentacles, rather than grow upward like a tree, this limb begetting that one and so on. When a woman is pregnant, she travels trodden paths, and the place at which she first feels the baby kick she marks. She chisels a symbol in the bark of a tree, piles rocks in circles, plants rows of sticks in soft mud, and all the other people who first kicked their mother's wombs at that same spot are the baby's relatives. It's a peripatetic determination, a matter of walking. The baby's kick is its first step, its choice of kith. If the path intersects with a kangaroo trail, then the baby is also thought to count kangaroos among its family members. If the mother sees a bird circling the sky at this moment, the bird too is the baby's relation. The hot sun and cracked earth, a sister, an uncle to the baby to be." Martin looks up from Ruby's hands and fixes on her eyes. He stares with such concentration, Ruby thinks the color is draining from them, thinks her irises must be running down her cheeks like green tears and her eyes will soon be empty.

Ruby stands. "Aborigines," she says. She has to ask: "What if the baby's a quiet baby who sits still and doesn't kick no matter where the mama walks? I bet you were a quiet baby. Maybe you were a secret your mama didn't know she was keeping."

Martin continues to stare, and Ruby feels the heat of his look in her chest, feels her bones huddle against it. It is the same feeling she gets when she pretends the moon is a giant eye staring her down, the sky's other eye closed in a nocturnal wink.

Martin scratches his chest, his belly. "You are bent on complication, aren't you? I might have been an active child. A hellion even. I could have been a truth that had to be told, not a secret, I wasn't a secret, my father didn't care for secrets. No, rather a child perfectly molded to his father's longing, to sate his hunger for extension, just as . . . just as the glass is the shape of the glassblower's breath, sire of his suspiration. It's not *so* unthinkable." Martin turns his head. "Go."

Ruby puts the glue print in her knapsack. She gently places her foot on Martin's bare stomach and taps it with the toe of her sneaker. "Kick, kick, kick."

The end of the trail empties out onto another street in another neighborhood. Ruby Tuesday has never followed it to conclusion, or origin. She examines the tree closest to the street so she will recognize how to get back. She runs her hands along the bark. She pretends it is a Braille message in a special blind gorilla language. "It says, 'You are here,'" she tells herself. Then she sees whittled letters farther up the trunk, human letters: *M* + *A* inside a carved heart. She steps onto the asphalt.

Ruby walks along the street and looks at houses and yards. They are slightly larger and farther apart than the houses in her neighborhood and the grass seems shorter, more like carpeting than grass, and there are fewer broken objects strewn about, but really, she thinks, it all looks so similar to the houses on the other side of the woods. Ruby hopes the children here have bigger bodies; she hopes their hair is more neatly combed.

Ruby walks and looks. A boy hoses a car in a driveway, a dog barks and leaps at a fence, a woman hangs clothes on a drooping line. Ruby stops at the end of a driveway. In the middle of the cracked cement, there is a reddish-brown stain that's splattered in odd shapes and seems to creep toward the front door. The house is dark. Newspaper covers the front window. Ruby kneels and touches the stain. It reminds her of a giant birthmark, a port wine stain, like the one she envies on the face of her classmate. Carla Totten's cheek and throat are covered in purple-red pigment, and Ruby thinks it's pretty, purple skin, dramatic as eggplant.

Ruby walks to the covered window. She tries to look inside, but there are no cracks that allow her sight through. She looks at the papered glass. She wants to know what lives behind a curtain such as this, behind the black headlines, wants to know who prefers yellowing newsprint to sunlight. She covers one eye and scans all the pages, letting herself see only one or two words at a time: *War in*, *watch fobs*, *honey-glazed*, *miracle*, *yesterday*, *32*, *homicide and*, *Metroplex*.

Ruby walks back to the driveway and sits on the center of the stain. "All gorillas must sit on this spot," she says, "before they are allowed to go home." Then Ruby notices that the giant birthmark she sits on is made up of a herd of small shapes; they clump together in a russet cloud that spreads across the concrete. Ruby sees a shape she knows, a pair of disheveled wings, misaligned, as if cast off at the end of a trying day. She sees small circles that crown and bleed into the body of the wings, reddish pebbles, like toe prints, and she remembers her mother's sleeping feet, wings she parts and looks through at night to watch her mother's even breathing. Suddenly Ruby feels a rumble and slap in the deep pit of her stomach, a sharp and frenzied churning. She slips her knapsack off her shoulders. She lies down and puts her hands on her belly, closes her eyes.

Ruby feels pain like fast fists boxing her insides. She tightens her hands against herself. She is suddenly afraid, so afraid she is going to break wide open and lose herself, lose the inside self held in by skin and ribs, and her lost insides will run away from the ruined body, a shattered bottle, run down the path and into the trees without her, throw peanuts randomly over the shoulder it has abandoned, and then she'll be all outsides, nothing but blown-open skin, and will have to stay with the torn-up leftovers of herself, a doggie-bag body, until someone sees she is broken and tries to stitch her back together; but it will be too late, hopeless, because the inside of herself will have escaped, will have run back to her life on the other side of the woods, will be pretending to be the Ruby Tuesday it peeled itself from, walking around and eating bananas, singing and telling itself jokes, brushing its own hair in a motherly way, it will be, will be too late.

Ruby Tuesday screams, but she does not know if it is a hearable scream, a loud scream out of her lungs, or if it is a quiet scream, a see-ya-so-long scream the inside makes as it exits. Her stomach erupts – *whoosh and clank and the feathers whirring cracking the hard dirt clink under roots cleave-cleaving seeds sproing shifting the earth tamped under hooves clacking in water fallen from sun splits duckbill burble marsh while revving the clover gloaming echolocation and chlorophyll –*

Ruby can hardly inhale between the sharp jabs slicing her breath, but she wants to see her last shape, the magma of Rubyself slipping away, so she lifts her shirt and looks, looks at the loud and viny jungle pouring out of her stomach, sees the turbulent tide of purple birds and twisting trees tenting her shirt, thick melons wobbling down fields of lit-up flowers and gorilla-faced blossoms whose petals spin like propellers, and lemons, lemons everywhere, launched and rolling and floating in water.

When she opens her eyes, a man is holding her hand and smoothing her cheek. He is a clean man with slicked-back, gray-templed hair and square, silver-framed glasses. He is wearing a white shirt and black suit coat and pants, wing-tipped shoes puckering beneath his kneeling legs. A gray bow tie sits cockeyed at his throat, and Ruby thinks it makes him look like a human present, a man gift. He holds a dog-eared Holy Bible to his chest.

"Speak, child," the man says.

Ruby Tuesday sits up and rubs her stomach. She touches her chest and her legs, her shoulders and face. The pieces are all there, gaps closed, atoms held together, she hopes, by the self-same glue of being she came with.

"Praise be," says the man. "This driveway has the smell of Gethsemane about it, the unmistakable scent of suffering." The man pats Ruby's arm. "Can you hear me, child? Can you tell me your name?" The man has a fatherly smell – aftershave and old books.

Ruby sees the contents of her knapsack spread out around her, the peanuts, the bottle of glue and magic markers, the copy of Martin's palm. In her lap, she sees a lemon, a large and shiny lemon so yellow it hurts her eyes to look at it. She offers the lemon to the clean, kind man. "You are my aborigine," she says.

The man's brow and lips wrinkle and squinch and his face looks to Ruby like that of a person learning to read. The man takes the lemon from Ruby, looks it over. "Who are you?" he asks.

Chapter Twenty-One. Rachel and Martin
Urticaria

A boy, a man maybe, came to see me today. He told me he knows Ruby, met her in the woods. He came for a rub. When he took off his clothes, I could see he was covered with hives. His back and his arms, chest and legs, bubbled with welts. I put my hand to my mouth. The angry skin, it was surprising. He said, "I know. You'd never guess that beneath this blemished canvas lies Grade A skin pure as an infant's." We had a conversation.

I said, "How'd you get this way? Do you have an allergy?"

He said, "I was lying in the woods."

I said, "Naked?"

He said, "Largely."

I said, "Why?"

He said, "I was searching for someone."

"I can't rub you," I said. "It might spread. Might go inside. You need medicine."

He said, "I thought perhaps you could rub my feet or my hands, reflexology. Aren't there buttons on the foot you can press to stimulate healing in the North?"

"Maybe," I said. "It will hurt."

He smiled.

So I worked his feet over, kneaded the soles, the toes, the heels, his body's bumpy template. He winced and smiled, winced and smiled.

"I used to get sick with some regularity," he said. "As a child. Headaches. They made me perceive the world strangely. Objects were limned in blinding light. My pupils were plagued. They had to perform ocular gymnastics to keep up with the modulating brightness. Eventually, squinting was my only recourse, and the world disappeared behind a gauzy scrim. Once my father held my head in his lap and massaged my temples. When I cracked my eyes open, I saw him glowing like a saint, torturously beatific. He propped the newspaper to the side and breathed baseball scores into my ears. He whispered, 'George Brett thinks he's hot shit 'cause the girls whistle him onto the field. Me, I prefer an average Joe solid citizen like Cookie Rojas, Freddie Patek, any goddamned day of the week.' He kissed my ear, sang, 'Shh-shh-shh.'"

This boy looked up at me.

I said, "I never liked George Brett either. Something about him."

He said, "He's gone."

I said, "Yes."

He said, "I don't like baseball."

I nodded.

He said, "I had beautiful skin."

I said, "He's not coming back."

He shook his head. "No."

As I rubbed this boy's feet, his history mushroomed in front of me, and in the map of his foot, his body's parallel universe, I read consequential occurrences, reverberant acts. Pressure to his big toe would send a tingle to his head. Rubbing his instep would soothe his intestines, his pancreas. Each gesture would sting on site and ricochet relief elsewhere. With every triggering grind of my knuckle, a healing twinge would telegraph its way along a circuit and distant pain would break loose, go tumbling out of his body, avalanching soreness. In this boy's foot, I saw his face as a child, serious as granite. I saw a man and a woman warring in a kitchen, the woman wielding a bread board, the man pulling at his suspenders, the boy crouched beneath the table, reading *James and the Giant Peach*, imagining how joyful it would be to live in stickiness, to be able to snack on the walls of his home. And I could see that years from now, when this boy has grown to be a man, unmistakably, an old man, the neighbors in his brownstone will sit on the fire escape in the summer heat, bellowing about money and food, infidelity, disorder, roaring, "Shameless cunt!" and "Worthless bastard!" as this man will sit beneath his kitchen table eating peaches, waiting to drowse off to the metronomic thumps he knows will follow, the lullaby sounds of fucking.

My hands traveled to the latitude of his eyes, below the toes, and there I found knots to crumble. I pressed hard. The boy exhaled audibly and sat up, worn slick by pain, its doggedness.

My mama said, "Watch what you open your eyes to. There's no injury in blindness, but sight can cause a mess of damage. The darkness of not seeing can be as a lovely sleep. If you must look, careful where your gaze falls. The view might have teeth, might just as soon gnaw at your heart, take you by the throat, as let you live peacefully. And then you get lazy-blooded with your heart all chewed up and pumping irregularly. Tired. So tired, some mornings you debate the value of rising. Mind."

Chapter Twenty-Two. Ansel and Ruby
Revelation Ranch

Mr. Dorsett dreamed of the strange child he'd found writhing on Mrs. McCorkle's bloodstained driveway, dreamed of her every night since he'd found her. When he awoke, he only remembered bits of the dreams, images, stills: her hand held out, offering him small white pebbles (or were they teeth?); fruit falling from the sky, cats and dogs dodging beneath bushes, under cars; a large purple bird with the child's small face; the child sitting hunched in a gold-wire cage, brushing her hair; nonsense mostly, not the sort of thing of which one could make meaning, the night mind's garbled film. Ruby, her name was, Ruby Tuesday, she'd told him. And what was that supposed to mean?

After she'd offered him the lemon, the lemon he could have sworn he saw bubble up from her abdomen and burst forth from her churning jacket in a startling fruit birth, he found himself asking her if on Saturday she would accompany him to the Cattle Drive on 49th Street, Newton Ambrogast, Jr.'s attempt to drum up a retirement fund for his inherited livestock.

Newton, longtime friend and neighbor of Ansel Dorsett's, had been a vegetarian for forty years, and though he'd never taken the moral high-ground with his father when it came to his cattle ranch, which had been progressively dwindling and which his father had tended only halfheartedly for the last twenty years of his life, Newton suddenly found himself in charge of the welfare and fate of twenty healthy Herefords, a bequest from his recently departed father. But it cost money to raise cattle, a great deal of money, particularly if it was your intention to let them die a natural death – thus the Cattle Drive, some manner of cow pageant that people could pay to see, cheap but well-intentioned bovine entertainment on a Saturday afternoon.

And when Ansel Dorsett looked at Ruby Tuesday's moony cheeks, the pale, round, quizzical face of this befuddling girl, this Martian child, he felt he was meant to swing her in circles in the presence of earth-brown cows, chewing, dawdling, farting cows with a taste for Kansas sorrel, meant to show Ruby Tuesday the aerodynamism of her small body. Why cows, white-faced and idle? Well, why prairie dogs? Why a plague of squirrels? Why Lemon Ruby, as he had come to think of her? He couldn't say, only knew that he must follow the instincts of his feet, presently pointing east toward the fertile pungency that wafted right into his garage on breezy days, the rank and weedy winds scented by the Ambrogast ranch.

And here it was Saturday already. The residue of last night's dream – an Armageddon number featuring apocalyptic horsemen garbed in jean jackets, twirling black pigtails with their wraith-frail fingers, and an angel-faced dog saying, *Hurt not the earth, neither the sea, nor the trees, till we have sealed the servants of our God in their foreheads* – still clung to the muddy walls of Ansel's unconscious.

Ansel looked out his window to see Lemon Ruby sitting, legs crossed, arms akimbo, on Mrs. McCorkle's driveway. She looked so calm and meaningful, a child-shaped symbol of something portentous and big – redemption, love, God's good intentions, who could say? – sitting so still and self-possessed, as though she could wave her hands and charm the bloodstain right off the cement, conjure it into the air like a dancing snake that would rise obediently, fangs chastened behind scaly skin.

He walked outside and crossed his lawn. He stood in front of Ruby, held out his hand. She took it and stood up. "What were you doing?" he asked, then smiled and raised his eyebrows, afraid he might seem to her the kind of generic authority figure she would feel obliged to dislike. He felt his personality draining from him, felt his face whiten with the loss. He didn't understand why he was magnetized toward this child, but he so wanted her to like him. He wanted her to smile and say his name, crawl inside him and fall asleep.

"Thinking." Lemon Ruby tucked her hands inside the pockets of her jacket.

"What about?" Ansel couldn't think what expression to paste across his face so he nodded.

"Mr. Abatista."

"Your teacher?"

Ruby shook her head. "He lives by me and he has a garden. He's sick. He's going to die. Maybe tomorrow."

"Would you like to go visit him?" Ansel did not want to see a dying man today, did not want to see Ruby seeing a dying man today, knew he'd never get away with swinging her in circles or making her laugh near a dying man's bed, knew that that would surely be an unbearable contradiction for the nearby bereaved. He had nothing against dying men, per se, fully expected to be one himself shortly in fact, but today was a day, he thought, to wrap himself in his own thinning skin and shake life from his limbs. He was relieved to hear Ruby say, "No, thank you."

They walked down the road toward the Ambrogast ranch. Though they couldn't see the site of revelry, party sounds – laughter, music, barking, and a chirping din of voices – gently swelled as they neared it, and barnyard smells laced with a hint of treacle sweetness drifted toward their noses, as though they were being eased into the foreign atmosphere of another planet, a swirling stew of, say, Martian sensation that required gradual acclimation. Ansel thought that those who had driven cars and parked right in front of Newton's house had cheated themselves out of a habituating trek and must have been knocked still in their tracks as the sensory curtain slowly parted and sucked them through to the other side.

As they walked through the gate, Ruby said, "Knock, knock." Ansel could not quite decipher the meaning of this, though he had a vague recollection of participating in this ritual with his own daughter. He remembered the basic drill – knock, knock, who's there – but couldn't remember if he'd be called upon to say something off-the-cuff and clever at some point. His mind was awhirl, in no shape to whip up nimble-witted quips upon demand. He stared at Lemon Ruby, his mind empty as a pew on a Monday afternoon. Just then, Newton Ambrogast, Jr. approached them and offered his hand to Ruby. He said, "Hi there, little miss. Welcome to the Ambrogast Cattle Drive." Newton looked at Ansel and winked. Ruby shook Newton's hand and said, "Knock, knock." Newton shrugged his shoulders and an exaggerated look of puzzlement crimped his face. He said, "Well, who could that be? Don't nobody visit me no more save those hungry cows wishing to be fed. Who is it?"

Ruby said, "Hatch."

Newton said, "Hatch who?"

"Bless you," said Ruby. Newton chortled and said, "I'll accept that blessing, thank you," and Ansel smiled, relieved. Ansel pulled his bill-fold out of his hip pocket and handed Newton a five-dollar bill.

"You folks enjoy yourselves, and be sure to check out them pampered bovine before you leave." Newton placed his hand on Ansel's shoulder and said, "We guarantee one revelation per customer. If them cows don't speak to you, if you don't see the word made flesh there, we'll give you your money back." Newton laughed a big, red-faced laugh and patted Ansel on the back. Newton Ambrogast, Jr. was a lapsed Baptist and missed no opportunity to rib Ansel about his most firmly held convictions. Ansel had always taken these jabs in stride, though of late they'd been getting on his nerves. Newton resented the dour brimstone foundations, the a priori remonstrations, upon which every sermon was built, felt that faith borne of fear was simply blind submission to thuggery, not authentic belief. "By the time it actually happens," Newton told Ansel as he departed from the flock, "I figure I'll already have experienced the Rapture nigh on a thousand times. I'll have imagined in my head the poor unfaithful wandering below, seized by all order of apocalyptic, God-wrought calamity so many times it'll likely feel like business as usual when it strikes, but for now it makes it near to impossible to get a decent night's sleep. No thank you. I think I can worship just fine from the safety and comfort of my Barcalounger, where nary a tooth will be gnashed." Ansel actually sympathized with Newton's misgivings, but despite his own qualms he couldn't help but thrill to the eschatological emphasis of the church teachings. He figured this ambivalence was at least partially responsible for his ministerial failure, that ill-fated, partially delivered sermon that had staggered toward a strangely spur-of-the moment existential message unpopular with Shadyvale Baptists and left him shaking in the pulpit.

Ansel heard Newton's laugh trail off behind them as he and Ruby walked into the crush of people. He couldn't decide what to drift toward first. He saw a cotton candy stand, saw the white-aproned man spinning a centrifugal vat filled with air and sugar, shaping the frothy lavender strands into a nest of confection. A picture flashed in his mind of his grandmother's long-ago hair.

Next to this, he saw a toothless, wrinkled man wearing faded denim overalls lower a flaming wand toward his grizzled muzzle then push it full inside his mouth, smoke curling dramatically to the sides, the gray and wispy remnants of a fire tamed. The man pulled the wand from his mouth and smiled, his unsinged gums a pink and shining testimony. People applauded.

"Where do you want to go first?" Ansel asked.

Ruby pointed into the crowd of people and said, "Heaven."

Ansel felt a warm flutter in his chest, and he clutched the coins and keys in his pants pockets. He followed Ruby, the black swish of her hair, as she moved through the thicket of staggered legs with, he thought, the purposeful gait of an explorer founding a continent, her tiny arm a gentle scythe clearing a path.

Ruby stopped when she found a hole in the crowd, a spot directly in front of a stage, where four boys sporting white gowns and wings and lolling gold halos stood in each corner, billowing blue sheets and howling like wind. Suddenly, the angels dropped the sheets and a great tumult of activity ensued: a squadron of angel boys ran onto stage and sounded trumpets as foil stars snowed around them; a large hand floated in from the wings and from the palm issued pink smoke; ping-pong balls fell and pelted the rushing angels; wavy, cardboard water sawed back and forth in the foreground.

Ansel stared at this interpretive hullabaloo. He was struck by the everydayness of the props, imagined women walking the aisles of the local crafts store, looking for feathers, non-toxic epoxy, imagined them sitting at home stitching and gluing this drama together. He thought about all the behind-the-scenes labor that went into the making of miracles and mayhem. Then he lost the trail of his thinking and as he watched the people dash across stage dressed like the End of the World, he felt himself become leaden, moored to the spot, to the scene. He became acutely aware of fevered activity beneath his own skin, felt the blood rush then slow its coursing, felt it grow thick as mortar in his veins. His eyes dried with their gaping, and he had the distinct and curious sensation of watching a forgotten memory come rushing back, a disturbing augury both ever present and long filed away, pressed between the yellowing leaves of his mind. It seemed to him that his life had been lived to arrive at this moment – this was its sum and apogee – that everything hereafter would be superfluous, postscript. He looked down at his legs and his arms. He couldn't remember what one did with these dangling extremities, to what use they were customarily put, couldn't remember having ever even seen them before; they seemed the misplaced prostheses of a perfect stranger, and he shuddered at their cloying attachment to his trunk. All this was less a revelation to Ansel than the inevitable cleaving of once companionable polarities, body and soul, heaven and earth, matter and faith. He groaned.

Lemon Ruby took his hand. "Look," she said. She pointed to the side of the stage, where sunlight caromed off a steely surface and shot back into the crowd. Ruby pulled Ansel toward this bright patch, wove him through the bodies standing rapt before the drama. At the side of the stage, slouched against the wall, one leg straight, one jackknifed, stood a sullen-looking angel boy smoking a cigarette. His foil-covered wings stood beside him, angled open, wavily reflective like funhouse mirrors. Ansel looked at the detached wings, looked at the boy's face, and thought his wistful, angry expression was that of a recent amputee. The halo that bounced above the boy's head was a solid silver circle rimmed in white, a blank eye big as an offering plate following his every movement, shining back whatever it observed. This bobbing silver saucer threw sunlight in all directions as the boy moved his head. The boy stared at Ansel and Ruby as they approached, blew rings of smoke into the air, languid eyes blinking slowly like a cat's. The boy was fifteen or sixteen, bony and bedraggled, dark circles under his eyes, brown, pony-tailed hair, white vestments wrinkled and drooping. Ansel imagined the boy with his hands in his pockets, leaning his forehead against the wall, saying, "It doesn't matter, it doesn't matter," intransitive anguish and the desire for a fatally fast convertible visible in the clenched fists he'd pull from his pockets and slam against the wall.

Ruby stood in the reflective V of the wings, stared at her rumpled body in the foil. She looked up at the boy, then at Ansel. Ansel felt the pressure of her gaze, felt her expectation for him to perform some perfunctory adult gesture, make some show of authority. "Knock, knock," he said. Ruby nodded.

The boy snickered, pitched his cigarette into the grass, and said, "Yeah, who's there?" Ruby's eyes went round with anticipation. Ansel racked his memory in search of a punch line, thumbed through the hours spent with his daughter as a child, puzzles, jungle gym, sno-cones, jokes, there must have been jokes. "Euripedes," he said.

The boy frowned, made a sighing show of having just barely enough breath and interest to utter, "Euripedes who?"

"Euripedes pants, Eumenides pants," Ansel said, raising his eyebrows and cocking his head as though he actually were scolding the boy. The boy smirked; Lemon Ruby's face remained flat and placid as a pansy. Ansel could see the boy's lips begin to wind up for a wisecrack, and he asked, "You're in the play?" nodding his head toward the stage.

"No," said the boy, "I just dress this way so people will ask me about my good works." The failure to fend off this barb caused Ansel to look down at his shoes. They gave him no guidance.

Ruby took the boy's hand and looked at his palm, studied the lines. She said, "Your parents want you to serve God. They want you to cut your hair and wear white shirts. But you like delivering pizzas. You like the hungry people who smile at you and give you tips. They're always glad to see you. And you like the way the Pizza Man flag flaps on your antenna. One day you'll be a famous chef and you'll open a restaurant only for children. You'll serve taco crunch and creamsicles and red velvet cake and you'll marry a woman with a big skillet."

The angel boy yanked his hand from Ruby's and said, "Who the hell are you anyway?" He looked then at Ansel.

Who am I? Ruby mouthed the words. The pensive dip of her eyebrows, her serious eyes, made Ansel want to fold up her face and hide it in his pocket; then later he'd shake it out like a napkin, stare at it for comfort. "Tomorrow," she said.

"You are one spooky kid," said the boy. Ruby blinked and shrugged.

Ansel took Ruby's hand. "Mr. Abatista's sick," she said. "Zero took me to the zoo and we saw the sad gorillas. My grandpa died this year."

Ansel felt Ruby's small, hot hand in his; it felt like a sleeping animal, something sick he'd bring home to Dolores to heal. He didn't know what to do with Ruby's words, didn't know what to give back to her. He said, "Dolores has begun to rouge her cheeks." The angel boy narrowed his eyes. "My wife," Ansel said. He shook his head, looked at his left arm hanging silently at his side. "I've never cared much for made-up faces," he said. He looked up at the angel boy, who appeared disgruntled, or maybe fatigued. "I'll be fifty years old tomorrow," Ansel said. Ruby's hand fluttered in his palm. Fearful he had stumbled down the wrong conversational path, Ansel asked the boy, "What's your role in the play? Do you rush across stage like the others, beneath the falling stars?"

"Nope. I have a speaking part. I fly through the mist and cry, 'Woe, woe, woe.'" The boy's mouth turned up at one end in a half-grin. "Just a warning to all you doomed mortals that the final fat lady in the sky has sung." The boy chuckled through his nose and pulled at his ponytail. "Curtains for the sorry unbelievers below," he said. "Pucker up and kiss my apocalypse, brethren, that's all she wrote. You dig?" The boy laughed outright now, and his thin, wan face became more animated than Ansel would have thought possible, exposing crooked, overlapping teeth and deep lines that bowed around his smile, as though it were parenthetical. The boy's laughter stopped suddenly, and his flattening smile put Ansel in mind of a crowd pressing against the taut rope of a restricted area.

"God is a fat lady who sings," Ruby said.

The boy crouched in front of Ruby and asked, "What's your name, kid?"

"Ruby Tuesday Loomis."

"Christ Almighty," said the boy, closing his eyes. "Tough break. Your parents hippies?"

Ruby shook her head. "My father's an aborigine," she said. "Mama walked the wrong paths when I was inside her, but she rubs people's sore skins now, rubs 'em new."

The boy touched Ruby's cheek, then stood up and said, "My cue's coming up, got to go." He picked up his wings and headed behind the stage. As he walked away, Ansel noticed the straps and hooks on his back, the mechanics of theatrical flight. *Deus ex machina*, he thought.

Ruby and Ansel walked away, among the meandering people, toward the food stands. Ruby sat down at a picnic table. Ansel walked to the nearest booth and ordered a funnel cake and lemonade. He collected some plastic forks and knives and sat down across from his Lemon Ruby. "Want some?" Ruby nodded. She pressed her finger against the greasy cake and licked the powdered sugar from it.

Ansel gazed at his hands clasped and resting on the table in front of him. "Ruby, honey, what happened the other day on the driveway? Were you sick?"

Ruby shook her head. "I made things grow inside me," she said. "I sowed the good seed, but it came up lemon. Do you know that one where you knock and knock and knock and each time you say you're apple then you turn into an orange at the end and say, 'Orange you glad apple ran away?' That's a good one. You get to keep starting over, for as long as the person behind the knocked-on door will take it. My grandpa told me that one. He made it go on for six knocks, or maybe nine sometimes, but he would say 'ding-dong' when he told it. He said I was sneaky like that apple who rang the doorbell then hid in the bushes. He said I was part child and part something else."

Ruby poked her fingers through the holes of the braided pastry. "My grandma read me a story about a smart bird. To make up for that one she told me about all those birds they killed. He's a gray parrot with a big beak. They're watching him all the time to see what he'll say. He gets a lot of words right and tricks the new people into giving him treats when he's not supposed to have any. They never taught him the word for apple, but he knows banana and he knows cherry. They wanted to see what he'd say if they gave him a fruit he never met, so they put an apple in front of him and they asked him what it was. He walked around and around – he knew it was a trick question – then he tasted it and said, 'Banerry.' He put those fruits together and made a new one. They gave him extra treats that night."

Something in Ruby's earnest, instructive look called the Angel Lady, only recently exhumed, back to Ansel's conscious mind. But it made him ever fearful that Lemon Ruby was beginning to speak in a divine dialect he'd not be able to decode, that she'd advise him how to remedy his life, shed his fears, in riddles that had no earthly answers, fearful that his years of servitude to God, years spent trying to learn the language of grace, its slippery grammar, would fail him at this crucial moment, and he'd become trapped inside his own flesh, a foreign carcass to which he felt increasingly little connection. *By hearing ye shall hear, and shall not understand; and seeing ye shall see, and shall not perceive.* How have I gotten here? Ansel Dorsett asked himself.

Ruby ate the funnel cake and sipped the lemonade. "There's a lot to look at here," Ansel said. "Newton's put on quite a show."

Ruby pointed behind him. "Let's go there," she said. "I see a smart bird."

They walked toward a miniature high wire stretched taut between two wooden poles, atop which a green parrot bicycled back and forth. On the ground, a big blue and yellow bird with black and white striped cheeks roller-skated in circles and bobbed its head. People clapped and the birds squawked then caught and cracked open the rewards the trainer tossed them.

"Do you think those birds like their jobs?" Ruby asked. "Zero says a lot of people hate their jobs and get sad at home when nobody's looking. Do you like your job?" Ruby asked. "Does your mama call you on the telephone?" Ruby looked at her feet. She scuffed her shoe against the gravel. "Do you think God's happy? Sometimes," she paused, looked up at Ansel, then said, "I wish God was dead." Ruby looked at the birds, who held peanuts in their feet like ice cream cones. "I know it's hard being God. Sometimes it's hard not being God too."

Ansel felt a sharp stinging inside his head, like a rubber band being snapped against his brain, and said, "Oh, you mustn't say that, child. You mustn't ever say that."

"I know. Just sometimes."

Ansel took Ruby's hand and led her away from the parrots. He was beginning to feel as though he were weaving through a minefield of faith; at each new attraction some fresh crisis would pour from Ruby's mouth or hands or eyes and bend his thinking, invisible perils around which they must tread gingerly lest they inadvertently detonate them and blow themselves out of this world. He felt his bones creaking inside him as he walked; his flesh felt loose and tentative. He sensed a shifting, as though his bones were lodged in hardened dirt that was turning to mud. He looked at Ruby, at that small body that would expand, the small face that would soon broaden and stretch. Where would it take her? I'll be fifty years old, he thought, half a century, not so old really, but who am I after all these years? What do I know? Is there any certainty? My life, the God business: dwindling Sunday collection accounts, tarnished plates, disaffected youth groups, waxing the pews, new organists, font maintenance, scripture for any occasion, bland kindness, updated hymnals, grief management, cracked asphalt, potlucks, God's will; my family: Dolores and Judy, the way they look at me now, so reticent, as though fearful their looking emitted a noise that might unhinge me; the prayers and retreats and revivals: desperate renewals; my country: What thing of significance have I produced? What enemy have I vanquished? How have I been consequential?

Does God have a sense of history?; my fallen father: do all men reach an age when those things they've swept from their vision – answers to the questions they could never bring themselves to ask (there was a life to be hewn, expectations, the size of planets, to remain bent but stalwart beneath, temptations to ignore) – shake them by their stooped shoulders, and they give up, play golf? What has led me to this place, Feet? Tell me. Why do I so often dream of sleeping? Why does my body insist on sticking by me? This world and then what? What happens next?

Is God happy? This suddenly struck Ansel as an apt and pressing question. He stopped walking and looked down at Ruby. "*Is* God happy?" he asked.

"I don't think so," she said. "If he is, he's not very considerate. At school some kids laugh when other kids get swats, but it makes my stomach ache. The paddle is a piece of wood all splintery with the holes in it, the way it swings so fast through the air and cracks against someone's skin. It makes me mad at those kids. I want to smack the laughs out of them." She looked up at Ansel. "Just sometimes," she said. She said, "I think dying should come first. Then nobody'd laugh."

Ansel bent down and hugged Lemon Ruby, terrifying oracle child, and she patted him on the back. "Hey look!" she said. "Just like my key chain."

Ansel stood up and looked behind him. A stout young woman with short, wiry, yellow hair and heavy, black-framed glasses sat at a table covered with Rubik's Cubes of varying sizes. They were all solved, each side of every cube a single color.

Ruby walked up to the table and said, "Do you like your job?"

"What?" said the woman. She looked at Ansel and asked again, "What?" She shook her head and shrugged her shoulders. Ansel tried to conjure a look that said, *I wish to be obliging, but I haven't any answers.*

The woman handed Ruby a cube and said, "Mix it up as much as you can. Twist it all up." Ruby looked at the ordered planes of the puzzle. "Go on," said the woman. "I'll put it back together in under a minute. If I fail, you get to keep it." Ruby handed the cube to Mr. Dorsett.

"What do you do again?" he asked.

The wiry-haired woman sighed impatiently and scanned the rest of the crowd, looking, Ansel imagined, for more obedient and attentive volunteers to aid her in this demonstration of her sideshow skills. "Just keep twisting it until all the colors are mixed up, and then I'll put it back the way it was in record time."

Ansel twisted the cube until the colors on each side were variegated, each row randomly mixed. He held the cube out, and the woman plucked it from his hands and began furiously manipulating the sections, twisting them with the intuitive fervor of a safecracker who hears sirens in the distance.

"Ta-daa!" The woman slammed the solved cube on the table and held her hands in the air. "Were you timing me? What was it, thirty seconds, twenty? I nailed that one." The woman laughed. Braces crowded her smile and seemed to Ansel to lend her face a silvery sweetness.

Ruby Tuesday pulled from her pocket a tiny Rubik's Cube key chain. She held it out to the woman and said, "Can you make yours look like mine?"

The woman held Ruby's key chain in her hand, turned it over in her palm. "There's no order," she said.

Ruby nodded.

"It doesn't work like that."

"But that's the way I like it."

"Any monkey can mix the colors up," the woman said. "That's not hard."

Ansel could see Ruby's face tighten. "The colors aren't mixed up," Ruby said. "They're just . . . blue red orange yellow white green and . . . green blue orange yellow white red." Ruby touched the spots of color as she recited the order. "Instead of blue blue blue blue blue blue. I like them that way." Ruby held out her hand. "You shouldn't speak for monkeys."

"You're missing the whole point," the woman said and dropped the key chain into Ruby's hand.

Ruby nodded and took Mr. Dorsett by the hand.

As they wandered again, Ansel noticed costumed people mingling with the carnival civilians. A boy clad in flowing white angel togs and wings walked by them lazily swinging a censer, eyeing the foot-long hotdogs people cradled as they moseyed. There were several angels with trumpets loitering near the skeeball area, as though looking for something to herald. Ansel noticed the nervous way the young women in the kissing booth held their elbows as long-haired men with the wings and legs and thoraxes of grasshoppers and the tails of scorpions, wearing armored breastplates and carrying gold crowns to the side, smiled widely and neared the booth.

Pictures floated behind Ansel's eyes: lion-headed horses spewing brimstone from their growling mouths, the curly leavings of Dolores's hair and the faint peach stain of her cheeks on the pillow of a morning; the sun-leathered skin and muscled curves of his father's arms; brass feet; wispy souls awaiting a hearing; Judy as a baby tottering toward him with the delight and uncertainty of an incipient skill, arms flung out in front of her. Ansel felt dizzy with stimuli and shadowy vision. Then he heard a soothing crooning as the lowing of cows quietly added itself to the whirling circus of his thoughts, a reassuring cynosure that pointed the needle of his body in the direction of the pasture. He put his hand on Ruby's shoulder, and they headed toward the melodic rumble. A bass croaking also accosted their ears as the cows came into view. Dozens of beefy bullfrogs leapt in and out of the scum that capped a small pond nearby, scum so green it made Ansel sneeze. They creaked their frog sounds, paddled the brackish water, sunned themselves on spongy leaves, lassoed with lightning tongues any winged thing that buzzed their way. The pond boiled with frogs, and this amphibious glut seemed to Ansel some manner of frog resort, a cartoony spectacle, frog holiday, a reward for shedding tails and growing feet and preferring air to water.

"Looks like the watering hole has been invaded," Ansel said.

"Grandma Nedra says too much of a good thing makes it go bad and that drastic measures have to be done for the big good. Excess killed the cat," Ruby said. "Made him get fat and pop."

"Your grandmother told you this?"

Ruby nodded. "Ribbit."

Ansel could see, between the human bodies, snatches of reddish-brown and white, mouths slowly chewing and drooling, snapping tails, could begin to see the cows, sliced into visual slivers by the weaving of the crowd.

Ruby and Ansel wound themselves through the hoi polloi, finally arriving at the fenced edge of the pasture, where spectators milled about, pointed, laughed. Clouds listed overhead, and the afternoon sun came sizzling out from behind them and lit the scene, largely washing it out of sight. With a halting palm, Ansel dimmed the shine to a manageable brightness and saw before him glowing white words hanging in the air, suspended, like laundry drying on a line.

"Oh!" Ruby exclaimed.

Ansel's eyes adjusted and he saw that these words were painted on the brown and swaying sides of the carnival's guests of honor. Ansel stared at the graffitied cows, who moved about with a sluggish disregard that suggested to him they were little mindful of this curious branding and their fundraising purpose.

Ruby read from the bodies of the front line of cows, recited the bovine text aloud: "Happy . . . Moon . . . Blinks . . . table? No, what's the first part? Blinks's behind is in the way. Vegetable! Beauty. Happy moon blinks vegetable beauty." Ruby jumped up on the wooden fence. "Cow words!" she said. *Cowards?* thought Ansel. *As in yellowbelly?* Ansel pictured the word in his mind. *Or moving in the direction of cow?*

This accidental poetry of grazing cows made Ansel rub his chin. Although Baptists didn't place much stock in relics, Ansel had always secretly loved the story of the photographic cloth that captured Jesus's final likeness with the ink of his sweat and blood, and he wondered if this was perhaps another veil of Veronica, if God had wiped his face with the hides of these slaughter-spared beasts, leaving behind a linguistic likeness, the Vera-Logos. Surely within these cows, these peaceable hay-fed bulletin boards, lay the revelation he'd been seeking, the license to give himself over to the peace of the idle, the grace finally granted the spiritually vexed. But Vegetable Beauty? It sounded to Ansel like fortune cookie profundity composed by someone who'd flunked haiku.

They walked the length of the fence and Ruby read the cows as they walked. "Sleeping. Future. Future's following us," she said. "Big. Free. Absence."

A sign said, "PICK A WORD AND PAINT IT ON. JUST $4 $3." People stood at the fence and fed the cows alfalfa. Money and Luck and Love were the most sought-after cows. Ansel felt a little disappointed in the predictability of this. Why not Hunger? Why not Absence? Where was the line for Charity (Charity!)? Weren't they likely more needy than Money? But people always gawked at the world through the fisheye lens of their own desires. As people fed these cows, whose special portent they hoped to fatten, they tickled their slimy velveteen noses, scratched between their eyes; they whispered instructions and pleas, maybe Christmas lists, or a litany of disappointments they sought to reverse, into their twitching ears. Ansel thought he saw desire flash in Love's doleful obsidian eyes, desire to return to the interactive semantic possibilities that awaited her with the rest of the herd.

Ansel took out his billfold and handed Ruby three one-dollar bills. "Want to?"

"Okay." Ruby gave the money to the man at the gate, and he lowered a paper sack down to her. "Pick just one," he said. Ruby put her hand in the sack and closed her eyes. She pulled a slip of paper out and handed it to the man. He unfolded it and announced, "If."

"If?" Ruby asked.

"So it says," said the man, holding the paper out to her so she could see.

"Okay." The man gave Ruby a bucket and brush, and pointed her toward the blank brown slate of a grazing Hereford. He patted the cow's neck and pulled hay from the pocket of his big red apron. "I'll keep her happy," he said, "while you paint."

"If is too tall," Ruby said. Ansel hoisted Ruby in the air and lowered her slowly. Ruby striped the cow with a straight white pillar of "I," sleek and simple in its evolution, Ansel thought as he gazed at the heaving page of the cow's belly. Then Ansel raised Ruby again for the anchoring flagpole of the "F" and its vestigial flaps. The cow snapped her tail against her side, catching some of the paint and tipping her tail white.

They repeated the process on the other side of the cow. "There we go," said the red-aproned man. "Let's see if she helps the sense of things. I think we've unleashed too many rogue nouns."

"Is there a Then?" Ansel asked.

The man pursed his lips and looked up toward the sky and said, "Uh, no, not as yet. I believe there's one in the bag, though. I think it's right that the If should have come first," said the man. "Don't you?"

Ansel nodded. He felt strangely satisfied with having helped to broaden this roving lexicon. The man slapped the cow on the haunches and walked back toward the gate.

Ansel leaned and Ruby stood on the fence and watched If wander among the slow, russet bodies.

Ansel saw Ruby's lips move as she read the cows. "If you read them from right to left, they make more sense," Ruby said. This brought to Ansel's mind an old printing press. We should have painted the words backwards, he thought. Make it all the more challenging. I bet the Rubik's woman would have liked that. It pleased Ansel that these words made more sense backwards, a kind of breech-baby syntax. The randomness of all this suddenly seemed to liberate something inside him, made him feel a little less heavy with the onus of Self.

"Hot Rabbits Sleeping Dream Quiet Risk." Ruby pointed. "Dream and Sleeping are sticking together," Ruby said. "Do you think they planned that?"

"Maybe," Ansel said.

"Look, look," Ruby said. If sidled up to Song who was just east of Seed.

"Eats . . . Ear . . ."

"No, the other way," Ruby said.

"If Song Seed . . . Plants . . . Ear Eats."

"Is that from the Bible?" Ruby asked.

"No, honey, just a chance grouping of words."

"Good group." Ruby hopped down. "I'm going to go watch the feeding people," she said.

"All right." Ansel saw behind a cluster of cows – Skin, Walks, Coat, and Under – a young man prodding them to keep them shifting, keep the words recombining like a wily virus.

Ansel looked up into the sky, which was reassuringly blue and draped with a fraying gauze of clouds that made it look as though the sky had worn through its bandage. I need this child's love, he thought. I need to antidote the vanity of living. The love of a strange child, a child who thinks things grow inside her, there is fertile purpose in that. Ansel stared at a long, thin, curving cloud. *Why do I feel apologetic upon waking?* It was evenly sectioned, like vertebrae, with a sharp coccyx at the end. He trembled to think he was looking at the sky's exposed spine. Ansel felt vulnerable and thin. He was weary of the inside of his head, which felt both too full and empty. What is most genuine? he wondered. What is most true?

"Why the hangdog phiz?"

Ansel looked down to see a cow with a question mark on its side standing before him. Love, Foreclosure, Eats, these words struck Ansel as perfectly at home on a marquee of cow. But ?? Punctuation seemed to Ansel somehow to defy the spirit of accident that directed the ruminant syntax. A question mark put a definitive end to things and rendered the jumbled sentiment uncertain. But whose words had suddenly halted his parsing of the sky? Ansel swiveled his head around. He was standing apart from the crowd. He looked at this cow's blank, white face. The red-aproned man stood at the gate, and Ruby was feeding Love at the other end of the fence. The voice had been deep and euphonious, with a vatic timbre, and Ansel felt his toes curling inside his socks.

"Nobody here but us chickens," said the cow, unmistakably.

The air near Ansel's head seemed suddenly to thin, and he felt as though he were about to hiccup. His arms and legs and feet buzzed with a coming numbness. "What's that?" he asked.

The cow yawned, exposing a thick, pinkish tongue. Ansel jerked. He'd seen cow tongues before, but only in his grocer's meat case, silent and plastic-wrapped, resting on a bed of Styrofoam like an arrested insult. "So." The talking cow rubbed its neck against the fence. "For me, things are looking up. I'm free-range, off the feedlot for the rest of my days, and saved from the fate of a pneumatic nail to the head, never to see the inside of the kill shed at the abattoir." The cow sighed. "But you, you look like a man condemned, resigned and ready to meet your oblivion. What's eating *you*? Perhaps I can help." The cow's mouth chewed.

Ansel stood stiffly, his lips and tongue the only parts of him seeming to retain motility. He said, "I think the fact that I'm speaking to you . . . suggests the degree to which I am beyond help." He popped the words from his mouth slowly, and they felt small and resistant, as though he were shucking premature peas from the pod.

The cow stopped chewing and looked up. "No call to be supercilious. I thought you were a man in need of astonishment. That's what your face and posture broadcast. I'm usually a good judge of this. You can imagine the consequences should I pick the wrong auditor." Ansel thought he saw a shudder ripple the skin of the cow's neck and withers.

Ansel didn't want to talk to this cow. He didn't want to go to work tomorrow, didn't want to pray, eat lunch, pay bills, didn't want to dwell on damnation. He didn't want to kiss his wife good night, didn't want to know if evil walks among us, he didn't want to floss his teeth. He didn't want to take the choir robes to the dry cleaner, didn't want to mow his lawn, didn't want to think about the meaning of free will in a universe created by a foreknowledgeable god, didn't want to wait for his erection to ebb of a morning so he could urinate, didn't want to save the believers whom the Spirit had newly moved. He wanted to sleep. Just wanted to sleep. Sleep.

"I had a dream," said the cow. "In the dream, behold, I stood upon the bank of the Kaw. And there out of the river came seven pharaohs, fat-fleshed and well-favored, and they fed in a meadow. And, behold, seven other pharaohs came up after them, poor and very ill-favored and lean-fleshed, such as I never saw in all the land of What Cheer for badness. And the lean and the ill-favored pharaohs did eat up the first seven fat pharaohs." The cow's tongue slid through its lips and licked something from between its nostrils, and Ansel felt his own tongue moving erratically in his mouth, as though he were dodging the dentist's probe. "And when they had eaten them up," said the cow, "it could not be known that they *had* eaten them as they were still ill-favored, as at the beginning. So I awoke." Ansel let the cow's words drop at his feet. He looked at the cow's long eyelashes and thought of Rita Hayworth, thought of her twisting on satin sheets. "We've all got a little famine inside us, eating us up. If not that, a 'grievous murrain' awaits us. Why don't you unburden yourself," the cow said, chewing, chewing.

Ansel let go of the thinning leashes of Reason and Skepticism and Education and a whole bellowing kennel of other notions straining at their collars, notions that lent order to chaos, principles he couldn't even name right now, and he found he did have something he wanted to say to this cow. In fact, he did.

"In my Bible, my King James Red Letter edition with the gold-embossed cover, there is a typo." He'd never told anyone about this before. He thought perhaps this cow, this biblical dreamer, this *question mark*, would understand, would somehow relate to a mistake of this nature. Ansel did feel a gnawing emptiness inside him, a hunger that turned its head anytime he tried to spoon nourishment into its gullet. He did need to unburden himself, just a little.

"Go on," said the cow.

"The typesetter must have been late for a deadline, typing so swiftly, must not have been familiar with the material. It's almost a plausible mistake. You wouldn't catch it if you were reading quickly. It's a common word."

"Angel to angle, God to Dog, heaven to heathen?"

"Revelation 10:9 and 10," Ansel said. "'And I went unto the angel, and said unto him, Give me the little book. And he said unto me, Take it, and eat it up; and it shall make thy belly bitter, but it shall be in thy mouth sweet as honey.

"'And I took the little look out of the angel's hand,' the *look*, 'and ate it up.' In my book, John eats the angel's look. He swallows the look the angel is carrying around and then gets a sour stomach." Ansel's limbs began to prickle with the sensation of having been asleep. "But I have always, secretly, liked that version better. He couldn't stomach the look the angel held. It was too harsh, like a fiery pepper. Maybe the angel held a grimace in his hands, or a look of wrath, or judgment, something so inclement and irreversible he feared to wear it on his face, feared its foreseeing surgery to his features. Maybe his look said, This is one fast-sinking ship – take to the sky, quick. Maybe it said, Beneath the fleeting veneer of beauty lies the inevitable devastation of unprepared-for endings." Ansel exhaled breath it seemed he'd been holding inside him for ages.

The cow nodded. "I'll tell you something I've learned from my transmigrational travails: the Book of Life has many a misprint, and in the translation back into flesh, something is *always* lost. The return, it's not an exact science, there can be hitches. *You* pin your hopes on Parousia, yes? But you may find he's not as able a judge as you'd hoped. Perhaps he tires easily now, becomes capricious when taxed, and cannot be bothered with mitigating details, like repentance, a vigilant conscience, can scarcely conceal his boredom when it comes to the accounting of good deeds. He recollects little about carpentry and in fact cannot suffer the thought of wood, putting forest rangers and ship builders and Dutch cobblers at a disadvantage at their moment of reckoning." Ansel looked into the cow's glimmering black eyes. "Or maybe he'll have the lightness of heart that eluded him the first time around, and he'll pardon us all straight away," said the cow.

Ansel imagined holding the cow's eyes in his hands, dropping them on the kitchen floor, thin glass shattering, black ink spreading across the tile. He was struck by an impulse to kiss the cow on its gooey, bristly, white lips but held back, asked instead, "God, is He happy? Do you think?"

The cow bent its head forward, perhaps for a scratch. Ansel stood still. He was afraid to touch this cow, afraid he himself might start mooing. "We are what God dreams when he sleeps a troubled sleep," said the cow, after some thought. "Perhaps it's God's happiness we all fear." The cow snorted. "There are questions roaming around out there I've got to abut," said the cow. "It ain't easy being interrogative."

Ansel watched ?'s snapping tail as it shambled away and tried not to think of this garrulous animal as the product of a tormented un-conscious. He did not recriminate himself for conversing with a cow, any more than he'd chided himself for sermonizing to prairie dogs. They had been extremely attentive prairie dogs after all, and the cow had approached him first, had chosen him. He did regret, however, the stern and jerking wordlessness he was often gripped by when it came to discussing issues of consequence with fellow human beings, Dolores, Charlotte McCorkle, Pastor Rawley. He felt so disconnected from people these days, as though he'd been amputated from the race and now existed as only a phantom ache, insubstantial, unpleasant reminder, a dull throb the body swatted at in its sleep. Ansel remembered as a child trying to help his father recover from whatever had spooked him into enmity with his own body. As time wore on, his father's estrangement from life and limb cut a Lewis and Clark trail of undiscovery across the waning terrain of his body, an unremembering, an anatomy lesson untaught. Whose hand, this? Whose tongue, whose navel? Whose sternum houses the alien thum-thump that keeps me awake at night? Ansel remembered trying to rub his father's leg back to life, rub it back to familiarity. He'd felt the generative heat of his own boy's arms as he pushed and kneaded and hoped he could bring it back to life, could jump-start his father's juices, and in so doing could assure himself a meaningful future a little less booby-trapped with heredity. There was a single hopeful moment, Ansel recalled, when his father looked at his body, then at his son, with flickering recognition, a thoughtful narrowing of his eyes as he said, "The time *is* at hand," then whispered, "I'm tired of being a man" before slipping into the permanent silence inside his dreamy head where he would seal himself up the balance of his days. His father never carried himself upright again, never lifted his body from the bed, never again touched Ansel nor spoke another word to him.

Ansel looked up into the frothy sky. The air smelled moist, the scent of renewal. The sun shined, clouds whitened. Lemon Ruby walked toward him with her palms upturned and at her sides. She stood next to Ansel and took his hand. "Cows never stop chewing," she said.

"Are you having fun, Ruby?"

"Yes. I think those people are feeding Money too much. He's going to get big as the world. Are you having fun?"

Ansel smiled. Ruby turned Ansel's hand over and said, "Your turn." She closed his hand and opened it again and said, "Uh-oh." Ruby licked her finger and rubbed Ansel's palm. She looked up and said, "The paint was changing things." She traced the branches of his future's imprint with a finger. A large drop of water splashed against Ansel's palm. Ansel and Ruby looked up into the sunny sky. "You need a good job and a swivel chair on wheels so you can get around the office even when your feet fall asleep," Ruby said. "You want to be the weather man on TV with the sky blinking day and night behind you when you talk. You want to point to the world and know what will happen. You'll know when the mountains are going to shrug their shoulders, and you'll tell people to stay in their rooms and put their breakable objects under the bed. You'll tell them to cover their hearts and heads when the shaking starts." Rain started falling now more steadily, pelting them with heavy drops that burst against their arms and cheeks. "You'll tell them God has a hole in his pocket. He's got nothing left to give."

Ansel breathed in the warm, moist air. He scanned the cows for any messages that might have formed when he wasn't looking. Love and Money, finally sated, were mingling with Tomorrow and Mouth and Sneeze. Beauty had hooked up with Hunger and If was nosing the ground near Quiet. I *would* like a swivel chair on wheels, Ansel thought. I need a new chair. Things would run more smoothly if I had a moving chair to make decisions from. Maybe it's simple as that, a feel-good chair, ergonomics and castors, things could be different then, I'd understand things, see them more clearly, not be confused by so much meaning.

Definitely need a better chair, need a new Angel Skin Coat? Ansel's mind paused, his eyes resting on Angel, then churned again, taking up where it had stopped but soldering these new words to his old thoughts: That's what I need would protect me nothing lighter than angelskincoat? Keep me from harm.

Ansel watched the white tip of If's tail as it whipped its back. The rain began to fall more forcefully, and people shrieked and scattered. The cows all at once stopped their chewing, lifted their heads and began to sing, mooing into the air. Coat's moo was the loudest and continued increasing in volume and pitch, bordering on a howl. She moved her front legs from side to side, back and forth, her back legs anchored in place, as though she were stamping accounts PAID. Ansel wondered if a power line had been knocked loose nearby, wondered if there was electrical current trickling beneath her addled hooves. "Look there," said Ansel. He watched Ruby's slow, precise lips as she read the cows. An gel s kinnn cooat, she mouthed. "Is that allowed?" she asked. "Can you get a coat like that without hurting them? How many does it take?"

Ansel imagined the jagged jaws of a steel trap hidden beneath a deceitful weave of sticks and weeds. He saw an angel, a shadowy form, more energy than mass, step into the trap, saw it try to gnaw its shadowy leg off. What is instinct to an angel, what survival? Maybe an angel would give up its airy guardian skin gladly to aid a heavy human. Ansel looked into the sky where the sun continued its defiant shining. The cows were moving round and round now without prodding, their throats stretching with every moo, aimless but somehow organized too, as though they were being stirred from above. The painted words began to bleed down the cows' sides, making them appear wounded, and the bleached gore dripped onto the grass and turned it white.

Ansel felt his body – shins, arms, eyes, penis, knees – felt his cells dislodge, release, and, struck with the lightheaded spontaneity borne of watching random prophesies fade, watching the blankening brown slates of fate and mystery and divination sway and protest a demystifying downpour, he lifted Ruby into the air, her little body, lighter than his own arms, significantly lighter than a conscience grown ponderous with theological stalemates, lifted her up and spun her around, said, "Abide in me and I in you, child, for I am the vine and you are the branches," circling, circling, and Ruby laughed and chanted, "Angel skincoat, angelskincoat, angelsincoat, angelscot, angsco . . ." until the words blurred with the whirring air, the landscape turned to glowing brown butter, and Ansel saw stringy ghosts climb out of the ground, scramble up the sky through the sickly spun-sugar sweetness of the wet air, and squirm toward heaven.

Epilogue
Canticle for Matter

Prayers rode the lips of the sleeping people of What Cheer, a thin mist, a fervid humidity spinning forth from their gently churning mouths, aimed at nothing, aimed at something, aimed at ears both local and stratospheric. This fine smoke of invocation rose, swirled through hypnagogic fingers clawing the air, fearful of their own groggy hunger. It drifted up and hung in the sky, this cumulus juju of collective need, wafted and mingled, pooled its energy, a spinning vector of the long-locked incantations of scared people. Particles grew thin, permeable, swapped electric intent, then spread through the air, snapping like bed sheets drying in the wind. This Sunday morning whirlpool of dislodged desire and hope sank back into the breathable air close to the emancipating mouths, settled onto shoulders, slowly, quietly, like a careful succubus trying to tread unnoticed, hunched and tentative from years of misunderstanding. It entered the bodies of these people before they could wake and protest. It rushed their limbs and organs, invaded every cell, an assailing virus, unleashed, breaking life-long quarantine, this seizure of love, bodies, soft and yielding as ripe persimmons, tossing in sleep, infection muscling through, breaching the limits of skin. The bodies heaved a breath and sank into a gauzy stillness, riddled with possibility.

And then?

MARTIN TENDS HIS SORES

Martin LeFavor sits on his bed in baggy shorts, dabbing calamine lotion on his ruddy, hived extremities. He imagines engulfing his father in a rash-dappled embrace, his father wriggling out of the alien arms, terrified of contagion. Though perhaps his father would favor his besieged body, tender skin marbled red with inflammation, be pleased by the vulnerability having risen to the surface. Or maybe it would anger him, cause him to question his paternity, as he was often wont to do when piqued by this or that – the absence of his favorite confection in the pantry; the threat of additional taxation; the ineffable, rainy-day pains in his barometric knees. Martin decides to be pleased by the clownish cast of his skin, the motley of his body. Being charmed is merely a matter of choice, he thinks. His skin makes him want to tell riddles only he can answer, riddles to make a sphinx sag and crumble. He plumbs himself for jester instincts but comes up empty-handed.

Out the window, he sees his mother. It seems to him she is delaying her ablutions a little more each day. He can see there will come a time when she will cook supper draped in chenille, no longer mindful of the days' seams, though she will likely cling to the diurnal churning of chores, domestic routines. She stands in the front yard in her flowered housecoat, her husband's paisley pajama bottoms drooping beneath, bunched at the ankles. Martin sees the top of her pin-curled head, the curls in back flattened like book-pressed mementoes. She stands with her arms at her sides and looks up at the yawning, cloudless blue. His father's clunky metal watch hangs loose around her wrist, sagging against the splayed fingers that keep it from slipping free. She lifts her arm and cups her hand, as if begging, or testing for rain. The watch droops like a halfhearted handcuff. Martin taps on the window. His mother stares at the sky and leans into the slight spring breeze.

He thinks of the woman who rubbed his feet, feels the aftertouch of her strong hands pressing into his heels. She is a woman with some-thing inside her, he thinks, something incubating or stored for later use, something that stirs palpably in the tips of her fingers. Her body, the flesh and bone of her, struck him as a formality, a nod to conven-tion, something she wraps around the thing she conceals, a convincing skin to keep people from gawking. And he thinks of her daughter, the sweet menace of her, her uncanny gift for saying the very thing that can make a body ache. Martin draws a circle on the window in calamine lotion and presses his face to the glass. A portal. To where? He taps on the window again.

Carrying his bottle of lotion with him, he goes to his father's closet and drags out his cracked and battered black leather sample case. On many a Christmas or Father's Day, his mother had tried to replace this dilapidated bag, offering up different makes, colors of leather, hoping one would snag his eye irreversibly, but Art always made her return the shiny new model with its lure of slick, aromatic elegance, the jazzed-up compartments, added crannies. Martin's father believed a worn valise inspired trust, that the customer could see in the weathered skin that he was a humble potwalloper, a regular Johnny Punchclock with nothing up his sleeve, just putting in an honest day's work, and would be more likely to listen attentively to his pitch.

Martin opens the case and looks at the disarrayed samples, clear evidence that his father is somewhere far away. His mother had rummaged through every drawer and box and envelope bearing any connection to his father, looking for clues to his whereabouts. Vials and boxes of medicine to raise and lower blood pressure; emergency syringes full of fast-acting fluid to treat anaphylactic reaction to allergens; burn creams; single-dose, long-acting antibiotics; stool softeners; and many newly developed drugs with which Martin is unfamiliar. Martin picks up a box of pills that are both anti-depressant and vertigo remedy. The package features a stylized blue and green, egg-like figure tipping, arms out, to one side. All his life, Martin's house has been littered with notepads, pens, paperweights, folders, even baseball caps, tote bags, T-shirts displaying the names and insignias and tag-line claims of different medications, the air forever full of cure.

Martin takes the calamine lotion with him downstairs to the kitchen. He sits down at the table and uncaps the bottle, pours the lotion over his limbs as casually as if he were saucing a steak. Bubbling streams of the worm-pink liquid drip down his arms and legs. He rests his wrists on the table and watches the excess liquid drip to his lap and onto the linoleum. He blows on his arms and waits for them to dry. His skin shimmers dully with the simulated ham-pink complexion of the recently embalmed.

The phone rings and Martin stays put; he's still moist. He hears his father's voice and starts out of his chair when he realizes it is only the answering machine message, unchanged since the machine's purchase a year ago, the recommended script followed to the letter, a source of jollity for callers, who often laugh and remark upon the stiff, rehearsed sound of it.

It's Millicent Dawkins, the woman from the advocacy group. *Just thought you should know we've gotten a few calls about Art. I feel certain they're cranks, which, you know, is all I figured we'd get. People see a grown man's face where they expect to see a child's, it just brings out the tomfoolery in them. Well, you know all about my reservations.* Anyway, *it's a man who says Art's doing fine and not to worry, asks us to pass this on to the family, simple as that. He's called twice now. He talks fast then hangs up quick. Probably worried he's being traced. I don't know where people think we get* those *kind of resources. Well, I do too know. It's that* America's Most Wanted *show. Don't we wish! Anyway, honey, give us a call if you have any questions. Not much else to tell. Talk to you soon.*

Martin gets up from the table and goes into the living room. The machine blinks a red number one. He listens to the tape re-spool then plays the message again. It rewinds back to a static zero. Martin walks outside, toward his mother. She stands in the yard and stares at the sky. He pulls at the loose watch at her wrist. "Come inside," he says. She looks down, touches her son's chalky arms. A jet whirs overhead. They look up into the wide Kansas sky and walk back to the house arm in arm.

CHARLOTTE WASHES HARLAN'S FEET

Charlotte McCorkle sits in the wheelchair next to her husband's bed, staring at her healing hands. The wrapping has thinned now to allow scabby fingers to poke through. She looks to herself like a beggar woman protecting aching hands with ragged gloves, fingerless for easier filching. Charlotte broke glass and crawled on it. It was painful, the skin of her hands and feet and knees giving way like ripe fruit, stabbed and razored, but it was a warming pain, the kind that follows the thaw of a frostbitten limb.

Harlan lies silent, sleeping, his skin moist and loose, pooling around him, the skin beneath the restraints on his wrists and ankles an interminable purple, injury renewed upon waking. Buttery light spills through the window beside his bed and illuminates his body in such a way that he resembles a wax figure, shiny and inanimate, an exhibit of an ailing man. Charlotte has removed the blue and white fleur-de-lis dressing gown that loosely blanketed him, and he snoozes in striped shorts and white socks. She thinks of those lifelike sculptures of everyday people, like the one in the museum in Kansas City, the figure of an elderly museum guard who stands idly in a corner, boxy, black-framed glasses concealing fraudulent eyes, hair convincingly thin and neat, liver-spotted hands folded over a sloping paunch. She remembers how foolish she felt the first time she asked him for directions, how she flushed when she touched his clammy fingers, testing for life.

Harlan sleeps deeply, his chest rising slowly and evenly with each breath, a brief peace. He had received pain medication before Charlotte arrived. She wonders what pictures his frayed mind conjures during these drugged slumbers. She remembers the dream she had just before waking. Harlan sat at the kitchen table in boxer shorts and house shoes eating bread. Beneath his chair black ink puddled on a newspaper, as though he were a car leaking oil. He ate slice after slice of spongy, white bread, some toasted, some plain. Charlotte asked him if she could get him something to drink, get him some grape jelly, a poached egg, but he wouldn't answer, sat chewing and swallowing. Then he stood up, walked to the bedroom, wordlessly, and Charlotte followed. He lay down and rolled himself in the sheets until no flesh was visible, just a padded shape rustling. Next to the bed sat four ceramic jars, the heads of jackal, falcon, baboon, and man bedecking the lids. Charlotte opened each one and looked inside. The first held marbles, and she stuck her hand in to discover they were actually eyeballs, sticky with fluid, unable to blink. The second was filled with tiny, white birds that chirped and pointed their beaks at her hungrily, beady black and yellow eyes studying her. The third contained metal letters, weighty, bygone type, jumbled together, spelling nothing, a heap of accidental, unspeakable words. In the last, lying in the shadowy bottom of the urn, was a black and white photograph of Charlotte, grinning, dressed to the nines, standing on shapely pins, leaning saucily against their old Hudson, lips parted slightly, sassy and dark with color.

Charlotte looked at Harlan's mummified body. It seemed to throb with life in its disappearance. But there was something else, a refined pulsing, something slithering beneath the wrap. She pulled and pulled the sheets, an endless bolt of fabric, until there was nothing more, no body, no movement, the disheveled wrapping piled on the floor. And then, sticking out of the white folds, she saw a small picture of Harlan, his face and arms old and inky, dressed in soiled overalls, waving, standing beside his corn.

In the dream, Charlotte had the sharp and sudden knowledge – the way such demi-revelations come to you in a dream, as if you'd known all along but were being reminded – that these pictures were to help them find each other when their bodies had lost their shape, as Harlan's undeniably had. As she picked up the photograph, it began to darken, as though it were reversing its development, chemicals separating and stealing the image back, and Charlotte sensed she was too late.

In the morning, she searched through photo albums but could find no such pictures; they were just a convincing fabrication of the unconscious, to which, she feared, she was often a dupe. She did, however, find a nice photograph of her and Harlan and Gabriel. They sat on a green sofa, crowded together. There had been a birthday or celebration of some sort. Plates with the crumbled remains of cake sat on the coffee table in front of them. Harlan's resistant grin suggested the photographer had just uttered something he couldn't help but smile at despite his best efforts to appear sober and respectable. His right arm looked tan and strong across the small back of his nephew. Gabriel, five or six, wedged between the adults, rested his head on Charlotte's lap. He wore a red and blue striped rugby shirt, blue shorts, and Red Goose shoes that dangled above the floor. His corn-silk hair had a distinctly feathery quality and his large, sad eyes seemed filled with a pained, premature knowing. Charlotte looked at Harlan, her hand on his cheek. Her navy blue, white-dotted Swiss dress with its wasp waist and A-line skirt made her appear clean and efficient, settled.

The three of them were ringed almost visibly by a circuit of strong feeling, looped by the love that flowed one to the other. Harlan had adored Gabriel and was stricken to the point of long nights of aching sleeplessness when the trouble with the gnarled growths began. When

Gabriel died, everything about Harlan grew a shade darker, and he began to drag his body around as if he were a pack animal bent beneath an imposed heft.

Charlotte places the snapshot on the table next to his bed, leans it against a bright turquoise bottle of liquid laxative. She takes a washcloth from one of the drawers and moistens it with water from a plastic pitcher. She pats it along Harlan's arm and chest, presses it against his face. His skin sags on his bones, and he looks to her to have entered some intermediate stage between human and something else, his body dissolving into a new design adapted to the demands ahead. With the tips of her fingers, Charlotte touches his skin, gray and papery as a wasp's nest. She wheels herself down to the end of the bed and removes his socks. She dabs at the feet and between the toes, unwalked on for many days. She bends down to a foot and kisses the instep. His foot feels smooth as soap against her lips. She rests her cheek against the warm sole and waits for the sun to slide back out the window.

IVY KISSES DUNCAN'S SCARS

Ivy and Duncan sit beneath the enervated limbs of a willow at Pamona Lake, plucking from the branches the long, serrated leaves that loll in the warm wind like green, reptilian tongues. Yesterday Ivy discovered a dead bat in her backyard, and she and Duncan have come here to bury it. She opens her backpack and takes out the bat, stiff like dried chamois. Ivy pets the bat's reddish fur and touches the rubbery velvet of its membranous wings. She studies the fuzz of its wizened face. It does not seem to be at peace. It appears to Ivy to be frozen in anticipation, as though its tiny heart gave out just as it stretched toward the first moth of the evening. She wishes she'd known this bat better, had known something of its career piloting itself through the night. She looks at the rippling water and imagines the ingenuity of the bat's echolocation, the boomerang hum of its navigation, and she imagines this bat a clever multilingual forager, bouncing out a vibration that says *love, comfort, food, sex* to a dragonfly, box elder bug, *right this way*. A breeze sweeps through and ruffles the tall grass, making it appear as though it were trying to talk, a shivering green glossolalia. "If we were a painting or a book right now," Ivy says, "they'd say we were 'pastoral.' And if we were reading us in Mrs. Elliot's class, she'd point out how we'd 'fled to the Eden of nature to escape the oppressive soot and machinery of modern living' and that that's why we're enjoying ourselves, because we're getting a break from working-class industrial bleakness." Ivy smiles and rubs the bat's nose. She likes Mrs. Elliott and the way she tries to adapt everything they read to the circumscribed lives of the students of first-period English. "Okay, imagine your parents – management, bourgeoisie – made you – lowly wage-laborer – mow the lawn on one of those 98-degrees-in-the-shade days in summer with one of those heavy manual lawn mowers with a rotary blade . . . ." Mrs. Elliott is in her late forties, has shoulder-length platinum blond hair and skin that strains against the bones and cartilage of her face, wears sunglasses indoors, lives alone in a split-level house on Lake Quivira, wears long, silky scarves that wave behind her when she drives her white convertible with the top down, and is rumored to drink her lunch, the closest thing to scandalous glamour Catalpa High has to offer. Last year hackles were raised when she included *A Clockwork Orange* on the Advanced English reading list and during its discussion argued in favor of "the unfortunate necessity of homicidal cullions in a free society," inciting school board and parents alike and resulting in the book's mandated replacement the next term with *A Separate Peace*.

"We're only on the outskirts of What Cheer, Ive," Duncan says, "which isn't exactly industrial England. And anyway, we're *not* a book or a painting. We're real life."

"Yeah, that's what you keep telling me." She lays the bat on the ground and straddles Duncan, who leans against the trunk with his hands behind his head. She wishes to modify the good-girl image her earlier rejection of his advances may have left him with, though she's not entirely sure what figure she's now prepared to cut. Each of her fifteen years courses palpably through her body, the nooks and byways abuzz with feeling, suggesting to her she has reached a threshold, though she remains puzzled by the actual shape and meaning of it.

It is something other than the bare burble of hormones, though there is that too. She inches back on her knees until she reaches Duncan's ankles and looks down at the scars that disappear behind his thigh. Every day she inspects his legs to see if the lines have crept forward. The scars' advance appears halted for the moment, but she can't help fearing that one day he'll show up at her house a maze of looping trails, compression scars having tunneled his body throughout the night like busy moles, and his vulnerable insides will suddenly tumble out of the perforated flesh and fall at her feet. Ivy knows now the exact topography of the skin around the scars, knows the landmarks of mole and birthmark, the swirling vegetation of hair that thins at his calves' peak, the hillocks of skin covering his veins. Everyone's body should have its own geographer, she thinks.

Ivy leans forward and lowers her face to Duncan's knees. She puts her mouth to the scars, the split seams, and kisses them slowly and softly, as though she feared waking them. She moves up his thighs, her own arms and legs braced against the ground. She continues to trace the raveling flesh with her mouth and feels the prickly grass poke her skin, the hair of his thighs tickle her nose and lips, and in this animal pose her life and body begin to make a certain sense to her, a sense that sitting or lying on her back or stomach or standing upright have never prompted, something about bent knees, forward movement, contact with the skin of another. She is unable to grasp in her mind what it is she's feeling but thinks somehow finally she has stepped into an order of things that suits her, is fitted to her as aptly as her very circumference, the shape she carves from the air, and she looks up at Duncan's face, lips curved in contentment, eyes closed, and thinks that the calid satisfaction of this moment, as though each nerve had been struck to life by its fondest stimulus, that which peaks its capacity for transmitting sensation, is too much for their bodies to contain and collides between them. Ivy feels a pressure rounding against her stomach, the storm of the mingling ingredients of Self, hers and Duncan's, and in her arms and legs planted on the ground, caging his body, she feels a determined belonging, an ineffable clarity that seems the origin of sentience, irreducible. But the minute she fixes the feeling with thought, this brief aperture closes, and she feels just as awkward and fraudulent, uncertain and exposed as she has always felt.

Duncan opens his eyes, and Ivy swings her leg around and sits, leans back against the tree. She picks up the bat, lays it on her legs, and thinks about Grandpa Engel, his kindness, his teeth, underground.

ANSEL DORSETT GRIPS HIS ARMS

Ansel Dorsett rifles through the previous week's accumulated mail and reflects on this morning's sermon about the bedeviled (Reverend Rawley's word) translation of the Bible into English. Reverend Rawley, Illinois Lutheran turned Kansas Baptist, claimed kinship to outlaw translator William Tyndale and liked to tell the story of his ancestor's courageous flight from sixteenth-century England to Wittenberg, Germany, where he worked, under the auspices of that original reformatory rabble-rouser Martin Luther, on a translation of the New Testament. Ansel watched the spittle fly as the reverend worked himself into a lather, and he worried the pitch might rise again to a denunciation of "pestilent popery" as it had once before, but the reverend pulled up short, not emphasizing directly Tyndale's weighty foes but simply his noble plight to "put the common ploughman more directly in touch with the Scriptures, to help him get his hands, browned and callused from working the earth, on a copy of the New Testament he could read for himself," leaving it at that. Ansel tries to fathom the strength of Tyndale's convictions, the pure dogged belief that drove him to risk his life smuggling translations page by page back into England. The idea of acting with such cocksure certitude about anything, even far less consequential things, is mystifying to Ansel, and he tries to imagine what Tyndale must have felt when he was captured, incarcerated, what went through his mind as he was strangled, condemned a hell-hound from the devil's own kennel. Did he feel the hero his distant descendent now paints him to be? In these sermons, Reverend Rawley always drew a dashing picture of his alleged ancestor, a righteous swashbuckler for God and the common man, the reverend's voice rising histrionically with each description of Tyndale's derring-do, and then he'd finish summarily and pat, tagging a hasty moral to the ending – pen mightier than the sword, courage of one's Christian convictions in the face of overwhelming adversity, and so on – to make it seem fitting material for the ears of a late-twentieth-century, rapt Baptist congregation and not merely genealogical gloating. This was something Ansel actually admired about Ben Rawley, the way he could combine shameless self-interest or -promotion with a thinly aphoristic lesson he could always coax parishioners into finding meaningful, indispensable, timely; "a spiritual investment whose stock is sure eventually to split" is how the pastor once put it himself.

As Ansel continues to mull over the morning's homily, he comes upon a letter addressed to A. Dorsett in blue ballpoint pen, the letters B.V.M. and N.Y.C. in the corner, nothing else in the way of a return address. He opens it, and written on wide-ruled notebook paper, in an endearingly wobbly script distinguished by the shaky loops of the elderly or mildly palsied, he reads the following:

Dear A. Dorsett,

Thank you for your recent inquiry. I am sorry to hear of your tribulations. I know how discouraging they must be at this particular juncture in your life and how terribly desolate you must feel (as do we all) as we prepare to shuffle out of this millennium. (I do hope the trouble with your waste management has by now been cleared up.) But I am pleased that you were able to see (as so few are) that this is no hoax, and that you have reached out to me for help.

The fact that you are not Catholic makes no difference to me, A. Dorsett. While it is true that the Catholic religion has, over the years, cultivated a tighter alliance with me than have the majority of the Protestant sects, I am blind when it comes to denomination. It is not my aim to get embroiled in that old feud. Simply put, I don't play favorites.

As you know, I will be appearing live in Central Park, in New York City, New York, later this month. It would benefit us both if you were able to attend – the larger the audience, the more likely my message will make it to CNN and therefore be heard round the world (snippets at least) – but, barring that, I have enclosed a donation envelope so that your support in the form of Christian charity, if not your actual physical presence, can be felt and news of your generosity passed along to the more important <u>Powers That Be</u>. *Although Good Works provide no absolute guarantee, "we are justified by a faith that worketh by charity," so this donation is sure to help ease your own troubles, for you know who God helps (and since my mission has the well-being of all creatures great and small in view, particularly spiritually unfulfilled but hard-working, middle-class, tax-paying Americans like you, A. Dorsett, to help me is to help* <u>yourself</u>*).*

If you are unable to attend but wish to receive a copy of the oration I will deliver, include a self-addressed stamped envelope along with your contribution, and I will be happy to forward that on to you. ·

In God's Love,

Mary

Ansel looks up from the letter and around the room, as though the joke or joker might whirl up out of the dust of the corners and reveal herself to him. He looks at the postmark on the envelope and is disquieted to think that there is a prankster in Grand Rapids, Michigan, with inexplicably acquired knowledge of his sewage peccadillo. The donation envelope is directed simply to "Mary" at an illegible address in N.Y., N.Y. Ansel knows no one living in or near Grand Rapids, Michigan or New York City. Ansel, temperamentally a lone wolf, has few enough local connections, fewer yet far-flung acquaintances. Mary? His mother's name, Mary Grace, raised Catholic, jumped ship when she married, not renowned for levity. Every day a new confounding. How to live? How to live in the face of persistent mystery?

He takes the letter to show Dolores. Level- (if perm-) headed Dolores with a nose for bamboozle will give him sound counsel about the meaning of a missive from Mary, an elderly virgin, or one with a taxed nervous system to judge from her handwriting. It is, in fact, a feminine script, Ansel decides, with a certain tendency toward voluptuous flourish beneath the unsteadiness.

As he walks into the living room, he sees people crowding together and rearranging themselves behind furniture, like bumbling, embodied ghosts preparing for a haunting. The curtains are drawn and the light from one small table lamp does not afford him enough illumination to assess what he is seeing. He feels his feet begin to float up and out from under him and then he spots Dolores, her hand outstretched, mid-gesture, and he watches as her face draws tight with stricken surprise when her eyes light on him. Meeting his eyes, she flutters her hands upward, and people move out from under tables slowly, bumping heads and shoulders nonetheless, jump up from behind couches, chairs, the television, and yell – not in unison, more like a domino chorus – "Surprise!" sounding not entirely convinced.

Dolores frowns and frets her hands, says, "You never spend less than an hour sitting and thinking in your office after the service, Ansel," and sighingly adds, "Is there nothing I can count on anymore?" Coming on the heels of the letter from Mary, the exact meaning of this display does not fully register with Ansel. He stares, droop-lipped, at Dolores, who smiles reluctantly, throws up her hands, and says, "Well, anyway, surprise." Someone peels back the drapes, and Ansel looks around the room: Mother Dorsett, daughter Judy, Reverend Rawley and various members of the congregation, neighbor Morris Myers, next-door neighbors Tom and Pauline Engel, and Newton Ambrogast, Jr. He looks at Dolores's face creased with aggravation and love and wonders how it ever even occurred to her to stage something as fanciful as a surprise birthday party, his sensible Dolores, whose faithfully clipped coupons are cross-referenced by type of product, amount of savings, and expiration date and filed in a recipe box, Dolores who throws away nothing, turning soda bottles into bird feeders, cracked ice cube trays into sprout starters, excelsior into doll hair, sweet Dolores who has always worn a brassiere to bed because she read years ago in *McCall's* that it helps breasts resist the ravages of gravity and will only cast it aside when she reads in *Redbook* that breasts need to breathe of a night.

The people gathered, though now fully upright, stand still, frozen in the confusion of the foiled surprise. Ansel half-smiles and nods politely, cuing the guests to mingle. Dolores continues to worry her hands and stares at the creased letter Ansel holds loosely like a bird with a broken wing. He walks to her and asks, "Do we know anyone in Grand Rapids?"

Dolores pinches her earlobe and says, "There was that couple from St. Paul we met at Branson. Is that nearby?"

Ansel shakes his head vaguely. He squeezes Dolores's hand, kisses her on the cheek. "Thank you for this party," he says. "It is indeed a surprise."

"I know this is a hard passage for you, Ansel. I thought a bit of fellowship might ease it a little." He nods and walks toward the couch where Reverend Rawley is seated. On the way, his mother catches his hand and stops him. She looks him over thoroughly, like a physician checking for signs of disease, guides her gaze along his arms and face, down his legs, back up again, finally training her eyes on his. "Tired?" she asks.

"I'm okay, Mama." He hugs her and sits down next to the reverend.

"Seems you're the surpriser rather than the surprisee," Ben Rawley says.

"Seems so." Ansel folds the letter and stuffs it into his shirt pocket. "Why is it we don't have much truck with Mary, anyway? We don't really linger on her trials too much, but she's an important figure, wouldn't you say? Well, sure, at Christmas we pay her a bit of lip service, but mostly we seem fixated on Jesus. Well, and then hell too, persuading people it's a place they want not to visit. Not that Jesus and hell don't deserve due consideration, certainly, I just wonder . . ." Ansel's voice trails off and his thoughts make a desultory stagger through his mind.

Reverend Rawley stares at Ansel a beat, waiting for him to wade back out of the murk of his words, then says, "What exactly's on your mind, Ansel?"

Ansel sighs, crosses his legs, stares at his knee, smoothes his pants. "I don't know," he says. "I got a letter from the Virgin Mary, though of course it wasn't the Virgin Mary, but she sounded very sincere and she knew of my plumbing troubles, and, well, you know my faith has been faltering of late, though now that I think of it maybe that's not an accurate accounting. Maybe I've never really known faith at all. Maybe all I've ever possessed is some feeble precursor to faith, and faltering's as far as I've gotten. And there's my father, in my thoughts so often these days, how he gave up when he was around my age, and the angel I thought I was counseled by as a child but who left me knowing less and less yet as I think about it – don't think I've ever mentioned her to you – and dear Dolores now trying to find a way to reach me and me wishing to be reached but feeling as though I'm thinning with the passing of every minute, but then to balance there was a sweet and alarming child I spent the afternoon with yesterday who helped me to feel the thinnest tether of connection and hope. And your William Tyndale, for example, how full of righteous direction he was, how impassioned and decisive – where does that come from? Was he always like that or was it acquired, forged in the fire of the Church's resistance? Maybe that's it, that nothing resists me or my actions, evidence that I am a man of no consequence." Ansel looks into the reverend's face, hoping to see there the antidote to these thoughts, waiting for a verse to cure him, show him his error, but Ben Rawley just looks at Ansel then down at his lap, rubbing his cheek.

Suddenly the reverend stands and clears his throat. The guests turn toward him. He looks at Dolores, who has brought out a fluffy, white cake and is garnishing it with blue candles, and says, "It has been my great pleasure to know Ansel Dorsett some fifteen years. His fundamental curiosity and hunger to understand the workings of God and man have led us into many an edifying debate, which, ever the gentleman, he ends always just this side of drawing blood." The reverend's bushy gray mustache, a touch of flamboyance that worried his flock when it first appeared, rises as he smiles, a small animal stirring to life. The partygoers chuckle. "Kidding aside, Ansel is a loving husband, father, and son, a devoted member and officer of Shadyvale Baptist church, and a man of penetrating insight, all the more worthy of being heard for his questioning, his particular take on the human condition."

Ansel continues to stare at his knees, his hands clasped in his lap. This is what it's like to be eulogized, he thinks, and then he realizes a request is about to be made of him, feels the expectation building around him. *Desolate.*

"When a man reaches half a century, he is entitled to say his piece, to share his thoughts with the people who love him." Ben Rawley holds his hand out to Ansel, passing the floor. "Say a few words to us, Brother Dorsett." People clap and cheep, "Speech! Speech!" perfunctorily.

Ansel stands, holds his arms, thinks, I'm going to say it, going to say it, my mind, what's been churning there, if they want to know, I'll speak it. This is what I have to say:

"I speak," pause, breath, "with the tongue of neither a man nor an angel, as I am certain neither of this world nor the next, ill persuaded by the very substance of myself, a wraith who blows words through flimsy lips." Ansel looks into the faces that hover around him. They are blank, furrowed with worry and consternation, young or serious, marked by their own concerns. Dolores clutches small, blue candles in one hand. Ansel notices a dusting of flour on her left shoulder. She blinks at measured intervals.

"The charity I have to give is to confess that I am neither psaltery nor Aeolian harp. No plectrum nor whisper of wind will vibrate the strings of my oratory meaningfully. I am a body and here and you are here and it is but now and that is all I can say with authority, and shaky it is, for I have no gift of prophecy nor penchant for hindsight. I stand here verily spindled and blinkered by the moment and do not understand all mysteries, though I see them eddy around me pleading to be solved. What sadness to be sentenced to insolubility, to circle around minds too small to do more than vaguely perceive the gauzy spoor of everywhere mystery! How disappointing never to be grasped, by minds advanced beyond mere sentience yet inchoate, closer to bacteria than to God when it comes to the cavernous latitude that divides us. And though I have lived now half a century, I possess precious *little* knowledge save that which tells me to breathe and to sleep, the stowed-away, default secrets of instinct. What more can I claim? What is faith but the desperate hope that *if* mountains move it was meant to happen? I have not charity – who am I to be charitable? Charity is luxury, implies a surplus of something, and what have I to give but the frank admission of nothing to give – rather I am the embodied cry for charity – *caritas!* – all absence and gap, concavity. My eleemosynary limbs droop for the want of its unconditional sustenance. I am nothing.

"If my soul were food it would make a slim repast, disappoint runt fleas with its false promise of nourishment. For I have not charity but am the breathing need of it. And there is no profit in a burning body when it is immolated by darkness and drought, a Stygian blindness.

"And though the suffering of charity is great, it cannot compare to that of the absence of the *possibility* of charity, the sense of being vanquished by having naught to offer. And while admittedly the absence of charity cannot help but be envious – this its vocation – it is, however, an earnest and modest hope for some saving increase, not a craking covetousness, but rather a middling ambition for some small addition that thwarts bald extinction. And what is there, when a body feels sapped to the marrow, to bluster and strut about? There is blood, ache. There is nothing.

"Perhaps if we knew and understood at least a part, the whole would not seem so heavily looming, impossible, would seem to have us reassuringly in mind; if we could claim to be even fingerlings, have an undeniable niche in the vastness however molecular. But we are nothing, and when that which is perfect and whole shall arrive we will remain so, a nothing no powerful lens can make visible, magnify into being. We disappear and disappear.

"When I was a child, I spoke as a child, I understood as a child, I thought as a child, but when I became a man, I put away childish things and now am neither man nor child, barely a dream of incubation.

"For now we see through a glass, darkly, so darkly – reflective, and what we see, the image that springs back to us is that of the glass itself, infinitely regressed, and we appear in none of the smoky portals. The presumption has been that before the glass stands *something*, occluded but there, but the glossy darkness hangs free of features, eyeless, a gaping hiatus hard to deny. And if the hope is to know as I am known – and to know me is to know nothing – then I fear it is an infinitely swelling empyrean of unknowing that awaits me.

"And now abideth the absence of faith, hope, charity, these three; but the greatest of these is the absence of self implicit in having nothing to give."

Ansel feels the skin of his arms beneath his clutching fingers, grooved with their grasp, and he relaxes his hands, sees the bloodless stripes, looks at the silent people gathered around him, smiles, light, warm.

ZERO DULLS EVELYN'S PAIN

Zero and Id walk along the railroad tracks, picking up flattened coins and bottle caps. "I wonder why people go to the trouble of putting these things on the tracks if they're just going to leave them behind after they're smashed." Zero looks at the elongated face of Abraham Lincoln, his distorted jaw and beard.

"You have attachment issues, Zero," Id says after a pause, a diagnosis. He throws a pebble down the length of the tracks side-handed, as though he were trying to skip it on water. "Well, when the train doesn't derail after all, maybe they lose interest."

"What?"

"Didn't you do that when you were a kid? Set something on the rails, thinking you could upset the train, maybe make it slip off the tracks? You hoped it wasn't a passenger train, of course, never exactly sure of the mysterious windings of Amtrak, but you took your chances and waited, feeling powerful, waiting perhaps to topple the new models from General Motors, thinking, anarchically, wreck American, *be* American, hoping to interfere with the coast-to-coast flow of commerce, from the safety of a darkened ditch, maybe make the evening news. You know?" Id breathes.

"No."

"You never did that?"

"No."

"Hunh. Yeah."

Zero parks himself on a railroad tie. He presses his hand to the wood then brings it to his nose. He inhales the reassuring smell of creosote. He likes its sturdy pungency and the fact that railroad ties everywhere smell the same. Angels, plural – Gabriel can't have been the only dissident, he thinks – dying grisly human deaths, unable to accept the fate of being better, floating above the fray, winged, their onerous lot. What's a person supposed to *do* with such a destiny?

"I thought every kid did that," Id says, looking off into the distance.

Zero recalls the oily velvet of Gabriel's wings, his musty breath, the mourning that ringed his eyes. "What do you really think about angels?"

Id pitches another stone, looks at Zero. "I don't."

"You don't."

"Never."

"Your monologue?"

"Well, sure, I thought about them long enough to come up with that, you know, but it's not like I sit around and ponder them *actually*. I'm an entertainer, man. More a man of breadth than depth. I aim to provoke. I leave the long answers to you, Copernicus."

"What do you think about gravity?"

Id grins down at Zero and crosses his arms.

"Don't say, 'It keeps a good man down.' Don't say something clever. Just don't."

Id sits next to Zero, puts his hand on his shoulder and squeezes. "What's up, bro?" The area beneath Id's hand feels warm and malleable, like paraffin. If Id leaves his hand on my shoulder long enough, Zero thinks, it will begin to melt, drip down my arms and into my shoes. Zero thinks he will kiss Id. And then he thinks, no. What Zero really wants is for Id to look inside him, crack open his past and his present, study the relationships tangled within him and give them numbers, map them, or stretch them into a discernible shape, then diagnose that shape, tell him what kind of person has been fashioned from this particular putty of living. That's what Zero longs for at this moment, to have his vicissitudes charted and graphed, thereby fixing him more definitively in the universe, to be shown the exact longitude of his ontology, and to not feel so acutely the fundamental diciness of every move.

"Nothing," Zero says. He lies back, turns on his side, lays his head on the track, cheek to metal.

Sunday night passes slowly, drowsily. Zero lies awake in his bed, willing himself to ascend, flutter up into the golden wings of the pedestaled angel, slip through, straight to Berlin, where he'd fall in love with a trapeze artist and have discerning chats with men who knew what was really at stake in being human, men who played rumpled detectives on television and happily baked pizzas, men without regret for having shrugged off the heavy, eternal feathers that followed them, for having swapped them for the transitory and fallible flesh. And he would speak and understand all languages, verbal and otherwise, reptilian, alien, seraphic, arboreal, communicate something with every twitch and whistle. Zero strains against the heavy detainment of his skin, presses against his contours, impounded in flesh. He remains moored on his own continent, in his own life, a collection of befuddled cells puddled in his sagging mattress, leaden as wet sand.

He aches to be touched.

On Monday, Zero heads to the DMV from which he obtained his first driver's license years ago. It is afternoon and crowded. Two sets of numbers are being called. People sit in metal folding chairs, hunker in booths, walk around the directing ropes. Zero takes a number. He looks for the woman who administered his eye exam but sees no one who resembles her. All the employees here, in fact, seem to him much younger than he remembers them being. They seem to wear their uniforms more smartly, seem to be the sort of people who work out and eat health-consciously. He wonders what happened to the old guard, the defiantly slovenly chain smokers who wore under their eyes the dark circles of overwork and high cholesterol, rubbed them with a fatigued air of honor and durability.

During the wait, Zero reads a brochure with safety tips, "for new and experienced drivers alike." It recommends never leaving evidence of travel in plain view, luggage, atlas, an invitation for trouble. It advises motorists to carry gallons of water and nonperishable foods like beef jerky and Twinkies in the trunk in case of emergency.

After forty-five minutes, his number is called and Zero walks to the counter. A young woman whose nametag reads "Fiona" asks him how she can help him. The parlance of service, he thinks, is unnervingly loaded. "I'm looking for, I'm, a woman. I mean *I'm* not a woman,

I'm, that's who, I'm looking for someone who's a woman." Uniformed women in a position to render him service make Zero stammer. Fiona blinks expressionlessly at him. He can see she's prepared to remain silent until he gets to the part that more obviously involves her. "I think her name was Evelyn," he says, hoping this will spur Fiona to speak. Nothing. "She worked here, well, it's been a few years since – "

"I've only been here six months," Fiona says, looking over Zero's shoulder. People with more pressing driving-related needs shift their weight and cross their legs in the chairs behind him. He can see Fiona yearning to put her fledgling expertise into action. "She was about so tall," Zero says, hovering his hand over the invisible, shoulder-high eye examiner named, he thinks (or was it Eleanor?), Evelyn. He has no idea why he has offered this bit of useless information to a woman who clearly cannot help him.

"Ern," Fiona calls. "He's the senior officer here. Maybe he can help you. Can you step to the side?"

"Eighty-three!" she barks.

Zero leans against the brown-paneled wall and waits for the senior officer. Next to Zero's right ear, there is a peeling bumper sticker that reads: 55 Saves Lives, under which a bored vandal motorist-in-waiting has scribbled the rejoinder *At 75 the dead come back to life*. Zero feels the impulse to sweep his shoulder, give it a quick whisking, as if to free it of insects or ash.

Fiona has walked back to speak with a man standing beside another small counter beyond the reach of the public. Though Zero is discomfited to be pointed at with a nod of the head, he's cheered by the girth of Ern's belt-eclipsing midsection. The man walks to the end of the counter and lowers his head slightly to look at Zero over his bifocals. "Yes, can I help you?" he asks, drawing out the "you."

Zero thinks he should be definite about the name so that Ern does not suspect his motives. It suddenly occurs to Zero that his tryst with Evelyn, though watershed for him, may not have been unique; perhaps Evelyn has an appetite for the young and newly licensed, perhaps even a reputation. Zero shrinks from the question then says quietly, as if asking for contraband, "I'm looking for Evelyn."

"Evelyn Popovits? You a friend of hers?" Ern asks, and the sound of his voice makes Zero think he has narrowed his eyes, though they remain round. "Or what?"

Zero nods.

"I guess you been out of touch a while," Ern says.

Zero nods again.

"Evelyn took early retirement about a year or so ago. She was sick, in and out of the hospital. Lost her hair." Ern looks down at the counter and shakes his head. "She's at home now. I can't give you her address. You know, you could be like a Richard Speck or something, have it in for the ladies of the DMV."

"No, that's okay," Zero says. "Thanks. Thank you."

"She was a real nice lady," Ern says as Zero turns to leave. "Always a kind word, though she didn't take no guff. Twenty-three years of loyal service, spotless work record, a real gem. And she bought us Dunkin' Donuts once or twice a week, the full assortment, more than we could ever eat. The ones with sprinkles almost always went begging." Ern pats his waistline nostalgically. "A real sweetie."

Zero remembers where Evelyn lives. He drove by her house numerous times while still in high school, the fateful license tucked above his visor, though he'd only been inside that once.

He stands on the front step and runs his hand along the wrought-iron railing. Though it is aged with rust and worn, he doesn't recall it being here before. The house seems a lot smaller than he remembers it being. He opens the screen door. The wood of the front door is warped and peeling. Fraying strips hang loose and look like the shedding bark of a tropical tree. *Every second another acre gone*, Zero thinks. Zero rings the doorbell, the kind that houses a tiny bulb to help guide the fingers of night visitors, the glow of this one dimmed.

He waits for several minutes before ringing again, and then tries the door, which is, in fact, unlocked. What will I find inside? he wonders. Maybe she's bathing? Maybe she's . . . He pushes the door open and sticks his head inside. The same lamp – gold pole stretched between ceiling and floor, sprouting three bulbs beneath cylindrical, turquoise plastic shades, staggered like the arms of a cactus – stands in the foyer. "Hello?"

"Ye-es, come in I said," rasps a breathless voice.

"Evelyn?"

"Bedroom, to the left," she says. "Whosit?"

Zero walks back to the bedroom and sees a woman with thin graying hair lying beneath heavy blankets in a hospital-style bed, bent at the knees and raised at the back, metal guards lowered. She appears much older than Zero knows her to be.

"I thought you were the gal from Hospice," she says. She runs her eyes over Zero, squinting.

"I'm . . . we met when I got my first license," he says. "You checked my eyes, and . . . I heard you retired."

Evelyn looks at Zero's face, relaxes her eyes, smiles. "I retired all right. Seems you brought some of the sun inside with you. I can barely look at you." She points at the window. A swath of sunlight cuts across the foot of Evelyn's bed, and Zero thinks about floating, lifting up into the mild heat of the afternoon, skin soaked with light. Maybe she's convalescing, Zero thinks, getting back on her feet after a long, hard battle. Zero closes the blinds, and Evelyn lifts a hand and waves her finger in circles. Zero takes this to mean he should angle the slats open so that the light is tamed but not extinguished. He swivels the wand of the jalousies.

"You were the boy who needed comfort," Evelyn says, vaguely nodding her head. She picks up a small, white console and pushes one of the blue buttons. "I always wondered if you'd be back." The bed unbuckles, a slow-motion jackknife, and her legs begin to lower and straighten. When the bed is flat, she pushes her body to one side and pats her hand on the other. She peels the blankets back on the empty side and doubles them over her.

Zero is slightly alarmed by the feeling that this is the right thing to do, to crawl in this bed with sick Evelyn. He sits on the edge of the bed, near her knees, facing her. She continues to pat the spot next to her. "Oh, come on now," she says. "We're old friends."

Zero does as she wishes. He removes his shoes, turns around and scoots back, swings his legs up on the bed and reclines next to Evelyn.

"You haven't changed much," she says. "Little taller, skin's cleared up." She pushes another button and the back of the bed raises up. She stops when they are nearly sitting upright.

The bedroom is small and except for a picture on the wall, depressingly nondescript, nicked and scarred blond dresser and chest of drawers crowded in corners, bottles of perfume – Ciara, Evening in Paris, Moondrops – and prescription medicine cluttered atop them. During his previous visit, he hadn't made it any farther than the front room. All these years he'd wondered what her bedroom looked like. This reality resembles none of the various pictures his mind had invented.

In a frame painted gold, hung in oddly close proximity to the ceiling, is a glinting picture of a woman in a flowing robe that caps her head and hangs to her feet. It is a strange picture, layered, covered with a piece of tin that has been tooled from beneath to show the outline and pattern of the robe. Flocculent whorls carved in the tin adorn the corners of the picture and look to Zero like the characters of an alien alphabet, meaningfully bent and arced. On top of the decorative silver is an aureole of gold bonneting the woman's head. Cut from the tin are small openings where the woman's face and proffering hands show through. The woman wears on her face a look of tranquil indifference, as though she were well beyond something so human as concern. The forward stretching hands offer the viewer a golden dish of almond eyes, disembodied duplicates of her own. These eyes, which seem no less at home on this platter than cocktail onions, gumdrops, assorted nuts would, reproduce the woman's equanimity, and their free-floating placidity is unsettlingly resolute, as though they wished to convey that being unfaced was the best thing that had ever happened to them.

"Like my saint?" Evelyn asks.

Zero turns his head to look at Evelyn. Her own silvery eyes possess a certain pacific flicker, as though she couldn't be touched by the mundane, the irksome habits of the flesh – belied, however, by the wan skin beneath.

"Paraskevi. She came along some years after Christ, during that time when devotion to a certain singular deity could get you into hot water.

She hit the streets and set to warbling her song of praise anyway. She was quite a looker, charismatic, and people listened. Converts aplenty." Evelyn runs a hand over her forehead. Electrified wisps of hair fly around her head, and she reminds Zero of a crackling current. Thicker strands of damp hair lie pasted to her cheek. "Does it feel hot in here to you?" She tosses back the blankets with a surprising show of strength. A pale yellow nightgown covers her thin legs. "Gussie! One minute I'm 'bout to freeze, next minute I'm a furnace. I can't ever get comfortable. My damned thermostat's on the fritz. 'Long with everything else."

Evelyn's drawn body unveiled jars Zero, and his surprise is akin to the shock one receives upon the first washing of a heavily furred dog that turns out to be little more than quivering bone beneath. Very sick people tend toward emaciation, appetite itself a ghost, Zero knows this, knows they put distance between themselves and the world they're about to leave, its pleasures, but the billowy emptiness of Evelyn's thin summer gown makes Zero want to carry her out of this state locked by land and into one with a white beach and endless sun, bury her up to the neck in warm sand, force-feed her fresh fruit and leafy vegetables, whole grains. Zero looks at Evelyn's body, desiccated, brittle as a cracker, but he finds himself filled with a palpitating longing the minute his eyes light on her enormous feet, bona fide whoppers! He had forgotten this detail about her, those size-eleven gunboats, now sitting stoutly with continuing purpose and meaning, untouched by illness, at the ends of her dwindling legs. Feet that never fail or falter, flat anchors in a turbulent world.

"Paraskevi's luck took a turn in Constantinople, where Antonius Pius, staunch pagan, fell hard for her good looks but thumbed his patrician nose at her message. He even wanted to marry her, so smitten was he, but only if she agreed to renounce her one and only God, which, of course, she would not do. She'd not be hanging on my wall right now if she had. So he had her tossed in the dungeon and tortured, a pastime she took to easily, never even showing so much as a scratch after the day's flogging or stretching or burning. It's a little like that children's story about the Chinese, what were they, brothers? Cousins?

Though Paraskevi is all those miracles rolled into one and then some.

"Anywho, Antonius, much miffed by her resilience, decided to witness for himself the strange mettle Paraskevi was apparently made of. He ordered her thrown into a boiling cauldron of tar and oil, and when she sprang up unscathed – *Ta-daah!* I always imagine her saying, though I'm sure she was not the type to crow – Antonius's eyes nearly popped out of his head."

Outside, as if to signal the climax of the story, there is a loud crash, glass breaks; a child shrieks. Evelyn shakes her head. "Just the hooligans next door. If you didn't know better, you'd swear they'd been raised in a barn. Probably burn down the whole damn neighborhood someday, house by house." More tinkling of glass, more shrieking. Zero listens closely to the screaming. It is equal parts elation and fear, surprise and uncertainty. *This* is the sound that was always absent at home, he thinks, testimony to the startling nature of sudden violence. Zero leans forward and peers through the blinds. He sees children waving neon plastic water guns in the air. He thinks about Rachel and Tuesday, wonders where they are this afternoon, what they're doing. He hasn't spoken to either of them in several days. He imagines Rachel kneading the tight muscles of a body beset by tension, common shoulder-clenched edginess borne of the generic scratch and scrabble of everyday living, Tuesday accompanying the methodic motion of her mother's hands with a verse of "O Come All Ye Faithful." I should teach Tuesday to scream, he thinks, teach her to caterwaul.

"So Antonius, thinking it was all smoke and mirrors, demanded Paraskevi douse his own doubting self with this same burning oil. He, of course, being a nonbeliever and so lacking the preemptive balm of God, went blind, which is what, paradoxically – as these parables often are, to keep you listening and off-kilter – brought Antonius enlightenment. He pledged everlasting belief in Paraskevi's God if she'd restore his sight, though really he was just wanting to save his blind ass most likely," Evelyn says, her voice growing increasingly breathy and halting.

Zero stares at her feet and takes her hand. He pats it and says, "Maybe you should rest a little. You can tell me how it ends later." Zero begins to worry he is more a source of pain than solace for this sick, small woman. He feels selfish and vacant and deserving of a loveless future.

"On top of the dresser there . . . some adhesive squares." Evelyn gestures toward the end of the bed. Her breathing and speech are now distinctly labored.

Zero gets up and searches among the brown bottles strewn across the dresser top. He finds the squares behind bottles of lotion, Oil of Olay, Vaseline Intensive Care. He brings one to Evelyn, holds out his hand. "Peel it," she says. She begins to unbutton her nightgown. Zero tries to separate the plastic backing from the adhesive patch, carefully, but his short fingernails prove useless in this task. He fumbles the patch, picks it up.

"Please," Evelyn says, "hurry," a note of panic shrilling her words.

Zero sees she is in pain she was before concealing. Sweat beads on her face and chest, rolling down her spotted, crepey skin. His fingers shake as he handles the patch, no longer at all delicate in his maneuvers.

"Oh, please," Evelyn cries.

Finally the plastic comes free and Zero quickly affixes the patch to Evelyn's chest, the skin there so sheer-seeming he wonders if it will tear when the patch is removed.

Her breathing begins to slow almost instantly. She rubs circles on the patch with one hand; Zero holds the other.

"Okay, it's okay," she says. She breathes, slow and deep, in and out. Her lips tremble. "Sometimes it just creeps," breath, "up on you, like a masher, all of a sudden," breath. "I don't like," breath, "to complain prematurely."

Zero sits back next to her and holds her arm, rubs it softly. Outside children are laughing.

"Whew, now I'm ringing wet." She hikes her gown up slightly, over the knobs of her knees. "This must be quite a sight for you." Evelyn attempts a thin smile, her face visibly taxed. She sits quietly, breathing. Zero takes her hand and smoothes the knuckles.

With effort, she inches forward and lifts the side of the blinds. She stares outside, her back heaving with each inhalation. "Hunh, life," she says, then leans back against Zero. He rearranges himself and holds her in his arms. He gently pulls her legs around and holds her like an infant, tucking the sticky hair behind her ears. She feels like heavy air in his arms. A sharp smell of ammonia and sour vitamins stings his nose.

"So there's some disagreement on what exactly happened next," Evelyn says, her voice slow and somnolent, eyes closed, "but this is how I tell it: Paraskevi hopped out of the cauldron and walked over to that whimpering emperor. She pushed her fingers back in her head and extracted her beautiful eyes, then she held them up to his, rubbed them right against his blindness. See, she offered him vision, held it out to him in her own hands. So doing, she extended to him her faith, the things she saw, the way she saw them, and the emperor's sight returned pronto, and he rejoiced and was true to his promise of faith. A hard sell, but it worked.

"Pretty story," Evelyn says. She opens her eyes and looks up at Zero. Zero looks at the fading bolts of yellow in the irises of Evelyn's eyes. "Well, of course, God-charmed though she was, her luck runs clean out eventually. It was still no picnic to be a Christian, especially one on an apostolic mission, in Rome at this time. After Antonius, that old dog Marcus Aurelius came along and started persecuting Christians with renewed enthusiasm, blaming them for every herd-thinning pestilence that swept through the land, and so poor Paraskevi eventually lost her head. Some scrapes even God, well-intentioned as He usually is, can't get you out of."

Zero touches Evelyn's clammy forehead. She blinks groggily, closes her eyes again. He closes his. He feels the warm, loose weight of Evelyn in his arms, then feels her begin to lighten, disperse. He tightens his hold and makes himself heavy, digs his heels into the bed. Evelyn sleeps, her tongue clicking against the roof of her mouth. Zero settles into his stiffening skin.

RACHEL TOUCHES RUBY

Rachel thinks of the different stages of her father, as though he had been a slowly evolving grief. When she was very young, before starting school, he had had little to do with her. He'd moved around her warily, a moody, watchful animal, sniffing out adversaries, cagy and cautious, fearful of ambush. Her mother was the envoy meant to bridge relations, arbitrating affection, pantomiming the paternal role, double duty, kissing Rachel on one cheek and whispering, "Mama's baby doll," a robust pinch to the other, laughing: "Your father loves you." "You're his sweet chicken," she'd sing, "his dumpling, Daddy's little pumpkin." I am food, Rachel thought, meant to be eaten.

By the time Rachel entered kindergarten, her father had moved in closer, studying her, clinically at first, at a slight remove, then suddenly too close, like the anthropologist who has lost himself in his subject and can no longer distinguish his habits and needs from those of the tribe he observes. Rachel thought this would please her mother, thought the fact her father's eyes never left her would be a source of relief, decrease her mother's workload, and that her endless song about the father's invisible love and devotion would have its final refrain. But instead it grew more shrill, insistent, and was spoken sometimes to a wall, the television, when Rachel wasn't even in the room. "He works like a Trojan for you." "Loves you more than his own heart."

The space between Rachel and her father shrank until it seemed he'd moved inside, taken dominion, raised his flag on the soil of her, so that he was always in her thoughts, coursing just beneath the skin. It hurt her to think about anything else.

Rachel's father took a job as a mechanic with Gosnell and Son's Garage when Leonard Sr. passed on. He came home each night still dressed in greasy coveralls and smelling of gasoline and pulled Rachel onto his lap, smudging her cheeks and legs and arms. Rachel leaned against him and inhaled his scent and felt happy.

Rachel loved to visit her father at work, loved to watch him slide back and forth on the dolly beneath the cars. The men at the garage kneeled before her and shook her hand and gave her salty peanuts from a machine inside the office. The office was dirty, with a big wooden desk littered with papers and carbons and scarred with the burns of a hundred neglected cigarettes. There were cracked orange and turquoise plastic chairs scooped and rounded like half a hollowed pear and a long-outdated calendar with a picture of the Grand Canyon that hung crookedly on the wall, time forever stalled. In the summer the air conditioner rumbled so loudly that Leonard Jr. had to shout to be heard over it and turned it off when the phone rang, waiting for it to cough to a stop before picking up. Rachel was especially enchanted by the shiny hydraulic pole that lifted cars into the air. It shifted her sense of gravity and made her think the light weight of children must cause them to sink, keep them close to the ground.

Once her father was injured on the job and had to recuperate at home. It was the happiest he'd ever seemed, limping around the house, visibly injured, wounded in the line of duty.

When business at the garage began to flag, Leonard Jr. had to lay off help. As top mechanic under Leonard, Rachel's father was not let go, but he had to start tending the pumps more, spent more time towing lame vehicles than fixing them, and this caused him to brood silently at night, kick chairs and pace.

Rachel's father next went to work for the city. The summer he began, the temperatures and humidity broke records and claimed the lives of low-income elderly and asthmatics who had no air conditioning. The air was thick with pollen, yellow and stifling. It was Jackson's job to maintain the ditches and islands and green peripheries along the city's streets and highways, cutting the grass and spraying for weeds. For him the airless days, though choking, were preferable to the breezy ones. Rachel could always tell when he'd worked against the wind. Every day he came home in clothes almost entirely darkened with sweat and reeking of herbicide, but on windy days he spent the evenings retching, the vomit stinking of chemical toxins strong enough to keep the vegetation flanking the city's streets free of noisome weeds. During this summer, her father's skin changed color. Even after the leathery tan faded, his skin retained a carotene tint.

As Rachel grew older, her father began to tell her stories of his life, an accounting. Not the laughing, angry stories he used to tell about men with powerful guns and whiskied breath and weak women who followed behind them and swept up. He sat on the edge of her bed, moved his finger from scar to scar, and spun tales of a damaged boy with crooked legs who'd been whipped with studded belts and laughed and spit at when he tripped over his big shoes, braces buckling, and made to eat raw liver, swallow still-shivering fish whole. A boy smotheringly cosseted by a mother whose ruddy cheeks were always wet with tears, a large woman with strong arms and legs who hid her face in his stomach and dandled him into his teens. A boy who other boys naturally despised and shot BB's at and on whose stoop they lit sacks of manure on fire. Her father sat hunched, looking at his knees, and Rachel watched his hands as they kneaded his legs and rubbed his joints. She waited for noise. In this pose, he made her think of a Jack the Ripper comic book she'd read. In the last panel, Jack sat on a stool in a cramped room before a fire, back to the reader, faceless, a source of continuing speculation, like God, bent in remorse, cold and tired after a night of slaughter. Rachel wondered if Jack had had a daughter he'd told stories to, stroking her small throat with gloved hands, testing himself.

At the end of one of these stories, Rachel asked her father what happens to a person after death, and he answered, "Nothing. Nothing to fear because nothing happens. Easy money. Best to do all your living now."

The story of their life together had changed too. He had gone from helping her to feel life fully, feel it scratch her skin and hear it as it shattered around her, to teaching her how to weather its assaults, offer up a thick, impenetrable hide that sustained only superficial licks. She'd succeed where he had failed, he'd said, learn not to feel, be bigger than sentience and nerve endings.

Rachel and Ruby sit on the sofa. Nedra sits in a rocking chair beside them. She rocks and leafs through a magazine. "Lobsters are a thousand times more sensitive to odor than humans," she says. "I can think of some places a lobster probably couldn't bear to live downwind of. Smashed mud snail tissue releases a substance that warns other mud snails to burrow. Hmm-hmm. Seems snails are more clever than people." Nedra looks up. Rachel is rubbing her own feet and Ruby mimics her.

"A giraffe's heart weighs twenty-five pounds, mercy! More to break.

When they bend down to feed, valves in the heart stop the blood from sliding toward their heads. Can you imagine a dizzy giraffe, Rachel?" Nedra looks at Ruby and smiles.

"There's volcanoes a mile beneath the ice in Antarctica," Nedra says. She flips a page. "Well, I knew that. Sperm scramble and fight and elbow each other out of the way, always in a tussle to reach the egg. They're quite vicious. Only one winner. See, we start out in violence and competition from the very get-go. Not much hope for 'love thy neighbor' with that beginning."

Rachel leans forward over her knees, stares at the space between her feet.

"Rachel?"

By the time Rachel was in high school, her father began to move back, watchful, as in the beginning, and Rachel began to think of other things, but she felt lonely without his stories, felt boneless, found it hard to stand up without him stretching inside her.

One night she was reading in her room and her father came to her. He walked around and picked things up, her alarm clock, her brush, set them down. He walked to her bed, took her face in his hands. This was familiar to her and she rose up on her knees. He smoothed and smoothed her cheeks with his thumbs and stared at her. He lowered his face slowly to hers and closed his eyes. He kissed her gently with trembling lips. This was unfamiliar and she pulled away.

"I'm afraid . . ."

Rachel moved back against her headboard as though something threatening, a sooty, enveloping fog, were advancing toward her.

"Maybe it wasn't the right way."

Her mind leapt again to Jack the Ripper. She wondered if he had felt regret, considered his youth misspent, wished to take the rips back, button up the gashes, take back the spilt blood. This belated thoughtfulness seemed to her an idea more appalling than murder, the horror of which was also sheened with a certain glamour.

"What happens when you die?" she asked.

Her father shook his head and looked away.

"Nothing," she answered. "Nothing to worry about."

Her father put his hands on his own cheeks.

"Comfort should hurt," she said. "Remember?"

She felt herself small again, looking up at her life from below, underfoot, fixed to the ground, but now her father seemed just as small and sadly moored and in the very place, it seemed to her, he'd wanted not to end up, standing at the side of her bed, stooped with a shapeless remorse. He was growing old, graying hair and yellowing, bloodshot eyes, muscles gone flaccid, chronic rattling cough. It was unbearable to see the fight inside him extinguished, fists no longer swinging randomly through the air, instead hanging chastened by his sides. Rachel covered her mouth but couldn't stop the laughter from coming, and her father backed out of her room.

Ruby has asked about the end of the world, and Nedra rocks and says, "God'll swoop down and gather us into his infinite mouth when we all least expect it, when it's on the mind of no one, when we're slumbering lambs, forgetful of the wages of sin."

The television is on, a Sunday afternoon movie about mysterious desert rocks that grow, become mountainous over night when left in water, and topple when looked at by people, crushing them and alarming the neighbors.

"I was a bad mama," Nedra says, staring at the television. Her face is drawn in puzzlement, as though she were trying to keep hold of a distressing thought she'd had once long ago and that has now finally come back to her.

This look makes Rachel think of the rusty set of car keys she found below the windshield wiper of the old Fury when she was cleaning leaves out from under the scooped hood. When Rachel was eight and Zero was three, they'd taken a vacation to the Ozarks, Bagnell Dam, and her father had raged one afternoon after misplacing the keys, house and car and work keys all on a round silver ring, gone. And her mother had neglected to bring spares, which made her father fume so darkly Zero didn't speak a word the rest of the trip. Her father had apparently set the keys on the top of the car and they'd slid down the windshield out of sight. And here they were, years later, bobbing to the surface like a dead body, mystery solved. Rachel took them inside, and her mother's smile went slack when she saw them. Then a faraway expression gathered on her face and she looked around, slipped the keys in the pocket of her housecoat.

Rachel moves a leg around Ruby and begins to brush her hair.

"A bad mama," Nedra says.

Ruby sings, "Armageddon, Armageddon, Armageddon!"

"Don't, Mama," Rachel says.

Nedra looks at Ruby. "Why are you saying that, child?" Ruby bobs up and down on the edge of the couch.

"She's keeping the end of the world at bay," Rachel says. "She's saving us." Ruby nods her head at Nedra and smiles. "The world is ending, the world is ending, I'm thinking about it, I'm thinking about it!"

Rachel sets the brush down and puts her hands on Ruby's shoulders then slides them to her throat. She sees her hands squeezing, imagines them tightening until the face drains blue, the neck breaks, head falls limp, her own head sagging forward, too heavy, a sunflower on a broken stem. Her fingers feel thick. She wraps her arms around Ruby, breakable Ruby, and Ruby laughs.

Years from now when Ruby is grown and sitting alone on the davenport in her own living room, she will remember the feel of her mother's hands on her throat, will recall how they tightened gently, not enough to impede her breathing but enough to cause a slight pressure to build in her head, behind her eyes, and Ruby will long for the touch of those strong fingers again, will imagine her head giving way to their grip, and then she'll clutch her throat with her own hands and try to conjure what her mama felt when she circled her daughter's thin neck with a powerful grasp; Ruby will try to imagine the feel of her own skin against her mother's fingers, child's flesh softer than the ailing hides of her mother's clients, the skins Rachel kneaded every day, and she'll try hard to feel what her mama might have felt if she'd ever held her daughter's hands, if she'd ever rubbed her feet; she'll try to feel Rachel's lips squeezed tight against her cheek, and it will all come back to this moment, to the prickling heat on her throat, the hands pressing there, all ache and feeling returning to this kindled spot, but now Ruby can only laugh at the sensation.

Nedra says, "Squids have a major nerve fiber a thousand times bigger than human nerve fibers." She stares at the TV. "No, thank you." On the television, people run to escape the glowing monoliths that collapse around them.

"Armageddon!" Ruby chants. "Armageddon!"

SOURCE ACKNOWLEDGMENTS

The chapters entitled "Rachel in the Mirror" and "Ullalulla" appeared under the title "Rachel in the Mirror" in *The Gettysburg Review* 13, no. 4, Winter 2000.

The chapters entitled "Ivy in Kansas" and "Ivy on Mars" appeared under the title "Ivy on Mars" in *The Santa Monica Review* 13, no. 1, Spring 2001.

The chapter entitled "Graft" appeared in *Inkwell*, no. 17, Spring 2005.

The chapters entitled "Jesus's Skin" and "Digesting the Father" appeared under the title "Digesting the Father" in *The Kenyon Review* 27, no. 4, Fall 2005.

In the *Flyover Fiction* series